THE BOOK OF NEVERMORE

THE BOOK OF NEVERMORE

APÓCRYFA

ANDREW J PIXTON

unmapped
THE KINGDOM REPUBLIC OF NEVERMORE
KARAQUIOK VALLEY
BARBATHOR MOUNSTAINS
SHRUUMOTH FOREST
here be monsters
MAOLGON
TROISACK MOUNSTAINS
CANTLGRYM CASTLE
VOIUM
MANTLGRYM
OVIEDOM
KOURII MARSHES
unmapped
BOGGORN
THORNWOOD FOREST
CASTLE COVADONGAR
TOLGRYM
CANTABRYN
ONIS

PROLOGUE

Based on *Camila's Last Testament*, cc bastica 1;
Scars of the Martyrs, cc bastica 890;
The Nordvargor Testaments, cc bastica 660;

15th of Novumbre, 230

The Razhod. They were coming.

Camila felt it true in her bones and shivered. She cradled Syago tight in her arms as rough waters rocked their ship, *The Nascendante*. The presence of her family gave comfort. Her husband, Odiru de Boligar Parlain, was ready for anything, with the Holy Judgment Sword, Alexandre, sheathed at his hip.

Wind whipped at her dress, lashing her own braided black hair and chilling her brown skin. She had powers of her own to protect and attack with. Her love for her family wasn't merely latent; it was reciprocated by the love the surrounding ocean had for her. The fear in the winds also mimicked hers, a bad sentiment but one she could use. And the anger—there was always hate and anger to use. Nature, cruel as it was, moved at the behest of her scepter. However, she worried that the ocean feared the enemy more than it loved her.

They'd been forced to leave Cantabryn. The Razhod had gained too strong a hold—Amaruc's murder had proved it. The people, too worn and afraid to fight anymore, had given up. She felt relieved to be going home to Tolgrym after so long, and with the betrothal agreement made for Syago and the de Bovua child, her family would be in a good position.

Odiru stood by Fal'iek and Matias, the three that remained of the companionship. All watched a growing black cloud behind them in the gray sky. Ahead, their destination was in sight—the woodland docks outside of

Tolgrym—and the crew prepared the ship for the approach. The turbulent sea brought its own dangers, and Camila felt relief that no sea monster attacks had befallen them. Of course, the Razhod could change all of that, even at shore.

"I don't sense anything," Fal'iek shouted above the wind. The two other warriors shook their heads; they too felt nothing amiss. But Camila knew better—the growing dread in her stomach told her. Then the wind told her. Hate and sorrow always followed and preceded the witchlords. She saw strains of it in the wind, amidst all the fear.

"The winds bear their sentiments," Camila said.

Matias asked, "Could you be mistaking ours for theirs?"

"No," she said, twiddling her fingers with Syago's to keep him from fussing.

"Go below with Bartolon." Odiru's eyes met hers, he drew Alexandre, which now glowed with sacred light, another ill omen. "The Trastamuirs can watch the baby while you help protect them. Hurry."

She did so, praying to Deova Bondua to bless and protect them. What if Barthandeon, the master and high priest of the Razhod, came too? Odiru might finally be able to end it by slaying him with Alexandre. They'd slain him before several times, but he'd somehow come back to life, each time more vile. Perhaps the Holy Judgment Sword would stop that cycle, if old Devilface didn't destroy them first.

Below deck was dark and cramped with trade-cargo boxes and rats and spiders that lurked in any remaining dry corners. She made her way through the lurching hold to sit on a box next to her cousin, Bartolon, who dozed in his cloak. The candles' illumination behind the boxes told her the Trastamuirs must be holding a makeshift mass in the back. Syago whimpered, and she quieted him, cooing and swaying him while her eyes watched for movement in the shadows and her ears listened for any unnatural sounds. Huddled in the corner, she kissed her infant on the forehead and nudged Bartolon. "We're almost home, but trouble comes."

Shouts seeped in through the deck above. It had begun.

Camila dropped to a whisper. "Bartolon, wake up."

Still nothing from Bartolon. Why wasn't he responding? She felt a chill and gave him a hard shove; he fell forward onto the floor. She froze briefly, then pulled back his hood. Blood smeared his face: His eyes had been gouged out, along with his tongue. She stifled a gasp and rose to her feet, clutching Syago tight in her left arm and her scepter in the other. No shadows moved, no planks creaked. Not even the scampering of a rat hungry for the dead flesh. She couldn't afford to mourn him now; with her heart pounding in her ears, it was suddenly far from her mind.

It could only have been the Razhod, somehow already on the ship, which meant that the others were already dead. She moved away from the cramped boxes and shadows on the walls and into the light cast by a main deck grate. She heard only her own thunderous heartbeat. *Where is he?*

The light behind the boxes, toward the prow. Not a mass of the faithful but a black mass of the damned. Her stomach twisted. She knew she shouldn't approach the witchlord, especially with Syago in her arms, but with everyone fighting above, striking first might be her only option. She edged around the boxes, scepter ready, and made fervent silent prayers. She couldn't normally take one alone, but if she could surprise him, cornered him mid-ceremony, she might have a chance. Peeking around, she saw on the floor a red decagram star inside a perfect circle. A bloody tool lay in front of her. Candles glowed, and in the center were numerous bloody eyes and tongues alongside the burning effigy made of a blackbird's skeleton. Behind the circle knelt a man in worship, muttering low chants. He sat straight then leaned forward and then straight again, bobbing up and down in hellish prayer. Camila watched, transfixed and unbreathing. She took a step backward without meaning to. *What are these people, really? What do they want?*

The Razhod witchlord called Aldith ceased the motion and stood up, clothed in darkness and marred with scars on pale skin. He chanted, eyes closed, a dedication of the slaughter to one of their greater spirits, Belfegor the Behemoth.

Snapping out of her shock, Camila pushed her fury through her scepter and ignited a bolt of lightning around the witchlord, a sustained crackle of blinding sparks meant to ensure his death and stop the offering.

Her assault faded, and she gasped for breath. The Razhod stood unaffected, the power of his soulgauntlets already protected him. Through the smoke and gloom, the Razhod's telltale coal-eyes that glowed red in the dark gazed through her as they had in her nightmares for the past six years. Panic set in, and she backed away. The presence of the summoning closed in around her, the shadows bending like reaching claws, then withdrawing as the spirit materialized behind them. She screamed in surprise when another Razhod, a woman they called Fala, appeared.

Fala smiled eerily with those hell eyes, holding up a large bloodstained sack. "Why leave? I brought your friends." She emptied the sack: The heads of the Trastamuirs thumped onto the wooden floor with gaping faces. "An unfortunate roll of the dice. Perhaps you'd like to reroll?"

Camila felt the spirit move nearer, but the woman didn't stop her from running up the stairs. Dimly aware that Syago was crying, Camila reached the main deck, but all her attention focused on the battle at the prow. Odiru, Fal'iek, and Matias were confronting a towering maelstrom of water reaching from the sea to the heavens. Inside the water lurked a shadowy figure: Barthandeon. Wind and rain beat at them beneath black skies, and foul spirits swarmed around the ship in a struggle against those defending them. She turned, and suddenly Aldith slid a jagged knife into her gut like it was the easiest thing in the world. He withdrew, and Syago wailed.

She clutched him against the wound to stanch the bleeding and with the other hand shot lightning into him again. With Aldith stunned, a nearby soldier cut him down with a battle-ax. Fala then gleefully chopped that soldier in half before being attacked by another. Everything was chaos.

Gasping in pain, Camila turned and saw Odiru avoid a tentacle of water and leap at the cyclone with the shining holy sword raised. It sliced in, cutting through the monster's chest, which exploded in light, ripping a hole in the front of the ship. She had only time enough to see Odiru perish in the burst as the ship tilted forward and began sinking. Hands and legs trembling, she kept her grip on Syago and jumped out onto a drop boat. When it achieved the shore, Camila's father pulled her out and carried her up to the village.

There in Tolgrym, as she lay dying, Camila recounted to her father, of the fall of *The Nascendante*, the end of the Razhod and her family, except her child, Syago, saved by her. Perishing with grief, immortal with hope.

CHAPTER ONE

A Hunt in Hell

Based on *Annals of Syago*, cc bastica 2;
Scars of the Martyrs, cc bastica 896;

18th of Septimosk, 246

Sixteen years later, Syago grew up.

Syago de Odiru crouched behind a mossy fallen log, minding its thorns to peer over it. Worried that the gleam of his armor might give him away, he pulled his cloak tighter. Ferns sat unruffled, leaving the woodland deceptively calm. Although it was a cold morning, he was sweating. His gauntleted hands trembled, but not from the temperature. His morion helmet, chest plate, and gambeson hid light-brown skin, black hair, and hazel eyes.

Fortify, Syago! You've faced worse before. You've slain a malwolf, for Deova's sake. And nobody slays malwolves. The whole village is depending on you.

He tipped back his helmet to wipe his brow.

Thornwood was a labyrinth of great thorntrunks that towered over them, splitting into brambled canopies; the thick, spiny vines descended to the forest floor, where monsters hunted other monsters and people. With age, the briars' green darkened and the barbs grew longer, sword-like, and here they reached overhead like gnarled claws. Fog was common and snow less so; both lay before them now. Syago's hunting group had been tracking a white rabbit when they heard the roars of a mabin'guarik and located its lair in a small outcropping under a thorntrunk, the thick roots leaving open a small owl cave. Now, only a corpse of one lay in view, staining the snow red, with no predator in sight.

Two crossbowmen stood ready, arrows notched. This ancient tract of Thornwood was a grim place. Eerie silence amidst the chirps and clicks of bugs and birds weighed Syago down. On the other side of the small clearing, a large malwolf skull and bones jutted out of the ferns, lichen and fungi clinging to the pale skeleton.

As leader of the hunt for the first time, Syago surveyed the safety of the area. Looking left, he nearly jumped—a line of venom ants carried a dead acid slug nearby. He backed away, then motioned to those behind to move closer. They'd already bagged some quervosks and gurows, but the black-birds were poor meat and not enough.

With their morwolf hounds on the other side of the clearing, he prepared to give the signal—but a quervosk swooped down to peck at the fresh corpse. It screeched and quickly flew away. Something had scared the blackbird. A fernbush rustled near his hound, Bethory, but she held, well trained and wary of being a small beast in a forest of giants. Even a rabbit could kill her with its claws.

Moving low, he edged around the decaying log and line of ants. He wielded his shortspear and crossbow, as did Tomas, Andras, and Henric, who moved with him, the archers filling in behind. Walking between two tines of a forked, mossy brambletrunk, he halted at a stretch of fresh mud as the monstrosity came into view. On the other side of the flower patch stood what he'd not seen: a dead mewil'ishyuuks, its body held up by the vines and flowers that had taken it. The graceful beast of antlers and sleek fur had made an uncharacteristic mistake in touching a wound to the flowers of another planted animal. The deadly pollen had entered it and taken over its body. Vines and flowers laced the decaying corpse and would make it move, even attack, spreading the poisonous pollen into new living hosts. But for now, the verdant corpse alerha remained still. A black rosebud sprouted from one eye; two more hung from its gaping mouth. But alerhas were rare in darkemorg season.

A crackling of wood followed by crunching sounded from inside the small cave. There, in the shadows, behind the dead mabin'guarik, emerged a live one. Its challenger and victor held the log up to the large, yellow-fanged mouth on its stomach, stripping bark and preening seedpods. The ten-foot beast was a study in intimidation with thick red-and-brown fur, short legs but bulky chest and arms that ended in long claws. Scars laced its body, some still fresh from the fight. Its bulge of a head held a single eye whose pupil darted around the forest as it fed. It was noticeably bigger and older than the dead one at its feet.

It swallowed, huffed, and discarded the log. Syago tensed when it sniffed the air, but it gave no indication that it caught his scent and it began pulling apart the dead mabin'guarik, tossing aside a leg, then its heart. Syago knew the others waited on him to initiate the attack, but he couldn't impel himself to interrupt the gruesome activity. Fear shot through him. *What if I can't do it? How does anyone confront these things?* He crossed himself with a silent prayer for courage. Intestines splattered into the snow near his hiding spot, then a sickening crunch and tearing of flesh as the mabin'guarik ripped the other's head off, making Syago jump slightly. It stopped, its own cyclopean head swiveling in his direction, and breathed heavily.

Syago didn't even breathe, but his sweat poured and his skin crawled as the creature paused to face him. It tossed the head and exploded out of the cave, roaring and beating its chest as it came down on him. His dodge wasn't enough, and a burly arm knocked him away. Syago rolled over in the snow, gasping for breath, but stopped as the flower corpse came to life and also charged in, lowering its antlers to gore and germinate him. Syago grabbed his spear and swiped at its front legs, causing it to stumble. Bethory bit its leg from behind and pulled it back as it rose to its hooves. As they fought the alerha, the mabin'guarik threw a log at the other hunters, who now encircled and shot arrows and bolts into its thick fur.

But as Syago moved to engage, cursing that he'd dropped his crossbow, the mabin'guarik instead bore down on him, knocking away his spear and grabbing him in one bloody, massive claw. Armor that had softened the blow now pinched in the grip. The beast shook Syago hard, disorienting and straining his neck as he struggled to reach his sword with his free arm. Bethory and the other morwolfs attacked; they were smacked away as the rest of the hunters charged forward while the flower corpse charged them. Under an assault of arrows, the monster held Syago up as cover and took him into the cave, which Syago then realized was not a cave but instead a large rabbit hole that went down and deep into the root-laced dirt. Rabbit bones lay scattered about the entrance, and the beast crouched to squeeze in. Unable to see, Syago felt the walls close in, smothering him. The beast huffed, growled, and shook him again.

Syago hung in frozen terror for a moment, the beast's breath hot on his face. He felt claws clasp his free arm. *Is it going to pull my arm off?!* Syago twisted, grabbed his hunting knife from his boot, and jammed it into the beast's neck beneath the eye, and again as blood splattered onto him.

The mabin'guarik roared and smashed him into the dirt wall, releasing him. He came to seconds later, when Tomas helped him up and Andras pulled his spear out of the monster's body.

Dusting himself off, Syago assured them he was fine and thought of how horrid the beast was, with a smell to match its appearance. Some Asturions spoke of mabin'guarik with hushed admiration, but at least they didn't worship them as the Kimoc did.

They dragged the corpse out of the hole and leveled it onto the net to be carried along with the other slain beast. Tomas had a gash on his side and Henric limped, but a quick tourniquet had stemmed the bleeding of both. Lugas had fallen on the venom ants and was drinking an antidote. Two morwolves had been injured. But when they turned to leave, Syago realized Bethory wasn't following.

"Bethory, come," Syago commanded.

She whimpered and sneezed, whimpered, then sneezed again. He ran to her. The other dogs watched but stayed in the lead of the group, as they'd been trained. He rubbed her around the neck and looked at her wounds. The gashes on her side and leg weren't big, but her sneezes increased in frequency and strength. She had taken in some of the pollen from the alerha; it would kill her, then take control of her body to spread more pollen. He had a cure that could heal her, but it was likely too late and with the injuries she'd taken, she wouldn't be able to walk back with them.

His heart sank as he realized what he had to do. Her eyes looked into his, pleading. He stroked the side of her face. "You were amazing," he said sadly. "But I can't save you. I'm sorry."

Bethory seemed to understand his tone, if not his words. She whimpered and licked him through the bloody mess of her snout, and he kissed her on the forehead. Her eyes already started glazing over. She didn't shy as he drew his axe, the sneezing all but over as her body convulsed, fur rippling from the roots growing beneath the skin. Taking careful aim, he let her lick him as he swung down. She gave a final yelp before going still. Eyes blurring with tears, he had to swing again to completely sever the head.

When he finished dismembering her limbs, he set them on fire. Now she was ready to run in Deova's spirit fields and her body wouldn't serve hell's army of nature. He wiped his eyes and turned back to the group. They waited, understanding the pain of the master's task.

"Good work, everyone," he said as he rejoined them. "Let's go."

Some few hours later, the hunting party approached the northgate of Tolgrym, their home. The men held up the net that bore their hunts on wooden posts above their shoulders, and Syago walked in front—it was his day. Though he'd long anticipated this passage into manhood, he now appreciated but little of the glory. Bethory's death, a heavier pain than his arm and neck, had left him feeling like he'd won nothing. Townsfolk gathered on the wall and cheered as the large door of wood and iron slid up, with the portcullis rising behind, revealing more cheers. He forced a smile and continued to the main square to deposit the meat to the town butchers. Shortly after, the gathering party returned, sponsored by Baron Milgalic, with a good harvest of Thornwood plants.

Their town of Tolgrym was encased by a garrisoned stone wall. All towns feared the outside getting in. Syago had lost most of his cousins outside the wall and even on it.

The town was originally built of wood, then that was replaced by stone bricks with wood supports and thatched roofs, all fitting close together for want of space—though the wealthier had clay roofing. King Pelaiod the Victorious had commissionsed the town, needing to maintain access to the sea and the woods as well as prevent attacks from the forest savages. But instead of sending an army, he sent a group of priestesses and knights to establish a mission. Since then, the forest had nearly grown over the village, while the mission and its subjects had intermarried with the villagers and settled down, becoming Syago's ancestors.

Once he'd set down the catch, Syago saw Elisabet's small form running toward him. His cousin, really more of a sister, was too shy to push through the crowd, so he moved to embrace her.

"We prayed for you," she practically shouted in his ear. "And you got so much without even getting hurt!"

"Well, I felt your prayers helping," he replied.

"Where's Bethory? I have a treat for her."

He then made the inevitable confession.

Grandfather Goidiberic walked up, seeming to understand from the lack of Bethory's presence and Elisabet's crestfallen face. The men of Syago's group clapped him on the back, and even the girls smiled at him, but he was in no mood for any of it, leaving the fanfare to go home.

Thoughts of Bethory brought him to the town cemetery. Standing alone, Syago wiped snow off his parents' tombstone.

Here Lieth the Remains of
Odiru and Camila
Noblest of Heroes
and Most Beloved of
Friends and Family
Fifteenth of Novumbre, Year 230

"I will honor you," he whispered. "Even if it kills me." He didn't remember either of his parents, but the stories of their valor and strength stuck. Being locked in the safety of town walls, stories, games, and music were their lifeblood. Stories of Odiru wielding Alexandre, the Holy Judgment sword, alongside his companions in the war against the Razhod witchlords inspired everyone. Syago's dream to follow in their footsteps and be worthy of Alexandre's election was often derided as a fantasy or even an obsession. But he didn't care. It was his, the only thing he had.

He brushed snow off of his cousins' stones and made the sign of the sun wheel cross.[1] One of the best duelists in the town, he'd squired to Count Toriacus and felt more eager than ever to finish his knight training at Castle Cantlgrym. He thought that then Alexandre would choose him and no more hounds would be lost. Yet he couldn't go. Bound by his grandfather's need for him in the workshop, the dream had to wait.

He saw Fal'iek approaching from the cemetery gate, smiling. Just shy of forty years, Fal'iek had aged well, retaining his long, dark hair, with beads and feathers strung through it. His healthy brown skin, much darker than

---

1   A history and layout of the graveyard can be found in *The Tolgrym Charters.*

Syago's, was lined with tribal tattoos and the occasional faint scar, which now only enhanced his looks. He wore leather pants and shoes; his light fur cloak concealed his bone armor and weapons, save the skull necklace and quiver of arrows on his back.

The two survivors of *The Nascendante* greeted each other, embracing tightly. "*Kolch'imaq*," Fal'iek said.

"We lost Bethory," Syago replied.

"Hm, sorry to hear that." Fal'iek's tone was of the indifference of one accustomed to death, a trait that irked Syago. "I hear this was your first day as a lead hunter."

Syago smiled.

Fal'iek did too. "Well, how fared you?"

"Great. We brought in two mabin'guarik and some birds." They began walking out, making for the cottage. "No thanks to you, of course."

"What you don't know is that we herded them to you, set it all up." The hellhunter grin deepened. "They paid us to do it."

Syago slugged him. "You're full of lies, like always." They both laughed.

"Really, I'm glad you had a good hunt," Fal'iek said. "Thornwood is never kind. Anyone who ventures out, let alone one who conquers, is worthy of fame."

"Well, I owe much to you. You've been a great mentor."

Fal'iek scoffed. "Is that a compliment from young Syago? This calls for a celebration."

"Oy, I give compliments all the time."

"Yes, to yourself." Fal'iek dodged another playful swing from Syago with a snicker.

Syago's mood soured as they neared his family cottage, where Bethory would've enthusiastically greeted them. The smell of fresh bread filled their nostrils as they entered the round hut. They sat at a wooden table inside the cramped room with Elisabet, who was working on her numbers.

Grandfather Goidiberic—Goia for short—brought the pot of stew to the table next to the pan of egg tortiyas. He set a bottle of cider down and served them each a portion, starting with their guest. A kettle of water began to steam, reminding Syago of one of his only remaining cousins, Eliana—Elisabet's sister—who loved tea. She'd been married off three months before to Theordoric, now in Mantlgrym, with few letters sent since. Goidiberic pretended not to notice, but Syago knew better.

With the table set, Goia motioned to Elisabet, who set aside her work and offered the prayer of blessing and thanks as they stood. Syago loved hearing her do it; her faith was so simple and sincere. Thin and gangly for her age, she had long, dark hair and darker skin, marking her and Eliana mastozans, like him.[2] He looked at Fal'iek, who watched her admiringly and, curiously, even made the sign of the sun cross with them at the end. He wasn't of the sacred knowledge like they were, or even a believer in his own tribe's traditions.

Upon resuming their seats, Fal'iek nudged Elisabet. "I see our young lady is studying well."

A faint, quick smile passed over her wan face before she hid it and nodded.

Syago asked, "Are you ill, Elisabet?"

She nodded and sipped her soup. "But I'll get better. I can still do my numbers."

"And do them well she does." Goidiberic beamed. "How fare you, Warchief Sequo'iek?"

Fal'iek snorted at the title. "I'm well, thank you. And I'm sorry to hear of the loss of your hound. I liked that beast."

"Yes, it's tragic, but all life comes and goes in the Deova's own measuring."

Unable to resist the opportunity, Syago added, "Of course, if I'd been better trained from time at Castle Cantlgrym, it might not've happened."

"Soon, Syago." Goia sighed. "The angels willing, but I still need you here. My joints are too old for these tools and I lack an apprentice."

Fal'iek and Elisabet said nothing during the silence that followed. The tense subject between them rarely failed to resurface. Syago had finally saved the money needed to make the journey to Castle Cantlgrym and attend for a year, but he'd still been needed in Tolgrym, and his money was spent on rebuilding the house and shop when they burned down. Count Toriacus also needed him for wall duty and the hunts.

Syago understood but still grew weary of being confined to the only walls he'd ever known, kept out of his family legacy. Noblemen overlooked them while delivering true service to the realm, such as the count's son, Andras, who was to leave for Castle Cantlgrym's esteemed university of knights and elementists. His family ought to be nobility, Syago thought,

---

2 Mastozon (male) and mastozan (female) are less derogatory at this time of writing. They still mean mixed skin, or blood, but not in the disgusting way as before.

and effectively had been in the past because of Alexandre. But without it, they were just regular mastozon serfs. *A life of these hunts and you'll never even make old bones*, he thought.

"It would seem one adventure at a time still isn't enough for our champion here," Fal'iek said.

"Well, neither could I wait at his age," Goidiberic said. "There are great blessings in store for you. But focus on your duty here and Heavenly Mother will bless you, else the hells will slap some sense into you. You represent the Parlain name well so long as you're not fighting the other boys or wasting time on tourneys."

"Basically, just don't do anything you normally do," Fal'iek chimed in with a grin and a flinch from Syago's jab.

After dinner, Syago and Fal'iek walked to the village square to join the post-hunt assignments.[3] Syago's task was to help skin the beasts, drain the blood, prepare the hide, clean the meat, and store or toss the bones and other materials. It was truly dirty work, which all loathed equally. The barons and count, who owned it all, would then distribute it or sell it to merchants.

Around the small square, women in woolen dresses and cloaks and men in furs and long leather coats gossiped and joked or consulted quietly. The family morwolves bounded on each other, snarling in play, and Syago looked away. Not far off, the children gathered around a traveling minstrel in a jester's costume. He performed acrobatics, juggled, and pretended total foolishness, to the children's delight.

Near the well sat a statue of Pelaiod, with smaller statues of Saint Columbar and Saint Culon branching off.[4] At the rear of the square was the Cathedral of Saint Amarias of the Holy Blood, a grand structure of two stories and a bell tower. Its buttresses held angel statues that wept in prayerful supplication, except for the angel over the front door, who wore an expression of vengeful protectiveness, broken sword extended. The stained-glass windows glittered under pointed arches.

The church bells tolled assembly. Syago approached Count Toriacus, who was conversing with the barons and priestesses. The thin count, tall with whitening hair and an elegant but simple robe, turned to him. He

---

3   See also *Keltion Keltibeerion*, 36

4   See *The Book of Tolgrym*, cc bastica 30

didn't smile as he shook Syago's hand—he never did—but Syago could see the approval in his eyes. Syago felt they'd become close in his time as the count's squire. Well, as close as anyone could get to the hard man.

"You did well," the count said. "You may sit out the next one if you'd like."

"Thank you, sir, I'll consider it," Syago lied. If sitting out was offered, then there was nothing to consider.

Count Toriacus nodded and turned to Fal'iek. "Warchief, always a pleasure."

"Likewise, Count Toriacus," Fal'iek said in return. The respect that flashed in the count's eyes was even more noticeable than the fondness for Syago—a glimmer of respect Syago aspired to. Syago had received armor and weapons following his squireship, though not as good as what the count's son received, of course. He still had to borrow swords to train swordwork, otherwise he was left with his ax or javelin. That was unique about the nobility in Tolgrym: They took comparatively good care of their subjects, even occasionally going out on expeditions with them.

Syago left them to converse while he joined the cleaning group. The only man of Syago's age was Andras, the count's son, who was set to leave for Cantlgrym the following day. They wavered between friends and rivals, and right now it felt more like the latter for Syago's jealousy. Andras, however, had joined the hunt and now the cleaning group too, much to Syago's surprise; the count's son was likely trying to end on a good note with him.

Dark-haired and strong with a light tan, he approached Syago. "Well done, Iago."

"Thank you." He forced a smile before turning to the rest. A few older men who usually led hunting and gathering expeditions—Henric and Lügos the Flayed—delegated the assignments. Like the daily wood harvests, the gathering expedition would work separately. Syago had already led one on his last outing with great success, even during the middle of darkelan, when plants and fungi blossomed more fully, making crop gathering more dangerous. Although less intense and less interesting, gathering gave him nightmares.

"It would seem you're the new miracle worker of the outside," Tomas said to him. "My question is, will you make the same quota next time or run out of miracle?"

"You're forgetting the skills part," Syago said, straightening a bit. "I've got enough of that, as your sparring bruises can attest."

"So next time should be just the same then?" Tomas's face developed a slight, teasing sneer. "Or will you be too craven?"

"Come now, Tomas," Andras chided, eyeing Syago. "None can rightfully call him craven after that. And I'm sure he'll be fine next time and each one after."

Although Syago would normally be grateful to Andras for his sudden advocacy, he'd hoped to sit the next one out. But now he couldn't. "I have results to my name, Tomas, and will have more yet."

"So you will, then." Tomas put his hands up in mock resignation. "At least you didn't have to get us out of trouble with the Kimoc again."

It was true, though likely he'd have to do it many times more. His mixed heritage and friendship with Fal'iek, old friend of his father, had helped ease his own mind when it came to the distant forest tribes. Meeting Fal'iek's wife and children had convinced Syago they weren't the savages he'd thought. His Kimoc friend found acceptance in Tolgrym because of his reputation and moderate departure from the traditions of his tribe, but the open arms extended no more than that, and even then, many still didn't like him. Syago wished it different and hoped the truce would change to an alliance or friendship, if for no other reason than to convert the tribes to the holy light of the Church.

The gathering before the church fell silent. Bishopess Myrian, Archprelata of Tolgrym, ceremoniously stepped forward on the chapel steps. Raising her hands in prayer, she said, "Our Heavenly Mother, Deova Bondua, blessed Sanator and Matron of Angels, we ask thee to damn this cruel world. But bless these, thine children. They have gone forth into the hell outside and slain the enemy, making war in thy service. We thank thee for protecting them. As thine ordained minister, I thank thee and ask for a blessing on the bounty. In thy graces, amen."

Count Toriacus, standing between his barons, Milgalic and Roberochester, cleared his throat and said stoically, "I too am glad for such an impressive return and congratulate Syago on it, as well as Robertoim for their gathering harvest. May there be many more yet. Now, let's clean it and prepare to feast!"

The square erupted in cheers and set to work, with Syago helping to drain the blood, skin the mabin'guarik, and hand off the furs for tanning. He was laying out extra meat to salt and sun-dry with Andras and Tomas when he noticed Donmal the Drunk waddling up to them. Evidently, he'd done another night of public drinking, for he now bore the Fool's Helmet and Boots: an iron box for the head providing limited visibility and iron casings placed on one's feet that made it difficult to walk. The helmet resembled a face gone mad. Only counts, barons, or constables had the authority to place these torturous devices on malefactors.

"P-please," the man begged, holding out his weathered hands. "I haven't eaten today. If you could provide..."

The group immediately dispersed toward the cathedral with someone grumbling that he ought to beg his wife first—for forgiveness, then for food.

Andras muttered into Syago's ear, "He rambled on about my father again. He's going to have him swear another oath of fealty once done with the punishment."

Syago felt a stab of pity for Donmal, but they'd been told not to give aid. The constable would see that he was sufficiently provided for. Yet Syago couldn't resist slipping the convict a strip of dried meat when the others weren't looking, himself having been through similar punishments before.

CHAPTER TWO

Dark Powers in Innocent Hands

Based on *Leyta's Journals*, cc bastica 6;
The Nordvargor Testaments, cc bastica 555;

17-18th of Septimosk, 246

In a gloomy chapel, a young woman prayed for cruelty.

Leyta[5] knelt before the altar in the Chapel of Saint Nubeiru, supplicating Deova Bondua. Despite the hanging candles and the dying light of dusk creeping through stained-glass lancet windows, the interior remained dim. The Church never dispelled with the gloomy atmosphere and grim messages, but Leyta had still enjoyed the mass. *But I'd have enjoyed Master Davagis's funeral more,* she thought wryly. The harshest master of the castle, his piety made relentless lessons even worse. *The mausoleum would breathe even better than this chapel.*

The evening ceremony, sacraments, and sermon on hope in salvation reminded her that her struggle was humanity's struggle. She needed that faith to sustain her against the mounting anxiety for her final trial in becoming a dynast.[6] At seventeen, she was young for such an ordeal, but none studied as hard as she did—and none wanted it as bad.

Leyta finished her supplication and rose, signing the wheel cross over

---

5 Leytamendras de Bovua Trastamuir la Eliot was her full name. Longer names were usually a sign of royalty. With most of that bloodline being dead, the tradition has faded. Even Leyta shortened her name.

6 Dyne from Old Asturion connotes power or, specifically, motion. A dynast then has authority over motion. They command the motion, and the elements obey. But the authority has a darker connotation still, likely from the Church that persecuted it before subsuming it. Dynasts went from being priestly pagan rulers of the hell worlds to being the dark agents of Heaven as directed by the Holy Church—its angels of death, as it were.

17

her chest with a dab of holy water before turning to leave. Silently, she took her staff from the hold by the door. As soon as she exited the front portal, she heard shouts along the wall, punctuated by wild screeches. Breaking into a run, she crossed the courtyard to the stairs.

Using her staff to push between the soldiers along the western ramparts, she saw the commotion on the lake below: Bats swarmed a small rowboat. The rower and his passenger ducked low into the hull while swatting at the vicious, dark menaces. If she'd not recognized the screeching, she'd have thought them to be birds or bugs, so fast did they flutter in the dark. The soldiers drew arrows but hesitated; the black flurry proved impossible to target.

"Bring the boat to port!" the Seneschal, Davagis, shouted from further down the wall.

Leyta could aim for the bats with a fire or lightning burst but feared she might hit the two as well. She could use the water to attack but risked swamping the boat. The bats started attacking those on the walls, hitting, clawing, and biting with fangs and corrosive saliva. Blood-red eyes and foaming mouths made them a frightening sight, in her face one instant and gone the next. Leyta yelped as one tangled in her hair, clawed wings beating and a hideous face snapping and slobbering until a soldier cut it away. All on the wall ducked as the assault increased, until a surge of wind directed by Davagis blew the bats upward, disrupting their flight and giving the keepers an opening.

"Cover me!" Leyta yelled, and two soldiers shielded her, swords cutting at anything that drew near. Staff in hand, she entered the Vision and saw the sentiments of the water as calm and friendly in spite of the attack. She pushed love into it. The emotion was difficult to muster in such a harried moment, but she'd trained five years for just such an effort.

The water bulged beneath the rear end of the boat and guided toward the dock despite the bats' frenzy. Leyta descended the stairs two at a time as Davagis and another adept used dyne to blow the bat swarm away, causing it to dissipate.

At the gatehouse below, the portcullis and doors flew open, and the rushing guards pulled the two in. The boatman's armor hadn't completely protected him from the bites; his unconscious form was rushed off to the infirmary. The passenger, an Unakan boy, stood weakly. He muttered numerous apologies before he too was hurried off to the infirmary. Leyta crossed herself, whispering a prayer for them.[7]

"Good reaction this time," Davagis muttered to her as he swept past. He then called back louder, "Except for the bat in your hair!"

"Yeah, thanks," she said, but he was already gone.

"Why you think the bats attacked them?" one of the guards asked another.

The other replied, "The Unakan's cursed."

"Or it brings evil known only to the bats," said another.

"Don't be ridiculous," Leyta snapped. "Those bats may not have been the kind to suck blood, but they've always attacked us. Every single monster on gierra attacks us for no reason at all, flesh eater or not. Blame our hell-world before you do him."[8]

In the growing darkness of the bailey, she could feel more than see their glares as they departed, but she cared little. She did wonder, though, why the bats so spontaneously swarmed them and why the two had come out in so vulnerable a manner as that. It would've been better had they stayed in the docking fort on the other side of the lake and waited until morning.

The following morning, she returned to the wall and walked the battlements with a calming wind. The land exhaled, blowing back her long dark-brown hair and chilling her pale skin. Lake Laomain, more long than wide, shimmered across its magnificent reach. Castle Cantlgrym sat on Isle Inveruglas, and Isle Ivow to the north hosted its mausoleum, with a small catacombs beneath.

Her brown eyes tightened as she noticed an odd cloud far across the fields to the east. Dark and foreboding, she could barely see the distant black swell hovering over Shruumoth Forest where sat Bokhor, the village of summoners. The cloud looked different than what she'd seen before, though she knew little of the forest's patterns or colors; their pollen storms rarely reached as far as Cantlgrym. Still, she would've liked to see them redirect it by calling down their greater spirits. But she had no time—she had to prepare for her trial.

Her trial... She shuddered.

She descended the steep, narrow steps to the field, where the keep loomed. The giant block-like edifice was intimidating, with tight windows,

---

7   See also *The Schiltron of Magodeoz*, 67

8   See *La Epica Eluveitia de Sepultura*, 63

a high pointed entryway, and crenelations on top—she drew strength from its imposition. Behind the front keep was a roofed hall, then a rear keep, with three pointed towers. The gray stonework was a remnant of the time of Pelaiod the Victorious, though it'd since darkened from age. The outside was magnificent if grave while the inside beautiful if gloomy. Cantlgrym protected her and gave her the lifelong dream she'd sought.

The sound of yelling children tore her gaze from the facade. A group of four kids gathered up against the wall around someone they'd cornered. She walked over and pushed through them as one yelled, "Go back to your home, savage!"

And another, "Our friend's hurt because of you, little digger!"

"Stop," she commanded, then looked at their target. The Unakan boy from the boat stood against the wall, arms folded and bandages slightly browned. His calmness surprised her. She turned back to the group. "Go on, leave him."

The four grinned at her and walked, one muttering, "Whatever you say, *my lady.*"

"Are you all right?," she asked the boy. "I apologize for that. You must be the new keeper. How are your wounds from last night healing up?"

"Yes, I heal good. I come far to be here, for-for to study," he replied with a placid face but friendly voice. A full foot shorter than her, with dark-brown skin, he looked like a younger Virgow, the only other Unakan at the castle but gone to gather the new recruits. Tight, dark eyes looked up at her; his long black hair was pulled back by a headband that gave him away as a dynfist friar. The worn fighter's garments fit his lanky form tightly, and a small sack was slung over his shoulder. He started speaking again, then stopped, then again. He stumbled through the language. "I sorry about..."

"It's not your fault. They just need more cleaning duties. I'm Leyta de Bovua, the archkeeper, or lead of tenants. Come sit with me for dinner." He nodded solemnly in gratitude and hastened to walk at her side. Already, Leyta found him adorable.

"I am Qosku," he said with a hint of pride. "Orphan of Chuqi'kirau."

Chuqi'kirau. isn't that the mining colony that's known for its uprisings? Maybe I should look in on his past then.

"A pleasure to meet you," she said aloud. "Of course, you already know the abbey where you'll stay. We eat in the great hall." They walked toward the large entry of the keep, where wood and iron doors sat beneath its soaring archway and she continued, "I'm actually an orphan too. In the last war, the Razhod hunted all royalty, including my parents of the Trastamuir royal line. I was adopted by the Eliot barony in a town east of here called Voium."

"So you are princess then, is truth?" he asked.

"I was, sort of," she said with a laugh. "I was the Infanta... er, heiress, but not anymore, which I think may be a good thing. They'd arranged for me to marry a boy named Syago, the son of a legendary knight, since the male infantes and most noblemen had been slain. I was only two years old and never even met him. My adoptive parents wanted to arrange one for me too, but I got them to send me here first so I can study."

"What do you study here?" he asked as they entered the keep. Candles on wall sconces and chandeliers illuminated the hall filled with tables and benches, which were moderately populated for midday dinner. Tapestries and banners of red, gold, and silver lined the walls.

Leyta took a seat at an empty table. "I study dyne. I'm a dynast, a type of elementist. In fact, I have my final trial today. I'm really nervous." Not nervous—terrified. She didn't want to do it, but if she couldn't, if she backed out—as she had last time—she didn't know if she'd get another chance. They weren't supposed to let her, but the masters had been understanding. However, it certainly hurt her position as a leader to the keepers and her prospects as a successful elementist.

Trenchers and goblets were set before them by the kitchen duty. "Commanding and ruling the elements of the world through your spirit, your sentiments, is never easy even in the best situations," she said. "The trial will confront me with the worst."

"I know dynast. We have dynast in Chuqi'kirau. What is you trial?"

Her voice dropped. "I have to execute a prisoner."

"Why?" He looked unsurprised, a reminder of where he came from. It unsettled her.

"It's a test to see if I'm cruel enough to administer justice. And society is cruel by design so... or is cruelty social by design?" He stared at her blankly. She sighed and dragged a chunk of bread through her stew. "A full dynast is like a ruler of the power, over hell. I may need to defend a town against monsters or barbarian raiders, so I have to be able and willing to do what is necessary. Yet if I fail to kill him or take too long—or even if I seem to enjoy it too much—I am banned from dyne forever. Dyne is a power of violence, so I must *do* something evil without *becoming* evil in the process." She stopped for a sip of watered-down wine.

"I suppose they also want to make a show of what happens to certain criminals, let people vent on a scapegoat." She shrugged at her own cynicism. "But they set up a series of trials to ascertain that I don't go mad with power. All of it after years of study and practice, and a lot of money from my parents. After this, I can both wield and teach it. Right now, I can only wield under close supervision; after, I'm still under the archdynast. Most elementists just stay at that first stage. But I won't." She looked at him and asked, "Do you go through any big trials as a dynfist friar?"

"I left before trial. But on way here, I had to kill much animals and monsters," he said and then quieter, "And people."

She nodded and said, "Power corrupts, but so does survival."

Castellan Alkant and Davagis entered the hall.

"Sirs," Leyta said as they passed, "this is Qosku, one of our new keepers."

Both towered over them in their distinguished, long leather surcoats. Alkant, his hair and beard both white with age, wore his with a thick cape representing his position as master of the castle, the castle shield of a crown emblazoned on the back of his cape. Brown eyes set in a pale face smiled down at Qosku. Davagis remained impassive as always. Master Alkant greeted them. "Hello, young one. Welcome to our fortress of knowledge and wisdom. Have you been treated well?"

"I am well, sir," Qosku replied, looking up at them curiously. Leyta couldn't tell if he misunderstood the question or lied to avoid problems.

"Good," he said and turned to her. "And are we ready for the big trial?"

"Yes." She tried to sound resolute, but Davagis's watchful eye unnerved her. He would be presenting her Ordeal of Trial. "It will not be a problem."

"I am sure," Master Alkant replied. "Nevermore has need of leaders and dynasts such as yourself. We look forward to it. Best of preparations."

They strode off, Qosku bowing then turning to his food. She bid him continue on his own and returned to the small library. She missed her parents' manor in Voium and her old friends. Most of them had married off, some to violent men. Leyta persuaded her adoptive parents to send her to Cantlgrym instead. The baron had never beaten her but was very controlling, locking her in the red room whenever she'd misbehaved; it wasn't unlike his treatment of his own mother, Woana the Mad, whom he kept in the attic. Dyne was Leyta's way out, her path to independence. She accepted that as heiress to the barony, she'd likely not escape marriage unless she took holy vows, but dyne would still free her considerably. Women only held authority as dynasts or priestesses, or perhaps as pagan chamands, and even then a husband would be head of the house. The only other option for women was submission.

But it was no longer just about her. After tricking a rival girl into marrying a man of the drink, she'd seen the pain she'd caused and felt guilty, but at least the act had confirmed she had what was necessary to be a successful dynast—spite to act on. She didn't want to hurt other women anymore, only support them. And children, whom she adored. Their innocent laughter lightened the weight of the world. She wanted children of her own, but, spurning marriage, was satisfied with caring for others'. Being a dynast would let her teach them. If only she could be a mother and not a wife... *Well, I could learn to hide a body.*

Laughing to herself, her thoughts returned to her ambitions, which could easily be her undoing. She feared ending up locked in the attic with Woana, or in Foucal Asylum Abbey for the Lost. She didn't want to be quarantined away and pitied like those other failed elementists. She was careful but also powerful, and that meant she was especially vulnerable to it; she could lose herself and harm others.

Still, the question of quitting hardly ever entered her mind the way it did with other elementists. She loved academics, uncovering mysteries and seeing how things worked, especially things that society needed. Dyne enchanted her, and the threat it brought into her life only enticed her more. Once she'd come to these conclusions, dynast was the only thing she could be.

Three hours of practice later, as the last vestiges of sun began to fade, Leyta waited for her time inside the guard tower. Again, she wore the Black Gown, elegant and simply embroidered with the appropriate silvery symbols of her elemental authority—an inverted pentagram on her chest, grail emblems alternated with winged serpents entwining along the body of the dress, and leviathan sulphur sigils around the hem. And of course, the sun wheel cross on her necklace and hair circlet. The unspoken history of the symbols was that their pagan, devil-worshiping origins were adopted by the Church to minister justice and safety to non-ecclesiastical societies using the powers of hell. She secretly found it alluring and aspired to it with pride, if coupled with trepidation. A minister of hell.

For all her preparation, she couldn't shake thoughts of killing this nameless human. Davagis's words came to her: "Every society has to decide who to punish and how to do it. It'll be your task, under the direction of the Church and the nobility, to ensure that we mete it out accordingly. The Black Work is yours." She understood the rationale but couldn't agree with it, not since the first attempt. This Black Work somehow felt wrong. So she'd been able to refocus how she saw it. She couldn't simply kill another human, but she could protect children from someone doing them harm. She'd do anything for those earnest faces.

From outside, Master Davagis called her name. Unable to see anything through the dark hood placed over her head, she heard the doors swing open, as loud as her beating heart, then both vanished in the clamor of cheering keepers. Sister Katti, her priestess guide, said, "You'll work wonders, Leyta. With the blessing of Heavenly Mother, you're unstoppable."

"Thank you, Katti," Leyta responded. "I hope you're right."

Katti stood in front, her voice sweet but firm. "Make it right. The power is in your hands now."

Banesa and Mariaciela, her fellow practitioners and ceremonial escorts, voiced their agreement. Katti blessed Leyta, and the three imitated the prayer sign as they led her out of the guard tower door along the parapet. Church bells tolled justice. After ten paces, Banesa turned her and pulled off her hood.

She stood on the wall facing inward. In the field below stood the young castle residents, rowdy except for Qosku, who she spotted on the edge. Along the wall stood the masters and keepers of the castle, resolute and judging. And across from her, on the opposite side, waited the criminal, bound to a wooden post over a pile of sticks.

So death by fire is my task.

Fire involved the most screaming and probably the most pain, but her expertise with it could make it a quicker death than drowning and less bloody than crushing. Taking a deep breath, she pulled her shoulders back. She would do it this time—no more being skittish about what was necessary, about her duty or her dreams.

Remains of rotting food and feces covered the man, and her heart sank. He'd already been subjected to the Tormentor's Box in Voium, the stocks and dungeons. Though he looked better than others she'd seen, she still churned at the sight.

He looked at her pleadingly. Instead of looking away, she faced him; it was now her place to judge. This man had stolen and murdered. She met his gaze, firmness without meanness.

"Leytamendras de Bovua, care of La Eliot," began Seneschal Davagis. He stood between Master Alkant and Bishopess Gladys Yanet. "You are summoned here to demonstrate your ability, willingness, and capacity as a dynast by the use of dyne for the supreme task of murder. It is the burden every elementist must excel in: the duty to perform evil so others don't have to. Your sacrifice is to enter the darkness to protect those in the light. Do you accept this task?"

"I do," she replied loudly, forcefully.

"Then condemn and execute by fire this foul man."

She raised her staff, almost forgotten in her sweaty hand, a symbol-etched tool of dyne that she'd crafted herself and now pointed at the nameless criminal, bound and weeping. With the commanding rod in hand, she could see the world in its reality, as bodies of matter imbued with sentiments. In the Vision, she saw the stone wall, calm and dark in its indifference with a tinge of blue sadness. The energy projected by the people's jeers slowly changed the blue tinge to a greenish anxiety. But that green was weak in comparison to the buzzing green fear of the wood, nervous in anticipation of what might happen and unsure if it wanted to cooperate. Feelings similar to hers that first time she backed out. But not this time.

Feeding on memories from a difficult life, she found that dark and dangerous well of hate and anger inside herself and approached it, taking what she could without surrendering. Warily, she regarded the background. Below, she saw the people in their animosity. They didn't look like people, but she knew it was them by the way they shined as beacons of sentimental energy, fluctuating, pulsing, and changing.

Leyta opened her eyes and shouted to the prisoner, "Criminal stripped of name and legacy, you have been caught in the act of taking property not yours and smiting to death one not hostile. You have been found guilty of these acts in the eyes of the people and the barons and counts of the Kingdom

Republic of Nevermore. Your life is forfeit and I hereby end it with fire. May you obtain mercy in the hereafter. Deova Bondua save us all!"

Not daring to pause, she pointed the staff at him in a hard thrust. At the same time, she pushed her anger into the kindling and wooden post with enough power to change the anxiety of the wood to an explosive red anger. On starting that initial spark of heat, it burst into flames.

He screamed.

She saw the wood's remaining fear, bright green. The man's thrashing had frightened it, and it was about to quit giving itself to the heat when she stoked it with more red. She ignited with her rage, switching to brown hate for its sustaining power, making the burning wood despise him too. She couldn't target him directly, since a body is too dense in its complexity, with lots of elements that don't easily receive outside sentiments. This took considerable concentration and effort from her, for she had to push away distracting and disheartening thoughts. She wasn't strong in hate, so pushing toward such a limit taxed her physical as well as mental energy. She called up memories, memories of victims of crime, of the people in her life who had tried to hurt and control her. With these, she tried to create more hate and anger in an effort that simultaneously repulsed her. She flared the flames so they fought the cold wind, which wanted to save the dying man.

He screamed.

His agony distracted her, weakening the sentiments she could give by arousing sympathy. However, with the blaze strong, the wood was persuaded more easily. She paled at the terrible sound and sight of him—no, *it*. Better to not see the target as human.

The fire now threatened growing out of hand, with the wind blowing flame and smoke toward the nearest tower. She tried some sorrow, and it began to calm.

He screamed no more.

She withdrew from her sentiments, leaving that dark place of her heart and the visionary world of souls. Then she breathed. Chest heaving, she watched the fire die. Nothing moved, and the burnt corpse hung out from the post even farther now that the bonds had burned off.

"Mistress Leyta," shouted Davagis. "The Masters of the Dynal university of Castle Cantlgrym and Bishopess Yanet of the Holy Church deem your deed complete and your authority as a dynast sound. Congratulations."

Leyta felt many things, but exultant was not among them. The charred, hollow face gazed at her. A breeze came, and the body crumbled into the embers, eliciting one final cheer from below.

She walked back to the tower, each step heavier than the last. As a new authority of dyne, she would be in charge of others. Her mandate to teach and protect children was now offset by the risk she posed to them and herself. Hate and fear were her only feelings for this new power she'd just achieved, and that was exactly as it should have been.

CHAPTER THREE

FROM FALSE LIGHT

Based on *The Hunter's Parchments*, cc bastica 203;
Writings of Qosku, cc bastica 35;
The Nordvargor Testaments, cc bastica 780;

18th of Septimosk, 246

When Fal'iek walked out of Tolgrym and the gate slid shut behind him, he concealed a sigh of relief. Yet Tek'ouk and Mour'ikik, joining him at the portcullis, misread his mood. The three Roah'riik, veteran warrior-hunters, walked from the wall.

"Tired of pretending to like them?" Tek'ouk asked heatedly, both of them smiling too casual for Fal'iek's taste. *All Roah'riik ought to be less high-strung, especially in the wild.* "Or did they finally kick you out, like we've been warning you?"

"I believe your warning was that they'd either execute or enslave me," Fal'iek replied, stringing his bow while looking around above. No birds monitored them; it was safe to talk, for now. "Neither of which has happened yet."

"Yet." Mour'ikik prepared his blowdart pipe. "Did you at least steal something? Maybe their next hunting plans?"

"Well, I always get that done," he said with a half-smile for the half-truth. "They're going to continue hunting south of Quoak, so we'll follow on their north flank to the river. And I do actually like them. The Castilions that like me, anyway. Odiru's family isn't bad."[9]

"Not bad for palemen, you mean," Tek'ouk quipped, thumbing his scepter and hand-axe.

---

9   The Kimoc and Unaka at one time called Asturions castle-builders, or Castilions.

Fal'iek inclined his head in gentle agreement as they moved into the forest, weapons ready. He didn't care for the paleman moniker, particularly because Syago and most of the village weren't pale—they were just paler than most Kimoc. And lacking their traditions. But then, so did he sometimes.[10]

His thoughts turned grim. *Perhaps tailing them like this will avoid having to make more trespassers disappear like last year. We only retaliated, then the body of one of ours was found with a sword wound. And on the spiral goes.*

Hours later, they arrived at the great river just north of where their canoe was tied. At the river, Fal'iek waited while Tek'ouk and Mour'ikik prayed, offering trinkets of wood and bone before dipping their hands in for a drink. Mour'ikik wore traditional hellhunting leather, light and laced with bones. However, he had a penchant for extra tattoos that ran geometric lines over nearly his whole body. Tek'ouk, the only dynast in the group, wore his hair back, better revealing the face paint he often favored. Neither commented on Fal'iek's non-participation in the prayer, but Fal'iek knew it was on their minds. It stopped the more important activity, paying attention to one's surroundings.

On this river, he'd once been fishing with three others. He'd turned around and one was simply gone, never seen again. The forest never ceased speaking; even its rare silence spoke like legends, pushing awe into the Roah'riik hellhunters as they noticed the quelk striding up to the water to drink. Its broad, gnarled antlers lowered with its head to the water.

They watched it without reaching for their blowdarts; it would've been too much to carry back to Quoak, even if they'd had the presence of mind to kill it. But they were not the only hunters prowling. The waters rippled, then bulged as the serpentine body of Yacumama rose, though to Fal'iek she was neither an eternal from the stars or great spirit from the World Below. She was just a horrifically overgrown creature that he would've gladly slain. Moon-quiet, her long scaly form rose out of the water, rearing a great head of feathers, horns, hooked beak, flickering red tongue, and heartless slitted eyes—eyes that reminded him why he'd stopped venerating in the first place. But even he could not pull away as the Great One of the Rivers reared. The quelk, sacred beast that it was, realized the danger

10 *See Gybiaaw Blackbraid: Born of Winter, 10*

and burst away, but too late. The massive serpent didn't bite—didn't have to. It was already close enough to lurch and wrap around the fleeing beast, choking its cries and dragging it soundlessly into the water, where both disappeared with hardly a ripple.

All three Roah'riik stared and wondered if it had truly happened at all. Tek'ouk and Mour'ikik put gifts into the river again and turned to Fal'iek, saying with their eyes, *Will you really deny that? Can you still rebel against a great one like that?*

Fal'iek responded with a blank stare, then turned away and walked down to the canoe.

Qosku trained late in the courtyard, honing his Takanaku, or what others called dynfist. He often delayed sleeping for the nightmares that it brought—trauma not just from nature, which was bad enough, but also that induced by the worst: people. Yet he couldn't wander the small corridors of the abbey forever. The abbot didn't like that, and every mortal needs sleep, warriors in particular. Tossing and turning on his straw mattress, with a single thin sheet, he eventually succumbed.

He dreamed in memory, a nightmare of the day before he'd arrived at Cantlgrym. Standing on a mountain ledge as dusk settled, illuminating the shape of the castle's pointed towers in the distance beyond the last of the jagged peaks, a dense fog crept over the ground below. The group of Asturion trappers he traveled with were setting up camp on a plateau near what appeared to be an old Unakan farming dell, but with a ruined Asturion tower covered thick in green overgrowth and hiding a recent, hastily abandoned camp. Both disturbed him as possibly cursed but didn't seem to bother the trappers. Called Moray, it sat on the side of a mountain in the Apugakas.[11] He'd been seeking out his parents, or any ancestor, with Chaska, his twin sister. And not only had he not found them, he'd lost her in the process. Lost his other half, his yanantin.[12] The grief at least distracted from his other struggles.

---

11 Known as the Barbathors in Asturion.

12 A dualism featured in Unakan myth.

But Cantlgrym had sounded promising as a place to recover and start anew. At this point, anything would feel better than the group of Asturion trappers he'd joined. They'd stopped asking about who he was or mocking his girlish writing and poetry. He hated being in the outerwilds and longed for any type of enclosed home meant for people. Even if Cantlgrym was similarly unwelcoming, he would take his time to rest from the constant watchfulness necessary for trekking the outerwilds. But at least the constant danger diverted his mind away from his inner turmoil.

"Oy, Qosku!" shouted Bodon, the burly mountainman who openly disliked Qosku the most. "Get us some water from that pond we saw."

Mungo, a mastozon and the only one of the eight Asturion trappers who showed any measure of sympathy, looked at Bodon. "You can't make him do everything, Bodon. Ease off the boy. I'll get the water."

"It's no bad," Qosku muttered, walking toward the brush where the pond had been. "I will go."

Mungo walked with him anyway, the smallest of the group made bulkier by his fur coat and armor. Qosku liked him, but even he got bothersome when drunk at night, and since the campsite was considered sufficiently secluded, they'd likely finish their drink stores this night.

They pushed through the grass, ferns, and vines with great caution, weapons up in defense. Such a field, even one small and high on the side of a mountain beneath radiant sunshine, could hide uncountable, unknown dangers. The ferns opened up to a beautiful field of flowers with white petals and yellow stamen. The ground was thick with them around the pool; unnerving in their delicate sweetness, they were also very small and so unlikely to pose a serious threat. Still, they avoided the flowers, with eyes and ears open, and stopped at the edge of the crystalline pond.

The grove glowed with warm sunshine, and the water was the clearest he'd ever seen. It rippled slightly against the stillness, and Qosku realized someone was swimming in it. A graceful man swam gently, elegantly in that crystalline water with a teal tint on the visible bottom, a perfect swimming hole. Long, beautiful black hair flowing behind him, contrasting with light-brown skin, he smiled warmly, mischievously, and came toward them. Qosku dropped the pail he'd been holding without notice.

"Never have I seen such beauty," Mungo said and crossed himself. "Especially in the outside. You, m'lady, are a gift from heaven, sent to weary warriors in hell." Mungo's gaze wavered not, and Qosku agreed that this person was quite handsome, though it was a man and not a woman, as Mungo hadn't yet noticed—the water blurred his sex. Qosku saw Fernandric standing behind them, mouth agape. Qosku, however, felt shame in his attraction to this man.

"Why don't you join me?" asked the nude swimmer softly, kicking back in the water, exulting in it.

"I-I think I shall. The water does look lovely." Mungo began undoing his pants, and Qosku began to do so as well but remembered his obligation to fetch the water.

He put a hand on Mungo's arm. "Wait, first I take water." Mungo paused, face scrunching up. The swimmer came up to them and reached out a beckoning hand.

"Well, I'm not waiting," Fernandric proclaimed and jumped in, fully clothed. The swimmer laughed at the splashing and the thought that they were seeing something different made Qosku realize the entire situation seemed wrong. *This person is not real but a poison dream.*

He called out, but Fernandric's screaming had already begun. On entry, he turned in the water and clawed at the sides, trying frantically to get out. Qosku then noticed piles of bones resting on the bottom of the pond, blending in with the dirt and rocks. Small vine flowers emitted faint puffs of golden pollen, barely visible. He sneezed and saw more naked people of flawless beauty walking around them, tempting them daintily.

Qosku turned to help Mungo, who quickly lowered a branch to Fernandric, but the sides of the pond suddenly shifted and pushed him away. Qosku recognized the pond, like a lethal am'bas'dubh plant with venomous spores of deceit. But instead of jawtraps, it had a leaf bowl of acid to act as its stomach. Qosku could see below the water, around the frenzied man's waist, a growing cloud of red, the acidic water eating through his skin. He reached out to stop Mungo from falling in when the man tripped on vines around his legs. Qosku grabbed him and held Mungo up as the sides of the pool shrunk, increasing the slope. The twisting vines encircled Qosku's legs, and Mungo slipped down but kept hold.

The other trappers ran in, tripping or jumping into the pond. Fernandric fell beneath the surface of the water into his blood cloud, with eyes glazed over and senseless death whispers on his lips. Five other unfortunate men shouted, struggling to get out, and their own blood clouds swelled and faces melted from their own frantic splashing.

With the vines and Mungo's hand on his leg, Qosku was getting pulled in too. After struggling to pull himself up, and failing even with dyne in his body, he knew he couldn't. He tried again, moving anger, hate, anything through his limbs, but to no avail. "Mungo, I no can pull you."

"You have to!" Mungo's voice was panicky. "Just pull, give me a vine!"

The others had by now stopped screaming, dissolving in silence, and the one man who hadn't fallen in ran away. Bodon was fighting the vines, crawling through it with a snarl and kicking up golden pollen everywhere. More naked men appeared, sensually urging them into the water, stroking their faces and arms. Qosku fought to ignore them when Mungo placed a belt-knife in Qosku's hand, begging for him to cut the vines and clear a path up. But he noticed Mungo's feet had fallen into the water, blood clouding around them. Even if he escaped, he'd be useless in the outerwild now. Tears fell from Qosku's eyes as he looked into Mungo's. "I very sorry, Mungo, but I no can help to you."

"No, no, no!" Mungo grabbed his leg tighter, pulling him down in an effort to climb. Qosku kicked at the hand and pushed his fear into his leg, twisting out of the man's grip. Mungo now had only the one vine in hand, and it slipped away before he fell into the acid water. Qosku pulled himself out, fighting through the vines and trying to not watch Mungo choking and sputtering in the water behind him.

Then Bodon was there, his hand wrapped around Qosku's neck and pulling him out of the vines to look him in the face. The trapper's eyes had gone wild. "All your fault, dirty little dugger!" he growled, choking Qosku. "I know you're hiding something. What are you really? A witch disguised as a boy?"

Qosku rammed Mungo's knife into Bodon, who kept him aloft. He flailed and kicked Bodon in the crotch and was dropped as the trapper doubled over. "I no witch," Qosku said as he crawled through the brush. "I girl in boy body." *Or a boy cursed to feel he's a girl.*

Qosku ran, stumbling, and Bodon's screaming followed him. Then somehow Chaska was there in chains and rags, stalking, haunting, accusing. He tried apologizing, but she wrapped the chains around him, squeezing.[13]

---

13 See *Losnin Liberado Kani,* 63

He woke thrashing in the blanket that had wrapped around him, panting and sweating. He sighed in relief—the dream was different. She'd not been there when he'd last admitted his secret, one of his secrets.

He then realized that everyone in the abbey room was watching him, of course his screaming probably woke them. He rolled onto his side, facing away from them and thinking, *Wonderful, now they have more reasons to tease or shun me.*

CHAPTER FOUR

THROUGH THE HELL OUTSIDE

Based on *Annals of Syago*, cc bastica 4;
The Scars of the Martyrs, cc bastica 666;

18th–19th of Septimosk, 246

Gierra, a world wholly malignant, sustained and killed its people at the same time. Both seasons brought on a different terror in Nevermore and beyond. The nights were fading from darkelan, the season of poison, the season they called the Long Hunt, when natural life in all its cruelty burgeoned forth. This meant an early onset of darkemorg, the season of bone, where each night all life hid and all corpses rose and wandered. Both seasons brought much pain and loss to Tolgrym, to Nevermore, but the turning would be celebrated in a few days' time at the Somhoin Festival of Saints, something Syago looked forward to.

With the success of Syago's first hunt came a great feast that night. One worthy of note in the Chronicles of a Thousand Suns,[14] the joke went. The gathering party also did well in herbs, vegetables and fruits, and wood; gathering stones would happen the next day.

That night, the celebratory feast was strong. Everyone ate in the square around a brazier that burned warm and bright in the night, allowing them to roast their catch. Both parties had brought in enough to last days if rationed well; what meat they didn't that night eat would be dried. Syago felt exhausted from the days' work and eager to enjoy its fruits.

Syago's victory was subdued by Bethory, who should've been play-fighting with the other dogs over some leftover bones behind the benches. The loss

---

14 A vastly underappreciated text, I believe. It can teach us much about our struggles. I'm fortunate to have one of the three extant copies with me in Voium, and it has profoundly shaped my views.

stung deep. Why was nature so cruel? The outside always took from them. It'd taken almost everything from him: family, friends, dogs, and dreams. It confined him to these damned walls. Elisabet too, who was a maid in Baron Milgalic's home. She was even less likely to leave than he, though she seemed less eager for it. His being of hero's stock got him a squireship with the count, but he still lacked time at the realm's castle of arms—and Alexandre. He felt a small measure of pride not only for the catch but also completing such a hard decision in taking Bethory's life. It seemed the kind of leadership of his father's caliber. Hopefully, Alexandre would recognize that in him next time he approached the grove to draw the sword, if he ever got that chance. If he'd had Alexandre already, Bethory might've lived.

As people around him laughed and sang, he brooded both for Bethory and Elisabet, who was sleeping off her illness. He still had faith and treasured the sacred revelation he'd received from Deova, but he doubted the Criod for cursing and torturing them in this way.[15] Surely, his fallen uncles and cousins weren't deserving of their punishments. Perhaps Alexandre would make it all clearer to him when it chose him. He was glad to have hunted when nature was most dangerous, but the outside would've been less of a threat to Bethory during the Grave's Night of darkemorg.[16]

"Don't be so glum on your victory night, lil' Iago," Tomas said, slapping him on the shoulder before taking a swig from his cider jug. "Dead dog still eatin' you?"

"No." He also drank from his goblet as Andras approached. "I was just enjoying the food."

Andras looked at him. "Really, you did great. That was quite an ending too. A hunt worthy of tales for children of many generations to come."

Syago shrugged—he hated to admit to appreciating Andras's praise. They both laughed at the gesture.

He forced the question out. "How do you feel about leaving for Cantlgrym on the morrow?"

Andras gave his own shrug. "You know. Excited, anxious, maybe a little afraid." He swirled his goblet, then drank.

---

15 As a gnostic religion, the Church of Deova Bondua relies on faith after knowledge, expecting each of its members to obtain in their hearts the revelation themselves and then living by faith in Deova the Savior.

16 See also *The Schiltron of Magodeoz*, 67

"Afraid?" Tomas asked. "What would you be afraid of?"

"Well, first there's the journey there. I can fortify through that, though. But I've heard the castle is harsh. And they do strange trainings, like they pull out corpses or... I don't know." He drank again.

Syago had heard similar things, but he'd learned to be suspicious of far tales. People told even stranger stories of the Kimoc. Yet Fal'iek's family certainly didn't seem that way. "It's probably only half-true, if that." He bit into his bread.

Donmal tripped in front of Syago with a loud clang. Lügos and Robertoim helped him up, and Sylbia fed him through his head cage, which, wisely, would come off on the morrow when the festivities had finished. Syago felt a renewed pride that the folk of Tolgrym took care of their own. If only that man could get himself together, they wouldn't have to torment him this way.

He shook his head, chewing the last kernels of corn. Spiced cider washed it down, and he started feeling better as a bard's music rose above the noise. The bard, now out of his clown's costume from earlier, gathered the children in tighter for one of his famous stories. As his assumed name implied, Tongunabiagüs loved the exaggeration and theatrics of his profession, so the grave fable held even greater weight. Even some adults moved closer, and Syago could already feel the energy of dyne coming from his tremulous voice.

Listen on and heed me well, for no tall tale do I tell.
Lest you imitate its choices poor—
Learn this tale dark and muddy of a fail so stark and bloody.
Their self-incurred hell so ruddy, follow them not, do I implore.
Burden of no small weight to bear, as a warning I spell this lore—
That you forget not the Whore of Nevermore.

Once upon a forgotten time, there fell a town of rotten clime
Behind guarded gate did they nightly quake in horror
There arrived in the evil hour, monsters of great size and power.
At death of day they'd cower, battle, and pray aught for no more.
Worse than our nights, they rightly fought, ere it became unholy war
And they long wept their fate of gloomy war.

From horned plant to tentacled titan, the beasts came to eat and frighten
They would rage and rumble, snarling and snaggling at gated door
To rake, snatch, and feed would they by night's abyss slake, hatch, and breed.
They were unable to sate such greed, in all manner of form to abhor
Beasts of Outside had nightly reign. Thus long the clergy did implore,
"Please, Holy Mother grant us succor!"

Solace and solution explored—to purge undesirables, light restored.
Thus the faithful prayed for safety in their hollow of Nevermore.
And a survey of all the people did they take from their holy steeple
To ensure a holy people before their Church of the Savior.
And of those poor souls they then caught, unwanted and unneeded, the
   town whore—
Disheveled, distraught, and sorely sore.

The woman in black coldly found, locked out to die on tenebrous ground.
Yet she stayed at the wall and pounded at barb'rous door
All who came to see off the gate heard her beg clemency of fate
But in place of mercy gave hate. Her wailing they could not ignore.
As the day wore long under the despair she bore—
Even seeing her pain still denied the door.

Massive monsters slithered and marched through encompassing wither-
   ous marsh.
Unnamables stalked village prey, looked and lurked they through murky
   moor.
Timorous watchers watched for nightfall, guards armed well prepared
   the fight of wall.
Mad monsters mauled a frightful gall; with darkness, they fed on sad whore
Swallowed fearful town's offering, offered outside that hollow's door.
Proffered for desperate peace evermore.

What pause they had would soon surcease, pause their violence and
   pause their peace
On following night porous mammoths pounded parapets louder than before
But the town was not alone in their homes of wood and stone—
Thereupon came a bloody moan, from ghost empty of mortal gore.

T'were the black gown that haunted, gown torn of her by odious boar.
Thus shame and horror shook them to the core.

Rent and riven by ravenous horn, spectral gown amorphous floated forlorn.
Neither vacuous nor vital—this was a phantom to deplore
When wailing phantom haunting came, woeful wailing wrought daunting
*   shame.*
Prayers barred not her daunting name, with that title called Evanore.
Hideous howling brought such dread, they failed at waging rueful war.
Their past callous actions they did abhor.

But pressing pleas had earned them naught and defiance only fury
*   fraught.*
So ended said town as the gates broke with final wail and roar.
There entered hell in walled hollow, they fell, used as gall to swallow
Each of you, I pray without wallow, do not as they did to Evanore
But defend all of like entreaty. Regress not the honor you forswore—
That we're all kindred here in Nevermore.[17]

It was by no means the best Syago had heard, but he did like its energy, not just of dyne but the rhythm and potency of words. Dyne normally interested him, since it was so rare. Tolgrym had only three elementists: Roberochester, an archemist; Milgalic, a dynast; and Toriacus, who was the town's archdynast, as all counts had to be. They were decent enough for the town, but if he understood right—based on his trips to Mantlgrym—they were comparatively weak ones. It made sense. Being isolated in Thornwood, Tolgrym was usually left out of the advancements of the towns. He longed to see such rarities as the bard's song or other dynal feats done by elementists, but his sadness overwhelmed any such curiosity. Alexandre was said to have powers; if only it would call him as its wielder, as it had his ancestors for generations, then he could discover such majesty himself. He'd harbored a creeping fear that it would never call him due to his mastozon blood or dirty skin. The priestesses had spoken of the purifying effect this had on the pagans, making their children holier and whiter. *But does that mean I'm too dirty for the Holy Judgment Sword? If my skin is light enough, then I could be the first mastozon to wield it.*

17 Taken from *The Words of Tongunabiagüs the Bard,* p. 3

Goidiberic approached, shaking him from his musings. "Syago," he said. "It's worse."

"What's worse?"

Goidiberic's voice dropped to a whisper. "Elisabet, her illness."

Putting down his plate and goblet, Syago made to jog for the cottage, but Goidiberic grabbed his arm. "Wait, Syago!" Taking Syago aside, he said quietly, "It's not just her. Several women have taken ill with the same symptoms. Go first to Roberochester. He likes you and might guarantee you get hold of a cure before it runs out. Meet me in her room."

"But what is it? What do I ask for?"

"By the rood, I really don't know. But they've seen her. Just explain that she's now got a fever and take whatever treatment applies."

Syago nodded and headed for the baron's manor. He did notice few women participating in the festivities; neither Roberochester nor his apothecary wife among them. He arrived at the manor, one of the few homes with a gated yard, and passed through to the front doors. Some windows glowed from candlelight, human silhouettes moving within.

Rapping the door's knocker made an unwanted sound that echoed through the dark streets. Young Lügos, the baron's son, opened the door.

"Lüg, I must speak with Master Roberochester," Syago began.

"Father is busy caring for Mother," Lügos said. "Are you here for the medicine? We haven't got any."

"And my wife is too ill-disposed from the pregnancy to make some," Roberochester said from behind his son. "Though I'm not sure she knows what it is in any case. Should we have some, you'd get it, and everyone else."

"What's happening?"

The baron's sharp gaze rose from Syago to see beyond. Syago turned to see several people gathering at the manor gate. Henric and Lügos the Flayed walked toward the front door.

Roberochester stepped out beside Syago and boomed, "My friends, perhaps it'd be best we meet in the hall. It appears we've a serious matter to discuss."

Mutters fluttered around, but as they migrated back to the square, Syago instead went home, where he found Goidiberic sitting next to Elisabet, laying wet rags on her head. Syago's despair grew at the sight of her: eyes closed, body wrapped up in blankets, her light-brown skin tinted pink. Goidiberic looked up expectantly.

"They don't have any," Syago said. "They don't even know what it is or if they could make a cure for it. They're meeting in the hall." He felt her hot head. It couldn't be pollen which usually killed quickly—they didn't get worse like this. "When was the last plague, Grandfather?"

"Thirty years past," Goidiberic replied without taking his eyes off his little granddaughter. "The consumption, they called it. It looked like this. This made her numb and slow before going to sleep, so I don't know. If the baron's wife isn't sure, then maybe not. And with her sick too, she won't be able to bleed the others. I might be able to bleed Elisabet with leeches, I've seen it done so many times..."

Damnation, she looked frail. She was always thin and timid, so Syago had always worried about her. But now she looked as though she might just fade back into the blankets. He'd never taken ill; none of them had. He hated that he could stop a mabin'guarik but not this.

"Suppose I'll go to the council if you'll watch over her?" Goidiberic said, rising on stiff knees. "Pray for her again, won't you?"

"No," he said, resolution taking shape. "I'll go. I'm going to see this—this curse stopped." Their eyes met for a moment, then Goidiberic nodded.

Syago donned his fur coat over his leathers and moved quickly through the frigid night air to the town square. Fluffy snowflakes flew in his face. *Damn this world*, he thought. *And to the hellpits with the Criod!*

He found the great hall a mess of emotional conversations that the count and his barons were finally getting to a calm. Candles along the walls of wood and stone cast shadows and dim illumination elsewhere.

Toriacus cleared his throat. "By the raise of hands from those here on behalf of someone, I want an indication of the number of our sick... That's sixty-six. Let's get names."

One by one, in an impatient succession, the men named wives, daughters, and mothers. *All women*, Syago noted. *How? Why?*

The realization of this peculiarity wasn't lost on anyone else, and conversations began anew. The barons hushed the crowd.

Roberochester stepped forward. "But let us take note, there are women who are not sick. For example, our Bishopess Myrian and my daughters, or the count's women." de Oviedom said, "But we're here for those that are."

The bishopess stepped forward. "Of course, we must look within and ask what is Deova teaching us? Why punish only women and only certain women? I've said for some time now that a new pride and lust of flesh has risen. Aspiring women and girls who walk in pride must expect chastisement from their matron and Heavenly Governess."

Syago knew Roberochester well enough to see the displeasure on his face. "Perhaps we ought to consider other possibilities as well, Bishopess." This thought resonated with Syago, who didn't think Elisabet was anything even remotely like that description.

The baron continued, "For example, our women every day bathe in the bathhouse, fed by the stream. They roll bread from grains of the forest. They wash our clothes. It might have to do with any of these, a bad seed or potion slipped in."

He stopped to see if anyone voiced a suspicion, but none did.

Toriacus moved forward then. "Then let's take count of who did what."

By show of hands, it was narrowed down to those lacking sickness had bathed that day or the day before, or in the case of most of the noblewomen, they'd had private water stored up. A pall of silence settled over the hall.

"But how?" Milgalic asked from Toriacus's side. He in turn looked at Roberochester, who also didn't appear to want the burden of having an answer.

"I suppose," he began, stroking his goatee, "the source could be coming from the stream… in which case we'd need to investigate upriver."

Henric asked, "You mean to send a group out at dawn?"

"No," Syago said, also standing. Expressions of surprise faced him. "We must go now; tomorrow may be too late. I'll go out. I and those who fortify well enough."

"We—we can't leave the walls at night," Lügos said, his badly marred face recalling the dangers that had earned him the title of Flayed.

Henric stared at Syago, then stood and nodded. "Boy's right, it won't do to wait. With enough people going out, and not far, we should be fine."

"I'll go too." de Oviedom also stood. When none else volunteered, he chided, "Are we of Tolgrym really this craven? I thought you stronger than this. Fortify and stand with us."

At this, several more stood, including Lügos. With twenty-four men, it was decided that the gate would open in half the hour, time enough to armor up and bid farewell.[18]

---

18 See *Luskmord: Atriom Carcerio*, 32

As Syago donned his armor, he thought of his training and regretted how little of it included fighting in the dark. Usually they didn't even go out of their homes at night except for guard duty, let alone past the walls. All knew that if you were without the walls after dark, you died in the gullet of some creature or became a lifeless.[19] He kept reassuring himself that a group of their size could handle it. They were trained, and even a pack of malwolves would hesitate against a ready group large enough. He realized then that his fear, same as before, faded before his new resolve: Elisabet lying there, withering away. He knew then he would die for her.

Goidiberic yanked the last strap on Syago's plate. "Ready," he muttered. They prayed once more, then hugged. He tied on his fur coat, kissed Elisabet on the forehead, and left.

The light snow had stopped, but the air was still cold and screened with a light fog. The town at night had never seemed so forlorn. Even with people in it, the life was gone. Gathering at the gates, they lit oil lamps instead of torches, which could blind the eyes and show like a beacon to anything on the hunt. Checking to make sure oil filled the lantern's container, he lit it and closed all but the front shutter.

Henric was the lead, seconded by de Oviedom. Syago stood with them, lantern and spear in hand, still longing for Alexandre. With a count off and a nod, Northgate groaned open a crack, iron hinges shrieking, and they filed out, forming ranks and marching warily along the wall to where the stream passed underneath through a grate. The stream's gentle trickle accompanied the crunch of their boots on soft snow and faint hooting of owls. The gray sheen of the mists made the forest brambles and brushes look even more haunted than usual.

They trekked along the stream and came to the first levy, a small dam that allowed them to adjust the flow of the river Nabia. Viewing the clog of sticks collecting there, Henric sighed, "We need to clear this."

"Now?" Syago asked.

"Yes. What we're looking for could be in that mess." Henric looked about the group. "I'll take half with me up to the second levy nearby. If we find nothing, we'll come back." He counted off those staying with de Oviedom as second lead. They began pulling out branches as Syago, even more

---

19 Referred to as the bodies or lifeless by Asturions and as lifeless by Kimoo, Chamands, and Unaka.

uncomfortable now that the groups had halved, followed Henric. *We'll be fine*, he told himself, looking around warily. *We're still close to the others and to the gate.* The howl of a malwolf, calling through the night for the moon, froze them in place till it faded.

The second levy had a couple sticks and a dead malwolf cub. Its hollow eyes stared up blankly, fanged mouth agape and tongue lolling. Black fur glistened from wetness, reminding Syago of Bethory. It twitched, reaching for them. They pulled it out, breaking its legs off, and cleared the levy.

Syago noticed a pair of glowing eyes watching them through the bushes, and he tightened his grip on his spear. But the eyes winked out, and after a moment's pause, he turned back to the body. The corpse still twitched, a reminder that this night began darkemorg and the bodies rose. A dead body could be what made their women sick, but they'd have diagnosed and treated it by now. And besides, the cub's body was too fresh, the levies having been cleared that morning by several men while Syago hunted. They'd cleaned the levies, as was done daily, and hadn't seen it.

Syago looked out into the night forest, an act that he'd thought was bad luck as a kid. He took in the giant thorny stalks in the distance amidst gnarly bushes, logs, and rocks, all of it clouded by fog. Upstream, something protruded out of the water. "Wait, what's that?" he called.

Henric followed Syago's gaze and led them to it. A jug had fallen into the stream, snagged on a branch. Or was it tied there? It was difficult to tell and, in any case, it hung on with contents already spilled out. Lamplight revealed the last few drops of dark liquid at the bottom of the large jug. They recognized it immediately: trap poison.

A collective gasp was quickly silenced as Henric gingerly pulled out the jug. Someone had probably left their poison jug in the river during the expedition. It'd carried down in the stream, only to collect in the women's bathhouse, where it poisoned the women of Tolgrym. Syago looked at the men who'd been on that expedition, feeling rage swell in him.

The conclusion hadn't needed to be spoken, and all looked at those who'd been in the gathering group. One shook his head. "I've no idea. We passed by here. Many of us did several times. But I didn't see nothing here."

Syago moved toward him. "You—"

Henric grabbed his arm. "No, not here." Syago let his breath out. They both looked the jug over. Then Syago saw past the jug a human-shaped figure in between two thornstalks. Spear and lantern in hand, Syago pushed through the others toward it. Seeing his target, they followed behind. As Syago neared the silhouette, however, it vanished and reappeared some distance away, deeper in the woods—too still to be a lifeless.

The calm sent a chill up his back; the greatest dangers of the outside were half as quiet and in control as this that watched them now. Again, the form faded away, soundless, and the thought of how easily it could kill him kept Syago's skin prickling. He turned to the others, who stared past him in the same direction. Henric merely shook his head. He took comfort that their faces shared his unease.

They returned to the lower levy. The second group had just finished clearing it and followed them back to town in silence, each mulling over the implications of what they'd found. Syago knew one of them now likely planned to avoid prosecution for this crime. *But why poison Tolgrym's women? I could imagine a man trying to kill his wife over a dispute, but trying to murder them all? Why would anyone incur such dishonor to hurt a woman. Well, boys picked on Elisabet for being different, so why not others? Or what if it was that phantom we'd seen? Could a ghost have pinned it down in the river so well?*

The groaning of the gate ended in a heavy clank, and they presented the jug to Count Toriacus and the masses of people in the hall.

"Who carried the poisons?" Count Toriacus asked.

Numerous names were shouted out and their owners pointed at. Six of those called out rose to their feet and answered questions about what had happened with their jugs. No conclusive answer was found due to the chaotic unpacking of the returning expeditions and subsequent feast preparations. Milgalic was missing a jug, but it could've been carried by anyone.

Finally, Henric observed, "It might be that someone else did it. For why would one of these men do it if the jug could be traced back to them? Anyone in the expedition could have pulled it off of their pack and left it."

"I think we're missing something else as well," Lügos said, rising. "We found the jug and immediately assumed this was on purpose. But could it not have been an accident? In that case, even the carrier wouldn't know. None would. We can't just assume evil intent at every bad turn. Reading conspiracy into everything does us no justice."

"The jug was tied to a branch in the water," Tomas asserted. "It was put there."

Henric looked skeptical, and Syago spoke up. "No, it wasn't tied, it was tangled." The rest of the group affirmed his correction, but Tomas didn't look satisfied. Syago added, "Of course, that could've been the ploy."

"Then unless we've any witnesses to the contrary," Roberochester said, "we must admit that it could've been either intentional or accidental."

Once again, the hall filled with heated conversations. Thoughts of his little Elisabet waiting for them to debate drove Syago nearly mad. But it wasn't just about her. Gleidy had mended his clothes, Yanet had baked them cakes, Rociol had tutored him, Gladis had treated him when sick, Mylagros had given him girl advice, Sylbia and Esmeralda were pretty and fun, and on and on. He cared for them all.

The cruel unfairness of it also struck Syago. Even if just an accident, it only affected the women. He remembered Eliana talking about how only women had to bathe every day in the River Nabia because they were expected to always be clean and beautiful. Men used the well and could be clean at their leisure. It also had only affected the poorer women. The count's and barons' ladies and daughters had private baths and so their own private stores of water, save the two who sometimes joined the rest.

Syago stood and shouted above the din, "We need to find a cure!" Several turned to him. "We can punish later, but we're wasting time here. Now that we know what it is, we have to cure it." He focused expectantly on Roberochester.

On news of the poison, Roberochester had immediately administered the cure to his sleeping daughter. It was not much, and not something they could simply reproduce, either. None blamed him for spending it on his wife, or giving some to one of the count's daughters, both of whom had been poisoned by using it to clean. He had obligations to family and liege lord, as did they all. But it also meant that there was none left of that batch for everyone else.

"I'm afraid I don't have a way to make more of the antidote. We've never needed it before."

"Then find a way!" Tomas yelled. "Make one."

"We don't know the full recipe and don't have the ingredients we know of. We need to send a group to Mantlgrym on the morrow. They'll have one."

"No, now." Syago remained standing, and the faces in the crowd were incredulous. "We go now. I'm not waiting. She—they can't wait."

"Lad," Henric said. "It's night. We can't go now."

"SHE'S SICK FROM A POISON MADE TO KILL A MABIN'GUARIK!" Syago yelled. "I'm... I'm..."

"We know, Syago," Toriacus said. "We're all at risk of losing someone. But it'd do us no good to go out at this time of night and it's only hours until dusk anyway. The night is almost spent and it may take that much time to prepare the wagon. We'll leave early, before the point of dawn, and will continue our investigation of the culprit in the meantime. Meeting adjourned."

Syago sat, wiping away tears as the envoy was picked and everyone left to their homes.

CHAPTER FIVE

A Strange Storm's Brew

Based on *Leyta's Journals*, cc bastica 10;
Scars of the Martyrs, cc bastica 900;
The Nordvargor Testaments, cc bastica 670;

18th of Septimosk, 246

Leyta stood in the observatory, a darkened room atop the central rear tower.[20] The open windows chilled the stone room as dusk settled; she gazed through a large bronze ardatum, Balgor's newest and most successful invention.[21] The two watchtowers had two ardatum: each a bronze pod and a tube with nobs and levers for adjusting the angle. Dyne controlled the image, the value of which depended on the elementist using it. The instrument had symbols and connecting lines that made it a dynal focus. It was like her staff, except it was an archemical construction with the single purpose of imaging. The instruments recreated images of faraway objects and places projected into the water inside the pod, providing a slightly better illusion than the previous crystal globes used. The main setback was that the images had to be pulled from a straight line of sight. Dyne allowed her far sight even in darkness, if with greater difficulty, though a clear image was hard to make any time of day.

It was hours after her trial, and a mixture of sentiments floated inside her: joy for finally becoming a dynast and anguish at what she'd done for it. She found that channeling her sadness into the ardatum produced a clearer image, so she used that.[22] She caught the image of Virgow and

---

20 See *Luskmord: Atriom Carcerio*, 36

21 For a list of Balgor's archemical inventions, both attempted and successful, see his *A World Reworked* and *Moonspell Hell Light de Lostregos*.

22 See *Thy Light, Therion!*, 65

Balgor's caravan leaving Lake Laomain toward Voium; colors were hazily portrayed, but the image focused on the shapes.[23] She twisted a dial to distance the focus and then swung it north to view Shruumoth Forest, home of the summoner's village, Bokhor. The images always took a few moments to become discernible and even then remained slightly blurry. The height of the tower with the reach of the dynal tool, depending on what sentiments she fed it with, allowed her a near-perfect yet one-sided view of the small, humble village.

She saw people around the village preparing decorations. The turn of the season meant an equinox celebration, a Festival of Powers, whence all the different summoner orders gathered. She twisted a knob on the side for the sight to move out so the village became very small on the view. Then she saw it.

A funnel cloud hurtled south toward the village. It surprised her, for she would've thought the cloud had blown over hours ago. But there it was, bigger, darker, and closer to where Bokhor sat. Squinting, she thought it looked more black than the usual dark brown and concluded it was a different one from what she'd earlier seen. She'd never seen a black cloud before and followed it, enlarging the image but unable to see anything inside the swirling vortex. She then dipped cup into the nearby water basin and poured the water into an opening on the ardatum's top. The water entered a small hold where the image projected, now bigger. She moved the sight back to the village. It was difficult to tell, but the chamands weren't summoning anything. If the storm was perplexing, the lack of activity from the village was even more so.[24]

"Mastra Anaruth, come look at this. Something's wrong," she said loudly. Anaruth's plump figure came up the stairs from the room beneath. Leyta moved to the right while Anaruth looked.

"Whatever that is, it's moving toward the village," Anaruth observed for a moment, moving the sight around. "That is odd. I know of no creatures that can do that. I'm damned if I know where it came from, though. There's nothing north of there. It could be one of their own summons or a weather phenomenon we haven't seen before. But I doubt it."

23 Discrepancy. Either the date or the caravan is incorrect here, they were leaving Mantlgrym that day.

24 Some water damage here has smudged the ink. Fortunately, I'm able to see most of the words, but some are questionable. Where I can't read I use context to determine what was meant, but others are more in doubt such as: funnel, decorations, and summoners.

Leyta looked out the window and hugged her body against the cold. "I can't see anything from here."

"Did you check if it's a flaw in the ardatum? Some blotch creating darkness?"

"Yes, it's not." Then she smiled. "But when will it see the darkness inside us?"

Anaruth either didn't hear or just ignored it. "There is…" she trailed off.

"There is what?" Leyta asked.

"The other, more distant possibility that this is the work of an other-worlder, a demon maybe, or anything not of gierra. But it's beyond me why they'd seek out their most dangerous enemies like this. As a preemptive strike, it doesn't seem very impressive. The Razhod created something like this once. Two of them wiped out half an army with that cyclone."[25] She continued to peer into the ardatum. "Leyta, get a message to the village, through Voium. I doubt it will get there in time, but it's all we can do for now. And get Alkant."

Leyta wrote a quick message on parchment, then went to the adjoining room and pulled a quervosk from its cage. It was small for its species but still bigger than Leyta's head. After warily attaching the parchment to its leg—for, though trained, it could still easily peck her eyes out—she set it to fly out to Voium. As she watched it go, Leyta felt a strange sensation. Her skin crawled as though she, in turn, was being watched. The chamber was empty, save for caged birds, and nothing could see her through the window so high in the tower. The feeling persisted, giving her goosebumps and raising hairs on the back of her neck, but she brushed off the superstition as coincidental to the evening. She shivered, rubbed her arms, then called down the stairwell for a keeper to get the Castellan.

Moments later Alkant watched and said, "It has to be an attack. The vortex has set on the village, just hovering there and obscuring it completely. It almost looks like a pollen storm, but it's too dark and at the end of the season."

Leyta thought on storms she'd been through. The worst snow or rainstorms were just thick and wet. A pollen storm could be poisonous, acidic, or harmless. In all cases, they'd only need to go inside and seal up their homes.

"It has to be an outsider, a fiend," said Davagis as he peered in. "Dynasts could potentially do this, but none would spontaneously attack Bokhor."

---

25 *ibid*, 44

Alkant stroked his beard for a moment, considering every option, as he always did. "It must be some new fiends that have been released. They would have to think themselves powerful or they wouldn't march on Bokhor. In either case, there's nothing more to be done. Voium has been sent a message and will respond when they're able; likely their standby army will arrive at Bokhor on the morrow. I want Anaruth to keep the watch. Davagis will come with me. Leyta, I have decided to approve the carnival group for entry to the castle. They *are* odd but I think they can be trusted. But watch them all the same."

She nodded. As archkeeper, Leyta held responsibility alongside her studies to arrange the seasonal ceremony, this time involving carnival performers.[26]

At nearly midnight, Leyta expected little sleep but was now used to not getting enough. Leadership and studying robbed her daily of these, though she traded it willingly. She went to her chest in the women's residence for a warmer fur. Pulling a locked chest out from under her bed, she rummaged through it, then froze. Out of the corner of her eye, she saw a figure, tall and dark, watching her from the doorway.

"I'm not going to undress for you, if that's what you're waiting for," she said, loud enough to draw attention from anyone nearby while pulling her coat on. Though it didn't respond. She turned, and it was gone.

The same as in the messaging tower, now following me? But who in Cantlgrym was as tall and dark? Davagis? Alkant? But they wouldn't just watch me. Was I imagining it? Probably, though that was little comfort, dynasts had to watch their sanity very carefully. A real stalker was its own problem; an imagined one something else entirely.

She passed through the main hall, then out into the bailey, where some late-night training was taking place—

...[27]

—feeling annoyed as ever, disturbed even, she walked away. She adored young kids, but sometimes she wanted to throttle them. And while Alkant and Davagis were always hard men whom she respected and learned from, she felt this was a little too strict, maybe approaching abusive. But they

---

26 *See Luskmord: Atriom Carcerio, 2*

27 An entire section of probably eight pages here was deliberately blotted out, with no explanation given. It's impossible to say what's under the ink markings, but the extent and context speak volumes.

were the authority, so she kept her mouth shut. For now, it gave chills, and she doubted she could forget it or let it go.

She walked up to the abbey and entered quietly. Luminous at night, it was a place she loved walking into to look around for just a moment before sleep. Almost more of a priory, it was a small room enclosed by pillars and residences. Candles hanging by thin chains provided the only light, and the walls muffled any sound.

She walked through rows of meditating friars until she saw Qosku sitting with his eyes closed behind two pillars. She'd heard he trained differently than the others. His meditation was a prayer to his gods while theirs was to Heavenly Mother. They trained with fist and weapon. He only trained with his fists and fought with clawed gauntlets, which she'd not heard of before. She was concerned both for him and about him. So many things felt off, and with how dangerous the Unaka were reported to be in the mountains, she couldn't help but wonder why he was really there.

The abbey was Deovan but was intended to be open to other worshipers, as its practice was dynal and not theological. But, of course, the Order of Nine Angels still housed the Asturion creed, which meant symbols of Deova Bondua and the Sacred Blood adorned the shrine. A sun wheel cross, black roses, and amaranth flowers subtly decorated the arches and reliefs. But they weren't as prevalent as the similar, dark symbols of pagan origin that the elementists used, such as winged serpents and filled grails.[28]

"Pretty, is it?"

She jumped slightly at Qosku standing next to her. He looked up at her with a mixture of curiosity and seriousness. "You no like it?"

"Oh I do, but where did you start learning this?"

"I started at five, which is lowest possible in Chuqi'kirau." His bare upper body bore Unakan symbols—which gave him his dynal powers—instead of Deovan markings, she noticed with some disquiet. She was trying to not fall into the same thinking as other people, but it was getting harder to trust him.

"Do they train many Unakan dynfists there?"

"More is now because monsters attack mountains and caves and they are need help."

"So then why did they let you leave if they need you?"

---

28 *ibid, 6*

"They no let—no, they let me for to train better. They say I go," he muttered, rubbing his arms and looking off to the side. Common traits of liars; however, the conversation already had difficulty with his shyness and lack of proper Asturion. She still felt sympathy and that he deserved a chance.

"M'lady," a young man interrupted from behind her. She turned to see Drest waiting expectantly, wringing his hands and not meeting her eyes. "Sorry, m'lady. But may I... can I speak with you? In private, I mean."

"Of course, Drest."

He led her to a tight hallway adjoining the main hall of the abbey and into a room at the end. She noted his hesitation at the door.

"Drest, what is it?"

"It's, well, maybe nothing. Maybe I should go get Master Constantin."

She caught him before he left. "Show me."

He looked into the room, so she walked in ahead of him. The abbey had dorms like Cantlgrym—beds in tight rooms with space only on shelves and beneath the beds—but even tighter in the case of this priory of wood and plaster. However, Leyta recognized this tiny room as the isolation training quarter: a simple room with no bed where a trainee would live in solitary confinement for weeks at a time. He had a single cushion, candle, and chamber pot, but no windows or anything else. The one door was opened to bring in food and switch out the pot every morning. The trainee wasn't to speak or interact.

Looking around, she saw that the cushion was gashed and the candle had burnt out. "Drest, who was this?"

"Navidsom, the younger one from Cantabryn."

"Why did he do this? Where is he?"

"We don't know; he was gone when we brought him food."

"What do you mean? Nobody saw him in the morn? Nobody knows where he is?"

He shook his head, then Master Constantin and Mastras Roza and Anaruth entered, followed by more boys. The dynfist master fingered the cushion and muttered, "A blade, or..."

But he wasn't allowed to have a blade in there, nor was there any way for him to leave the room without the others noticing. Its only exit was the door. Leyta then noticed on the floor, by where the cushion had been, four long scratch marks that ran parallel on the floor planks, as if from a claw. The gouges in the wood were bright in their freshness in contrast to the old planks. The boys gasped, and Leyta resisted the urge to cross herself with them.

Constantin looked at it, his old face impassive, deducing. Anaruth and Roza surveyed the room. Finally, Constantin looked at Leyta and she realized she was biting her nails. She quickly withdrew them.

"Go tell Alkant," Constantin said. "It appears we've a phantom to be rid of and a body to find."

CHAPTER SIX

FORBIDDING PEOPLE

Based on *The Hunter's Parchments*, cc bastica 203;
Writings of Qosku, cc bastica 35;
The Nordvargor Testaments, cc bastica 800;

19th of Septimosk, 246

The three Roah'riik sped down the woodland river on canoe toward Quoak, moving fast in the fading daylight. They'd not intended to stay out so long and now night stalked them, an inescapable hunter. They moved quietly, calmly despite their haste, for the river held dangerous secrets, violent if disturbed.[29] Though the forest loomed on either side of them, the river at least opened the canopy for some starlight. The moon too, though weak it was on this eve.

They put in at a point nearest to where Quoak was located. Moving into the eerie bramblewood, they paused to get their bearings on the retreating wildlife before continuing on, running. Birds sang and bugs chirped year-round, but they quieted at night during the season of bone. Whether out of fear or reverence for the dead, it was not known, but retreat they did. Yet the Roah'riik slowed their run when they arrived at the potted dell, a small dip in the forest where various clay pots sat beneath overgrowth, some nearly as tall as a standing person.

Each were painted and held the bones of dead ancestors. When a Kimoc died, he was painted, burned (depending on the season), then sealed into a jar and kept there until it was time to place him in the forest. Sometimes they were brought back into the village for a few moons, then returned. The big jars held multiple family members at a time, something done more

---

29 See *Luskmord: Atrium Carcerio*, 4

and more of late as pottery was not in practice as much as it used to be. These were all very old.

The Kimoc looked over the graveyard, some pots broken, most covered in vines, all eerie. But several had their lids removed. This was not supposed to be; the disconnected bones couldn't move of themselves and were not appealing to scavengers either. The lids were heavy and tight-fitting. Someone had removed them and, as the Roah'riik inspected more closely, taken out the remains. There were no scattered remains, save some from the broken ones, which may not have meant anything. But to Fal'iek, it was clear their tombs had been desecrated. Tek'ouk and Mour'ikik looked at him and each other, eyes passing along the unspoken questions of *Who?*

Other Kimoc tribes or the Asturions could only be the culprits. But the hunting and gathering parties hadn't gone near here, at least not recently, and other Kimoc would have no reason to. It made no sense.

They abandoned their investigation, but only temporarily, as night fell and twitching lifeless began to rise. Animal corpses leered at them through forest shadows, moving toward them in search of flesh to tear. At first, the three Roah'riik moved quietly through the woods, focusing on stealth and safe paths. Then, as their lifeless pursuers increased, they broke into a run. Lifeless came after them, clumsily but noiselessly. It wasn't long until the three reached the safety of Quoak, where the reported atrocity stirred calls to action.

Qosku dreamed a memory once again, this time a nightmare from before Mungo and Bodon.

The Apugaka Mountains jabbed at the sky with snowy peaks over forested valleys. On these ridges, Qosku ran from Izquchaka to the nearest tambo fort following his betrayal of Chaska there.[30] He ran along the dangerous stone-laden trail. Although he couldn't stop crying, he managed to fight off the atocfox that had attacked him. It wasn't very big, about

---

30 There are several points here where her name is written as Ch'aska instead, one of the remaining spelling variations in an otherwise consistent text.

as large as he, but alone he made good prey for the quick and clever. He tightened the leather gauntlets on his arms, utilizing them as bandages for bleeding hands.

Clouds overhead, gliding between mountain peaks, promised an imminent rainfall. He reached the tambo, a small tower with a sun gate and granary, encircled by a wall atop terraces that stacked down the mountainside like a giant staircase. All made of tight-fitting stone blocks, well-crafted though not the masterworks of the temples and palaces in Izquchaka or Chuqi'kirau and incomplete with ruined thatched roofings. It was empty, as he'd hoped. *Is that a good thing? Can I survive alone in an empty tambo?*

He moved through it all, quick to find a good place to defend if the atocfox came for him. He hid in the granary, which was empty of grain as well. He didn't know what to do about food; he'd never wanted for food before. Had never been outside civilization before. But he couldn't be in Chuqi'kirau or Bictos or Izquchaka anymore. Not now that he'd been exiled and lost Chaska, his twin sister, by his own fault. He ached for her, and for his body. Lacking his twin, he was even more off balance, even more wrong-bodied. The curse making him think he was actually girl never felt so profound as at that moment. He wept until he could not anymore.

Exhausted, he dozed off without meaning to.

It was not a creature on the prowl that woke him but something more sinister. People were chanting outside. Quietly, he peeked out the small window, then backed away. They were coming out of the tower, but it'd been empty and it didn't look as though anyone had arrived or he'd surely have heard their approach. The rain and hail had stopped, and it was getting dark. They were all in religious garments, dark woolen tunics longer than the typical Unakan wore, and with steel helmet feathered headdresses over clay masks. They formed a circle outside the sun gate, oddly lacking soldiers.

They chanted words from a language he didn't recognize—it made his skin prickle.

Then they raised up the head of the atocfox on a pole. The priest then pulled the skin off and put it over the head of a figure in yellow, like a mask in place of the headdress. Realizing who they might be, Qosku backed away from the window. The Saqra's Cult, the renegade group of Unakan priests. Necromancers, it was believed, that summoned Yaoltmictlan to aid them here on kay pacha, the world. Yet Saqra was more mischievous, while these figures were solemn, dark.[31] *Zupayk's Cult, then?* More animal heads were held up: an ozor, a yama, a black dog. But these were not skinned or put on; only the atocfox, which became the Saqra while the other heads were set up as posts around a pit others were digging.

And in that pit, a girl.

The sacrifice was younger than him, a girl he didn't know. She was gagged and crying. They were burying her live but without quieting her pain or putting her to sleep first. Qosku knew little of the old rites, except that it was a prayer, perhaps to Zupayk or Amaru. He wondered if he intervened, then he might be able to return. But no, the weight of his betrayal was already too much. And for this, he was too afraid. He understood nothing of their chanting or hand motions, didn't understand why they weren't starting it on a waka altar, didn't like that they wore steel armor, and, despite the priests, didn't think any of it was even truly Unakan.

Then he had an idea. Since the Apus and Great Ones hadn't helped him, perhaps these priests could. But would they? He could offer himself as a sacrifice to fix his mistakes, fix him, and maybe even save Chaska.

He ran out to them. "Stop, please! Sacrifice me instead, I beg. I'm ready and willing, and she is not. Take me!"

His heart thrummed as the masks turned with unnerving calmness toward him. The weight of it pressed on him, sacrificing not just his life but also his soul. The girl's eyes pleaded with him while hard, dark masks regarded him. The foxheaded Saqra approached.

Qosku backtracked. "Wait I-I only meant—I just want to save my sister. My twin, to bring her back. Can you do that?"

The Saqra in yellow said nothing but instead motioned to Qosku, then the girl. He stood confused, then went to her, cupping her tearstained face in his hands. He began digging her out. But the Saqra raised a scepter and whacked him unconscious.

He jolted awake, lying in the same spot beneath a star-filled sky. It was beautiful, but where were the priests? A leering face of shining eyes and teeth, those of some kind of fox, watched him from the darkness before vanishing. But the priests were not there, nor were their posts or ornaments, but their sacrifice was, buried up to the head. The dead girl's eyes were unmistakable.

---

31 See *Losnin Liberado Kani,* 36

Not a stranger. She was Chaska.

He screamed, stumbling away. Slowly, he walked back to her, to feel her. *But this is impossible, I saw her. It was a different girl.* Removing the cloth and paint revealed more of her. Cold in death. He crumbled, weeping over her until he fell asleep once more. Her body was gone when he woke near the empty pit. He searched but she was not there, nor were the priests. He determined by the tracks in the dirt that someone had been there just before the group of Asturion trappers found him.

But which was the dream?

Lying awake on his mat in the abbey, following the sequence of nightmares, he was as tormented by the memories as he was by betraying Chaska in Izquchaka—ill-fitting puzzles he tried to piece together as confusion and horror mixed. Had he dreamed of seeing the cult and their sacrifice only to wake up to the reality of Chaska being murdered by him? Or had he dreamed her dead body as the sacrifice while she was still in Izquchaka? He wanted recourse but accepted that he could no longer save her, for if she were still alive, this was clearly an omen of what was to come and she was already gone from him regardless. But then how now could he save himself, if not her, being exiled and shunned by his people and their eternals?[32]

---

32 *ibid,* 23

CHAPTER SEVEN

THE HELL OUTSIDE AND IN

Based on *Annals of Syago*, cc bastica 9;
Scars of the Martyrs, cc bastica 906;
The Nordvargor Testaments, cc bastica 620;

19th of Septimosk, 246

Syago prayed over Elisabet again, asking Deova to heal and preserve her. She was noticeably paler, still warm regardless of being bled. The baron had devised a potion to ease the symptoms, to grant them more time, but only the cure would be enough. Without having slept much, he made to leave. Goidiberic prepared him some food and saw him to the square, where the wagon waited.

The church bell tolled sunrise, this time marking when the wagons bound for Mantlgrym were meant to lock and leave. The wagon waited in the square by the road and took up almost half the available space. The woolly bulk of two horned bomogs were harnessed to the ten-foot-high steel and wooden structure.

The driver's box on the front better resembled a cage. Its top lid opened, and the small Unakan form of Virgow climbed out.[33] A leather coat hid most of his dark-brown skin, and his eyepatch and scars attested to his hardened experience. Emerging from the back of the wagon was the massive, fur-clothed figure of Balgor de Danteligeir, the ohancanu. He was called one, being from the Fomorions, but Syago didn't like it; they were known to be violent and follow pagan rituals. Balgor was a giant cyclops but civilized. He braided his long, thick beard and hair, and studied ancient texts of multiple languages. With Virgow, they made an odd pair but were always accepted at Tolgrym for their annual visit.

---

33 *Kachateo Qoyorik at birth, but he went by Virgow.*

60

"Syago!" Balgor boomed when he saw him. He turned and embraced Syago and then Goidiberic, muffling their faces in his bulk of fur-covered gambeson and beard. Syago still sometimes found the single eye unsettling.

The giant hefted supplies in and out of the wagon, negotiated by the town's trade deals, while looking Syago up and down. "Are you ready to move on then or what now?"

"Oh, I wish it," he mumbled. "No, I go with you only as far as Mantlgrym."

"Ah, we'll get you next time then." He ruffled Syago's hair and went to speak with Count Toriacus.

Everyone going had someone close who had been affected. Balgor and Virgow would continue on with those set for Cantlgrym, already being sched-uled to leave this morning anyway. Andras, Lüg, Deiba, and Sylbia would go on, while Syago and Tomas would stay in Mantlgrym on behalf of the town council.

At the sound of a horn, the crowds quieted. Tongunabiagüs the Bard stood atop a roof, shed of his jester's motley for the farewell. He raised an unfurled banner with a large red circle and hammer painted on it, and other smaller symbols of dyne along the sides enabled him to sing a dynal Song of Might in a healthy baritone:

Bought and born, ire and angst designed
In frightener's fires refined
We are stronger than pain and fear
There'll be no faltering here
Fighting war, you beat out more strong
Burn off all the weakness and wrong
Die heavy, untamed, and live hard
We the people of iron scarred
Bear that crown, the furnace goes long
Face the beatdown, the heat burns strong
Harden on, fie slowness, be gone
Get weakness gone and thunder on
Fight on, conquer, and bear that scar
Forward with force and fly far
Warring, you kill that weak more strong
Heavy on, warriors, fast and long
We are the strong, we are the strong![34]

---

34 *ibid, 66*

His voice sounded more like a chorus of men singing rather than one individual: louder, deeper, and richer than natural. With dyne, his sentiments of strength and courage filled all who heard him, as if being warmed by fire. If performed with sufficient skill and power, such songs were said to shift the winds of battle, still riots, and move enemy forces to surrender. When his song finished, he closed the banner and took a slight bow to brief applause.

Gathered around the wagon, the town delegation approached, with Count Toriacus at the head.

"With great confidence," he said, lifting a small brown pouch, "I present the town funds that we've collected for this purpose and place them in the hands of Syago, whom I charge with leading the group."

The crowd's cheers turned to laughter at Syago's stunned expression. His blush changed to a sheepish grin, however, as he was handed the bag and given the count's medallion to signify the authority invested. He couldn't help glancing at Andras, the count's eldest son and would-be carrier, but who remained impassive in the pass over.

Count Toriacus continued, "I would give it to my own, but he is to continue on to Cantlgrym. And Syago, having squired under me as well as conducted successful expeditions, is worthy of the responsibility. Many of us, too, would go. But we must care for our afflicted and protect the town. So I trust you will be quick and sure in your journey. Do not let us down."

The young men responded in the affirmative and, amidst more cheers, climbed into the back of the wagon. The back door of the wagon slammed shut and was locked twice from within.

The fanfare of the town now behind them, the wagon's rattling became the only sound. Each passenger kept quiet, eyeing warily the woods around them. As darkemorg season dawned, the woods browned and hardened in plantsleep, in preparation for the seasonal resurgence of things in decay. The moonlit nights of darkemorg woke the bodies, lifeless, at night to roam destructively across the realm of Nevermore, dusk till dawn.

The wagon's sturdy, thick frame protected them well enough, and Syago felt only slight anxiety. He felt reassured by the competence and familiarity of the group. Despite their tiffs, they were close as kin and would die for each other if need be.

All eyed the spears that hung along the walls. Through a crack in the planks, Syago spotted a group of gurows. At some point, the group relaxed enough that light conversation filled the wagon. Syago tried not to think of how most of the group was heading on to Cantlgrym without him. The blackbirds continued to scratch, peck, and shriek on the box roof overhead. It unnerved them at first, but they came to ignore it and talked quietly. Syago sat between Andras and Lüg, whom Syago was surprised to see leaving Tolgrym. Andras had been speaking of the tournaments at Castle Cantlgrym.

"So they let you use real weapons but with full armor. When we do that in Tolgrym, I always win, so I know I can beat Voium's best."

Syago couldn't hold his tongue anymore. "Andras, the only reason you always beat us was because your pa got you nicer weapons and armor. And it's not even always."

At this, everyone chuckled or rolled their eyes, not surprised by the exchange between the two. Andras's eyes narrowed. "This again? I can hold against you with regular arms well enough. 'Sides, it's not like squiring under my father and being the son of a hero hasn't done you any favors."

"You try fighting someone in your armor and tell me that," Syago said over grumbles from the rest. Andras let it go, so Syago kicked back lazily—until a sudden jolt in the wagon bounced him into the planks, hitting his head.

Balgor called out from the driver's seat, "Sorry! Didn't see that stump."

Hours later, the wagon slowed to a near stop, and everyone hushed, listening. It was too soon to be at Mantlgrym, which meant trouble outside. Syago opened the front hatch. "Why'd we slow?"

Balgor pointed in front of them. "There's a tree by the path."

Syago saw the gnarled oddity towering over the road. He quailed. "Are we to fight it, then?"

"No," Balgor said. "You'll have to show off another time, lad. We'll move around it."

Syago had been face-grabbed by one before in the worst, most humiliating experience of his life. These bore little resemblance to the mythical plants known as "trees" in Kimoc and Asturion legends. Those trees portrayed beauty and peace, providing shade and magical fruit. This tree was like a clawed arm sticking out of the ground, waiting, leafless and still, a bringer of death. It even had a desiccated human skeleton hanging from its branches, which reached out and scraped the wagon reins as the bomogs pulled by, scratching at the wooden box for six terrifying seconds. And then the creature was behind them.

Balgor stroked his beard. "Unusual for trees to move out here like that during darkemorg. I'll ask Anaruth for her opinion when we arrive." He turned a cool eye to Syago. "I'd prefer you stay inside and help back there next time, lad."

A little red-faced, he retreated to his seat. With Alexandre, he'd have more respect and authority. Goidiberic had said that the corpses of those that died on *The Nascendante* came to Tolgrym, having washed up out of their ocean grave and begun stalking as they do every darkemorg. The Grave's Night. They came at the walls, driven by unseen energies and were then destroyed by wall guards and traps. His uncle burned the body that had belonged to Odiru, then interred its ashen remains in the family coffins. Syago had occasionally wondered why the lifeless rose and gotten theological responses that never satisfied.[35] For certain it was stranger than the savage hate of the monsters of the outside, but only because that made sense, as explained in the scriptures. The lifeless were assumed to be part of the Criod's punishment of creation. And he'd received his share of scars, losses, and nightmares in that created world.

The wagon rolled for most of the day, almost eight hours, and they ate dinner without stopping. Syago got up from his bench and climbed over the bags to open the door to the driver's box. He sat in the cramped space between the burly form of the large fomorion and the small Unakan.

Virgow grumbled at his presence, but Balgor leaned down to mutter in Syago's ear, "You lose the bragging competition back there?"

"No, of course not. I always win those." He grunted as the wagon jolted from a rock. "Actually, I just wanted to get out of that box and breathe some air."

The road ahead looked clear, pushing forward through the newer thorn-branches that had begun to encroach on the road out of Thornwood. Dusk neared. Syago knew from previous rides they were just under an hour away from Mantlgrym. He looked off into the woods.

"Patience," Balgor mumbled without taking his eye off the road ahead. "Someday it may choose you, or it may never choose anyone again. Nothing you can do about it, only accept it."

---

35 *The beliefs on this vary, so it's not clear which he's referring to. They all have something to do with the constellations and phases of the moon during the season.*

"Yeah. Everyone else says the same thing. They don't have dirt in their heritage muddying up the legacy like I do, though."

"And of which dirt do you speak?" Both looked at him. Balgor's voice dropped to a growl. "Your mother's? Don't shame her like that. There's nothing dirty in your blood or skin, just as there's nothing dirty in mine or Virgow's. Watch what slander you believe, or it'll destroy you from the inside out."

But what if it's true? Forces of light and dark, good and evil, of which we are made.

"Ah, the Mounds of Fury," Balgor said. Some ten paces ahead, the path opened up out of Thornwood to crest and give an expanding view of the mounds. As they neared, the field of bulging hills below became more visible, giving them a good look at New Galica, Mantlgrym, among them.[36] Beneath gray skies, the field of mounds, stony, grassy, and even, allowed enough space for the wagon to weave between them.

From that distance, the walled city appeared as a dark-brown oval. The wagon left the hill overlook, leaving behind the gurows with the brambles, and began weaving through the mounds. As they descended and neared, rooftops and pointed towers became visible over the thirty-foot wall that surrounded the buildings. Virgow snapped the reins for a quicker pace in such an open area.

Sounds of heavy drumming and clamor rang out over the mounds from the city, the terrible sounds of battle. The wagon turned the corner, and they saw that the noise came from outside the wall. A herd of daemogs, fearsome horned bulls with eyes that burned of loathing, rustled and stamped around, working themselves into a rage in front of the southgate, which the caravan needed to pass through,

BOOM! BOOM! BOOM!

Three rammed the gatehouse, their large horns scarring it and throwing off wooden splinters from the great door. Smoke and embers plumed around them, mixing with the dust cloud. The vengeful herd obviously sought to take the city, or break its power before full onset of the Grave's Night. The fortifications held due to the well-built doors and trained soldiers who

---

36 New Galica, or New Galic, was Mantlgrym's older name. It was officially re-chrystened after the fall of the Razhod. The Mounds of Fury were also known as the Wokimigiks.

manned the wall. Smoke also rose out of the city with trumpeted signals and shouts from the soldiers.

The wagon stopped. Virgow said, "Looks even bigger now than when we saw them on our way out. Might be that another herd merged with it."

"We'd best have you get in the back, Syago," Balgor said, unlatching the top of the driver's box. "This could be a rough one. Have everyone get the spears out, we only need to last till we get in front of the wall." He pulled out small flasks with dynal symbols etched on them from his belt, symbols that held sentiments he put into them and exploded accordingly.[37] He opened the hatch above, then stood up while Balgor closed all but the front and top iron shutters. Syago retreated into the cabin without argument this time.

BOOM! BOOM! BOOM!

Several daemogs rammed the gate, splintering it while arrows rained down on the herd, felling none but sticking many. The arrows did little more than hurt the monsters except for the eye shots, but they allowed for fire or lightning sparks from dynasts to be more effective. Two beasts roared and spat fire at the top of the wall, where the men hid behind the crenellated battlements. As soon as the flames vanished, the soldiers rained arrows and rocks down on the attackers, and dynasts released a wave of lightning through the beasts. The creatures shook their large heads and then their furred bodies, rejuvenating numbed muscles and shedding some of their arrows, snorting puffs of smoke.

Syago watched the two drivers through a crack with the others as the advance began. Virgow managed the bomogs, and Balgor threw an exploding flask just as the herd noticed the wagon approaching. The explosions were muffled by the furious approach of the hoofed beasts.

On seeing the approach, each of the passengers gripped their iron spears, their knuckles white, and stuck them out of the side of the wagon, ready to prick anything that moved too close. Fear filled the air of the tight wagon box with the unspoken knowledge of how daemog herds sometimes tore apart wagons. They heard the grunting and snorting of the enemy as it surrounded them. Syago's heart pounded; he hoped to demonstrate heroic courage instead of the panic as before. The dynal blasts sounded about

---

37 *See also The Schiltron of Magodeoz, 36*

them as the wagon jostled on, and he knew Balgor had only so many. If a team of elementists from the wall couldn't fend them off, then one man wouldn't be able to either. He also had to protect the bomog team and driver's box, or they'd be stuck here in the hell outside. But they only needed to reach the wall.

The first fire burst hit the wagon in front of Syago, flames reaching in through the fire-resistant planks. He looked away, hiding his face behind his shoulder, but maintained his position. Two more came, then the first blow knocked through the spears and rocked the wagon. "Blood of the rood!" Syago swore, falling back with Lüg. The kid yelped, and Syago helped him up. Syago saw that his own spear had stuck in the daemog well enough that it got pulled out of the wagon.

Now lacking a weapon, Syago went to Lüg, who seemed afraid to even touch his spear. Fire hit the wagon, seeping through the planks, and Lüg jumped. Syago grabbed his hand. "Here, I'll help you. Hold it like this, left arm under, right over. And keep your face behind your right—there, that's it. That'll protect your face from fire. I'll stand with you. Now fortify!"

Fire and horns pounded at the other side; they were surrounded. Smoke entered through the floor as the clever monsters filled the cabin with it, stinging eyes and throats. Lüg's face was wet either from sweat or tears, but he seemed to gain more confidence while Syago held the spear with him; he didn't even flinch from the second fire blast. Syago gripped it on the other side in the same manner. "There, do you see them? Try for the eyes or shoulders. Here come two—"

Two daemogs charged. One aimed for the wheel but had to veer away from the spearheads and instead rammed right behind it, shaking the box and breaking a plank piece away with its horn. Syago and Lüg's spear glanced off the skull plate of the second, missing an eye but nailing the shoulder as it glanced the underside of the box. It snorted before backing away. Another took its place. Syago jerked the spear down just in time to catch its eye. The beast stumbled out of view. Syago shouted to Lüg, "We got it!"

A large burst of fire hit the other side of the wagon, followed by a heavy hit. Planks blew apart on the metal frame, and what remained started to burn.

Syago yelled out, "We've only got to last till the wall! Almost there, strong forth!" He noted Lüg's frightened look at the hole. "Keep watch on our side or same thing'll happen here. See? Balgor just extinguished the fires."

A boom from the wind flask rattled the wagon and popped their ears as the flames vanished, along with most of the smoke.

Syago and Lüg managed to ward off the monsters on their side as the other side became more frantic. Two spears got pulled out, nearly taking Andras too. Fire popped around the area that remained, Syago yelled for them to take cover and then return to post. Another frenzied exchange of horns and spears broke a hole in the back. It looked to be the end; they were nearly exposed on all sides, with only the iron braces left.

But through the haze and the hole, Syago saw lightning sweep through the beasts, followed by puffs of darkfire. He shouted, "We're at the wall!"

None cheered yet, still on edge and shaken. Somehow, the wagon reached Southgate without more trouble.

Southgate clanged shut behind the wagon. Through the broken planks, Syago saw soldiers straining to press the gate shut and renew the locks and braces as the doors thundered from the continued assault. Grooms led the wagon to a holding spot for unloading and repairs. The stables hid underneath the city, a smelly and tight labyrinth in between the carved-out mounds, walls, and columns the city sat on. Despite being dimly lit with lamps, and very compact, it had worked for centuries without fail. Even the last gierraquake had no effect on it.[38]

They pulled into a stall, and Syago heard Balgor speaking with stable-master Migel. "Still got your hands full, I see," Balgor said as he and the grooms opened the mangled rear door to check on the passengers and helping them down.

"Aye, fight's at three days now," Migel replied. "And they split to flank on north and south since you left. Nasty onslaught, that."

The crewmen took down goods to be traded from Tolgrym while other stable hands unhitched the panicky and wounded bomogs and brought them to the feeding troughs. "Would be sooner if the count would lend us more guards and elementists. They could even go out and finish the whole lot for some fine meat. They's usin' them for internal security, though."

Balgor helped the keepers out of the wagon. "How long can you hold?"

"'Bout three days, mos' likely. We stocked up good enough, but it'll strain me family for certain." He led away the bomog. Twice his height, the large

---

brute of thick brown fur could crush him and many others in the cramped stables if enraged. "Of course, the catch of a hunt is right there at our gates, waiting for a nobleman's permission. But I go on."[39]

Syago and three others hefted their packs and walked to a twisting wooden staircase that rose slowly into the ceiling. Shifting his bag to the other shoulder, he went outside.

Familiar sounds and smells greeted him, the frenzied bustle of a dense town with greater concern for the business of the day than an ordered and hygienic city. The streets teemed with citizen soldiers running around. Warchildren—any child deemed too young to fight but old enough to help with frontline duty—ran about with pails of water, bundles of arrows, food, and tools. A young black girl, probably a soldier's servant, bumped into Syago. She looked up, revealing charcoal smudges on her face beneath a tin helmet. "Outta my way!" she snapped.

"Sorry," he said. She hoisted her sack of bolts up and skirted around Syago, who tried to move but found it difficult with his bag in such a busy street. She ran off toward the din above Southgate.

Reminiscent of Tongunabiagüs in Tolgrym, a minstrel's voice floated over the town with the power of dyne, pushing courage into him. A group of young kids marched south through the middle of the street. Each marched in form, bearing their small armor and weapons with fearless faces.

Syago backed into an alleyway entrance where the latrine smell of the streets faded to garbage disposal and understable ventilation. His anticipation always dwindled on arrival in the Kingdom Republic's capital; the novelty of it wasn't as great as actually being there. Still, being outside of Tolgrym was always a welcome adventure. The city buildings were mostly brown wood and white plaster, built using various kinds of strong timber, mostly from Thornwood. The necessity of the wall made housing space scarce and forced them to build upwards using cruck support beams for taller houses. Every building and home had at least three floors and sometimes more, with wooden windows and shutters or cloth curtains over the occasional glass window. It also served as the economic center, as the dangers of the outside both forced and limited the independence of any civilization, so they specialized and traded.

---

39 See also *Keltion Keltibeerion,* 56

Syago was admiring the grandeur of Mantlgrym when he noticed a stiff, leather-cloaked figure sitting on a box in the tight alley behind him. The tall shroud crouched there like a predator bird, watching him. He couldn't see into the patchwork cloak but noticed two dark eyeholes. Wary of thieves and gangs, Syago stepped out of the alley and said, "Good evening."

Saying nothing, the form shifted closer to the wall.

A voice from the side startled Syago. "Sad, isn't it?"

Another man, whose presence had been obscured by boxes, huddled to the right. He leaned against the wall, a dark-red stitched blanket pulled around his body and a small cage clamped onto his head. Thin rusted iron bars crossed each other over his face as evident punishment for a crime, a minor one in that the cage only encompassed his head rather than trapping his whole body. Spikes jutted inward to prevent moving or removal, yet he'd managed to undo the mouth harness. Through the bars, an amused smile offset his grimy black hair and intense eyes. His voice rasped, "Are you a religious man, newcomer?"

"What? Who are you?"

"Call me Kask. One of the many city thugs fighting the never-ending battle against life, against the world." He nodded toward Southgate and, with a slight swagger, walked until he was in front of Syago. His gait conjured in Syago's imagination a deviant well accustomed to maneuvering dangerous streets at night, stealing when he saw fit. The man's eyes never left Syago's face. "Well? Are you a follower of Deova Bondua or the eternals or none?"

"I walk in the path of the Holy One, Deova Bondua. Whom do you serve?"

With stiff slowness, Kask turned and looked at the cloaked one. "My friend here starves every day because nobody will feed him. He can't acquire food the way you do because of his... condition. And yet you in your plenty believe in alleviating suffering. What do you say to that?"

Uncomfortable and uncertain, Syago felt he was being duped. So he made as if to leave. "I don't know. I—"

"Are you an aspiring man, young one?" The man turned and coughed.

"Yes," Syago said.

"That's good. You ought to be. But this world we live in is so vicious and brutal. It mocks any sense of justice. Only the strong survive." He nodded in the direction of the battlesong and paused his vehemence to catch his breath and look Syago over more. "But you're not ready for it. I pity you in your comfortable, soft life."

"You don't know how comfortable my life is or isn't," Syago snapped.

"Syago!" Balgor called to him from down the street. "We're heading down to Brair's Inn."

"I should go," Syago said, turning back to Kask.

"Of course." Kask nodded, smiling faintly.

Syago rejoined his group, thinking of how he knew what kind of world he lived in and didn't need a street kook to tell him. He deposited his bag in the room with the others, which they locked behind them, then headed back out. It wasn't dark yet, so he hoped to catch the last of the city council, or at least one of the noblemen.

Dismay found him when the doors of the Court of Ashor, the ancient-fortress-turned-city-court, closed just before he arrived.[40] The city's main square was full of people, many closing up shops and opening inns or going to a night mass at the great cathedral on the other side of the square. Warily holding the money bag at his side with an eye out for thieves, he pushed through the crowds.

With the others in tow, Syago ascended the city court steps and banged on the door while shouting about an urgent message, thinking, *Surely they'd allow an exception for this emergency. The nobles of Tolgrym would bestir themselves in such an occasion, so why not here?* They banged and yelled on the doors until a constable shouted them down, threatening to put them in irons. He laughed in answer to their questions. "Ye think they've time for you now? E'rybody knows they close by now. The day is done. Come back on the morrow. Get 'ere early enough and ye might get in."

Dejected, they descended the steps.

"Well, maybe if we can locate the doctors?" Tomas asked and looked around as if they might be there in the city square. "Or find the cure and be on with it and to the devils with the nobles."

Lüg frowned at the frequent nobility jabs. "We can't just buy it. All medicine needs approval to be traded out of town to allow for sufficient supplies here. And a cure for trap poison wouldn't be large in stock. I doubt any apothecary would know where it's at. Hells, we don't even know if that money will be enough; they might have to give it to us."

---

40 Ashor was likely a founder's name, a noble, but also an old Asturion word meaning councils, or more specifically, war councils. It held the Court of Counts.

"I'm sure we'll work out an agreement," Tomas said. "Something with trade and maybe a loan."

Syago pursued, "Does anyone know where the count lives or any of the barons?"

"No," Andras said. "In fact, that might get you the irons we were promised. It's different here. A bigger city with richer nobles has put more distance between them and the commons. You can't just call on them as needed, especially if they don't know you."

"Just go early," Lüg said. "At the crack of dawn. We're rising early in any case for our trip to Voium."

"You'll have to beat the lines," Deiba said, and everyone nodded in agreement.

Tomas clapped his hands. "So all's left now is for us to enjoy a night in Mantlgrym."

Sylbia went to her room, and the men began discussing bars and whorehouses, but Syago had stopped paying attention. Frustration and anxiety welled in him. He had to wait a day? He'd hoped to get the antidote the night of arrival and leave for Tolgrym the next day. This meant that unless he could get it done and still leave that morning, Elisabet would have to wait at least two more days. Could she?

The group agreed on a brothel first, since most in Mantlgrym also served drinks. Deciding to return to the inn instead, Syago felt a spike of anger at them for going after women while the women of their own town suffered near death. He understood there was nothing they could do about it for the night, but it still felt disrespectful.

CHAPTER EIGHT

A STUDY OF DEATH AND THE DEAD

Based on *Leyta's Journals*, cc bastica 10;
Scars of the Martyrs, cc bastica 912;
The Nordvargor Testaments, cc bastica 589;

19th of Septimosk, 246

Leyta couldn't shake the feeling all day of being watched.

That day, the quervosk from Voium returned. The letter confirmed that the strange storm was not theirs and, worse, it had blinded summoners to their spirit sight. The village of chamands was unable to communicate with the dead as well as with their emaions. That combined with the panic over the missing boy, Navidsom, created tension within the castle.

Unsure what to do about Bokhor and feeling responsibility for the disappearance, Leyta poured over her notes on necromancy. A reading candle burned low next to her inside its lantern fixture; it would finish up at her two-hour mark. Due to having lost many works to fire, it was now the rule to have all candles sealed up, and no oil either.

The library was one of the largest rooms in the castle, with two floors of rows and rows of shelves, the second being more of an open walkway. The old parchment pages were frail and glossy in her hands; she had to turn them slowly but liked the odd smell. The browning leaves had fading ink, but she could still read it with some effort. The text detailed elementist attempts to track and communicate with spirits, a non-heretical alternative to the summoners that ended up looking just as bad. Around the margins were various pentagrams and wheel crosses.[41] Stacked books surrounded

---

41 Likely the *Satyricona* by Amonamarth. The text is mostly instructive, but the version at Cantlgrym uniquely contains the curious account of the venom death of Immortal Dimuborgir the Waylander, a greater spirit and his archenemy, Lambogod the Aviator. It also lacks Saor Vader and Suidakro de Gojirak, both fables of the Old Man's children in the owl cave.

her on the small table in the castle library, a massive room made cramped by shelves and their chained tomes and scrolls. She'd just made it through one but had so many more to get into, and no time to do it, with the urgency of the castle's need. Alone in the gloomy library, she stretched in her wooden chair, yawning, then turned the page. The candle burned.

Elementism in general, once known as geomancy, had its own dangers, but its necromancy aspect was something else. An older field, and one vastly underdeveloped, it called to Leyta's ambition but scared her for the same reasons. She wasn't getting anything out of it, either. The extensive symbolism and old language made it nearly incomprehensible and demanded a mysticism she didn't share.

As a full dynast, she could now study it independently and without prohibition, although she would still be banned on practicing without the supervision of the archdynast. Much superstition surrounded it as the favored study of Barthandeon before he'd changed. But all dyne required care. Any dynast could potentially lose their sanity or mortality to the vile project. Her efforts now, in between duties as archkeeper, were to locate Navidsom, his ghost, his corpse, or both of the latter. After the discovery of the claw marks on the floor planks, the entire castle was on edge.

When the candle begun to sputter, she closed up the books and rechained them to their shelves. She took one last look at the trypticon of the iron psyclopean apocalypse, considering how they conveyed the foreboding she felt from the claw marks in the abbey. She looked up at the vaulted ceiling, the dark windows along the wall indicating nighttime.

After eating something from the kitchen, alone in her thoughts among the chatter of keepers in the halls, Leyta went to the bailey, to the wall. Standing between Fernandeon and Robertobrus, both on wall duty, she watched the corpse training begin below in the courtyard, her staff in hand. A fog was setting in.

"Now the fun begins," Fernandeon said, looking below into the courtyard. Soldiers were bringing out of the tower cell from the wall, near the carnival tent, some captured animal corpses and chaining them in the open for practice. The bodies of a pale rabbit, a daemog bull, and an ozor twitched and rose about senselessly. The ozor was gigantic. It had thick dark-brown fur and long black claws, with teeth that jutted out and, in the case of this lifeless, dark eye sockets gaping from a white, hairless face. It didn't roar and snarl as a living one might have, but mindlessly resisted the pegged chains that held it while the soldiers in training practiced maneuvering around it and attacking. All three corpses would've been prepared for dinner if not for the aged smell.

"Creeps me out every time," Robertobrus said.

"Still?" Fernandeon scoffed. "I got used to it ages ago. We've been seeing this our whole lives."

"Doesn't mean it can't still get to you." Robertobrus shrugged.

"Maybe it's something we shouldn't get used to," Leyta said quietly, musing on why watching it appealed to her. Robertobrus nodded, but Fernandeon snorted. "Or maybe better to laugh at it instead of each other."

Robertobrus didn't catch the rebuke. "But that's disrespecting the dead and glorifying violence."

"Come on." Fernandeon gestured toward the corpses. "Death happens to everyone. Being all squeamish and sentimental about it does nothing to prepare you for the inevitable. Better to learn to cope with it now than when it comes true for you and yours. Even throw in a little humor if you can."

"But you act as if you like it," Robertobrus said with a plaintive look at Leyta. He studied dyne under her and often sought to impress her, she believed. She liked him and loathed Fernandeon, but the constant quest to please annoyed her almost as much as the latter's obstinance. Robertobrus said resolutely, "You sound like the execution mobs."

Mobs were one thing, but Leyta had to agree with Fernandeon. Being squeamish and sensitive about the lifeless was weakening. Since the rabbit corpse was going untouched, she decided to practice darkfire on it. The fog in the air provided plenty of moisture, full of a calm fear which she could use. She raised her staff and sparked it to life on the rabbit. The cold fire, which grew blacker as it grew colder, froze the rabbit. She used the same darkfire to reach over and catch the bull's body as well, frosting its legs in place with small icicles hanging down from its belly. "There, I fixed them," she said. "Cold as death, but not a threat."

"Aha, that's it," cackled Fernandeon. "Now make them crumble." Leyta frowned at him. He shrugged. "What? You agreed with me."

Leyta thought it a good thing the boy wasn't studying dyne, though what kind of knight he would make she couldn't imagine. At least he'd refrained from taunting her.

Leyta descended the wall stairs to the bailey to examine the corpses. The training, she understood, was more psychological than actual practice. The body of a monster lost all cunning and ferocity on death. But her thoughts turned to what might've taken Navidsom. Regardless of what it was, it would've left sentimental tracks. She entered the Vision; it was the same in day or night because sunlight didn't come into it. A view of sentiments was separate and distinct from the other senses, though nighttime was usually darker for the fact that sentimental circulation slowed down at night in correlation to physical and social activity.[42]

The dark landscape stretched out before her: mostly black and empty, with some yellow fear and blue sorrow—leftovers from the tension of their missing keeper as well as common effects of a night in darkemorg. People were a dense bundle of sentiments compared to the land. Here tinged with yellow, which bled out around them, coloring the steps like footprints. Living bodies were usually too dense in matter and full of their own sentiments to affect with a sentimental push. Lifeless, on the other hand, were less dense in body and produced none of their own sentiments. She saw them as dark pits that sucked up what sentiments lay in the surrounding area.

The books hadn't told her of creatures as stealthy as this one had been. Most talked about was of an underworlder, a demon or devil. But if an outsider from the underworlds was here, she thought it would've taken more than just one boy. It might also be a monster or lifeless somehow loose in the castle grounds, but that would have been even more noticeable than a fiend. *So what was it then? What am I to look for? I've no idea, but everything leaves a sign.*

In scanning the courtyard, she overheard some of the training boys arguing, one saying, "We should've turned that Unakan away."

Another, speaking quite loudly, chimed in, "Yeah, we all knew he was cursed."

"Quiet! All of you," she snarled more sharply than she'd intended. "Is there anything wrong with him? Has he done anything wrong here?"

"Might be that he's what reason Navidsom's gone," one challenged. "How do you know he wasn't the reason?"

42 See *Luskmord: Atriom Carcerio,* 6

"How do you know he was?" Her reply was cold, uncaring for her appearance or his pathetic excuses. "Prove it."

"But he's weird and—"

"Unaka are bad. They sacrifice people and—"

"I don't care!" The rage was building in her, despite her own misgivings about him, her grip tightening on her staff. She paused to calm herself. "You either prove it or leave him alone."

They resumed their training without another word. Her attention fell on activity in the large tent that housed the carnival group, simply called Jester's Carnival, in the corner of the courtyard. She'd caught glimpses of some of the performers, a new group from the east that they'd never heard of before, and couldn't help but wonder if there was a connection. It was likely foolish, given their entering after the disappearance. Recalling it was her duty to arrange it, she approached the tent. The timing of the enigmatic troupe had been like a miracle for Somhoin, though Leyta also worried it would overshadow the festival, but miracle or no, they'd still put guards over the group.

She approached one of the tricksters just before he entered their large tent. "Did you find everything in order, sir?"

The big man, with a wide toothy smile on his face, put deliberate emphasis on each word. "Oh yes, it is all in place, really good. We be really good. You like."

She hadn't expected him to be an idiot, or lunatic or whatever it is they were. She believed the Deova Bondua teaching that it was a curse but had known only one in Voium. A kind boy that helped his mam with her shop, shunned by everyone else and hardly worthy of any curse. "Would it be possible for me to meet this jester before then?"

"Noooo, Master Jester ne'er reveals himself before he goes on de stage. Is part of de act. We has rules." His foolish smile never relented, like trying to grin between each word.

"I see. Well, then would I be able to at least meet the rest of the group? I just want to greet them."

"Nope. Def'ly not. Nope. Sorry, but you meet him and de others after de show, he says. Is how we got our success and reputation as de best group in de world." He straightened up with pride.

"All right then, I'll see him after the show. Thank you."

He disappeared into the tent flap without any response. Even more awkward than her Voium friend had been. As the flap swished closed, she glimpsed the inside. It was packed with crewmembers and equipment.[43]

She crossed the bailey toward the abbey and entered. She found her way through the long hallway off the side to the isolation room at the end. The door had remained closed and locked, the way it supposedly had been the night before. She got someone to unlock it for her, then entered alone with an oil lantern. The gloomy room had been untouched since. It creaked as she walked around.

Davagis, the only master with any necromancy experience, had already looked it over and determined nothing. If he couldn't find anything, Leyta was even less likely to, but she still felt responsibility for what was happening as archkeeper. She had to try.

In the Vision, the room was void of sentiments. She suspected it hadn't many to begin with but was caught off guard by how blank it appeared. Faded footprints marked the floor, though sparse in number. She ran her fingers over the claw marks. Those at least should've had something left over; they should've been even stronger than the footprints. Even the cushion, likely where the boy had been sitting, held some remnant of the fear he'd left behind. It was faded, but a close inspection told her it was there. But nothing from the claw marks.

If only I could learn stealth like this I too might get out of my castle duties.

She supposed if the marks were made from a blade instead of actual claws, then they wouldn't leave a very strong impression. An outsider would've left a strong impression, as she understood it. Outsiders were said to be powerful and left traces everywhere, but they were also strange and unpredictable.

But then came the other dilemma: *How did something with a blade enter and then leave with the boy? How did they do it so quietly, with no blood or alarms raised?*

She walked around the room again, carefully inspecting each timber plank down to the polished grain. What if the planks had been pushed up from underneath? This was one of the few rooms in the abbey, on the whole island, with a wooden floor.

---

43 *ibid,* 13

She froze when a plank behind her creaked. Looking, she saw nothing but the door that she'd closed behind her. No... she'd left it open—about a foot open—but it was closed now. She stood up straight; was she remembering wrong? Then she felt it again. Something was behind her, right behind her. Out of the corner of her eye, she saw standing there something solid and tall and dark. A long limb scratched at the floor beside her, and she jumped away. Turning showed her nothing. Not in the Vision or with physical eyes. She wanted to run but made herself check the area where it had scratched. Nothing. *Hells, I'm going mad! The power is already interfering with my sanity.* She felt her chest constricting under heavy breathing and ran to the door. She stopped at the doorway and forced the panic down, slowing her breaths. No, she would not run. She would not be shied by the harassment of some petty phantom, nor would she let madness take her. She opened the door to call for a weapon.

Walking over the floor, she stomped until one sounded more hollow than the others. Holding her staff, she couldn't see anything beyond the wood or do anything to it with dyne. Drest entered the room with a few others and left her a sword and a second lantern. She thought to ask them to do it, but given their looks of annoyance, she decided she could do it well enough herself.

Using the sword to pry the planks upward, damaging the wood but little, she uncovered a hole in the stone foundation. Her lantern revealed a stone staircase desending into darkness. Her heart stopped as it revealed a long staircase and something white and inhuman, sitting just under the floor. As soon as the light hit it, it was gone.

Staff at the ready, she jumped into the hole. The plank slammed down behind her, making her jump. She thought to turn back for help but knew that in doing so she'd lose her quarry. Her racing heart and tight grip on the staff betrayed the fearlessness she'd pretended to. She was a dynast now, a minister of hell—she could do it.

Eventually, the stairs opened up to a longer room with cloisters, along with dark and dripping water in the distance but otherwise silent. The stairs ended on a platform, and she saw that she'd entered the castle catacombs. They'd been long ago sealed off and forgotten in favor of a different tomb on Isle Ivow.

This place went deep. Just ahead, at the base of the stairs, was an archway with words inscribed on its stones:

She made the sign of the wheel cross and whispered a prayer, more for herself than for the dead. She shuddered, feeling cold and alone. The air was damp. She saw little more than the immediate area of her lantern, and the inscrutable darkness that encompassed her made her slow her steps. Walls opened up into large shelves and alcoves that held decorated stone coffins with engravings and statues of historical figures accompanied by crowns and the rood. She didn't recognize any of it. The stair walls had panels sealed off for additional crypts. She saw in Vision the place void of sentiments, save a few scratch marks on the ground, but whether these were rats or her prey, she couldn't be sure. Neither did they point in any discernible direction.

To her right and left led passageways that bore no signs of her hunt and possibly more dangers. It was already past nightfall in darkemorg, and while all remains had to be dismembered and sealed tight prior to burial, it did nothing to quiet the small, timorous voice in the back of her head. Just ahead lay an ossuary. Bones and skulls were neatly arrayed in the grim design of what looked like a flower or coin. She could only wonder at how deep it went. The side bore another inscription in Old Asturion.

Then she heard the sobbing of a small child, and her body went cold. *What. hell have I found?* The wrongness of it made her consider turning back, but she realized it could be another captured child in need of rescue. She looked up, and there, just above the ossuary, out of range of the light, she saw two yellow eyes glimmer and blink away. She rushed closer, and the lantern briefly caught the fleeing form of a thin four-legged creature with feathered wings, all white. A growl faded into the darkness.

Her hands trembled, but if this chamber held a child, she had to save it. She considered the platform behind the ossuary, a stone walkway that extended from an arched doorway into a vast opening. In the dark expanse, she heard the trickle of the waterfall and a faint shuffling. *Could this be a xana or cuelebre?* Xana were said to be good forest creatures, but sometimes they switched out infants for changelings. A fable she'd not believed till now. She steeled herself and descended the open-air stairs.

The staff and lantern flame felt reassuring as she stepped out onto the walkway, out into a morbid abyss. *Breathe, Leyta. You're a dynast now, I can do this. Weakness is my enemy, anger my arrow, hate my sword, fear my armor, sorrow my balm, joy my reward.* Following the elementist mantra, she crossed herself again and increased her pace. She saw little more in the Vision than with physical eyes, even though it was not affected by lightlessness. After all, she was still young in dyne and even the most experienced perceived but half their distance of physical sight.

The walkway extended out and down into the abyss on pillars from below and chains from the sides. Stairs descended and doubled back to avoid the crag ahead. It offered her no railing and left her feeling very exposed. She heard the weeping child again and paused to listen and look but saw only the eerie yellow eyes flicker in the dark, followed by the occasional faint scratch or flutter. She tried shooting fire at it but caught nothing except the brief flash in the Vision of a ghostly creature. It let out a low howl that echoed in the cavern and filled her with tremors and chills. Only the faint crying of a child from below kept her from turning back to get help. The shuffling below paused, then resumed with grinding and she continued the hunt.

Finally, she reached a set of stairs that descended into a small lake. As if the lake was fuller than it ought to have been. A small boat floated nearby, chained to a stone column, but it was out of reach due to the raised water level. The shuffling resumed just ahead and another baleful howl reached her ears. She pointed her staff at the water, using the water to push the boat nearer. Not quite close enough, she sucked in her breath, hiked up her dress, and stepped into the murkiness. Clenching her jaws against the cold and awful sense of what she was getting herself into, she climbed into the boat and unlatched it. Rather than use the oars, she moved the water and glided out between the rows of columned archways, shivering from her wet clothes. She saw the waterfall against a back wall, splashing down on the statue of a regal man with the inscription of *Raoul de Montresor.*

She recalled him as the first castle architect. Another statue stood on top of a nearby stone coffin, this one obviously a great king, but with a name that had chipped away. The entire thing was partially submerged in water and looked as though it might topple over. It couldn't be Pelaiod, who was interred in the Cathedral de Saint Casilda, in Mantlgrym.

As she neared these statues, a glance upward showed the water coming out of a gaping crack where a more sculpted spout had once been. *That's why the pond is full—something broke its source.* One mystery solved, but not the one she'd come for. The sobbing stopped, and the shuffling too. She moved her boat to where the sounds had faded away—a staircase that ascended out of the water and into a large archway made entirely out of bones and skulls. Dead candles sat in some of the skulls, and some parts of it had the decoration of a complete skeleton or a sun wheel cross.

As she neared the staircase, the shuffling resumed, louder. She hesitated and decided to stay in the boat, an easy retreat if this thing only stayed on land. The shuffling and grinding grew louder, coming from something big.

A massive shadow walked toward her. With horns, it was fully twenty feet tall and had wings, all of which barely fit through the large archway. It came into her light, an iron box sealed off its head but allowed the horns to come out. She'd no idea what it was, humanoid in form but resembling something half dead and bestial. Its body was bone-thin and dark green, save what was covered in the old and tattered habit of a friar. Her first thoughts were of angels and devils—it resembled what the myths said about them. But the way it stopped, stared, then reached long clawed arms, chained to dragging weights, into the water to pull out a stone coffin did not resemble any otherworlder she'd ever heard of. *The watcher of the crypts, a resurrected saint.*

She got out of the boat. If it was only a guardian, it was not responsible for Navidsom's disappearance and was only awake to clean up or fix the flooding. She watched it warily as she ascended to the archway. Inside the long hallway, she found the legendary Chapel of Skulls at the back. An altar fronted a victory cross, all of it made of stone and bone. Skulls everywhere watched her.[44] She bowed on one knee, made the sign, and turned to leave.

---

44 It is understood that the upper chambers rested those fallen to the Great Pestilence. It was closed off before the Razhod came and all of those fallen are in the other isle.

The feral eyes watched her from the entrance. She ran to it, staff raised. It vanished. As she exited the archway, lantern swinging light about wildly, she saw the watcher at one side and the pale form of the creature to the other. She put steady anger into the lake, causing an arm of water to reach out at the creature, bright with sentiments. Too slow, the water splashed onto where it had been. Chains rankled behind her and she turned just as the watcher swung an iron weight at her. She stepped aside and fell backwards as the iron thundered onto where she'd been with a clang that echoed through the chamber. Its footsteps thudded forward, and the second weight ground stone as it swung up over her. She rolled over and felt stone tremble as it came down right next to her. She shot fire at it as a distraction while she regained her footing. But the fire merely blazed off of its iron helmet while massive hands clasped around her waist. The laughter of a young girl echoed through the opaque chamber, its wrong sweetness grating on her. The guardian picked her up and turned toward the lake.

Powerless in its grasp, her mind ran frantically in search of a way out as it leaned to plunge her in the water. It was responding to her use of dyne in the sacred area of the catacombs but would take orders if she could give them. "Saint Franthiscon..."

It paused.

She'd guessed correctly its name and safeguard but was unsure of what else to do. "Uh, release me."

It set her down, roughly, and resumed care of the coffins. "Saint Franthiscon, you will let me use dyne here to defend myself." It gave no indication of agreement, so she continued. "There is a vile beast in here that threatens humans inside and above. We must get rid of it." Saint Franthiscon showed no response, and changing the words didn't help either. Her voice trembled. "Is there a child here? If there is, I must retrieve it to the grounds above." It gave no response and returned to the chapel. *Great, another useless saint-er, corpse thing.*

Regardless, the creature was gone, but the absence gave her little comfort when, on the way back in the boat, her lantern dimmed. Running out of oil and wick, her bubble of lamplight weakened until a small glow left visible only the bench in front of her. She used dyne to keep the ember alive but even with dyne, it still required a fuel source. The ember died out. She had no idea if she was close to the platform with the stairs or even moving in the right direction. Fighting panic, she continued her search in vain. Pillar after stone pillar passed by her, and she feared moving in circles. She prayed and called to Saint Franthiscon for help, but both were for naught. She found a wall and tried to follow its direction but despaired after a few minutes and tried to backtrack.

It was then that the last glow of her lantern finally went out, leaving her in total darkness. Still shaken from the fight with Saint Franthiscon, she couldn't see her trembling hand in front of her face. So she was stuck in the old catacombs, lost, and cold and wet on top of it. Worse, she'd left no indication of where she'd gone. It'd be hours before anyone noticed. Breathing deep, she sought for a solution she'd overlooked.

A cold chill swept through her as she heard wings fluttering and more scratches on stone. It had returned.

Well, if I'm to die, I'll do it with a fight. She found one of the oars and, using her staff with some anger, lit the oar's end on fire. *Of course, this wouldn't occur to me until the last second.*

Burning oar in one hand and staff in the other, she swirled fire above her as the ghostly creature suddenly appeared. The fire blinded her eyes, but a swish of the creature's wings blew it away and it moved through the flames unhindered. She swung the burning oar around above her just in time as the pale thing averted its dive. All she saw of its head was a mouth full of fangs, a flash of shimmering eyes. More girl laughter followed, this time the tone of sweetness had turned mean, bullying. She felt certain now that the sounds were not imagined but coming from this loathsome beast. The thought gave little comfort, for it was obviously clever, cruel, and good at hunting human prey. It laughed without lure; the game was up now that it had her. It flew out of sight in the darkness between pillars, but seeing its ghostly visage through dyne wasn't any better. It was all she could do to push back the fear and focus on more aggressive sentiments. With a great effort of hate, she sustained the meager oar fire while also pushing the water to carry her to the platform.

As she reached it, a bony tail, a sickle-like claw on the end, whipped out, knocking the oar out of her hand and into the water as another claw scratched her arm. She screamed. It let out a taunting giggle.

Jumping out with her staff, she set the whole boat ablaze, grabbed the other burning oar, and ran for the stairs. The fire on the boat died quick, leaving her with less light, isolated on the stairs in a black abyss. It swooped in as she whirled about, ripping her dress and tangling her hair over her face with another scratch, toying with her. She shot fire and swung at it frantically, nearly losing her balance, arms tiring. Shrieks of laughter cut the air like knives. It swept at her again, and she dropped her staff to sustain the burning oar with both hands. Unaware of the tears streaming down her face or that her knees had buckled, she screamed at it. Evil laughter surrounded her, but she still couldn't see it as it swooped out of the darkness, then again from another direction, knocking her down. Another dive, and the oar was ripped form her hands, vanishing. She screamed for help, having nothing else.

Then fire and lightning exploded above her. Roza and Anaruth were there, holding her as she melted and sobbed. Alkant and Davagis stood on the stairs above, their scepters raised.

They brought her to the upper level, and once she'd recovered herself, Alkant began sharply reprimanding her for entering a forbidden area and without a companion, but was interrupted by Roza sighting the thing as it disappeared into the stone chute whence came the waterfall.

Needing to see where it went, Leyta ran upstairs, staff in hand, with them behind. She rushed up into the abbey and out to frightened looks. But she didn't care.

Hurrying outside, she looked over the wall, listening and watching. Several keepers of the abbey followed her. "Look!" A boy pointed at the sky. Looking up, everyone saw the white figure gliding through the night sky on broad wings and long tail. It passed over the bailey and continued on, dark clouds above and faded moonlight making the pale figure more pronounced. The children watched, whispering about it, and one tried to throw something at it, but it was too high. Switching into the Vision, Leyta was still surprised by how it shone bright with sentiments, more other-worldly than any normal animal. White in physical sight, a brown-and-green-tinged glow in dynal sight. It flew in silence, but the cruel laughter flitted through her mind. She briefly considered attacking it with air, but it was already too far.

They all made the sign of the wheel cross over their chests as it disappeared from view. Could that have been what took Navidsom? It was clearly a physical creature; it probably had claws enough to mark the floor. But she couldn't imagine how it would go in and out of the room, leave no dynal marks, kidnap a boy, and all without violence or screaming from the young warrior in training.

Still shaking, she left them to enter the church. She needed solace, to pray and find strength and answers. Since the pews were already full of people attending evening mass, something she regretted missing, she decided to go above, where the choir usually sat. She didn't feel up to sitting through the mass; she was still thinking of her near panic in that room. The archbishopess's voice droned on below. Leyta prayed aloud but quiet enough for her cloister so that she could hear and feel it more strongly.

"Mother of Heavens... forgive me of my evils and mistakes. I'm a simple creature and in need of thee. Please. I need thy guidance and strength. I am nothing without thee. I'm trying to serve thee and thy children but am unable. Forgive me for losing one, please help me resolve it and protect the rest. And please save me from the void, don't let me lose my sanity. Aid me, please... Amen." She made the sign but kept kneeling. She wiped tears from her face. No answers came, but at least she felt better.

The mass below finished, and she waited till the faithful had left. She turned to go down the stairs but halted when she saw something on the window at the back of the choir rafter. Skin prickling again, she approached the window. She stopped when the shadow that stood outside drew nearer.

It was not the creature from the catacombs, not even remotely similar. The shadow had the undeniable form of a human, and the way her skin crawled, she knew it was the same thing that had been stalking her the past two days, real or imagined. It raised an arm and pressed its hand against the glass. Her breath caught in her throat. Though she wasn't supposed to bring it into the church, Leyta had her staff in hand. She entered the Vision and saw the form of a person, but no sentiments within it, a humanoid vacuum save two glowing dots where the eyes should've been. Leaving the Vision showed her it was still there on the outer windowsill where no human could possibly be. Her breathing was heavy, her heart raced as fast as her mind. *Am I going insane or being haunted? Angels of Heaven help me!*

The hand withdrew and it faded away.

What's happening here?

CHAPTER NINE

THAT AWFUL LABYRINTH

Based on *Annals of Syago*, cc bastica 9;
Scars of the Martyrs, cc bastica 810;

20th of Septimosk, 246

The rest of the group had gone on to Voium, and Syago was at the court doors just after dawn; already a crowd grew. *Damnation*, he'd thought it early enough to be first. *Rood's blood, I hate this place already.* He was further dismayed to find that it wouldn't open for two more hours. His stomach grumbled, yearning for food more than the bread and cheese he'd had, yet he dared not leave his spot lest the line behind him take it. He'd left his weapons in the room after being told they would prevent him entry. Feeling the bag of money secured on his side, he waited in mental agony.

The crowd in the square grew until it flooded the area in front of the doors. Syago couldn't believe how many came just to petition the city council. He knew the town was bigger and so would have more people, but this was something else. Were the capital's residents really that unhappy here?

As if in answer to his question, some started waving parchments in the air and chanting. "No more corruption, only the truth!"

He turned to an older woman next to him and asked, "What are they about? What's going on?"

She turned to him without breaking her weary frown. "Hmm? What's going on? You live in a crypt, lad? The corruption letters. They want answers."

"I'm not from here," he clarified. "From Tolgrym to petition for medicinal aid."

"Mmm, well you picked a right bad time to petition. Though I suppose I did too. I also want answers, but even more than that I want my husband out of the house or a different house for myself. If only I could get their attention over this mob, we could resolve it."

As the crowd grew with the daylight, so did the noise. The guards standing nearby looked tired and a little nervous. Then someone waved a handful of parchments in the air while shouting something about Count Gallegom having arranged for the deaths in hunting expeditions of numerous dissenters, unsavories, and even his own nephew, a popular nobleman of the town.

Suddenly, the woman near Syago perked up and snatched one out of their hand. "Let me see that."

Syago watched her eyes skim it. Gallegom was the city's count and as much a central leader of Nevermore as they've had in the last two decades.

"Well, damn me to the lowest pit," she said. "I was hoping that bastard would be on my side."

This sparked worry in Syago. *What of my own plea?* He took the parchment from her. The writing was sloppy, hurried with ink splatters all over. It also struck him that they'd used an ink that resembled blood. It was the first time Syago had seen dye, hopefully it was dye, mixed into ink, adding effect to the claim of murder by the Kingdom Republic's most powerful authority. As he skimmed it, however, he saw many claims but no proof. He understood enough about these things that there should be some way to check it, such as a witness or the count's dagger found with blood on it. This stated things about the count that sounded shady but could easily have been made up. He saw no author ascribed.

"So what happens now?" he asked.

"Probably nothing," the woman muttered in a raspy voice. "Nothing and nothing." The angry crowd began to encroach on the petitioning crowd who'd come early for the purpose of preceding them. The woman added, "Or maybe a little bit of everything."

They got pushed aside as the mob insisted on protesting directly at the door. Banging on it and the guards' feeble attempts at calming them availed naught. Syago saw Tomas on the other side, shock written all over his face. Syago had told him to come early too, but he'd said only one needed to be early in order to wait.

Finally, the doors opened, and a determined Syago pushed his way in through the mob to stand at the front of the court. A real mix of fear and frustration gripped him now as he wondered how he'd ever get his petition out, let alone granted. Furthermore, he was already getting hot from being in a crowded room of angry people who jostled and shoved to their own importance at the expense of others. His most hated aspect about Mantlgrym had always been the crowds, and now it was at its worst.

The well-dressed men accumulating on the dais, behind hearing pulpits, appeared stern and angry. The people in the hall continued yelling at them, and at one point, a heavy older man took one look at a parchment handed to him and with raised eyebrows looked out on the crowd, which went quiet. Syago supposed this was Gallegom just receiving word about his new charge. The count said, "Believe you everything and anything you hear, or do you think first?"

And, of course, the people raged at this, even throwing crumpled parchments along with insults and threats. Most of the accusations had to do with bribes and lies, but the new murder indictment gained momentum. They chanted "Truth" over and over again. The men on stage tried to quiet it but gave up and watched in visible despair as their power waned. Gallegom made ready to speak but waited for them to quiet. Syago itched for it too—and for those around him to bathe more often.

Finally, they quieted and Gallegom said, "If it is the will of the people, we'll spend the day addressing these charges and into the next day if—"

Syago and a number of others immediately shouted their opposition, to which the rest of the people also began shouting. Eventually, it quieted again. "We must allow for the speaker's respect rule or nobody will get anything answered. One at a time. Now, what say we hear out a couple quick petitions before moving into these claims?"

Syago pushed forward. "I have it, Lords of Nevermore's prime court." He held up Toriacus's pendant as if it were supposed to explain everything, but everyone just looked at him expectantly. Syago understood. They wanted him to delay, be a division among the assembly, and, most importantly for him, restore trust as they resolved his dilemma. "On behalf of my town of Tolgrym, I, Syago de Odiru, petition the Kingdom Republic for medicinal aid."

Faces in the crowd frowned. Syago's foreigner status wouldn't serve their needs as well, he realized. Or darker skin, as there were fewer mastozons than in Tolgrym. But what could he do about that? Once again he wished for paler skin. He cleared his throat and continued. "A poisoning has taken place, infecting most women of the town, including my cousin. They're pursuing justice for it as we speak but lack the cure. If the court grants me passage with the cure, we shall ever be in your debt—we'd be grateful." *Don't mention debt, you fool! You'll enslave the whole town.*

Gallegom said, "You need to ask at the Vargayos Manor about availability, then back here at the Trade Tower. They'll get your money."

"You give money to a mastozon foreigner, but not to us?!" shouted a man. Others took up the call, and the petitioners yelled back at them. Then there was pushing, and suddenly Syago was on the floor—someone had punched him. Feet moved all around, and someone stepped on him as he tried to rise, pressing him down. Yelling and fighting broke out on the floor while Syago was getting trampled. Now a more visceral fear filled him. He couldn't get out, couldn't breathe, and his body hurt from the beating it was taking. Covering his face, he tried to rise, but the room was so crowded that it was impossible. He was shoved hard, then pulled out of the crowd. He stumbled to his feet, only to be slammed against the wall with an angry bearded face right up in his own.

"They paid you, didn't they?"

"What?"

"You're their pet," he sneered. Awful breath came out of a mouth of crooked and missing teeth. His hand choked Syago, who couldn't slip it. "You're paid cover to keep up their corruption. The letters said they had these rats, and you smell like a rat. Almost look like one too. From Tolgrym are you? Riiight."

"The damnation are you talking about?" Syago broke free of the hand and twisted the man's arm to slam him into the wall, holding him there while he growled about dirtskins and rats.

Suddenly, a boom overhead silenced everyone. Gallegom held an ornate scepter aloft. He'd used a sound bubble to get everyone's attention in a rare break in decorum.

Grumbling, they all eased off each other. Syago slipped through the crowds to the outside, thinking about how he was to find this manor. Tomas appeared behind him, looking dazed. They nodded to each other, knowing what they had to do.

Getting directions from a guard, they began on their way. It was then that Syago recognized the name. This was Eliana's manor... well, her husband's, anyway. His spirits lifted at the thought of meeting her, along with some anxiety—awkward reunions always bore out short as they danced around the divide between them.

They moved up through the streets when Tomas asked about the money pouch. Syago felt for it. To his horror, it was gone, untied from his belt. He'd had his hand on it most of the time, but he'd been distracted in the crowds. *Damnation to the hell of all hells.* Their one hope entrusted to him, and he'd lost it. His first thought was of that last man who'd pinned him, but no, he could've lost it long before that. It could've just fallen off.

Tomas smacked him upside the head. "Thought you were watching it!"

"I was watching it. What were you doing, sleeping?"

Tomas shook his head and kicked a rotting apple down the street. It had started to rain lightly. "What do we do now?"

Syago was resigned to hope that maybe Eliana could grant them the money they needed or just give them the medicine. Otherwise, he wouldn't be able to return home. He didn't even have more money for their room at the inn. The thought made him nauseated.

After some difficulty in navigating the confusing city streets, they found the manor. Though hardly a manor at all, it was more tall than broad. Small inside the walled enclosure; barely wealthy and not nobility.

Syago knocked on the small gate door. An older serving lady opened the door, looking at him with raised eyebrows.

"Good morning, er, afternoon," Syago said. "Might I speak with the Lady Eliana?"

"Yes," a feminine voice said from farther in. "Who is it?"

"Syago," he called. "Your long-lost cousin."

A small squeal, and the serving lady moved aside. Eliana appeared, and she and Syago embraced. Nice perfume filled his nose, and he released her. Elisabet's older sister looked much like her, with the darker skin and black hair, but otherwise couldn't be more different. Eliana was less gangly and had a smile more mischievous, which Syago dearly missed. She curtsied to Tomas as they passed through the small garden area into the parlor.

Sitting in the greeting room, they exchanged pleasantries and caught up on gossip, including Eliana's recent pregnancy, before falling into an awkward silence.

"Iago, you didn't tell me you were coming," she said suddenly.

"Well, the truth is unfortunate events have brought me here. Elisabet has taken ill."

Eliana gasped, worry filling her eyes. "What?! What happened?"

Syago told her of the recent events in Tolgrym. "We've no cure," he concluded, "and I've come to, er, get it from your husband, actually."

"Oh, Theordoric would love to work something out with you. Slania, go get him, won't you?"

The servant went upstairs, and they waited while sympathies and concerns were expressed over Elisabet. Theordoric entered: a thick and tall man, with a large mustache and smaller, pointed beard. He looked every bit the wealthy apothecary and doctor that Syago had come to know him for. They'd never spoken in great detail, Syago's visits being short and few.

As Theordoric sat next to Eliana, Syago explained the situation in greater detail but held off on the money part.

Theordoric nodded. "I think we can spare some. For as much as you need, it'll raise the price. I think five hundred pounds should do."

"Well, see, there's another issue." Syago sucked in his breath. "I came with a bag of four hundred pounds collected by the town. But it was stolen on my way here."

"Stolen, you say?" The man twisted his short beard between fingers.

"Yes. I sought petition from the count and the crowds there made a storm about something—"

Theordoric frowned. "Are you in with that crowd?"

"No! I'm not even from here." It annoyed Syago that such a question should even be asked. "It was merely in the same room, and one of them took it while I petitioned."

"Indeed."

"Yes, indeed."

The man held out his hands in a helpless gesture. "And your point is?"

"That I can't buy it and need assistance. Surely, as family in such a dangerous situation, you can help us."

"Mm—no, I'm afraid not. The cure you need is expensive to make and maintain. I can't afford to give it away. You have my sympathies, and I might give you a discount down to the four hundred—a rather generous one, I might add—but nothing more. I have a business to run and a house to maintain, with a child on the way."

"Are there any others with this cure that we can barter with?" Tomas asked.

"I'm afraid not. Of course, I'm not the only apothecary here, but I am the only one with that cure. And though I would love to help you, I simply can't afford to."

Syago stared in disbelief and rising anger. Giving up a portion of his supply would hardly impoverish them or even reduce their status. "But they're dying! They're—" He looked at Eliana, who'd gone from watching the exchange with a pleasant smile to watching the floor. "My cousin, Eliana's sister, is dying."

Eliana put her hand on her husband's arm. "Couldn't we give them some?"

Syago added, "Or maybe the recipe so we can make it ourselves?"

Theordoric laughed at this. "Bah, give them the recipe for my invention? Why not just hand it all over, then? No, I'll not give ground to that bastard Roberochester who thinks because he's a baron he can push me out of the market. He won't get me that easy."

"But we're not here to 'get you.' We're here to save lives. Are you willing to let the women of Tolgrym die? Are you willing to kill your sister-in-law?"

"I don't see it so simply. Your tale raises a number of odd questions, and I rather think it your responsibility to protect your women and manage your money, not mine." With a pleading look from Eliana, he sighed and said, "All right, I'll give you one dose enough for a single person, to guarantee her survival. For the rest, you'll have to go and come back with the money—without losing it again."

"But we need it for the whole town!" both Syago and Tomas said together. "They'd be dead by the time I got it to them. What about a loan?"

"I'm loaning nothing to anyone who can lose four hundred pounds, if that is what happened. You might obtain from someone else, the Trade Tower perhaps, so long as you don't mention your loss. Still, your best chance is to take my sample and hurry back for the rest."

"I can't believe you'd be so callous. Can you at least give us money for passage? I tell you I don't even have that."

"Shall I rescind my offer due to ungrateful guests? No? Then take the sample, work in a smithy for a couple hours to earn passage, and come back with that money. Be happy you're getting anything at all." He rose and went down a hall to the cellar. Eliana watched the floor as they waited in the most awkward silence in the history of the world.

Theordoric returned with a small vial, which Syago took, pointedly not thanking him.

Outside in the rain again, Syago and Tomas walked hurriedly back to the Court of Ashor, getting soaked and lost on the way. Angry wet crowds still bustled about the square, but—warily pushing through—they found the tower just as the rain stopped.

Two stodgy men at a table heard their tale with impassive faces. They denied that they were able to give loans to the two of Tolgrym so soon, but in three days' time after approval—the minimum time to lend—they might. Tolgrym didn't have three days. Syago and Tomas then had three seconds to exit the room for those next in line or face the irons. And so they left. Actually they had heard that the city guard was out of irons because of the pressing mob. But there were still ropes, wooden locks, and other such punishing restraints. Even in Tolgrym, guards could be quite inventive.

The clear air turned to pelting hail, so they moved away from the crowds under a roof enclosure, eyeing the food they longed for being sold to people less desperate than they. Syago pulled out the vial, and they looked at it, a small glass container with black liquid inside.

"Listen," Tomas said, "I have just enough pounds in my pocket here to send a message. Look... well, we might have to bargain down the price of sending it, but if we can get a message to Tolgrym that we're out of money and need them to send a wagon, we can in the meantime get together some money for the supply."

"Four hundred pounds?" Syago ran his hand through his hair while fighting back tears and hating that he had to. "We can't earn that in a day!"

Tomas looked no less distraught, and Syago recalled that he'd come from a family of all men, his mother long dead, but he did have a love to whom he was plight trothed. "Well, at least a return now might be enough to save some. At least you could guarantee your cousin."

"I can't give this to her while the rest go without," Syago muttered, surprised Tomas would even suggest it at the risk of losing his Heideh. Or was he already giving up? "They'd skin me alive if I returned and saved just her."

"Hey, Lügos the Flayed don't have it so bad." With a look from Syago, Tomas removed his smile. "Sorry. But look, what else are we going to do? This wasn't supposed to be this hard."

"You could win the money," said a voice behind them. They turned to see

Kask sitting in the alley, the cage still on his head. "Tournaments can run up quite a sum. Tonight is melee sparring, I believe. I think you do have to pay to get in and they might make you bid in order to win something. But—"

"Show us," they both said.

He showed them the place, closed until the tournament began in the evening. It was a new theater house, a tall, round white building. Theater had boomed in the towns and demand for new tournament spaces brought this construction, according to Kask, who didn't appear like someone who'd know that sort of thing.

Syago turned to Tomas. "Everybody knows even small-time tournaments out here are quick money if you can pull it. We'll just have to find some odd wages to buy us entry. I contest and you bid on me... I wouldn't even have to win, so long as I hold out up to second or third, that should give us enough. And what else have we to do?"

"Well, we could lose the money we earned—aw, foda!" Tomas cut off, having just stepped in morwolf shit. He scraped his boot along the clay-plated plankway and continued. "But I suppose if the wagon's already on the way from our message and bringing more money, then we couldd still buy some of what we need. That's better than where we're at now." Tomas stopped the scraping and thumbed the stones marked as pounds, thinking on it. More thinking than Syago had ever seen him do.

Beside them, Kask coughed violently, drawing blood on the cage spikes. They regarded the street rat distrustfully.

"You," Tomas demanded, "why are you helping us? What interest have you in our affairs?"

Kask cleared his throat, but it remained raspy when he spoke. "I like supporting a good cause." Both snorted at that.[45]

They sent the message by trained quervosk, after a challenge of bargaining down the price. Seeing the bird fly away brought little comfort. Quervosk messages usually arrived, but not always; it wasn't uncommon for them to be attacked or simply forfeit their training and fly away. Given the luck and lack of divine favor they'd been having, he felt he shouldn't bet on it. In fact, his sword arm was much more reliable, when someone lent him a sword to use. He was the best at sparring in Tolgrym, save some of

---

45 See *Luskmord: Atriom Carcerio*, 16

the older men, and even they struggled against him. He didn't know the ability of these cityfolk but doubted their comfortable lives afforded them as much practice in weaponry as he'd had.

He would've practiced for the tournament, but the money was so much on his mind and if they didn't get anything he wouldn't even be able to enter it. He convinced a blacksmith to let him clean the furnace and shop while Tomas found work in a kitchen house. Syago finished, then ran to collect Tomas. Together they suited Syago up in armor, he stretched and did some practice swings, and he and Tomas ran to the theater house.

CHAPTER TEN

A WORTHY FOE

Based on *Writings of Qosku*, cc bastica 40;
Leyta's Journals, cc bastica 14; *Scars of the Martyrs*, cc bastica 913;
The Nordvargor Testaments, cc bastica 566;

20th of Septimosk, 246

Qosku remembered working in Izquchaka with a terrible mix of emotions. He missed the beautiful, magnificent yaqta. Masterwork buildings sat on the top of a mountain on a terraced plateau between two peaks. A river wrapped around it and mountain ridges knifed the sky, some in the north with snow, but most were forested. Everything about it was bigger than Chuqi'kirau, and busier too.[46]

But the pain of the memories—and not just from betraying Chaska before possibly sacrificing her. He was a mine worker, as most children were for their small sizes. Though because he was of the few that could write, sometimes he got to scribe inventories in the forges when the rain was too heavy, a gift from hanan pacha. The day before he'd betrayed Chaska and left, they'd been split up by the guards, he to the mine of iron and she to the gold. Both were dirty and dangerous work, and Chaska was afraid to separate from him, so they devised a plan to stay together. Cutting her hair and wearing boy's clothes, Chaska went with him to the iron mines. It was a fun idea, though he'd much rather have dressed to be a girl, thought he'd be good at it, but it she didn't think it a good idea and wanted to be a boy. Were they both in the wrong body? He suspected hers was more a brief flight of fancy inspired by him. She agreed to let him switch the next day. But after a day's labor, the Asturion guards grabbed him and Chaska and

---

46 *See Losnin Liberado Kani, 32*

roughly checked both his and her sexes with their hands. It always felt wrong to Qosku, to be examined and found not as he felt. Always male instead of female. *But maybe it's extra help needed to convince the rest of me I really am male.* Behind them, Qosku had seen the Asturion guard, the only mastozon, hand Mancopac some coin, his eyes avoiding theirs. He, another slave, had ratted them out.

The twins were both lashed that day, there in the cave entrance overlooking the steep cliff of vine-covered stone, with the yaqta on the opposite mountain. Qosku used what little Takanaku training he'd had to endure the pain. Chaska had no protection and wailed uncontrollably. They had brought out thirty ore, good enough for what should've been proof that they could work together effectively. But that wasn't the point; division and dissolution of the conquered was. Peace among slaves. Once back at the yaqta, they were made to live in different buildings, separated and prohibited from seeing each other for the first time in their lives.

Qosku remembered. *Wounds never forget a person; even after healing, they always find that someone, re-inflicting their pain.* He walked the streets of Mantlgrym, which reminded him of Izquchaka for all its dense busyness. It had other reminders as well. Iron and iron's bastard, steel, were everywhere, shipped in from his home. They held the structures of the town up and together. Guards were covered in steel, wielded it. It was effective, Qosku had to admit, as he'd eventually given in and taken the dead trappers' steel gauntlets and greaves for himself, and a smaller hauberk for his own. If he couldn't do anything about it, he decided he'd at least make use of that which he'd built.

Gold too was everywhere. What he'd risked his life for, bloodied his arms in countless hours under the whip for, and what had been stripped from Unakan temples in the beginning, people now traded around as coins for clothes, food, and any number of barely necessary items. Some even wore this oppression on their hands as jewelry.

This is the meaning of bondage, chains that stay with you long after you've escaped them.

He'd come to Mantlgrym to get some of that money to pay for more time at Cantlgrym, but now he searched for a place to train and sleep. He'd hoped doing service labor at the castle would be enough to earn his stay, but they'd said it wasn't. Luckily, he'd heard of a tournament in Mantlgrym.

If there was anything he could do well, it was that. Of course, he hadn't planned on getting tricked out of his money once he arrived, or having his bedding soaked through in the rain, or getting sick from bad food. But he was used to these things. In fact, he'd not planned on staying at inns in the first place. For a dynfist friar, a bed was a luxury—and luxury made one weak and complacent. Still, sleeping on the streets or rooftops was always better with a couple blankets for bedding. At least here, in so large a city, people generally ignored him.

He'd found peace at this abbey, and though the other friars admired his skills, they still disdained his not being a full convert. He told himself he actually preferred being the invisible kid. In Chuqi'kirau, he'd trained with weapons more common to Unaka. Slings and bolas were easy to remake, but all his maces, flails, and axes were repeatedly broken by the other children in Chuqi'kirau or by guards in Izquchaka, so he'd learned to use guarded fist and foot. It'd drawn unwanted attention at the abbey, which worried him. If they did figure out his truth, he feared he'd have to leave again.

He walked down a street between tall, square buildings and eyed with hunger some fruit being sold from a cart. The vendor's eyes narrowed at the sight of him. He moved into an alley and began poking at garbage piles. He had no money to pay that vendor anyway. So he went back to what he'd learned since leaving Chuqi'kirau—scavenging with the rats and dogs.

Finding a rooftop where he could eat his stale bread and train along a stony ledge, he stretched, then went through combat forms as the sun fell through cloudy skies toward the mountains. He still prayed to the apus on occasion, though he was far and had difficulty summoning up any rever- ence, given their lack of help during his years of pain in their stony care.[47]

The falling sun gleamed off of the dark skin of his bare upper body and black hair, tied back into a short tail. Sweat shone on his Takanaku tat- toos, each symbol necessary to tie his sentiments into his body, to power his arms and legs the way a dynast pushes sentiments into the elements or an archemist into his creations. He fed sentiments into his limbs as he worked forms, emptying his sorrow into it. Sorrow was better for heal- ing, but it's what he had and needed to get rid of. Pushing anger into his

---

47 But only certain peaks are apus and worshiped alongside other special natural features, with the focus being on the sun, moon, and stars as they traverse the three pacha worlds of the universe.

feet, a flying kick carried him halfway across the rooftop, almost hitting a weathered gargoyle drain.

After finishing more stretches, he felt ready to leave for the tourney. He donned his shoes and tunic, then eyed his gauntlets and greaves, padded leather gloves, and stockings with steel plates to cover his forearms, hands, feet, and shins. He put them on—the chestplate, too. They added bulk to his lanky limbs and made him look as tough as he felt. The gloves had detachable claws and the plates were strong enough to block a sword swing, though the impact could still hurt. He donned his habit and climbed down to the streets below using the ledges and ladders. He could climb anything, but he found it odd how easy it was to reach rooftops in the city. *What of robbers and murderers? Aren't they everywhere here?*

Qosku found the theater. He paid the men at the door what little money he had left, the price of his starvation, and entered a large room full of people milling about in animated betting. He didn't need to win a lot of money and so didn't need to bet. Any winner's earnings alone would give him a month at Cantlgrym's dynfist abbey.

On seeing him, a few people raised eyebrows, one scowled, and another looked on in amusement. He ignored them as he'd learned to do and plunged into the crowds, where he became invisible. The theater was a circle of audience benches, three floors, with a single platform in the center beneath an opening in the roof, a dressing room at its back. There would be up to three matches at a time going on, one on the stage and two just below, following the free-for-all round.

There was some confusion when he entered his first match without a more common hand weapon; they didn't think he understood or could compete without one. He had to explain every time, and they'd look it up in the rulebook, then confirm his right to fight. The fights themselves were hard, more than he'd expected. He'd trained much in beating off swords, axes, and polearms with his gauntlets and greaves, but these warriors were some of the best in the realm. His advantage was that they severely underestimated him and lacked training in fighting someone of his style. He had to refrain from using dyne, which became its own challenge every time he got cornered. Yet his mastery over himself prevailed, and he rose in the ranks.

The time came for his final contention, a contest for third place. Qosku wanted to see his competitor, but crowds blocked his view till he climbed a ladder. In the middle of the circle, two competitors dueled with axe and shield. Unlike sparring, the weapons were real; however, wounding was avoided, though it still happened, as did deaths—an unfortunate but unavoidable consequence of tournaments. Around them, people cheered and yelled.

The current reigning champion that would counter him for third had mastozon hair and skin, but hazel eyes, and was covered in iron and steel. All the competitors wore his sweat and blood on them, and he wondered, *Do they not know where their metal comes from? Or do they know and not care?* Qosku gave them the benefit of the doubt. His opponent used a hand-axe and shield of wood and steel but was quite good, if a little cocky. His skin was the darkest outside of Qosku's own, which made him feel slightly less alone. The boy called Syago bathed in everyone's adulation for his skill but tolerated their mocking as well, gestures and slurs that Qosku recognized. *Do you not rebel because you don't know your oppression, or because you've embraced it, having no alternative?* It felt like looking in a mirror, dark skin wearing metal from the mountains and complying with what they gave him. *Where is he from? What does any of this mean?*

He made a joke that Qosku didn't understand, and everyone laughed. The bravado amused, but something else deep inside Qosku yearned to experience that. For people to laugh not at him but at something that he said with intention, at something he *wanted* to be funny. He pushed the thought away; pride gave power but could be distracting.

Qosku watched the champion parry a thrust, spin his axe around the opponent's, and twist it under with a snap, deftly disarming his adversary in less than fifty seconds. If anyone had any right to be arrogant, it was him, even having lost the first and second places. He smiled, clearly enjoying his stream of victories as he vied for third.

Children cheered this Syago, who looked around for the next competitor. Qosku went down to the bottom of the audience box and clapped his metal gauntlets together, saying, "I am Qosku. It my turn for fight."

Qosku cringed as all eyes turned on him, no longer invisible. Among the faces, Syago's smile faded. *Earn the respect,* Qosku told himself. He jumped down, expecting the need to push his way through, but the crowd parted for him. Now on the stage, he faced Syago, who stared at him, as another man protested, "You need a weapon to compete."

"My weapon are these. I have gloves and greaves." He clapped the steel gauntlets together again and stomped his feet lightly on the stone floor.

"No, you don't understand," the man adopted an insulting tone, slow and loud. "This isn't your training group. It's ours. We use weapons here. Do you know what a weapon is?"

"It's fine," Syago said. "I saw him in other rings. You don't need to be rude about it. I'll just beat him like everyone else."

The man grumbled, and betting started. One of his friends shouted, "Beat that dirty digger, Syago." The kids followed their parents in picking up the jeers and slurs as the bell sounded and the two closed in, circling.

Not understanding most of their language anyway, Qosku had already transcended the group. He saw only Syago behind his shield.

Syago came in hard with a slash from the left. Catching it against his gauntlet, Qosku guided it away as he punched forward with a right cross. His steel fist glanced off of Syago's shield, then the shield pressed forward in a rush as the axe snapped low. Qosku brought both arms to bear against the shield, leaning into it, while raising his left shin to deflect the axe on his greave before snapping it into Syago's leg. Syago went down on that leg but adapted quickly with a thrust of his shield, clipping Qosku in the stomach lightly. As he backed away, the kids called point. With a horizontal kick toward Syago's back, Qosku skipped to shield side. Syago spun, regaining his footing and swinging his shield wide to knock the kick aside while thrusting the axehead.

Resisting the urge to funnel sentiments into his movements, a cheat in this, Qosku swatted it down. He switched legs and side-kicked at the exposed axe arm as it moved to slash his side. Syago shifted, awkwardly, to block the kick, but Qosku pushed it too hard for the blade and his armored leg plowed through, tapping Syago's shoulder. The audience called point halfheartedly, and Qosku realized they hadn't for the earlier leg blow. The thought was fleeting, his mind clear as he swept aside the axe that came at his chest, then pushed with both arms at the shield. Again he resisted the urge to put sentiments into it, make it stronger and faster. The push forced Syago back, but he retained footing—that is, until Qosku snapped a low kick that removed Syago's foot from the ground. Syago fell back. He rolled on his side in an impressive recover, but the advantage was already forfeit. Qosku landed on his axe, pinning it, while tapping him on the thigh.

Noting the lack of what should've been his victory point, he tapped him again. This time, they gave it to him.

Silence filled the room. Syago lay breathing heavily, a look of stunned frustration on his face. Qosku stepped off the axe and punched his hands together, bowing slightly and saying, "A worthy opponent. Grateful you fight me."

Syago glared at him, ignored the offered hand, and pulled himself to his feet. Because of the look on his face, Qosku feared he might do something to him in front of everyone, but he only brushed himself off.

Another competitor on the side said, "Hey, you're one of those dynfist friars, aren't you? You must've cheated then. I've seen what they do. They use dyne to make themselves faster. That's how he won."

"That is not truth, sir," he replied. "I could do this, but I did not."

"How do we know you're not lying? I say you're lying." He raised his voice and others muttered agreements.

"I show you." He crouched down, gathering his joy at winning and focusing it into his legs, then jumped and kicked up, moving inhumanly quick, then landing lightly on the ground. He'd been fast in the fight, but not like this. This was lightning—the flash of an arrow.

The other kids looked at Syago, who remained slightly reddened in the cheeks but mostly expressionless. He muttered, "It's fine," and walked out of the ring, vanishing into the crowd of disappointed faces. All around the audience, gold coins exchanged hands.

Qosku reflexively braced himself for more taunts and jeers, but the others merely departed to other tournament rings. Invisible again, better than a victim, but he still felt alone and not himself. *They don't even accept me as I appear now. If I looked more feminine, it'd be worse.* Well, he would pray and train for peace, anything to not self-abuse as he once did.

He left to roam about the stage area as the competition wrapped up. He hated the champion's ceremony, being presented a bag of gold up there in front of everyone and knowing none of them were glad to see him there. Well, none but two men that had taken a chance on him with small bets. Qosku's reward would give him about seventy days at Cantlgrym, including the trip back, assuming he didn't lose it again. He stood there next to the only two men who'd beaten him, wishing he could enjoy the victory more than he felt. A quick meal and night's sleep would make him feel better.

And more training to avoid dwelling on his miseries.

Leyta woke in the middle of the night with a start. Dreams of the execution plagued her: the man trying to talk to her while she burned him. She rubbed her face and shifted in her bed, trying a different position. Lying there, she thought about how quiet it was; it reminded her of the catacombs and that creature.

Actually, it was more quiet than usual in the quarters she shared with six other girls.[48] She couldn't see because the windowless room was pitch-black, but normally there'd be a fire and breathing, and occasionally light snoring from Banesa. Now she heard none of it. Reaching for her staff, she lit a candle. Slowly, light filled the quarters, casting shadows in its many corners. The faint light revealed empty mats around her. Her heart fluttered slightly in fear, but she knew the more likely answer was that they'd all snuck off. The boys on the other side were still there.

She put on slippers and ventured out into the back hall to look for them. She heard nothing and so didn't know whether to go up or down. With her staff in hand, she switched to the Vision and saw sentimental footprints so faint they were almost gone. They went into the library, and so did she. The air was so cold she shivered, regretting not bringing an extra blanket over her nightshift and feeling like she should've slept more and scolded them in the morning. As she entered the library, placing her candle in a lantern case, she used the Vision to find a number of faded trails in all directions. She looked about for one to follow, then saw something move around the corner of a bookshelf. Running after it, she said, "Oy, I know you're there. No use keeping this up, only making it worse for you."

She turned the corner to find it empty. Just a long, tall stack of shelves with chained texts, shadows everywhere. Her own tallow candle had time left yet but was weak and threw eerie shadows. She hurried to the next corner and saw down this passage the back of a leg, dark in the shadow, disappear at the top of the stairs around a corner. She began to move toward it, then halted.

The tapestries along the walls behind the shelves had been cut—no, slashed. Long tears ran through the scenes depicted. Her heart quickened. *What if*

---

48 See *Luskmord: Atriom Carcerio,* 26

these girls are in danger of being taken the way Navidsom was? She ran up the stairs and saw an open door at the end of the walkway, total darkness inside. One of the side rooms, used for storage and a privy. As she approached, the door slammed shut, but she was quick and caught the handle before it could lock. Her lantern swung wildly, casting shadows everywhere as she yanked it back open.

Her candlelight illuminated portions of the dim, tight hall. At the end stood the girls in their nightclothes in a half-circle, facing away from her. Above them in the dark were two small embers, or low-burning candles, it appeared, for they glowed but illuminated nothing.

"Girls," Leyta said, moving closer to them. "What—"

Her light peeled back the darkness to reveal a tall, thin man of shadow with embers for eyes. The girls gazed up into those eyes, saying nothing, moving not at all. With its long dark hands on the head of one girl, it bent down and kissed her full on the mouth, almost swallowing her head.

"Oy, get away from them!" Leyta shouted, sparking a fire over their heads. Her own candle flared, eating up more of the wick and tallow. At the increase of light, the ember eyes faded, leaving a blank, dark head. The girls snapped out of their reverie and screamed, falling back as she ran forward. The man, like living darkness, darted to the adjoining privy, and the shadows inside shifted and stretched pit to ceiling—and the phantom was gone. *NO!* She was so close. *How did it get away? I can't let it.*

After a quick glance at the girls to make sure they were unhurt, she ran to the privy.

"Leyta, what was that?" Banesa asked. Little Kel'feq began to cry.

"I don't know," Leyta muttered. *It was my query and it escaped.* In the hole of the privy, she saw cobwebs hanging down and something dark was smeared around it, something that looked a lot like blood. A quick shift into the Vision showed that the smear had a strong yellow glow: fear. *Well, at least this privy rarely gets used.*

"Bring me a rope, quick," she ordered the girls.

They did so, all holding it and bracing it against a chair while she was lowered in, lantern handle wrapped into the rope just above and staff in the crooks of her arms. The tight drop opened into a small ledge. The corners were all shadows and cobwebs, the bricks covered in dust, save the foul stains of the main chute, but the air was old in its unuse. She saw a trapdoor below, likely a forgotten secret passage. But what drew her eye after that was a blood-caked arm, this one clearly human, hanging over that ledge below.

Hand to mouth, she stifled a scream, then pulled herself up and saw that the arm wasn't just bloody but also severed. Several parts were laid out around a mess of blood. She fought the need to vomit and noticed that the limbs were clearly from an adult. But who if not young Navidsom? It was impossible to tell in the poor lighting.

Then she saw him. Navidsom shivered in a crouch in ragged clothes in the corner, but that meant he was alive. His head was down, tucked into his legs, and that he maintained this instead of looking up at his rescue gave her pause. Her skin prickled and breath caught. She swallowed and called on the girls to descend her down a bit more.

When she got to him, he didn't look up, so she put a hand on his shoulder. With a start, he knocked her hand away and gaped at her. Eyes wide, mouth muttering soundlessly. Even without having known him well, she could see the effects of his time here. Face gaunt and pale, and mind clearly disturbed. Wide eyes continued to stare, but not at her—*past* her. She waved a hand in front of his face and snapped her fingers while repeating his name in gentle tones to get his attention: "Navidsom. I'm Leyta. I'm going to take you back to the main hall, where you'll be safe."

He shook his head, still muttering. Then his eyes grew even wider, and he hid his face again. She turned to see above, in darkness, the ember eyes. They held her, and her body went cold with fear. She couldn't move. The candle flickered, darkness in the room grew, and the faint human form stretched out and approached slowly with impossible silence. Her gut lurched as she realized she couldn't move. Caught in the unwavering stare, she fought it without success. The eyes drew nearer, borne by an unfathomable being of material darkness that she wanted to be far away from. Tears streamed down her face. Then Navidsom touched her, pulling her back just enough to break out of the locked gaze.

She threw everything she had against it, creating a lightning spark that lit the room and crackled. Almost as fast, the shadow creature jumped back. She fought to maintain focus against the continued onslaught of the smoke. Then Navidsom grabbed her, pulling at her staff arm. She slapped him in the face, having no time to worry about whatever insanity

he was wrapped up in. She brought darkfire to bear from the moisture of
the privy chute and drew it up after the shadowman who now retreated
out of the small hold.[49]

It wasn't until Anaruth arrived minutes later, being summoned by the
girls, that they were able to get Navidsom out. Banesa confided to Anaruth
that when it'd briefly kissed her, it'd sucked all her sentiments out, leaving
her passive and cold as an empty shell.[50] None of them slept the rest of
that night.

---

[49] *ibid, 28*

[50] *Peculiar why it seems to prefer child sentiments. Children's sentiments are usually much more free-flowing but weaker. Perhaps they're easier to entrap in the gaze.*

CHAPTER ELEVEN

STALKER AND THIEF

Based on *Annals of Syago*, cc bastica 9;
Scars of the Martyrs, cc bastica 928;

20th–21st of Septimosk, 246

Syago pushed his way out of the theater, badly in need of air and to be away from everyone. Freeing himself of the building, there were still people everywhere. The city was never not full of people and their noise and bumping. He wanted to throttle them all.

Walking into an alley, he ran his hands through his hair, then kicked a box while yelling at the sky. At the Criod or the hells or anything that might've been responsible for such a failure. He'd been disappointed at losing out to the two now taking first and second but not entirely surprised. His position on third had been sealed, but he'd somehow still lost it to some mountain boy who didn't even have a real weapon. They'd be lucky to break even now.

In storming out into the alley, he'd stepped in morwolf feces. The gross squishiness of it and the putrid smell augmented his fury. He snarled and kicked at a box. *Why is this stuff everywhere? I've never been anywhere so dirty as this.*

Walking up to Syago after exiting the building, Tomas demanded, "What the hell happened?!"

"I foding lost it to that—that... gah!" Syago kicked another box, this one much heavier. The defiance of the box annoyed him as much as the pain in his foot, so he kicked it again, feeling some satisfaction in the crack he'd given it, as if it'd learned its lesson about resisting him.

"All right, calm down," Tomas said after a shopkeeper poked his head out a window and scowled at them.

Tomas waited till the man retreated back in and whispered harshly, "But how could you—ah well, it's done anyway. What now?"

"Nothing," Syago said, throwing his arms out to the side, his eyes big. "There's nothing we can do. We're foded, Elisabet and all the women of Tolgrym are just foded."

"There's always the darker way," called an old voice. From farther down the alley emerged Kask. He'd somehow removed the head cage, though a couple red lines from the spikes marred his face. "You don't need to play by his rules, you know."

"What are you doing here, Kask?" Syago asked. Both Tolgrymians' hands fell to knives at their belts.

"Me? I'm always here, always everywhere. Such are the poor and infirm, though they try to keep us out of the richer neighborhoods. Don't want the wealthy getting uncomfortable."

Syago rolled his eyes. "What do you want?"

"To help." Kask cracked a faint smile. "As I said. By the sound of it, you're in the exact same situation that brought myself into my current mess. Can't afford the cure, so you lose it all. I now encourage you to do what I would not. Steal what you need."

"That's dishonorable," Syago snapped. Tomas guffawed at the cretin.

"Honor? Your rules of honor were written by the same people who wrote the property laws and set trade prices. Both sets of rules are killing and impoverishing people left and right, including your..."

"Cousin," Syago said. "I'll not become the monster here."

"Would stealing to save your cousin's life make you a monster?" Kask stopped in front of them in the alleyway. They wanted to leave the rat, but his words held their attention. "Should you do this thing, who would truly be the monster? You or him? Look at it this way: There are two moral embargoes at play here, working against each other. Killing, or at best allowing to die, and theft. Now which is worse, a neglected death or a mostly harmless theft?"

A reactionary answer caught in Syago's throat.

Kask pursued his point. "Consider the broader pattern for a moment. Nobody logically believes theft is worse than murder by negligence, and yet in a famine, they'd punish thieves but not hoarders. And who does it benefit? The wealthy rule makers. They can neglect their subjects unto death, a process they often do while publicly expressing regret. You can do it too, if it's in line with their system. You and they will even commit to change, but they're not truly interested in change and it's too much trouble anyway, so life remains an unfortunate cost of a peaceful society. But property? No, for that is what they have and must not lose. It's the basis of their power, which they maintain by protecting it before life. They have all the power, the untouchable property. Property, then, is more sacred than life itself. And in a moral dilemma where two rights are in conflict, one must be sacrificed. So which will you now sacrifice on the altar of a harmonious and just society? A person or a property?"

Syago didn't answer.

Tomas looked at him, brow furrowing. "Iago, you're not seriously considering this, are you?"

He looked at them both. "I need to save my cousin. All of Tolgrym's women. That's my moral imperative right now. More so than these arbitrary property laws."

"Don't listen to this foding thief." Tomas looked at Kask while saying it. "And don't become one!"

"Why am I accused when I merely point out a problem and a way to approach it?" Kask questioned, holding hands up defensively, though his sly expression betrayed him. "I didn't say do anything violent or steal any more than for what you need. Just reconsider the view of right and wrong that you've been spoon-fed, then right the wrong. Am I bad for wondering why this cousin must be sacrificed for this property law?"

"Tomas, look," Syago began. "I don't know about property laws and people or any of that, but Eli-they need this. I'm only going for what we need, and if that condemns me to another hell, then so be it, so long as they're safe. If you have a better plan, then I'd like to hear it."

Tomas stared at him and held up a hand. "Fine. I'll cover for you and help you get back to Tolgrym, but I'm not going to break in with you."

"I understand. Wasn't even going to ask," Syago said. "I'll do anything to save my cousin."

They went back to the theater to get their prize of ten pounds, which was barely enough money to buy them another night at the inn or some food, but not both; passage to Tolgrym the following morning wasn't even an option. So food it was. Feeling famished, they'd need the energy to work the night as they planned—if they could find work for the night.

They barely registered that it was Somhoin, Festival of Saints, for while it would've swept up all of Tolgrym in reverential offerings followed by joyous celebration, here it only crowded the streets with processions followed by lots of raucous drinking. Syago longed to be enjoying that with his family and friends, yet here he was.

The tables at the inn were already nearly full. Syago had hoped to talk with some of the tourney attendants but couldn't see anyone he knew until he noticed the Unakan boy who'd beaten him sitting in the back, alone. Without thinking, he started toward the boy, hands becoming fists, but then he stopped. The boy looked younger and smaller than Syago recalled. And so much alone, as people laughed all around the room, that the quiet and glum boy inspired in Syago a measure of guilt and sympathy. He approached and asked, "Excuse me, may I sit next to you?"

He looked up. "Ary. I, uh, yes. Please, sit."

Syago sat down on the bench, still quelling the feelings he wished he didn't have. "I'm sorry, I forgot your name."

"My name Qosku. And you are call Syago. Is truth?"

"Yes." Syago smiled. "So why did you come to Mantlgrym?"

"I get money for to study dynfist in Cantlgrym and see find family." After a perplexed look from Syago, Qosku tried again. "Oh, see if my lost parents here is what is meant."

Nodding, Syago thought on the cruel irony of it: Of course the boy would be where Syago longed to go. "And how is Cantlgrym treating you?"

"People not always nice. But I know it already. I made one friend. She is called Leyta Trastamuir. She really nice."

Syago perked up with a laugh, recognizing the name. *So she's at Cantlgrym now.* He wondered what she was like.

Qosku noticed his reaction. "Why you laugh?"

Syago shrugged. "We-our parents arranged a marriage between us when we were really young; we were plight trothed. But it was canceled when they died, and the royals ceded to the counts. I've always been curious, though."

Qosku asked, "Why you have dark skin? You parents are refugee too?"

Syago froze. "*What?*"

But Qosku looked at him earnestly; there was no notable malice in those deep-brown eyes. So Syago responded, "Oh, uh, my mother had Kimoc parents. But she was raised Asturion and married one, my father."

"Which eternals she worship? You remember her rituals?" Qosku's enthusiasm for the old pagan culture was evident and unshared.

"No, she converted to Deovan faith when she received the holy witness." Syago left out that she'd reportedly held onto a number of the pagan traditions until she became an elementist.

But Qosku didn't take the hint. "My family, in Chuqi'kirau, we were warriors. We prayed to thunder and sun, like Kimoc. You pray with me?"

"Uh, no, thanks—"

"I can teach you, I know Kimoc too. It gives me great power and joy. You can worship like your mother."

"No, thank you." Syago changed the subject. "But well done on the competition." He had to cough to hide the crack in his voice.

"You not angry I beated you?" Qosku asked, devouring his mushroom soup.

"I am," Syago said with a sigh, "but you don't need to worry. You did what I would have done."

"What you do now?" He drank some cider but never took his eyes off of Syago.

"I'll need to work a night here to earn my keep. Otherwise I've nowhere to stay and no way to get back to my home in Tolgrym."

"I help you." Qosku fumbled at his side, then put some coins on the table in front of Syago. Syago stared at them. He didn't like accepting charity, but then why was he here? It occurred to him that he might be able to talk Qosku into giving him more, maybe enough to buy the medicine. But no, he couldn't do that to Qosku, who himself looked as though he needed all the help he could get.

Syago thanked him and took it. They finished out the awkward silence, talking but little more since Qosku was so quiet, except for simple questions and a pride in his ancestry that made Syago uncomfortable for reasons he couldn't pin down. On finishing his meal, Syago passed word to Tomas about the help, but Tomas decided to work some more just in case. It also helped provide a cover while Syago planned the necessary theft.

Syago then found his way to the Vargayos manor. A light fog covered the streets, clouding the night and making the search difficult. The manor somehow looked different—even gloomier and more forbidding. The moon hung over him, blurred by clouds but still providing light. The street was quiet and vacant, exactly the way he wanted it. Carefully, he scouted the place. He'd no experience in thieving, but sneaking around Tolgrym to pull pranks and spy on people, as well as hunting, had taught him well.

The manor had no lights on inside, no guards anywhere in sight. He wondered what kept it secure in such a city overrun with theft. Then he recalled the archemical devices Roberochester had made to protect his keep.[51] It was likely then that this manor had solid locks and archemical traps all around.

In which case Syago would be up to the task. Hiding in the tiny yard of statues and potted plants, he moved around to map the outside, forming plans and backup plans in his mind. Crouching, he looked one last time to check for anyone watching.

A ways down the street, in the fog, stood the dark silhouette of a man. Syago froze. The man was watching him. Syago felt a chill in his bones, and it reminded him of the figure watching him in the woods.

Then the shadowy figure vanished. Eyes wide, Syago jumped to his feet but saw nothing, only fog. Crossing himself, Syago returned to his project. Staying low, he peeked into a window. He believed it to be the room that would show him the stairs to the medicine hold. Using his hunting knife, he released the window latch and reached in slowly, feeling a small table with a flask that he pushed away from the window, gentle. He then softly hoisted himself up and in. The flask, disguised as a lamp, didn't explode in response to his intrusive movement. He decided Theordoric was a fool for not keeping a dog and left his knife outside. If he was caught, he did not want it be with weapon in hand.

Cringing inwardly at every floorplank creak, Syago moved to the stairs. His eyes drifted back to the window—and jumped on seeing the shadowy figure again. Heart pounding, Syago tripped on a rug and fell back onto the stairs, stifling a gasp. He kept his eyes on the figure as he reached his hand out for something to use for a weapon.

It stood there just watching him, and he could see better now that it wasn't just an obscure silhouette: It was a completely dark and faceless man. A living shadow, like material darkness taken into solid form. It stared with a face that now had eyes, or what resembled the faint glow of dying candles. It brought up long black arms and stretched in through

---

51   *See Luskmord: Atriom Carcerio, 33*

the window, soundlessly climbing into the room. Syago scrambled up the steps, praying to Deova Bondua that this thing couldn't touch him and wouldn't get him caught. Irons wouldn't help Elisabet, he couldn't let her die because of this.

He reached the top of the steps and turned—the figure had once again vanished. Looking down the hall, he saw nothing either. Stilling his trembling hands, Syago fumbled at the lock of the door with his tools. It popped open. He prayed under his breath, "Heavenly Mother, make it go away. If you can't save me, at least save Elisabet. For the love of light, please."

He entered and immediately scanned the shelves of jars. He eventually found what he was looking for, but it was only one jar. He looked frantically for more, then turned to other shelves—and there was the shadowman. This time, the eyes burned brighter. Like two low-burning candles that somehow grew in strength, the specks of light on its head told Syago it was never human at all but something else entirely.

Syago, petrified to the spot by the unwavering stare, couldn't so much as blink to pull his eyes from those of the shadow. An incalculable being of living darkness in the shape of a man, inhumanly tall, and still until it moved toward him. What would it do?

Movement and a yelp at the door snapped Syago out of it. It was Eliana, her white nightgown haunting but also welcoming. Syago held up his hands to quiet her. The shadowman was gone from the corner, gone from the room as Syago looked about. Such stealth frightened him.

"*Syago!*" whispered Eliana. "You can't be in here."

"If your little sister weren't guaranteed death, I wouldn't be," he snapped in a slightly louder whisper.

She looked down the hall, then back at him. "Hurry before he wakes. I don't know what I'll say if he wakes. I should just tell him."

"I only have half of what I need," he objected and resumed his hurried search. "I can't go back and save only half of the women. I should bring three jars, just to be safe."

She grabbed the jar from him, examined the label, then pointed at a jar on the far wall, where the shadowman had been. He walked over, examining the darkness of the corner before taking the second jar, and she pushed him out of the room and stood at the top of the stairs while he descended to leave.

At the bottom, he turned back to her. "Listen—"

She cut him off. "Syago, I am sorry. I do miss everyone and hope she gets better. I'll write soon; it's just hard."

"I know. I just wish…" He paused and shrugged. "Have you ever seen a man made of darkness?"

Her forehead creased. "What?"

"Like a living shadow with little star specks for eyes, you know, like—like the grimshades in those stories from when we were kids."

"Syago," she groaned.

He nodded. "Goodnight, Eliana. I hope he treats you better than he does everyone else." And then he was out of the manor. The shadowman haunted him no more that night, except in memory, as did Eliana and Elisabet.

CHAPTER TWELVE

A HORROR ON THE TRAIL

Based on *The Hunter's Parchments*, cc bastica 207;
The Nordvargor Testaments, cc bastica 824;

21st of Septimosk, 246

Fal'iek crouched down in the trampled forest brush of Thornwood and ran his hand through the dark-gray fur of a dead mabin'guarik. He marveled at the audacity of a gray color in a forest of greens and browns. The wet, soft fur could still be used, its glossy beauty stark against the snow. A magnificent beast that could move through the spiny woodland branches as though on wings. Preserved by the night's cold, it looked under a day old but still in good condition—despite the large, bloody gash in its side—a rare gift from the wild.

Fal'iek looked up at his companions. "Do what you can with it. But be quick, we need to keep on this trail."[52]

Guara'upik and Mour'ikik nodded and set to work on harvesting what they could of the dead animal. Fur, bones, teeth, but they had no means of carrying the meat. Kimoc wasted nothing of a kill, considering it sacred even if it wasn't their kill and not of the pure groups. Mabin'guarik ate only plants but were still aggressive and territorial; evidently, this one had opposed something beyond its ability. That something killed it, last night's snow hid it, and the Roah'riik discovered it. *But why wasn't it eaten or dismembered?*

Fal'iek and his men, all skilled warriors, hunters, and elite guardians of the Kimoc tribes, sought answers. The woodland's hellhunters and

---

helltamers; they were Roah'riik, the Brotherhood of the Bone. In searching for the stolen remains, a movement in the forest had drawn their attention. Herds of mewil'ishyuuks had fled, and trees wandered. Something big and unafraid had trampled through the thick, dark jungle of brambles of a youthful green with short, thick barbs. A light evening rain fell on the trail of mashed dirt and foliage before fading in the northwestern region of Mother Yoaom.

The seven Roah'riik bore similar characteristics of their tribe. They each had brown skin and long, dark hair in a range of shades along with beads, braids, and feathers that varied by family and position. Each bore various tattoos of familial design on face and arms. Furs and hide-armor vests laced with bone fragments concealed bone-crafted knives, small clubs, quivers of arrows, and climbing hooks. Only Lolish'ith had full wooden armor as well as parts of bone armor, but most relied on bone-riddled hides and shields. They crafted all tools out of bone and wood, sometimes using stone; all tools necessary for survival in the forest. A set of javelins lay in the snow beside the corpse.

But rank set Fal'iek apart from the others.[53] A thin scar on his face along with the earrings, warrior's beads, and leadership feathers distinguished his older days whence he'd fought all the powers of hell. He wore face paint markings, a dark band across his eyes, and others around the faded lines of his tattoos. Being the leader of the Quoak tribe—though not himself actually a Quoarn'riik—as well as the most celebrated warrior among them granted him their respect.

He surveyed the forest and the trail they'd followed. Three mewil'ishyuuks moved through the thicket several paces south of them. Their sleek green fur camouflaged them from predators and graceful movements prevented their twisting, jagged antlers from catching on the surrounding flora.

Tek'ouk, Lolish'ith, Ka'shuor'iik, and Yarok stood in a circle around the clearing, watching the boundaries for approaching threats while also considering the trail. Unusual in its width, the trail widened further in this

---

53 Kimoc rankings to this day are widely considered the most complex of any known society. Each status is a combination of multiple ranks. The various markings of beads, feathers, earrings, and tattoos makes it even harder to understand, and for this reason it has never been documented. They alone understand it, and it was one of the first proofs cited by Asturions a century ago that the Kimoc aren't savages in spite of not having a written language.

spot, marked by one large set of footprints and several smaller sets moving together. Lolish'ith, the tallest of the group, with a broad chest and serious eyes, turned to Fal'iek. "It's a herd. There's too much for anything else."

Yarok, the oldest and sharpest of the group, crouched down to peer closer, then shook his head. "Too controlled for a herd. A herd would've been all over the place. It has to be a hunting party, a group of Asturion soldiers and barbarian giant."

"But that makes no sense," Tek'ouk said. "We'd know if any barbarians were here, and even if they were, the two don't mix."

"Could've mixed in a spontaneous festival," Lolish'ith offered, and everyone laughed. "Castlemen always make messes when drinking, this is just the first time they left no refuse behind for us to clean up."

Fal'iek chuckled. The clearing was more like a crater of mud now. He knew of a giant that did mix with Asturions but strongly doubted that they'd been here doing this. Balgor was far more respectable. Fal'iek asked, "Ka'shuor'iik, what do you think?"

Ka'shuor'iik, the youngest and shortest, stammered a response. "I—I don't know. They both sound convincing. Do you think it could be a demon or the like?"

Fal'iek was already shaking his head. "The Razhod released a lot of devils into the world, and not all of them have been accounted for. But as we've not seen any since their defeat, we'd best not rely on those superstitions without better proof. Otherworlders get blamed for too much phenomena simply because we don't understand them."

The other Roah'riik looked at each other. He'd left much unsaid. Fal'iek would've been ostracized as a non-believer if not for his insurmountable reputation. Still, it was a source of friction between him and his people, so he patiently avoided the topic. He'd once believed, but a lifetime of traveling and fighting—fighting the Razhod in particular—had worn out his spiritual reserves. He'd tried to hold onto them like the memory of a deceased loved one, but he eventually gave up and accepted the doubts, one of many wounds. It struck the Roah'riik as strange, however, that his views hadn't disabled his spiritual capacity for hellhunting or helltaming. He still felt connected to the wild, even though he sometimes resented it for all it took from them.

He withdrew the bird skull that hung on his shoulder and hesitated. Spirit touching was never an easy or pleasant endeavor. Clutching the skull in both hands, he took a deep breath and gazed straight into it, connecting to the spirits of nearby gurows. He shuddered at joining the vile minds of the hungry carrion feeders. They remembered little of what had passed here and had fled when it approached. He grimaced, their violent hunger for corpses and bird sex, including with dead birds, made these connections difficult and often dangerous. He saw the world through their eyes and other senses in a bleary, raw mess of crude instincts. They in turn saw through him and affected him the way he did them. In their faded memories, a group of large dark things moved through the woods, trampling and destroying, accompanied by something so vile and frightening in the minds of the blackbirds that they'd blocked it out of memory after flying far, far away. He tried to make sense of their smell and hearing memories but could distinguish nothing more. It was beginning to affect him, making him hunger and harden. He pulled himself out with a gasp, heaving deep breaths and sweating. His hands had cracked the skull. *That's what you get for taking on so many at once.*

Yarok and Tek'ouk pulled out of theirs, the latter wiping away a bloody nose and the former hiding trembling hands. The rats and rabbits had given them the same result.

Fal'iek walked up to a brambletrunk of black wood and placed his hands on it. He got a general sense through the plant; its perception was only sentiments that were fainter—more vague and difficult to grasp than the animals'. But it was continuous, didn't run at the sight of danger, and had a much better memory. He could only get a frenzy of commotion, but at least here the connection wasn't so... violent. Plants were usually peaceful, if sometimes savagely hungry in a more subtle and patient way.

Fal'iek left it and pulled out his climbing hooks, made from the talons of a grim'iik bird. Jumping, he stuck the hooks into the thorntrunk, then placed his feet on two barbs before hoisting and re-hooking. He ascended quickly until he hung from a branch directly over the trail. From what he could see, it did look like a hunting party, but too big and disorganized for any hunting. *Maybe it was Balgor. I did see him enter Tolgrym. But why would he do this?*

Mour'ikik called out from behind the dead mabin'guarik. "We'll need one more hand to skin it."

Fal'iek climbed down and regarded Tek'ouk crouching down by the snow-specked mud and saw ripples in a puddle. Having the lightest skin of them with the most unique tattoos, Tek'ouk stood out, but it was Tek'ouk's hair, with its sides cut short and a braided tail drooping down, designating him as a dynast, that truly marked him.

"Tek—" Fal'iek began.

Tek'ouk held up his hand for silence and put his other hand on the mud. "Something's coming."

Fal'iek and Ka'shuor'iik put their hands on nearby thorntrunks. Fal'iek felt it this time, big and moving quick. He stepped away. Tek'ouk pointed west. "It's coming from that direction. And fast."

"I can hear it," Yarok said. They clutched weapons, ready and wary. The sounds of crashing branches and dull thuds resonated in the distance as some gurows flew overhead and the mewil'ishyuuks bounded through the thicket. The commotion grew like thunder.

Fal'iek shouted, "Climb!"

They jumped up the thorntrunks with their climbing hooks. Moving quickly, they reached the middle branches as a gigantic mass of pale flesh burst through the brush and rammed a stalk three had climbed. The blow shook them on their branches, but they hung on. Its throat shrieked an "Ao! Ao! Ao!" that hurt their ears. A wave of stench rolled over them like piles of rotting dead bodies.

Large, pink, tusked jaws clamped down on one of their branches and shook it furiously. The bough hit the tangle of interconnected branches and the forest trembled with fury, beating them against the wood they clung to. Fal'iek's body slammed into the branch, his armor softening the blow and thorn jabs. He twisted his hips to avoid a thorn near his abdomen but knew he couldn't keep this up, so he let the branch toss him away. Yarok followed from just below. They grappled another branch but failed to maintain the hold against the convulsions, dropped again, bounced off a lower branch painfully, and landed in the soft grass near a hole half-covered by a dead log. Fal'iek rolled in, Yarok dove in, both hoping it was unoccupied. The rest clung for their lives as the savage shaking continued. The thing belted its "Ao! Ao! Ao!" without ceasing.

Clutching their sides and covering their noses, they both grimaced at the thing's stench. Fal'iek now saw the monster in its entirety: A large flattened snout extended beyond long twisting tusks and black beady eyes. The stubby legs held up the bulk of what Fal'iek knew to be a muru'unkuy. It had thin, black fur over pink skin and cuts along its body from the thorns, where black blood seeped. It also sported a large gash on one leg.

It turned, moving fast for its size, and came to the ditch, its swiveling flat nostrils leading the way. Fal'iek and Yarok backed away and down into the ground, wishing the ditch were deeper. Their arrows and knives bounced off the grimy, thick skin. The snout filled the opening of the ditch and pressed against the log. It snorted, spraying them with snot. The hot odor made their heads swim. Large drops of blood fell on Yarok like black tar. The snout swept aside the log, opening up the entrance. Then the muru'unkuy shrieked and turned away.

Three other Roah'riik had dropped and grabbed the javelins off the ground. Standing together, they used the spearpoints to prod the beast while avoiding its attacks. The muru'unkuy spun, stomping the ground and kicking out. They backed into the brush, staying close to bramble trunks to avoid the rampage.

The last two Roah'riik dropped down but also had to back into the thicket, away from the tusks. As it spun, the muru'unkuy picked up the dead mabin'guarik in its mouth and threw it, narrowly missing the armed Roah'riik. They jabbed at its face; it kept turning and flinging mud, grass, snot, and blood. Fal'iek and Yarok used the distraction to climb out of the ditch.

Trumpeting a roar, the beast snapped its leg out and kicked Guara'upik away like a doll holding a twig. Fal'iek darted past the thing and grabbed Guara'upik's javelin as it whirled in the air. He turned to face the monster.

The muru'unkuy's giant head swung toward him, tusks leading the way. Fal'iek took a deep breath and leaped inside the open mouth, holding the javelin vertical. The muru'unkuy bit down, driving the point up into its skull and splintering the wood. Dark blood splattered. It let out a squeal of pain, and the gust of odious breath overcame Fal'iek. He nearly passed out in the mouth and stumbled on the tongue as the thing fell onto its side. Yarok jumped in and caught him before they hit the ground. When the head landed, Yarok quickly carried him out and into the brush, also nigh unconscious as the beast whimpered in pain. It worked its tongue and jaw, trying to get the javelin out; its mouth spewed a fountain of black blood. The stubby legs squirmed. Then twitched. Then still.

Fal'iek watched the thing's final agonized movements. He saw the pain of the creature and felt something. Tek'ouk and Mour'ikik helped him stand up, then Yarok. They covered their faces from the smell. Ka'shuor'iik retched.

Fal'iek looked at his men. "Resume watch points. Who's hurt?"

Everyone looked bruised and bloodied. Three held pressure on cuts from the thorns while they wrapped bandages over the gashes. Mour'ikik and Tek'ouk returned from the thicket with Guara'upik between them. Covered in blood and wincing, he couldn't stand on his own. Fal'iek went to him, pulling some bandages out of his supply pouch. They lay him down, raised the leather vest, and cleaned the wounds. Fal'iek tenderly wrapped them around his body and added a bandage. Guara'upik said nothing, holding back any sign of pain.

Lolish'ith looked at the dead beast. "What is it?"

"I think it's a muru'unkuy, or was." Fal'iek stood, studying it. "It's obviously too big to be native here."

"I've never seen one like this," Mour'ikik said. "Do you think it could be a furacán?"

All eyes turned to Tek'ouk, who shrugged. "I've seen no better candidate."

"What's-" Ka'shuor'iik began to ask, but Lol'ish'ith cut him off.

"They're creatures of the wild that Asturion dynasts bewitch into being more monstrous than usual to attack us. But none of that's ever been seen." Fal'iek disagreed with this but said nothing.

Mour'ikik agreed from his watch post. "I have seen them attacked by one before, so it wouldn't really make sense."

"And even then, they're rare. I've only seen a skeleton," Fal'iek said.

"That was the greatest move I've ever seen," Ka'shuor'iik said in young awe, looking at Fal'iek.

"A lucky maneuver," he replied. "And I couldn't have done it without my men."

Just then, two other Roah'riik scouts, Reed'luk and Kor'miir, emerged from the northern brush on the backs of mewil'ishyuuks. They lowered their javelins when they saw the men and dismounted. Kor'miir asked, "What happened? What is that?"

"A muru'unkuy. It charged us from the forward trail," Yarok said. "Gave us one of the closest fights of my life."

"So if this came from the east, and then returned to hunt us—" Mour'ikik began.

"The muru'unkuy didn't make this trail," Tek'ouk said from a branch above. "Look at the trail leading to this spot and then the one it left. They're completely different."

Fal'iek and three others joined him on the bough. The two sets of tracks contrasted sharply to the Roah'riiks' trained eyes. Even in the brush, the muru'unkuy had plowed through without thought, while the other group had moved in between everything, only occasionally cutting obstacles and leaving no blood.

They dropped back down. Ka'shuor'iik asked, "So whatever this was, it scared the muru'unkuy?"

"Scared or sent," Mour'ikik said. "If they're even related."

"Scared by their palemen smells," Lolish'ith quipped to some laughter.

"Thing didn't look scared to me," Yarok said, kicking it lightly. "Blasphemous wretch hungered for us. With a fury. We should refuse it the dignity of dismembered decomposition and burn it."

"It only did what it had to, Yarok. It didn't know," Fal'iek said.

"Are you sympathizing with this abomination? If furacán, it is not a natural of the wild, so what do we owe it?" Yarok asked.

"Not sympathy. Pity. It lived a tortured life. I pity it for being driven to this violence, no different than the mabin'guarik," Fal'iek said. "Either way, we need to know the connection between this and the trail."

Reed'luk said, "They probably are related, considering what we just learned."

Everyone's eyes locked on him. He continued, "Bokhor has experienced a blinding."

They gasped. Kor'miir explained, "Some kind of storm hit them with black clouds that hid even torchlight. They'd never seen it before and are calling it a True Night. And once it passed, the summoners couldn't see or talk to any spirits. Nobody's hurt and nothing else happened since, but apparently they're still spirit-blind."

Ka'shuor'iik looked at Fal'iek. "Do you think the Razhod have come back?"

"No." Fal'iek stared past them into awful memory. "We accounted for all the bodies. They're all long dead and their mementos destroyed. More likely that whatever the Razhod used is happening again, though I don't think they ever made a full True Night."

"You still think it's not a devil?" Tek'ouk asked, incredulous.

Fal'iek shook his head. "The Razhod were terrible and mysterious, but so is the wild and the weather. To jump to conclusions while excluding other, more likely possibilities is the abandonment of reason. Though this certainly sounds as dangerous as a fiend." Fal'iek thought of the direction of the forward trail. If it continued in that way, it wouldn't hit anything significant, just the marshes. But the mystery horde could veer off into Cantlgrym or into the Kourii marshes. But Fal'iek didn't like taking chances when lives were concerned.

Fal'iek turned to Kor'miir and Reed'luk. "We need to confront whatever led the trail before it's too late. And we need to send a set to Bokhor to learn more and inform them of our trouble here. They're likely connected, but we can't be certain yet."

"If possible, we should also send someone to the trail origin. There could be more information there," Yarok said.

Mour'ikik turned slightly from his watch position. "But those would each require a minimum of two of us. Better at three. And don't forget, we still need to take Guara'upik back to Quoak and send reinforcements west. That's at least three, better at five. And most of us are wounded."

"*Golk*," Fal'iek cursed and looked down the trail, then back at the others. "I'll have to hunt it alone. I'll take one of the mewil'ishyuuks. You four go with Guara'upik. And you three track the eastern trail."

"We can't let you hunt alone," Tek'ouk said. "Take one of us with you."

"I've hunted alone plenty, and I'll probably just stalk it until more arrive."

"Your wife asked me to not let you hunt alone anymore. I'm under oath, Fal," Tek'ouk said quietly. "And we don't really need to know the trail's origin right now. That information would come too late to be useful. Have me come with you. Yarok and Reed'luk will be fine without me."

Lil'iek. He fingered his feq'uok. The necklace had an infant's tooth from each of his three children and a lock of her hair, connecting him to them. He churned on the inside. It'd anger them that he stayed out in so dangerous a hunt, but any amount of family strife was worth protecting them. They were only safe if everyone was. "All right, fine. Let's go."

They broke into motion. Yarok and Reed'luk looked at the dead muru'unkuy before mounting. Tek'ouk and Fal'iek approached two of the tall mewil'ishyuuks and bowed in reverent salute. The mewil'ishyuuks touched their proffered hands, palms up, with its snout. Its four eyes gleamed. They then mounted it and sprinted off to the west, down the forward trail, leaving the dead muru'unkuy behind in putrid decay.

CHAPTER THIRTEEN

JESTER'S CARNIVAL

Writings of Qosku, cc bastica 42; *Leyta's Journals*, cc bastica 16;
Scars of the Martyrs, cc bastica 929;
The Nordvargor Testaments, cc bastica 655;

21st of Septimosk, 246

Qosku finished his goblet of cider, his favorite Asturion drink—but by no means as good as chicha—then stood from his place at the feast tables. He walked through the great hall and out into the bailey, all of it crowded with young people having fun together. He felt strangely disoriented, having just arrived back at the castle to find a carnival underway for some big festival involving fires and offerings to the Deova and the saints. Game stands lined the courtyard outside. He enjoyed some carameled fruits and tried to talk to some girls, but they avoided him. After the tourney in Mantlgrym, he was in no mood for the competitions underway in the courtyard. Nor did he understand the ahedreth board game or the newer games that used cards. His mood already low, nothing helped, save the food and a show of puppets that trounced around a miniature stage to the delight of the younger keepers who watched.[54] He won at a stone toss, leaving him as one of the few remaining in the hall while the others returned to the great hall for the performance.

He took the prize, a small clown doll, from the oafish crewman. Qosku couldn't remove his eyes from the few remaining yellow teeth of that witless grin, and he wondered why the entire troupe consisted of large, dim men and women—was the East all like that?

---

54 *See Reptilium Nimrød, 3*

He walked hastily back to the great hall, tying the doll to his rope belt, which looked absurd, but he didn't care. The dinner tables had been cleared and moved away to make room for an impressive if odd hexagonal stage. Fresh rushes lay strewn about the floor, most of them tied together to prevent drag. Rows of benches and chairs surrounded the decorated platform, with barrels of water sitting nearby, he guessed for either fire prevention or hydrotecnics. The platform itself was about five feet high and had royal checkered curtains draped over the sides to cover what hid beneath. Above and around the stage flew various banners of the nation as well as other nearby nations, such as the Unakan settlements in their totemic variations of a stone cross. Qosku realized the designs of the poles resembled scepters and the whole shape of the stage a crown. He also noticed the use of royal colors. Red, purple, white, and some gold or silver, traditionally signifying Asturion royal politics, or so he'd gathered. He'd taken an interest in the history in his quest for his parents. Looking at the decorations, he wondered if this was to be a political performance. But the dull shading of all the colors indicated a tragedy. The occasion, a celebration, didn't seem fitting for either. Only a large violet box sat in the middle of the otherwise empty platform. But he still knew little more of Asturion history—or theatrical mummery, for that matter—beyond children's puppet shows. He briefly wondered if acting in differing costumes would be a way for him to dress as a girl, but he quickly dismissed the absurd thought. On the walls behind the platform still hung the old tapestries of Otrantor and Pelagiod.[55]

The room brimmed with loud conversation, and he looked for a good place to sit. He saw none with whom he felt like sitting—until his eyes fell on Leyta. She was talking to two other women when he approached, so he waited for her to finish. She saw him and cut off, "Qosku, you must meet Katti and Mariacarmina. They were just ordained into the ministria last month."

Both were about Leyta's age and wore plain green-and-gold gowns with dark hair woven into a thick braid topped by a veil that fell back. Both Katti and Mariacarmina had mastozan dark skin. Both smiled warmly at him, and Katti said, "Oh, I'm so glad you're here. It's good for you to be away from the pagan rites of the Unaka and instead witness the light and truth that we have."

55 See *La Epica Eluveitia de Sepultura*, 13

"Oh Katti, don't be so forward!" Mariacarmina chided, and, judging by Leyta's look of annoyance, she agreed. "You'll scare him away."

"What? It's true, isn't it?" Katti looked at each of them. "I do hope he enjoys his stay here. If nothing else, it's better than being where they sacrifice to their demon idols and are on a path to another hell. We do a disservice if we hide a truth that he needs."

"But a bitter truth served first is spat out at once!" Mariacarmina said.

"And in any case," Leyta added, "I'd think the Holy Deova cares more about our kindness and understanding toward each other. For its own sake as well as to improve the good message. But now if you'll excuse me, I must begin the performance."

Mariacarmina said something Qosku didn't understand, then Leyta laughed and walked up to the stage. Mariacarmina reached out and took Qosku's hand. "But don't you feel unwanted with us. You're always welcome in our pews. Here! Come sit with us now." She pulled him to sit beside her and he couldn't help feel pleased to be suddenly a focus of interest, even if it was tinged by what his slavemasters had told him. Actually, he didn't care much for the religious jab, as he'd had his own doubts about his people's practices himself, if they even were still his people. He'd worried about losing the eternals' favor due to his lack of prayer or rites outside of the Apugakas and sincerely hoped he wasn't incurring their wrath. But he wasn't sure how to go on giving obeisance when he'd always been led by a priest. Even so, it hadn't helped when he did participate in the rites or pay tribute. Neither the eternals above, nor the apus, nor the forests and waters below, nor even the sun had answered his pleas for help. Otherwise he wouldn't be here in Cantlgrym.

At least the two priestesses were friendly. They chatted amiably a moment longer until the show began.

Leyta looked around at all the people in attendance, anxiety racking her. She worried about going ahead with the carnival while the phantom remained at large, and the white creature too, but she'd become convinced the latter was merely a brief occurrence, a creature that had slipped into the catacombs. Both warranted care during a public event, but the masters insisted since they felt the matter resolved and the priestesses had blessed the hidden room, then given thanks on Somhoin. They'd said that it would take everyone's mind off of what had happened. *But if the danger remains, why take our minds off of it?* They still didn't know the identity of the dead man whose body had been laid in some ritual formation. All of Cantlgrym were accounted for, so it wasn't one of them. The carnival denied missing anyone. It was possible that it had brought this man in from somewhere else, but how it could get even someone in there without anyone noticing was beyond her. Yet it had gotten Navidsom out of a locked room, so maybe this was no different. Unable to stay calm or coherent, Navidsom was locked in another room now. The poor lad had been driven mad by that shadow creature and showed no signs of returning. He would be sent to Foucal Abbey Asylum. It saddened her greatly.

She moved up to the stage and looked to one of the crewmen, who smiled and nodded that they were ready. She rang a bell and the talking died down. "Welcome to Jester's Carnival, our guests and entertainers for the evening. They've worked hard to bring us this show, so we ask that you remain respectful to allow everyone to enjoy the performance. Thank you, and enjoy Jester's Carnival."

The lights dimmed as she stepped aside and sat down.

The stage burst into life, emitting colored smoke and fire lights; dancers leaped up, seemingly from nowhere, and music spun into play. The six dancers wore tight clothing with frills, the same gloomy royal colors, and such an abundance of makeup to render any discernment of identity impossible. The chorus rang out beautiful tones in deep and high notes of indiscernible lyrics. Somewhere, the sound of drums, flutes, strings, tambourines, pipes, and maracas moved in tune to the vocals and dancers. The dancers flowed smoothly, professionally, but she noticed a missed movement here, a costume slip there. It only endeared, giving a beautiful harmony to chaos. It started slow, almost mournful, and then shifted into an energetic flurry.

The song ended abruptly. The dancers froze in place. The torches went out. Clapping and cheering followed, then faded as the torches flickered back on, revealing a boy sitting on a wooden crate. The "boy" whittled at a stick with a small knife, humming to himself. A gang of robbers interrupted his song, beating him, even burning him with fire amid their taunts and his screams. Finally, they let up. As the boy lay near death, the leader took the boy's sack and they ran off, leaving him blind and horribly scarred. He wandered through stormy streets alone, for want of food. After days of healing in a sympathizer's home, they kicked him out when they decided he'd healed enough. In getting no sleep or scraps to eat, he attempted to steal food and got caught.

The stage shifted again to a king's court.[56] New performers, in regal clothing similar to the dancers, moved about, discussing their frivolous lives of luxury and marvelous military achievements. The imperious king and queen then took position on their thrones, and the flamboyantly dressed attendants and guards surrounded them. Leyta reminisced on the obvious political point they were making here. Speaking to the people against the nobility—odd, given that most in the audience were of noble birth or wealthy means, herself included. She only smiled and enjoyed the performance.

A gallantly attired man walked up to stand before them and spoke in a loud, dramatized voice. "Oh, your Highnesses! We have brought another criminal to be tried before you as it may please your judgments."

"Bring the criminal forth, Neverthal!" The queen spoke in a deep, almost operatic voice.

Two men dragged him onto the stage in front of the king and queen, then one walked off. The king gave a harrumph, and the other seemed to remember he too was supposed to walk off and he hurried away, eliciting laughter from the audience. The boy thief in rags looked up at the rulers. Neverthal said, "This boy has been caught practicing witchcrafts and thievery."

"Very well, what is your defense, child? Why did you commit these atrocities in my perfect kingdom?"

"I—I was fr-framed, your Highness! I didn't do it. I swears!" His voice wavered in singspeak, a pitiful sound that floated across the audience.

The court attendant stepped forward. "You were caught red-handed, unawares. How do you explain that? And the witchcraft tools in your possession!"

"Please, your Highness, I'm just an orphan trying to make a living as an archemist, and I was only made to look like I'm stealing—"

---

56 Though I'm only summarizing, the entire play made several literary allusions. Most notably the courtroom scene, which draws on *Kameloch Within Temptation*, *Xandria Mansona*, and the birthday massacre scene of *Sirenia de Lacuna Coil*.

"As if the evidence wasn't enough, your Majesty, look at his face!" Neverthal pulled the hood off of the boy, revealing the mask of a horribly disfigured face. "That is sure proof of demonics!"

"Please, it's not my fault!"

"Enough! I have heard enough lies and heretical denials from the boy. He is clearly an enemy of the Royal State. Have him executed promptly." The queen rose and left, and Leyta joined the rest of the audience in shouting boos. The stage darkened around the boy as he sat in chains. The boy looked up, and in the most woeful tones any of the audience had ever heard, he sang:

O pretty world
You looked so clean and good for me
I adored and bathed in your glory
Until, from my mind
I found you differently
Underneath, unkind
I peel back this covering
This world picture distorts
An ugly form, discovering
My joy it contorts
And wraps around me
Bending, twisting
Winding, binding
Sooty world bent on breaking me
All truth and beauty smothered in time
Moving over me, it slays me
Enveloped in the grease, grime, and slime
Left behind
And I suffocate
I look around and see all the dirt
I decay in this filth
And all the hurt
Nothing spared, nobody clean
No sense, no innocence
All hidden beneath a shiny sheen
Until the foulness rubs off on us

The Song of Sorrow lulled the audience into a mournful state, mentally and even physically, for a minstrel's songs pervade the being when sung with dyne, and this bard was powerful. Leyta felt a weary sadness settle deep into her, as if the music numbed her muscles with despair.

The morning of his impending execution, the boy slipped through his manacles and then through the bars of his prison, having been starved so much. Thus,

---

57 A group of keepers must've scribed the poems as they were sung. Some, including the final song, probably were not recorded in full.

he escaped. Everyone in town opposed the destitute boy; the world became his obstacle. Within his hiding place of a pile of the town's waste, he lamented:

No stranger to pain
I wander in search of refuge
Heavy are my burdens
And endless are my sorrows
What I seek
I ne'er find
What I have
They take away
I am robbed of all
They have robbed us all
But die I do not
I fight and thrive
I assert my life

The guards spotted him, so he ran and jumped onto a wagon just as it closed up and exited the gates, all of it made of sticks, which fell apart as the stage hands moved them about on the stage. The caravan, and the boy, headed east. But Leyta noticed the stage clumsiness less and less due to the overwhelming power of the music.

This unseen master bard's voice penetrated Leyta's heart and mind with the experiences of the young hero. The emotional tale enthralled her so much that she forgot completely about her earlier troubles. She wondered at that one singer, immensely impressed and hoping that the minstrel would show himself soon.

As if on cue, fireworks illuminated the center of the stage, and there appeared the silhouette of a single dancing figure, the now-adult hero returned in triumph, to sing and dance for his once-forsaken home in personal conquest.

Dominion, I am dominion
Now you're to be my minion
I will have you for my ownself
No, not anymore for your self
Yourself, Nevermore

My own, my whore
Nothing more
Now lie and sleep in your body
Lie and wait, till you all rotty
Rest and wait
and wait
and waaaaiiii.

Creepy and haunting, the bizarre song crescendoed in elated chanting of the last phrase, growing louder and deeper with the glow of the firelights spinning around the dancer. Leyta lost all self-awareness in that hypnotic dance, completely entranced by the dazzling display.

The firelights ceased spiraling and lined up around him as the climax of the song built up and the dyne of the singer fed sentiments into them with hypnotic force. The dancer stopped and raised his arms. His voice boomed out across the entire audience with such power that Leyta felt a great chill sweep through her body and the audience gasped collectively. And then the song ended with an echo fading out through the hall. All music stopped, and he kept his arms up and out. The lights dimmed out into a faintly visible darkness.

Immediately, Leyta knew something was wrong, but it took a second more to realize exactly what: She couldn't move. Her body, out of her control, as if she were only a passenger, as if in slow motion, slumped down, then fell off the bench. Her head hit the floor painfully. Qosku landed next to her, Katti and Mariacarmina on the other side of him. Her senses still functioned; she could see the cracks and feel the cold of the stone floor beneath the bristly floor rushes—their fresh smell. She heard others of the audience also falling down in the quiet avalanche of people. Human bodies pounded softly against the terrifying silence. Leyta fought the paralysis with every part of her being, but nothing happened. She screamed mentally at her body to obey her, demanding it do something, anything.

Nothing!

Inside her motionless body, her mind raced through thoughts of why she couldn't move. She realized she knew next to nothing of dynal songs or hypnotism. The stillness lasted for what felt like hours before she heard footsteps nearby. Someone walked down the rows in front of where they lay. She heard shuffling as somebody neared, rearranging the hypnotized. Footsteps approached. Large, strong hands gripped her by the shoulders and lifted her up. The face of one of the stagehands considered her indifferently, then gently sat her down while leaning her against the back of a chair, propped against Qosku so that their heads held each other up, looking forward. She saw that they had a bunch of wood poles where they were tying the hands and feet of several motionless keepers. *Kidnapping? Slavery?* Leyta's fear materialized in the clammy sweat that drenched her body.

Now, she saw only the stage where the final dancer, a jester, stood in shadow. His costume consisted of a checkered patchwork of the tragedy and royal colors: dark reds, blues, purples, silver and gold. He calmly descended the small steps to the floor and walked over to where the Castellan and masters slouched against their benches. The clown suit covered his whole lanky form; not an inch of skin was exposed. The mask, a drawn jester's hood with bell-tails, clearly visible now in the dim light, obscured the face beneath. It bore a frown instead of a smile, with eye holes and mouth restitched to droop downwards. Dark, empty, and with little bells hanging off the extension tips of the hooded covering, he was a depressing sight in a terrifying moment. Looking at him made Leyta's limp head nauseous.

"Mm, I've waited a long time for this moment," he said, almost too quiet. That sorrowful face looked down at Alkant. He reached out and grabbed Alkant's face around the mouth.

"Cute. You almost escaped my song of sorrowful disablement. But alas, not even you were strong enough." He turned to Davagis. "You as well. Iron-willed leader? Not quite."

Then Jester came to Leyta. Fear tightened in her, fear of not knowing what he would do and being powerless to stop any of it. "And you! You're a pretty little thing."

She felt his wiry hands slide under her arms. He lifted her up and shook so that her head rolled to the side and her face could see the mask. Behind the mask was only black obscurity. She heard the ragged breathing and felt it through the stitched frown, hot and rancid, on her face. "You asked to meet me so many times. Well, here I am!"

He laughed, but it sounded closer to sobbing than laughter. Her mind scrambled to understand what he wanted. *What will he do with me? All of my practice with dyne, everything I knew about it, is doing nothing for me now.* She would've been trembling and crying uncontrollably had her body been capable of movement. Instead, tears poured down her clammy face and her mind focused on nothing except her one desire: to be as far away from him as possible.

"Have you ever just lost your mind? Hahuhuh. No, you've never known sorrow like I have, but you will. And you will learn and grow as I did. We'll have plenty more sad times playing together." He turned to a nearby crewmember and said, "Bring her too."

The crewmember took her over his shoulder, then tied her to a pole and fixed her gaze at the stage. Her abject terror shifted to a queasy fear and gratitude to be out of his hands, if only for a moment. From the corner of her eye, she saw Jester nimbly jump back onto the stage and sweep his arms around theatrically. His voice boomed out with an echo that sounded bigger than a single man. "I do enjoy such an attentive audience. You thought this play was a tragedy? A tale without a hero's victory? No, this is the victory, and we are the heroes. You and me. The only difference is that this isn't like all those lies your parents told you at night. Stories to keep you comfy and obedient. This is real. And it will both liberate and avenge."

His voice expanded even more. "Now ladies and gentlemen, boys and girls. You've seen our carnival, a mere dalliance compared to what comes next. Let me introduce the gang; my cohorts and your conquerors. First, you have me. Jester, the Mourning Jester! The Bard of Sorrow. The Minstrel of Misery." He took a bow to no applause.

"Second, we have Knave, our Nether Knave, the Demon of Undamnation." The white creature flew overhead, circling high on white-feathered wings, the very same she'd encountered in the catacombs. It swooped down, then perched lightly on the top point of the stage canopy. An underworlder of the Abyss, either an agony or a despair. It was small, almost her size, though its wingspan was enormous. But still, a real demon—the first one Leyta had ever seen. Its pale body was akin to the hunting cats that prowled the snow-capped Barbathors but completely hairless: white-tight over its skeleton. The bony tail, whiplike with a sickle-bladed end, snapped at the air above. But worst of all was the head—that of a young human girl with bright-blue eyes, fangs, and silvery-blonde locks of hair, which explained the child Leyta had heard. Seeing it fully now was far more awful than hidden in shadow. It snickered at the rows of people, licking its lips. A little girl's voice came out: "Tasty dolls."

Jester continued. "Third, we have Knight, the Thunder Knight of Might." Metallic thuds sounded from the entry hall as if wargongs approached. A full suit of plated armor ten feet tall emerged out of the dark corridor. The giant of a man, probably a Fomorion, stomped slowly and deliberately up to the stage. He stepped onto the stage, which groaned but held the weight. Through the opening of his helmet, Leyta saw an emaciated face of hollowed eyes. *Is that a lifeless inside?! But how?* The steel plates were complete and tight on him, with fluted rivets and sharp ridges. A massive cleaver blade hung on his back. He said nothing, standing statue-still.

"Fourth, I introduce Our Lady of Truth. Queen, the Fire Queen." A small section of the stage exploded in fire and smoke that faded to reveal the elegant figure of the queen who'd acted in the play. Her frilly, puffy red dress whirled in a regal curtsy at all directions. Her painted mask bore no expression beneath the crown she wore and revealed nothing of the wearer inside.

Queen stood with formal composure and said in a hollow but high-pitched voice, "Hurry up, Jester. We haven't all night for your theatrics."

"And the last but not the least of us," Jester continued, "Our Lord of Liberty. King, the Ice King." Another section of the stage exploded. King appeared, wearing thick royal robes and an ornate crown similar to the queen. His mask displayed a carved beard beneath a dignified expression. He stood with the others of the group, imperious and victorious. Jester said, "Conjointly, we bring something bigger and better than anything you've ever known. A grand revolution. Announcing the rise of a new order. The Order of Disorder, briefly holding court at Cantlgrym. Meet the Royal Chaos!"

The carnival workers clapped, a small noise in the quiet of the great hall.

"Good evening, my beloved people," said King. Like Queen, his tone was hollow but also old and deep. "I appreciate such willing acceptance of our non-reign. Tonight you have lost, but henceforth you shall win. We are the new supreme force of this world. I can assure you, we come not as authority but as anti-authority. Rule of any kind is immoral. We're here to abolish power. The only exception being the powers we retain for that purpose. We are your liberators from the captivity you have been blinded to.

"Your leaders and priests. Your teachers and rulers. They all lied to you.

They have used you and abused you, and you knew it not. They have kid-napped some of your young and staged it as the work of a ghost."

What is he talking about? Leyta wondered. *Is he referring to Navidsom? That wasn't us!*

King opened his arms in an all-inclusive gesture. "We come to expose them and open up the real world you live in. We will destroy those tyrants and any that stand in our way. For the first part of our plan, we are taking some of you with us for a more proper education, to learn these truths firsthand. We are the Royal Chaos."

"This revolution is yours," said Queen. "An end to the lies. No more leaders. No more rulers. No more rules. All of those traps will burn in the flames of liberty." She clapped her gloved hands together and opened them to reveal a small flame between her palms, whence the symbols were etched into the fabric, her dynal foci. By a trick of kindling, the flame grew and divided into several more flames that shot out at the flags hanging above, burning them. Smoldering embers ate up these sacred emblems, the symbols of their homes and peoples. A terrible rage swelled up inside Leyta. Unable to do anything about it, she felt as though her wrath might consume her body as the fires ate her flag.

From the instant the paralysis began, Qosku had noticed and fought it. He'd struggled mentally with his body until he realized the problem dif-fered from what he'd thought. Either his body had been put to sleep or it was simply detached from his mind. He stopped fighting his body and switched to searching for the disconnect.

Then, something beside him started to glow. It was Mariacarmina. The light came from her, engulfing her, and she moved, rising to her feet. Her bold voice echoed slightly throughout the great hall. "In the name of Deova Bondua, Holy One of Carracosa, I defy you. With light, I command you to leave this place."

"You command us?" asked King.

Mariacarmina rose into the air slowly, her gown ruffling in the holy light that enclosed her. Qosku watched in amazement; he'd never seen such power before, and it wholly distracted him from freeing himself. Her otherworldly radiance and voice filled the hall. "We do not want you here. Nor does the Holy One. This place has been sanctified by—"

Her call was cut off by the demon, who dove at her, unperturbed by the bubble of light. They crashed into one of the barrels, which collapsed in a gush of water that turned red and soaked Qosku as Knave tore into her, pulling out intestines and discarding a severed arm. Qosku felt the warm release of his urine against the gory wetness.

"It's best you don't mention your religions in Knave's presence," said King. "It upsets him."

Qosku stared in disbelief and horror, then returned to himself and pushed sentiments outward. At the moment, he felt mostly fear, usually the most useless sentiment, but in this case, it could help. Grateful that the meditation he'd done earlier had prepared him for this, he spread the fear, a raw desire to flee, throughout his body. His mind wandered through dark corridors of subconsciousness and began pushing out that strange presence of the sentiments pushed into him by the songs. His body twitched and trembled. Ignoring the cold, bloody water that seeped over to him, he continued using the energy to locate and push out the alien sentiments that repressed it. Finally, his mind connected to it and woke it up. After several more vibrations, he had his body completely restored to natural control.

As the demon fed and the banners burned, Qosku stood up.

"Stop!" he shouted, punching his gauntlets together. The sound echoed throughout the hall, and the enemies turned to regard him. He worked his mind, focusing on protective anger to build it up in place of his fear, memories of standing up to his abusers giving him power. "I am Qosku," he said. "And I do not let you hurt my friends."

"Impressive," said King. "If you think you can take us, come and do so."

Dashing between the rows of benches and people, Qosku gathered all the anger and courage he could, building into a quickened jump. Just as he left the ground, King clapped his hands, and a small burst of darkfire hit Qosku's wet clothes. Qosku landed on the stage and fumbled toward King as the freezing clothes impeded his movement. Knight raised a large armored hand and effortlessly swatted him away with a dull thud.

Qosku crashed through the benches, hitting people as well, before rolling to a stop awkwardly on top of someone, with splintered wood jabbing him in the side. He briefly struggled to maintain consciousness but returned in full to Knave's laughter: a high, girlish cackle. He turned, trying to get up but found his arms would barely work. He refused to give up.

"A valiant effort," said Queen. "But pathetic in the end. Your heart's in it, but you're too weak to stand up to us. Grow up first, then you can dream of such power. Jester, is everything ready?"

"'Tis, your Highness," replied Jester with a slight bow.

"Then let us part from this place. It bores me," said Queen, turning to King. Qosku managed to sit up but knew that the bleeding meant he wouldn't be fighting now, not well enough to accomplish anything. He needed to use the energy to heal, but that would take too long; they had to be stopped.

King faced the crowd again with a final address: "Your ancestors have wronged us in the past, and you now pay the price. But this isn't about us or them anymore. It is now about you. We bring a world of no oppressive rulers, no greedy lords, and no structured society to take away your freedom. War with us if you wish. You will not succeed and will incur severe consequences of death and dismemberment. We have nothing more to lose, as you have already taken it. So now it is your turn to lose something and experience a little of the sorrow that you have caused the downtrodden of society to push you into the better way, until you join. Since this castle has failed to educate appropriately, we're removing a select group of its keepers to our own new university. We leave you with a task to be done ere we return.

"Consider that your leaders, all of them, are not who you think they are. They have lied to you. Failed you. And they will continue to do so as long as you give them that power. Your assignment from us is to get rid of them and be free. Otherwise, we'll have to slaughter them ourselves and perhaps a few of you as well in a lesson on our imminent return. We bring freedom, which is a hard lesson to learn. So be free and enjoy the joy of chaos that belongs to you. We have set the board. The pieces are ready and the cards shuffled. The next move is yours."

King and Queen glided down the stage steps. Knight and Knave led the way, followed by Jester, down the entry hall in imitation of a royal procession. Then King and Queen exited with crew members and prisoners trailing behind, leaving the room abominably still and quiet. *My move,* Qosku thought. *My chance to really prove to everyone my value.* He tried to follow, but on standing, the world spun and then faded as he collapsed.

CHAPTER FOURTEEN

Hunt of the Night

Based on *The Hunter's Parchments*, cc bastica 208;
The Nordvargor Testaments, cc bastica 840;
Scars of the Martyrs, cc bastica 936;

21st of Septimosk, 246

Darkness descended quickly on the two Roah'riik in the cold forest of brambles. The mewil'ishyuuks carried Fal'iek and Tek'ouk along the tracks, a harmony of the wild made possible by the hellhunter's skull spirit-bonding. After the sun departed the sky, the only illumination came from the moon between clouds and soft fireflies. However, the moonlight was almost a curse in the forest, for it gave the illusion of sight while creating more shadowy pockets. Like black claws reaching out of the darkness, the brambles hid what might be stalking them through this older part of the forest, where the stalks were darker with longer thorns. Chirping bugs and the soft crunching of their footfalls hid what else might lurk with them in the dark. The Quoarn'riik had said the season of bone would be strong this year.

Night fell, and the lifeless began to stir.

They guided their mewil'ishyuuks under a rock overhang just big enough to permit the antlers without scraping. Fal'iek and Tek'ouk quickly dismounted and hid behind the mewil'ishyuuks to allow them rest and wait out the rising of the lifeless, half-eaten, decayed, and in search for something to break or tear. Most of the lifeless were animal. Corpses of mabin'guarik and mewil'ishyuuks roamed, searching mindlessly for any semblance of life to destroy. Occasionally, a bird, a malwolf, a serpent, or even a human would appear. The warding bones covering the two Roah'riik gave some protection, but only if they kept a quiet distance would they avoid the mass pursuit their appearance would draw. Tek'ouk whispered prayers over his bone coverings, and Fal'iek ran his hands over his. The protection was minimal, just enough to allow them to keep moving.[58] Their mewil'ishyuuks mounts, of course, wore their own protection. If they remained sufficiently still, they were all but invisible to the lifeless, one reason the Kimoc revered them.

This all happened naturally during every season of bone. The old Kimoc legends said that they were souls left over from the battles of the eternals, and the Deovan dogma that the dead rose as a punishment until the purging of hask'iiq.[59] He didn't know what did animate them, he just felt certain it wasn't any of that.

As sounds of branches and stones crackling reached their ears and the smell of old rot invaded their noses, they waited, barely daring to breathe. A pit formed in Fal'iek's stomach; despite seeing this his entire life, it still unsettled him.

Fal'iek and Tek'ouk sat wordlessly, waiting with the patience of veteran hellhunters. Peering from behind their mewil'ishyuuks, they saw that the lifeless were out and walking, but quite clearly moving in a single direction. The abnormal, unified movement chilled Fal'iek. *Is something drawing them?* Their direction appeared the same as the trail, and he hoped it would not be connected but knew better. He whispered, "Do you hear that?"

Tek'ouk nodded as he watched the flow of lifeless in astonishment. "Music, like a wailing."

"But so faint and without direction, it almost doesn't exist," Fal'iek said.[60]

Tek'ouk watched the forest as Fal'iek readied their blanket saddles. None of the lifeless even looked at them.

Fal'iek grabbed a rat skull and found the souls of woodland vermin in hiding. They hid as all did life at this time during the rising, but he'd hoped for more insight on the music. He got nothing except that they hated the song, feared it, even. It put an awful feeling in Fal'iek, and he withdrew shortly.

"We should just camp here," Tek'ouk said. "We don't know where this trail will lead or for how long. Movement in this weather is dangerous.[61] If we manage to get any attention, it's two against twenty."

---

58 See *Gybiaaw Blackbraid: Mutilated Tyrant*, 11

59 The Kimoc word for *gierra*. Unmentioned here is the Unakan and Amoyaran beliefs that mirror the Kimoc eternals, or Great Ones—that lifeless are part of their cosmic balance.

60 See *Luskmord: Atriom Carcerio*, 24

61 The rising and moving of bodies, or clouds of poison or acid, was often referred to as the weather.

"No. We need to figure out what's happening as soon as possible. It's the beginning of the season, so they're calm and weak tonight, and we're near Cantlgrym. We can veer off and stay there if we need to. They'll grant us shelter."

"Will th—" Tek'ouk cut off.

"What?" Fal'iek looked in the same direction, but only momentarily. "What did you see?"

Tek'ouk stared into the forest. "Nothing." He turned and climbed onto his mewil'ishyuuks; Fal'iek followed on his. "It'll be hard to follow the trail in this—"

Without turning, Fal'iek kept his voice low. "What is it?"

Silence.

"Something's watching us, other than the lifeless. It's moving… and hiding. Hold on." The dynast Roah'riik pulled a small tinderbox out of the saddle pack. A flame popped from his bone scepter as he commanded it to light the box, then he threw it. The burning tinderbox burst open against a bramble trunk, and shadows fled as the area lit up briefly. Fal'iek glimpsed something black dart away from the light and into shadow. Lithe and silent, as if the thing itself were a shadow. Fal'iek had to reassure himself it was not a trick of the mind but knew not what else it might be. The lifeless collectively stopped and stared at the flames, then resumed their mindless walk.

"Maybe not. I didn't see anything," Tek'ouk said.

"I did. Something fled. At the burst. Something dark and… humanoid."

"You think one of the other tribes is spying on us?" Tek'ouk asked.

"No, this was human in shape only. It's too stealthy and quick, even for Thornwood. In fact, I'm not sure it's part of the wild." He shifted in the saddle, wondering if they should burn again. He didn't like the thought of being followed by something unseen. Darkness was haunting them. "Let's go."

With the moonlight allowing the two Kimoc only a vague picture of shadows, they had to rely more on sound and the mewil'ishyuuks' night-sight. The mewil'ishyuuks sped out of the overhang, brush crunching under its hooves. With the agile navigation of the mewil'ishyuuks and cloaking of all four, the lifeless posed no immediate threat but always a potential one. Something drew their attention and in effect allowed the hunt to continue at full speed. Fal'iek felt it certainly would've gone bad had they not been so prepared. A few lifeless did take notice of them but weren't quick enough to begin chase until they'd long passed. Still, they kept weapons ready. The forest is keener than its rulers. More dangerous than its hunters. Even darker than its secrets.

Eventually, the trail led them out of the spiny forest, away from the flow of lifeless, and to the shoreline of Lake Laomain. The outline of Castle Cantlgrym stood faint in the broken moonlight. "No guards on the walls," Fal'iek said quietly. "And the lifeless are going the other way."

It appeared that whatever their hunt was, it had sought Cantlgrym, but this didn't explain the path of the lifeless or their shade stalkers. They followed the trail along the shoreline and stopped outside the docking fort, where they dismounted. At past midnight, no lights could be seen inside the fort or the castle. It looked like an empty shell in the moonlight. The faded trail went to the door and became muddled but did not appear to reverse direction, its disappearance at the docking fort indicating that its maker either remained there or had already left by a different route. The door to the docking fort was black and silent.

"Fal," Tek'ouk said, "whatever we find in there could be nothing, a mistake. Or if not, it is far beyond us. We…"

Fal'iek followed his gaze back toward the forest. Nothing moved, but a human figure stood out, blacker than a bottomless pit, with eyes like small stars gleaming in its head. The tall and slender shadow, incomprehensible to the unnerved hellhunters, stood perfectly still, watching. Only noticeable because of the moonlight faintly outlining it, it vanished after no more than five seconds. Again, Fal'iek almost doubted he'd seen it, actually hoping he hadn't, but Tek'ouk's eyes told him he'd seen it too. He breathed a prayer onto his necklace while Fal'iek felt his heart pick up speed at the return of the old feeling of being hunted by something he couldn't fight.

Fal'iek whispered, breathless, "Any more objections? Either all this is connected, or if not, we can't let it distract us."

"Are you sure it's connected to us? Or that the Quoarn'riik won't care about you going out of your way and risking our lives for the Asturions again?"

"I'm not sure of anything right now, but we can't stay here, the Quoarn'riik can be persuaded, and some of our kal'muq reside inside.[62] Let's keep moving." He knocked on the door. The ensuing silence was as out of place as

---

62 Kal'muq is a Kimoc term signifying the lending of a child to another people for that child to learn from them and build bridges between the two. Yet it speaks to the controversy that Fal'iek wouldn't abandon them here.

the missing wall guards. Fal'iek drew his hunting knives and pushed on the door, gently at first, then harder. The door slid open, roughly. Tek'ouk lit a small torch with dyne, and they entered. Moving quickly through the small empty rooms, they found the crew in the sleeping quarters.

The three watchmen lay in the same bed, underneath layers of blankets, while the other beds were empty. Confused, Fal'iek froze at the door. Slowly, he walked to the bed with Tek'ouk behind. As he felt a pulse at their necks, he sighed in relief. He noted that putting them together under all of those blankets kept them warm enough, though their arrangement seemed very tidy. It struck Fal'iek as not just comfortable but affectionate. A joke?

He shook them, but they remained asleep. Then he noticed that one had a swollen face, faintly visible in the torchlight. He imagined someone sticking him with a dart upon opening the greeting slot at the front door. He said softly, "Kliik poison knocked them out no more than five hours ago."

"We ought to move on, then," Tek'ouk said. "They'll wake on their own."

Tek'ouk tied up the mewil'ishyuuks in the stable and they went out onto the docks, stopping at the sight of the boats floating in the lake, let loose to prevent crossing from either side. "Can you move a boat to us?" Fal'iek asked.

"It's generally unwise to disturb the water with only two of us, but we'll have to do it somehow anyway. Freezing is best." He raised his scepter, the bone rod ended with a stone painted to resemble a human skull; feathers and hair stuck out the back. He thrust it forward at the water, and darkfire caught on the lake surface.

Within seconds, a path was frozen to the boat, not wide but strong enough to walk on if they moved quickly.

They stepped lightly into the small boat from the ice bridge and paddled gently, quietly, to the wall's gatehouse, where they ported and approached the door. Fal'iek pushed on it while Tek'ouk watched the walltops. The door resisted, shut tight. Neither said anything, but both pondered the best action.

The night was quiet, but the course of events bore strong likelihood that danger waited on the other side, rooting out the customary option of knocking. Fal'iek reviewed the wall, pulled out a quim vine from the pack, and removed his gloves. His hands felt the cold grains of the strong, thin ivy. He bonded to it, putting his mind in the still-living vine, and moved it up the wall. The vine moved like a serpent, sliding up the stone bricks until it reached the top and laced itself around a small nook on the edge of the battlements. Fal'iek had the vine tie itself into a knot, then pulled hard on it. It held, so he braced his legs on the wall and ascended. Tek'ouk followed close behind.

Fal'iek reached the top and, with one hand, drew his knife, grabbed the edge, and pulled up. After seeing the walk was clear, he hoisted himself over and onto the walkway in a crouch.

Tek'ouk slid down behind him and recoiled the vine as Fal'iek moved to the other side of the wall and surveyed the dark courtyard.

Empty.

Except for some broken carnival stands. He searched for tracks. The entire courtyard had seen heavy and confused traffic. He eliminated the possibility of a battle for the lack of blood; the tracks could be just from the training rounds earlier in the day.

All windows on the broad front were lightless. Fal'iek and Tek'ouk crept toward the wall stairs and descended, surveying the area. The large doors never looked so forbidding. Fal'iek pulled down the lever and pushed it open; Tek'ouk had his scepter ready. Fal'iek notched an arrow on his bow, which bore two bone spikes on each arm for melee confrontation.

The front entryway included adjoining stairs spiraling up into uninviting darkness. They passed into the great hall and gasped: Rows of corpses were strewn before them, in the middle of which sat an odd platform.

Examining the carnage, Fal'iek saw first a small Unakan boy lying sprawled on top of a broken chair as well as a little girl, her eyes wide but motionless. He knelt down to inspect the body and realized that the Unakan was not dead but merely unconscious. And also wet—water and blood soaked the floor. *Was there another Unakan uprising? No, they'd not leave it like this.* He shook the boy.

The boy groaned and put his gauntleted hand to a cut on his head. Fal'iek began shaking the girl he'd been on top of, but the girl did not wake. He found a pulse—she lived.

Paralyzed.

Everyone in the hall were paralyzed, not dead. Relief swept over Fal'iek as he asked the boy what had happened.

The boy muttered something in Unakan. Fal'iek noted the battle-ready cassock. A dynfist friar. Fal'iek pulled out some cloth and herbal medicine in a small flask and handed it to him. "Do you speak Asturion?"

The boy took the items and said, "Some. Who are you? Where are they?"

"I'm Fal'iek of Quoak. What happened?"

"We watched the carni—carni—"

"Carnival," Tek'ouk suggested, kneeling down beside them.

"Yes." The boy smelled the medicine, poured it on the rag, and applied it to his cut. "And he sang at us. And we all stopped. We no could move. But I meditated before so I broke out of the bind. And I fight them and they beat me."

"Who is 'them'?"

"Royal Chaos. They came with carnivals and sang and preached to us. Then they hit me and took some people. Nobody could stop it. But I try."

"I'm sure you did well," Tek'ouk said. "What's your name?"

"I am Qosku."

"Can you describe them?" Fal'iek asked.

"They appeared like..." He thought for a moment. "I don't know."

"Royalty," a voice rasped by the stage, where Alkant pulled himself to his feet.

Fal'iek rushed to him. "Alkant, are you hurt? Tell me everything." Alkant was of the few palemen Fal'iek respected, although still with wariness.

"I would like to see to the children's well-being first, then we can talk." He rose, brushed himself off, and surveyed those around him. "We already lost one." He indicated the scattered carnage lacing a pile of broken wood.

"A good priority, Castellan. But we're losing time in going after them..."

Alkant considered it while bending over Davagis. "I would call them destroyers, but they described themselves as freedom fighters. They wore the royalty costumes from their play, except for one giant in a suit of armor, big even for a Fomorion. They lulled us into paralysis by disguising the song in the play with our minds open and attentive. They gave a speech before leaving. They've kidnapped a number of our youth and, I suspect, stole some valuables as well."

Davagis awoke after some prodding. He put his hand to his head and sat up. Alkant then went over to Balgor, Roza, and Anaruth; they'd already begun to stir. Fal'iek asked, "Do you know if they took any of ours? Any Kimoc?"

Alkant spoke as he moved to check on others. "I didn't get a good look at everyone they had. I was paralyzed. It will take some time to account for everyone here. But they left out that way." He nodded toward the main hall entrance. "Hurry, for all our sakes. Your assistance is appreciated."

Fal'iek turned to leave but slowed when he found Tek'ouk facing him with folded arms. Fal'iek walked past. "I'm not debating this with you, Tek. They might have some of our kal'muq, and we don't have time."

Tek'ouk followed behind. "Might? Do you think the Quoarn'riik will accept that answer? Or Lil'iek? Is that even your real reason?"

Fal'iek paused, looking at Tek'ouk with a faint smile. "No. But it's the one you're getting."

"Even if I agreed with your goal of a new alliance or treaty, this is not the way to go about it. The Quoarn'riik would sooner strip you of your station than concede your point for more involvement. Can't we at least scan the area for the kal'muq here first?" Tek'ouk fingered his feq'uok, probably ruminating on his own family. Fal'iek did too, the necklace warm in his fingers. Could he justify this to them?

"I don't like or trust them either, but they need to understand the rules of the wild apply to the Asturions too. Give and take, Tek. We aid them now, they'll aid us in the future."

"You don't know that. They've never kept a promise before or even a good-will gesture. We don't want another Mo'jibwak Massacre, or even another Tolgrym."[63]

"We've barely given them a chance, not recently. Look, what happens if this continues, and they fail to stop it? Then we not only lose trading partners but also allies against barbarian raiders. Or comes after us. This 'my people first' approach only works if we didn't actually need each other. I'll just have to persuade them by doing it; I think they can humor me while I try. Somebody has to start."

They went to Qosku, who knelt in fervent attempts to revive his neighbors. Fal'iek assured him, "They'll wake in time, unharmed. We're going to hunt the enemy. Would you like to come with us, Qosku?"

"He'll slow us down!" Tek'ouk snapped. "And we have no authority. Honestly, Fal, this is too far."

Fal'iek looked him in the eye. "Are those really *your* reasons? Isn't this already bad?" He looked at the Unakan. "What do you say, Qosku?"

---

63 The Tolgrym settlement was seen as a blessing by some but the betrayal of Mo'jibwak by Voium in the year 112 was a major tragedy by any measure.

Qosku looked between them. "I—yes, if it is not bad."

Fal'iek shook his head. "You broke out of that paralysis on your own. And you know more about them than we do. We could use your help."

"He can't come, Fal," Tek'ouk protested uselessly, knowing Fal'iek's overpowering resolve.

"He is coming, Tek. He's competent, and we need this." Fal'iek looked back at Qosku. "We're leaving now. We'll be moving fast and at long hours if you are able and willing. And if Alkant permits it."

Fal'iek looked over at the Castellan not far away, who simply nodded without taking his eyes off of a youth. Qosku stood. "Yes, I come now."

Without another word, the trio left the hall and entered the cold.

They rode the mewil'ishyuuks along the edge of the lake in search of a set of tracks where the enemy crew had landed. It didn't take long for them to find a trail farther up from the docking fort; instead of a line from people walking or a wagon, it was messy and washed. The Roah'riik deduced that they'd used a sled. It led northeast across the grass and toward the mountains, a dangerous area to journey during the rising.

The mewil'ishyuuks that carried all three increased its speed to a gallop, hunting into the icy night.

CHAPTER FIFTEEN

THE RESCUER

Based on *Annals of Syago*, cc bastica 10;
The Nordvargor Testaments, cc bastica 840;
Scars of the Martyrs, cc bastica 936;

21st of Septimosk, 246

Hours after they took the medicine, Syago and Tomas got to the stables early to get a wagon for Tolgrym but found that none were available. All the wagoneers were at the Court of Ashor, angry about another letter, this one attacking the church leadership. The drivers they talked to wouldn't take them except for a ridiculous price. Panic welled in Syago again; the entire trip had been a pattern of defeat after defeat, risking more lives. It wore him out, and he hadn't the patience for it. He would've gotten into a fist fight if not for his exhaustion and expanding hopelessness.

It was nearly noon in the square. If they hurried, they could manage stealing a wagon, but the trick would be leaving the city. Their plan was interrupted when Syago heard his name. Turning, he saw Henric waving at him over the crowd of people. Pushing toward him through the crowds, ever mindful of his expensive pouch and that guards might be looking for him, he reached Henric and hugged him. "Never have I been so glad to see you!"

"Likewise, my young changeling," Henric laughed. "You can't be Syago, or how else did you become such a mess here?" Bathing had completely slipped Syago's mind during their efforts there. Henric embraced Tomas while Syago was jostled by the yelling crowd. The people got angrier every day, and so did he, already out of his mind with frustration.

Syago yelled, "How are they? Tell me they're fine and you've got a wagon ready to leave now."

"Elisabet was doing a little better when I left, but some have died. After receiving your letter, we left before dawn, so eager were we. Come, let's—oof—escape this madness."

Arriving at the understables with Lügos and his and Henric's sons, Syago was surprised to also see Milemeron, the count's second son. Henric began yelling at the stable boys because the wagon wasn't ready, like he'd asked. They said they didn't have enough hands; everyone else was above for the corruption ordeal. So they hurried to prepare it themselves, ignoring the stable hands' protests that it was too late to leave. They didn't speak of it, but all understood that by the time it would be ready, even a hurried pace would have them outside in Thornwood after dark. But such was their need to return that the risk wasn't even debated.

On the road by early afternoon, Lügos drove while Henric filled Syago in on the passings. Isabela, Casilda, and Sofiana had passed, three older women who'd already been in poor health. That gave Syago hope. Elisabet was young and healthy. Still, Casilda had been Lügos's wife, and here he was driving their wagon. "It's the reason he's here," Henric explained, "to be alone with his thoughts, though he won't say it."

"She was good to him," Syago said.

The quick pace of the wagon jostled and rattled worse than usual, so further conversation and sleep eluded them. The other three present, Matias, Milemeron, and Gabriol, were all a couple years younger than Syago and Tomas but not inexperienced. They were notably more nervous, however.

They perked to even greater awareness when darkness settled in. It being darkemorg, their path would be brutal but not insurmountable, Syago hoped. Most lifeless would be small and easy enough to push aside. Still, Tomas and Syago prepped the younger boys with spears and archemical flasks, and listened well while Henric sat in front with Lügos.

After some hours, Syago wondered why he hadn't seen any lifeless through the plank cracks, but it was dark. He settled his spear down and went to open the latched door, peering out beside Henric and Lügos.

"I don't understand," Syago said. "Where are the bodies?" An eerie emptiness filled the woodland around them, illuminated by their lantern.

"I don't know," Henric muttered, "but I'm not like to question our good fortune."

"Not in the outside," Lügos growled. "Out here in hell, a blessing is never good fortune but a warning sign that nature is heeding and we are not."

Suddenly, something appeared in their path—a man, a clown or jester. He just stood there in his costume, unmoving. A pit of fear welled in Syago's stomach at seeing something so out of place.

The wagon rolled to a stop. The bomogs huffed in place. All three men were too shocked to say anything at first.

The jester broke the silence. "You know what I like about Thornwood?"

Henric began, "What the hell—"

"During the day it kills you with passion beyond bounds," the sad-masked clown said. "But during the night, it has nothing but apathetic coldness and still kills you all the same. Wouldn't you say that's fair and just?"

"Who are you?" Syago called out, a crack in his voice betraying his fear.

"Your liberator." Jester whipped his arm up and something flew at them just as Lügos snapped the reigns with a *yah*—but it was too late. The flask hit their lantern, and it exploded in a burst of fire. Syago fell back into the wagon box and the front door slammed shut. He got up and peeked through a crack: Jester had gone, if he'd ever been there in the first place.

But the wagon, rolling forward and gaining speed, was on fire. The flames had caught under the goop of the flask and spread up the box. Everyone began waving blankets at it while others watched the sides with spears. The lacquered wood held in the cold of night. Though smoke filled the cabin, they got the fire under control, but the wagon's frantic jostling worsened.

Syago opened the front latch. Lügos and Henric sat calmly on their benches, and yet the bomogs ran without direction or light.

"Oy, I think we're heading for that thornstalk." Syago nudged Lügos. The man leaned over against him, and his head fell off. Splattering blood, it rolled into the wagon box. Syago banged his head on the door jam. Someone screamed and Syago grabbed at Henric, who slumped forward but whose head stayed connected by a thread of flesh, not completely severed. Syago swallowed the bile that rose in his mouth as he fell backward.

Gabriol was still screaming and Matias looked dumbstruck, his spear hanging loose. Only Milemeron and Tomas maintained clear heads, trying to get the younger two back on duty. A guttural growl came from the bomogs in front, followed by a sickening crunch—and the wagon jerked to a halt, throwing them all to the floor. *Holy Mother in Heaven, please no!* A loud bang, followed by deep crunching alerted them to the breaking of the smoldering wood above. And it continued to break—something big was crushing the wagon box. Their light gone, Tomas opened the back gate while Milemeron and Syago gathered up weapons and the two useless youths.

They blindly pushed their way out of the wagon, nearly stumbling on trembling limbs. A collapsing wagon would offer them no more protection than the open forest at midnight. Bumping into each other aimlessly in the pitch blackness, they were out. They clamped shut the mouths of the younger ones and push them forward. The moon and stars weren't out, so the sky was only a slight shade brighter than the utter void of the forest itself. The loud crunching of the wagon continued under the violent weight of this unseen monster. Syago pushed them away from it, in the direction he believed to be south. They still had hours to go before they reached Tolgrym and probably zero chance of arriving, but he had to try. He had the jars that Elisabet needed, and with his axe in the other hand, he would die bringing it closer to her, if that's what it would be. The consequences at stake instilled fear in him as never before.

They heard a sickening snap, then a great pounding of the ground followed them—a pursuit. The two kids struggled, panicking, but Syago quickened his pace, his own heart hammering. He debated leaving them; if he ran full, he might make the village with the medicine. But no, he wouldn't leave them and didn't want to be alone either. Still, the deep, dull thuds of the dirt drew nearer, chasing them and catching up. The boys screamed.

He changed course, moving in the direction he believed to be the forest itself. Whatever followed them was gigantic and would have a hard time getting at them in the thick brambles. Advancing into the brush with the thing nearly on them, he saw a light ahead. He didn't understand what the light could be, but it was his only possible salvation. Pulling the others toward it into the woods and away from the path, he hesitated, considering how the light did look like a torch.

Pushing through the brush, he prayed with the greatest fervency he'd ever known that he not step on some trap or deadly plant. The thuds grew louder and a loud crash sounded close behind them, leaves and twigs cascaded onto them. Even Syago yelped this time but they pressed ahead toward the lighted area, leaving the thumping and thrashing behind. The torch revealed the clown, Jester. He sat on a rock in front of a stone pile that held many torches, as if warming himself by them.

"Bad evening," he greeted pleasantly. "Would you—"

"I'll kill you," Syago growled, brandishing his axe.

"And forfeit your chance at safety for the night?" Jester picked up the torches and began to juggle them. "No, I don't think you will. I think you want my protection more."

"It's your fault we're out here in the first place," Tomas snarled.

"Blame games are fun, but they won't save you when all is said and done." He continued to juggle, circling the rock pile.

Syago turned to the group to gain their agreement for what he knew to be inevitable. But Matias was not there. "Where's Matias?" He remembered Matias climbing out of the wagon with them, even whimpering, but then nothing.

"It would appear," Jester said, "that the forest has chosen our friend Matias. So let's all wave goodbye to the chosen one. Bye-bye, Matias!"

"Shut your mouth!" Syago shouted louder than he'd intended while Tomas advanced on him, but Jester handed him a torch.

"Follow me, please," Jester said and promptly turned to lead a march deeper into Thornwood. "Unless you want more unpleasant company. It's already on its way."

And they could hear it. Brush crackled as something big pushed through not far away. So follow they did deep into the the woodland of every child's nightmares, to an old crumbling castle where a corpse in a suit of armor stood guard and a white demon prowled.

CHAPTER SIXTEEN

PRISONS OF PEOPLES

Based on *Leyta's Journals*, cc bastica 50;
The Nordvargor Testaments, cc bastica 799;

unknown day of Septimosk, 246

Leyta found herself in a vast dark room of violet curtains that stretched high beyond sight. She pushed through them in search of a way out. She didn't like it here. The curtains obscured much until she pushed them aside. Some of them moved, came toward her, then parted, revealing a tapestry of Jester's mask blocking the only exit.

She cried out.

The mask sobbed once, and the frown deepened, then opened. She tried to run, but it was too late. As the mouth began to suck her in, she grabbed a curtain and held on. She pulled herself to another curtain. Several thin tongues shot out of the mouth and grabbed her arms, dragging her across the floor. She wanted to use dyne but lacked her staff.

The mask called for her, saying her name over and over. She screamed for help and fought with everything she had, but it only held tighter and faster. Inside the mouth, a white creature ate her friend Mariacarmina and a criminal burned.

Something stung her face, and she snapped awake in a small stone room. Robertobrus knelt in front of her, with two others on either side. She stopped fighting, and they released her arms and legs. Robertobrus asked, "Are you all right? You woke everyone else."

Their prison cell had one barred window in the corner, with a hide covering to keep out the cold and a cast-iron door on the opposite wall with a small barred opening at the top. The floor of the room was full of blankets around the youths taken captive. None appeared injured; instead, they stretched and looked around, faces scrunched up in fear.

Leyta sat up. The room brimmed with kids waking, but Robertobrus was the only one still looking at her, one of her oldest and best students. She wished he would look away. Her mess of hair hung over the sides of her face but exposed the flush she felt in her cheeks. "Uh, I'm fine. Where are we?"

"It looks like an old castle dungeon. But I'm not sure where..." He looked at the small window, the only source of light pushing in from behind the small blanket. He then stood up and tiptoed past some kids on the floor toward it. Brushing some snow off the ledge, he peeked out the side of the blanket. "Oy, we're in Thornwood. I wonder where, though? We can't've been here much more than a day."[64]

She pushed the blanket off her lap to go peer out the tiny window: a dark stone corridor, entirely vacant. Their situation struck her then. Kidnapped by a gang of strange performer rebels who dressed up in flamboyant clothing but had power beyond anything she'd ever seen before. And that clown, that mask. She felt a shiver as she remembered him breathing on her while holding her in his hands, the parent of the nightmare she'd just had. And a sharp twinge of sadness for Mariacarmina. The sight and sound of her death remained, burned in her mind. Her hand trembled slightly on the black iron door as she tried to look through the small slot.

She heard some of the kids behind her crying and recalled her responsibility to them as a leader. She turned around as Robertobrus said to the younger ones, "Listen, I know this looks bad, but we can do this! We aren't going to let them dominate us, will we? We'll break free and show them they can't take us like that—strong forth!"

But a motivational speech didn't suit the moment. It didn't take them out of the crowded cell or reverse how badly they'd been overpowered that night.

She stepped forward. "Is anyone hurt?"

Nobody answered.

"Good, let's get our bearings, then," she said. "I don't know some of you, so why don't we say our names? I'm Leyta of Voium, Archkeeper of Cantlgrym."

The rest of them slowly rose off the floor and formed a haphazardly tight circle. She noticed one did not join them, a young mastozon man

---

64 The accounts seem to uncertainly suggest this all happened in one night, yet the logistics involved call that into question.

with messy hair and hazel eyes. The others started pressuring him to join, but Leyta noticed the dried tears that streaked his face and told them it was fine. But he wiped his face and rose to his feet. "I'm Syago de Odiru of Tolgrym. I and some others were attacked on our way back from Mantlgrym and were brought here to Castle Covadongar."

There was a stunned silence, muted at the name of their location and their present reality. All had heard of Syago de Odiru, but more so Leyta, who'd been promised to him in their infancy but which promise no longer held. Still, she felt a moment of surprise and wondered if he too knew and remembered it. Her thought was interrupted by Tomas, who went next, stating he too was part of that caravan, and so they went around the room, each stating their name and home. Of the sixteen people in the room, she was among the oldest, the youngest being ten. All except those of the caravan had been tied to the poles in Cantlgrym, put to sleep, and, it appears, carried to some place in the East of Thornwood. All were Asturion, except a young Kimoc girl named Kel'feq, whose brown, tear-streaked face looked very frightened. Leyta wanted to embrace the girl.

"I don't suppose anyone has a dynal foci?" Leyta asked. Everyone shook their heads. "All right, what do we have that we can use?"

No one answered. Some ruffled through the bedding on the floor and found not even an overlooked hairpin.

"What about that window?" Robertobrus asked. He pointed at the covered opening.

"S'got bars built into it behind the cover," Syago said. He stared at the floor, then looked up. "I've heard of people escaping from places like this. They dug their way out. So let's pry at the stones to loosen one. And maybe someone can try and pick the lock."

"Wait," Leyta said. "Maybe escaping the cell isn't the best idea. I mean, what would we do if we got out? If we don't get eaten, they'll just catch and punish us. We should learn their plans and make preparations of our own. Maybe send smoke signals out the window."

Robertobrus shifted in discomfort. "Well, if I don't get out of here soon, I'll douse my trousers. I need relief."

"We can't just sit here," said Fernandeon, agitated. Elegant dark hair always obscured half the boy's face. "I'm not waiting for *them* to make their move."

"I agree," Syago said, but then, with a look at Leyta, added, "But maybe we should think about it first. Why did they take us? What are they planning?"

"We're hostages for their rebellion, right?" Gabriol, a younger boy, said. "So they'll probably just keep us here until they find a use for us."

"In the castle," Katti interceded, "they said we were to be a part of their new school. Holiness above, they won't be converting me into anything."

"Don't be ridiculous," said Fernandeon. "They'd be half-mad before being serious about that."

"Are we sure they aren't?" Leyta said. "They seemed quite mad to me." Everyone laughed, though she was actually serious. Stories of elementists, lost to the power, floated through her mind.

Syago inserted, "Well, whatever their reasoning, I don't doubt we could become hostages should they feel the need."

"That sounds right," Leyta said. "So maybe if we begin an escape plan, we can activate it later when the opportunity comes."

"What would you know?" said Fernandeon. "Why are we letting her take charge?"

"Why shouldn't she?" Syago asked.

Tomas was perturbed as well. "Yeah, why shouldn't she? She knows most everyone. And she's doing better than you would."

Fernandeon scoffed.

Syago continued. "I think we should start with the loose stones and the door lock. At least it'll give us something to do and will make the beginnings of a good plan."

"Can we offer a prayer first, before we start?" Katti asked.

Surprise and agreement greeted her request, except for another dissenting comment from Fernandeon. They ignored him and the young Kimoc girl Kel'feq who stood aside nervously. Katti offered the prayer then made the sign.

Everyone picked up tasks on their own. Relieved that she didn't have to be the authoritarian figure they probably saw her as, Leyta joined them on the brickworks, pushing and prying. Fernandeon and another boy tried to pick the door's lock. After some effort, everyone went from working to standing and talking about options. From talking about options to sitting on the floor in hopes of a guard to bring food or a chance to use the privy. From waiting to complaining. From complaining to yelling out into the hall and banging on the door at around midday, hours after Robertobrus and Syago had used a chamber pot in the corner.

Fernandeon hit the door repeatedly and yelled into the hallway a mix of threats, shouts, and blasphemous curses.

Syago said, "Calm down, Fernandeon. We'll be fine."

"What's there to calm down about? We're rotting in a cell in the middle of the damn forest, and you treat it like a game. And that stupid clown's probably down there laughing at us right now. I hate that clown." He grabbed the door's window bars and yanked, growling. To everyone's surprise, the door moved.

They all stared blankly at the rusty door now cracked open—hardly able to believe that in the entire miserable time they'd been there, it was merely unlocked.

"What happened? Did you break the lock?" Syago asked.

"No," said Fernandeon, eyes wide. "The rust held it tight when I tugged it earlier, but it wasn't even locked to begin with. I can't believe we could've broken out at any time."

"How could they forget to lock the door?" Robertobrus asked.

"They didn't forget," Syago said, shaking his head. "Something else is going on."

"But why leave it unlocked?" Leyta said. "They left the door closed, it looked locked. But we figured it out fairly easily. Do they even want us to stay in here?"

Everyone stared at the door for a few seconds.

"Well, I'm going. Trap or not," Syago said, and he walked out.

A mutter of consent flitted around the room as everyone crowded behind him. Leyta felt less sure but followed anyway.

The stone hallway extended both ways around a corner and into darkness. A tallow candle hung next to their cell, nearly burnt out. Leyta pulled it off the wall and looked at Syago. He shrugged and started down the short, dank hall. She moved to catch up so the light would lead the way. He put his hand up and motioned for her to stay back so he could look around the corner without the faint light giving them away. Katti whispered a prayer, and Leyta motioned for someone to silence her. Robertobrus put his hand on Katti's shoulder. She jumped and quieted at a look from him.

They turned two corners then crossed a bridge that spanned an open chasm. A weathered staircase descended down into its cavernous darkness, and Leyta could see other stairs and bridges, or at least broken halves of them, crossing that abyss over pointed arches to other unseen areas. The sound of a small waterfall reminded her of the catacombs, and her stomach twisted.

The bridge brought them to a thick door at the end of the hall with another candle, which they took. Leyta pressed her ear against the door, listening. Then she pushed it open. Light spilled into the hall, revealing a vacant kitchen. They entered, drawn by the relief of a clean room and sweet smells.

Knives and pans hung from kitchen walls over stone counters. A fire burned in the center of the tight room beneath boiling pots and a chimney. Remnants of chopped vegetables sat on the tables in the center of the room. Bottles of herbs and spices cloistered around goblets and trenchers.

They took parcels of bread and vegetables. Leyta hardly believed their fortune—or how hungry she was. Syago put his hands up and whispered, "Don't touch anything. We don't know what's in any of this, and we have to get out of here before they notice us."

Just then, the door at the other end of the kitchen flew open, and a large burly chef walked in. Everyone froze. The man walked toward Syago with a stack of trays in his arms. Syago backed away, searching for a knife. The man put the trays on the counter, then began stewing some soup. The name Mungo was stitched into the back of his tunic. The group stared at the chef, then looked at each other. To Leyta, it was now obvious that they were not intended as prisoners here. So she asked, "Why are we here?"

"I don'd know. Don'd dalk du me," the man mumbled in a deep voice.

"Where are the leaders? Where's King?" she asked.

He pointed at the door he'd come through.

"Why would we go to King?" Gabriol asked, confused.

"Because he has some answering to do." Leyta and Syago led the way to the door as the others followed. A smaller but chubbier woman came in, also ignoring them; the name Crestina was stitched onto the back of her garment. As Leyta walked past the chef, he grabbed her torch.

"No figers allowed in dat hall," he said.

She looked him, confused. He eyed the candle, so she left it on the counter.

They passed through the door to find a room with more connecting hallways and a twisting stairwell that led up. Leyta ascended the stairs; everyone followed. The stairs opened up into a tiny enclave walled off by a thick red curtain. Pulling back the curtain revealed candelabras illuminating the lavishly decorated hall, which extended past several more thick curtains and around a corner. Like the royal halls depicted in paintings of old, a crimson rug ran across the newly painted black-and-white checkered floor. Small tables and suits of armor lined the purple walls whence works of art hung. But Leyta, who grew up with nice things, recognized these as mostly imitations, they had no weapons to steal.

She moved forward. The decorations of various mismatched sculptures, all old and chipped in places, unsettled her. More red curtains obscured doorways. Political tapestries lined the walls depicting the fall of an oppressive king, and one of the garden of paradise with Deovan symbols sloppily stitched over.[65]

Leyta moved on to the end of the hall, where a thick red curtain hung. She parted it to glimpse a dining hall: fancy, but not quite as big as the great hall she was accustomed to seeing. The room was empty, but she noticed a table set for tea and cakes and wondered if she should ask the others to wait. She understood enough about diplomacy to know that bringing a group of frightened children to a dinner meeting would be disastrous, but she knew they'd not wait for her. She went in, hoping that they would follow carefully.

Food glistened before them on old plates of brass and silver, surpassing anything she'd seen at Cantlgrym. It was mostly frosted white cakes, with a roast rabbit in the middle that smelled sweeter than it had a right to. Loaves of bread and candied wafers also tantalized them. Pots steamed with tea water, and a couple of wine bottles sparkled as well. Her stomach growled, but she fought the urge to partake. She had no idea how long it'd been since the feast the night before, but her body felt drained. She needed something.

"Do you think it's poisoned?" Gabriol asked behind her.

Syago shook his head. "They wouldn't let us come this far just to kill us. But they might've drugged it."

---

65 *See La Epica Eluveitia de Sepultura, 65*

"In any case," Leyta said, "we shouldn't eat because that shows weakness to our captors."

As she said it, Fernandeon pointedly took a piece of fruit and bit into it. He looked at Leyta with the faintest smile. "It's delicious." Then he turned to the kids. "Come on, I'm not afraid of anything. Why should you be? Eat up."

"That is right. Don't be afraid. This is all for your benefit." Queen's voice rang out from the far end of the hall. She emerged from behind a curtain with King in tow.

"Thank you for waiting," said King as he and Queen took the lead seats at the far end. "You may now be seated and help yourselves."

"We came to resolve this," Syago said.

"Of course," Queen said. "We'll commence with a tea party-feast."

"We came to take back what you stole," Leyta said. "We were free and fine until you arrived with your foolish games."

"What did we steal?" asked King. He brought a cup of tea up to his cracked mask, but it only dripped through the fissures. "Everything here, everything you've lost, was already yours and lost to begin with. We're simply giving it back to you. Now sit. We can converse more as we eat and drink."

Leyta took a seat next to Queen, who daintily picked at her cake with a fork and an austere composure. Syago sat beside Leyta, and Robertobrus sat next to him. Leyta remembered the firepower Queen had brought to bear in the great hall, burning the banners. She faced them and said, "Tell me where we are."

"Oh," said Queen after taking fake bites of her cake, which was smeared over the mask and dropping to the ground. "I dare not tell you what you can learn on your own. Self-determination is the first step."

"How can we do that when you have us trapped in a dungeon?"

"Trapped? No, dearie. You are able to go anywhere you like. You could leave and never come back if you wanted. But you won't. You're not yet ready. So enjoy the tea-party feast while you can."

"That's ridiculous," Leyta snapped. "It can't be both a feast and tea party, they're opposites."

Queen dumped an absurd amount of sugar in her tea while saying, "We have many new opposites meeting here, all my favorite paradoxes with more to come, so it only means this is the first of its kind!"

"Enters the clown!" Jester's voice echoed through the room as he joined the table. "Spots a tea-feast, sits right down. Chews into cooked beast and..." He looked at Syago. "Can I borrow a noun?"

Leyta shivered when the masked head turned in her direction, even after she looked away. She felt as though that same mask that haunted her nightmare would never leave her. She couldn't hear the ragged, putrid breathing, but she knew it was there.

In choppy movements, Jester picked up a spoon, buried it in a pile of crumpets, then rammed them into the mouth of the mask, splattering them all over.

Syago turned to King. "Why did you kidnap us only to... well, let us go?"

"You mean, only to set you free," corrected King, patting his mask's mouth with a napkin, insufficiently clearing some of his smeared cake. "That's what you were about to say. And it's certainly what we did. You merely have to accept it."

"Tolgrym needs me!" Syago growled. "I was trying to save my cousin, to save everyone from this poison, and now that I'm finally able, *you* had to come and ruin it. Why?!"

"It's for your own good," insisted King. Queen nodded.

"YOU'RE KILLING MY COUSIN BY KEEPING ME HERE!" Syago roared. "You already killed three of my friends and—" He cut off in a growl of frustration and ran his hands through his dark hair. Leyta felt a wave of sympathy for him.

"You can't expect to persuade us to join you," Tomas said. "Especially with a move like that."

King turned to Queen. "Isn't it interesting that people seek cages. Perhaps it's the sense of security they're after." Queen nodded tritely. Jester sat limp in his chair, as if dead. Cake and tea covered his mask.

"All right," Leyta spoke up, trying not to look at Jester. "If freedom is your mission, why did you paralyze everyone and kidnap us? You don't help people by hurting them. That's not freeing people."

"We never, never hurt anyone who did not attack us first," said Queen. "If they had not taken the offensive, none would've been harmed. And sometimes in order to free slaves, you must bind the slavers. But no, we are not violent."

"Although," added King slowly, "sometimes Jester does play too rough."

"Highness, don't embarrass him!" said Queen. But Jester gave no sign of even hearing it, sprawled out in his seat.

Leyta retorted, "Then why didn't you *free* everyone? And why didn't you start in Mantlgrym at the Court of Counts instead of the university?"

King put down his fork and stood up. He raised a glass and rang his spoon on it. "Attention, please. First, I would like to welcome you to the Halls of Rebellion, where we're holding court. And we induct you now as the first of our new university. Here you are always welcome as long as you abide by the rules. The rules are, first and foremost, the rule of no rulers. That is, no forms of power, except individual power, are allowed. And second, the rule of no other rules. The third not-rule you must obey is to always respect us, your not-rulers."

Leyta began, "But that—"

"Any questions? Good. You are, of course, welcome to anything we have to offer, or abstain as you wish. Stay as long as you want; more refugees like you are on the way. We will only intervene when we observe your freedom being taken away by something other than yourself. Here, you won't have to do as you're ordered or believe what you're told. You are your own authority now. No more lies and no more hypocrisy. So we hope you will take advantage of the opportunity to grow and enjoy your freedom. In time, you will discover how you've been wronged by those you have respected. When you find the skeletons in their chambers, the bodies under the beds, you will understand and even thank us. With our help, you can become strong enough to overthrow them and live as you ought. But we won't make you. The Court of Ashor will meet us soon, but we won't overthrow them for you. It is you, the people, who must do that. You must free yourselves just as you did from that cell moments ago. You have only to realize the door is not locked."

"You won't make us do anything," Syago broke in. "But you'll take us from our homes."

Queen muttered something about being rude, and King answered, "To taste freedom, young mastozon. Something you've not truly known as a descendant of slaves. That you swear loyalty and pay gratitude to your conquerors, thanking them for erasing your heritage even as they keep you down, demonstrates this need. You've even adopted their creeds and shunned your ancestors."

"But I like them and the Church has blessed me-" Syago was cut off as a couple of well-dressed servants came in and switched out empty plates.

One had a large overbite and foolish grin, with Arrochor embroidered on his tunic. The other had a shriveled arm, with Chester on his.

"Ah, yes," King said. "You may have noticed our stage hands, cooks, servants, and so forth are all simple. Idiots, I believe they are called. Such terms are not welcome here, though we won't stop you. They are people like you. These are they who your rulers both in Heaven and on gierra forgot. Born infirm, physically and mentally, neglected by their parents, abused by their masters, mocked by their peers, they would be dead or in chains had we not taken them in. They are one of us as all are accepted into the loving care of the Royal Chaos.

"We've excused Knave from dining with us. He has a nasty habit of eating our guests. And Knight is at his guard post, ever vigilant in our protection from outside oppressors. Now take—eat as much as you can. Anything uneaten will be consumed elsewhere. Anything unlearned will be used against you. Anything gained, well, for the first time in your life, that's up to you. So a toast, to liberty!"

King, Queen, and Jester raised their cups and drank, most of the liquid spilling onto their chests. The group only watched. The servants smiled, and it surprised Leyta that she struggled for a sufficient response. Jester's splashing of his drink repulsed her especially. She eyed him and muttered, "A fool's toast if I ever saw one."

"Now in the future, I expect better table manners," said Queen. "We are a forgiving royalty, but if you cross us and the freedoms we lay before you, we will give you over to the clown, a playmate even less enjoyable than the demon." This time, Jester's limp head swung to face them, and the frown mask looked as though it almost smiled.

CHAPTER SEVENTEEN

REALMS OF RIDDLES

Based on *The Hunter's Parchments*, cc bastica 212;
The Nordvargor Testaments, cc bastica 860;

22nd of Septimosk, 246

After riding all night and into the morning, the two Roah'riik and Unakan friar ambled wearily toward the Shruumoth Forest. Tracking all night while avoiding bodies exhausted Fal'iek and Tek'ouk—even the mewil'ishyuuks grew weary. They'd followed the trail from the lake going northeast until it faded into nothing. A decoy trail. Disappointed, they discussed whether they should turn back and look for the real one or continue on to Bokhor for help and ask after the reports of the True Night. Being at their limit and closer to the small nearby village of Bokhor, they pressed on.

As they approached the edge of Shruumoth Forest, its twisting toadstools towering in the moonlight, they hesitated. Watching the still fungal forest, they considered its dangers. Some had frilly ridges, and others with thin spines like hair, but Fal'iek had heard that they all interconnected their roots in a great ground web. Any could be lethal or hiding some terrible creature. Though at night during darkemorg would be the best possible time to enter, if it could be said that there was ever a good time to enter.[66] During darkemorg, the fungi closed up in defense and emitted less pollen—except for the few that preyed on lifeless.

A loud thud alerted them, followed by another thud, and another into a kind of rumble. They recognized the pattern of beating hooves, but these were loud, ground-shaking, and scaring their mewil'ishyuuks, whom they quickly moved

---

66 *See Gybiaaw Blackbraid: I Don't Conform,* 12

to remount. Then they saw it: To the south, through creeping fog, strode a gigantic daemog, at least thirty feet tall at the shoulder. Its thick neck had three heads; twisting horns formed a despotic crown atop, and the beast's three tails had long spikes at the end, casually snaking behind. It owned the night.

As the furacán moved toward them, its three mouths opened, revealing an internal furnace that flared. It breathed a deep rumble, snorting out smoke and fire that would let it safely eat the giant mushrooms or set an entire city ablaze. *Or obliterate a small group of unfortunate travelers,* Fal'iek thought, feeling naked out in the open. He'd seen many a strange beast of great size—a seven-headed wolf, Tehu Yagua, and others—but never such as this. He looked at Tek'ouk and Qosku. Both had fallen to their knees and now whispered prayers, wide-eyed, to what they saw as not a wretched furacán but a mighty ruler of the wild, an eternal that they were calling Ariq and Hatun Piyunkuy, respectively.[67] Even Fal'iek felt inclined to recognize it as one. But eternal or no, he refused to bow to it, to offer any kind of prayer to something that would crush him like a bug without a thought.

It thundered past, either not noticing them or not caring.

They watched it disappear to the east, hoping to never see it again. The three quickly mounted and entered Shruumoth with a mind that the giant beast would scare away any waiting dangers. And it was quiet, tranquil, deadly. The roofs of bulging mushroom caps blocked out much of the moonlight, creating pockets of shadow around them until dawn began to illuminate the sky. Some fungi glowed, providing their own light. What bodies they saw were stuck by the fungal mesh of the ground, being consumed by it. Though living things did stalk the forest, none threatened them, but many watched. From afar, the human intruders saw huddled forms and glimmering eyes.

They reached the convent village as dawn bloomed above. The summoner's convent was a hill fort in a southern area of Shruumoth.

Fal'iek tried not to be impressed by the eerie beauty of the place; it could be more dangerous than Thornwood.[68] The trio neared the wooden wall,

67 Meaning world breaker and storm maker, respectively. These are not known eternals but appear to be simply how they described something so awe-inspiring.

68 Unlike Tolgrym, which was built outside the forest and then overgrown, Bokhor was founded to be inside as the forest itself protected from more dangerous beasts so long as the pollen was avoided. The first chamand covens were mostly Kimoo but in the founding joined with Asturions and an unknown group from the sea thought to be Amoyaran, according to various sources.

laced with painted skeletons to ward off beasts, lifeless or living. A tall black man from the top of the gate, dressed in the guardian cloak and mask of a summoner, called out to them.

Fal'iek shouted, "Greetings, I am Fal'iek. Kimoc Warchief. We seek refuge and word on the state of Bokhor."

"Aye, then. You may pass, Warchief," the sentinel said.

"Many thanks."

The gate doors cracked open: A light mist hung over the village squalor. The humble religious colony, like the wall, consisted almost entirely of wood, thatching, and mud plaster. It was a dirty, impoverished collective of dwellings due in part to its founding as a holding for the region's outcasts: chamands and freed slaves. Exiled into a village separate from everyone else, the strange and dangerous pagans were allowed to live in the commune with occasional contact with neighboring cities—until the Razhod. Due to their vital aid in fighting the witchlords, they'd gained greater freedom and respect, but only by degree. Quoak even accepted some of its chamands, as did the other tribes.

Fal'iek and Tek'ouk had entered before, but on seeing it now, they stopped. All in the colony wore a cloak and some kind of mask. The masks were wood or skulls, often topped with antlers or horns and an array of feathers. Even the children who worked and played naked did so with facial anonymity. Fal'iek understood this was not always so, but now, it was like walking into a funeral—no village business or non-ceremonial clothing in sight. The deafening silence of the masked colony slowed their pace, and the mewil'ishyuuks had to be coaxed. A villager took the reins, and the beast resisted until Fal'iek prompted them with a soul touch, its strange, alien spirit leaving him disoriented. Another led the three to a small guest hut as Fal'iek stumbled through an explanation about their search to an unknown tender.

"I'll look into it. It sounds urgent, but your weariness eats you and you must first rest," said the villager.

Fal'iek and his companions took rest in the small hut. He woke in the afternoon, dusk giving a warm glow to the wooded village, illuminating his room through the window. Already anxious of time wasted, he left the hut in search of a leader.

In the village center sat a ghost portal: several branches woven together to create a large hole lined with decorative bones and feathers. Nearby stood

Thoroah, an archamand and sage of the summoner's convent council. He wore a full fur cloak with a large, antlered kulk skull on its head, with feathers sprouting behind.[69] A cape of feathers hung off his back and a necklace of teeth around his bare ebony chest. Fal'iek had to remind himself that "strangeness" was a perspective, not a fact, and not in itself bad. He'd also forgotten what the nightpeople were like, in this hovel they'd been condemned to after their liberation, since most of them now lived in Bokhor while others remained as debt servants in the Asturion cities.[70]

"Tek'ouk is over at that," Qosku said, suddenly at his side, rubbing sleep from his face and pointing toward a tall wooden tower Fal'iek recognized as the calling tower. He nodded but turned to approach Thoroah. Talking to masks such as these always made him uneasy. Qosku followed quietly.

"Thoroah, forgive our entrance," Fal'iek said. "It has been a long hunt that we are on. Are you well? I received a report of a strange storm that hit here while in search of a group that captured our friends."

Thoroah wore a painted mewil'ishyuuks skull, concealing his aged face. "It is no problem, Warchief, though we know nothing of this group you seek. And it was no storm but a great obscuring. A True Night."

Fal'iek felt some of his old apprehension returning. "You lost your spiritsight? When did it come back?"

"It has not, and we mask until it does," Thoroah said, turning. "Come."

He led them away from the ghost portal. The decorated posts meant nothing to Fal'iek. The chamands remained ever secretive of their customs.

As they walked, Thoroah began, "Only legends of blindings in times before. Punishment of individuals. Spirits mentioned nothing. No warning given."

"Why is spirits?" Qosku asked, and Fal'iek frowned at his nonsense question. They were in a hurry.

"What boy hunts with thee?" Thoroah asked, turning to him. They came to a clearing where several chamands prepared for a group summoning. They drew lines on the ground, poles held aloft decorated skeletons symbolizing who they intended to call; though Fal'iek recognized none of the emblems, the scene was an old but familiar picture to him. A scene from

---

69 Similar to mewil'ishyuuks, but bigger and usually alone or in smaller groups. Different from quelk.

70 It's interesting that most brown-skinned people, namely Kimoc and Unaka, referred to ebony-skinned people as nightpeople who usually preferred the naturalistic, or mythic, label over others ascribed to them. An affinity within the underclass.

the old war, one he'd always approached warily, even in the safety of an allied coven.

"I am Qosku. This place like abbey but nicer. Me feel safe here." Fal'iek watched Qosku out of the corner of his eye. *This place isn't scaring him? Maybe he doesn't know what they do at night.* The Unakan had not proved as useful as Fal'iek had hoped, only causing discomfort on their shared mew-il'ishyuuks. *If the boy likes it here, perhaps we could leave him and continue on the search without. That way the boy would stop being a burden without feeling put off.* Fal'iek inwardly wished he'd listened to Tek'ouk more.

Thoroah led them around the ritual area but spoke to Qosku. "You see things truly. See through the disguises. You would make a good summoner should you one day consider the path of no return." He raised a skull scepter and pointed it at the circle. "The spirits I speak of are our ancestors, await in death. The dead are hidden beneath the surface of Otherworld. Beneath, they lack the clarity of the surface but contain secrets of the ages. When we summon a spirit, it surfaces, and we communicate. Most of us hear and see, close but still far. Most, before. Since, nothing. No one."

"But where spirits go?"

"Spirits wander, spirits move, graduate, from this room to the next. From that room to another. That room to the next room. And on and on, through innumerable rooms. Lost in the endless labyrinth of existence." Fal'iek felt a chill, and a gratitude he'd left such myths behind. He'd concluded that no spirit was eternal after all, but that they all eventually faded alike their decaying corpses. *Everything crumbles and fades in time, why would spirit be any different? We're not special.*

"Now." Thoroah turned to a circle marked on the ground as summoners gathered around it. "Amidst the True Night, a sacrifice was made here. A sacrifice to block our powers. Now, a rite to reverse it and a call to a greater spirit. Together, we are sufficient."

"Then this was deliberate," Fal'iek said. "By… an intruder?"

"Yes, a mystery traitor." Thoroah motioned to the circle of chamands. "You know the ritualist, Hoyoche."

Fal'iek turned to see a Kimoc, his tattooed body naked in the weak sunlight. Fal'iek had known him by his Kimoc name, Kichuwa'koh. Hoyoche walked up and clasped Fal'iek's arm. "How are you, old friend?"

Fal'iek smiled. "I'm well, and you?"

"Not well." And his brown, sun-darkened face showed it, beneath his wooden mask. Tired and drawn, full of wrinkles and absent any smiles. "My wife, Heikewe, passed beneath the surface several moons ago. Because of my powers, I've been able to continue communication with her, though I had to change my chamand circle. With this blinding, I can't speak with her. I've no idea if she's in this world, the below, or the above." Grief ate at the man; holding on after death hadn't been good for him and Fal'iek pitied his fate, wishing there was a way to urge his old companion to move on. Fal'iek realized he'd been fingering his feq'uok again; he'd not seen his own family in days.

"Well, hopefully this will work," Fal'iek said.

Hoyoche nodded and greeted Qosku, who introduced himself with eyes on the ground, then perked up. "Can you summon my ancestors? I am seek my family."

Fal'iek looked at him sharply. "No, they can't summon anything. And they don't take requests." He turned to Thoroah. "Why would it affect both lesser and greater spirits? Aren't emaions different?"[71]

Hoyoche explained, "We aren't sure. I think the blinding is more than just our senses, like what Nimrød the Reptilium had done in the old war but all of us. It's a complete communication block, which makes this all the more disturbing. If I could summon Izilblisk, I might be able to lift the blinding. Instead, I've no idea if she's even aware of this."

He returned to the circle of chamands, that stood waiting. Fal'iek recognized most of them as the Ogouk, unique in their practice of physical blinding in exchange for a continuous spiritsight. Though now he understood they didn't have that either and remained completely sightless. They still wore the bands over their eyes, faces painted in place of masks, but walked with a hesitant awkwardness common to everyone without sight. It struck Fal'iek as extreme when they had the power and dangerous now without it. He couldn't imagine living in this way but recalled them as quite formidable when they'd fought together. Hoyoche was instead of the Anazakor, one of the more open groups. Fal'iek did note with some pleasure that many of them were Kimoc, along with many Unaka, Amoyara,

---

71 Emaion is another name for greater spirit and sometimes called eternal. These beings are ancient and mighty, and knowable only by covenant and a dedicated life. But even the most noble can still be dangerous to their sworn humans.

and some mastozons, the other half being nightblessed.[72] The one area
that oppressed people came together was chamands, if only to be impoverished and despised as witch deviants by everyone else. But somehow
they adapted and thrived in spite of it.

Fal'iek itched to leave, impatient and uninterested in the bloody rite. Blood
would add power to the effort of these two chamand orders, two of many
that used blood. But they never ritualized human blood, which had been
the primary dividing line of summoning between the chamand covens and
the Razhod witchlords. Still, Bokhor was a key bastion for the region against
outsider forces. Aiding them meant protecting his own people. His family.

Ten stood in the circle, which had lines pointing to the triangle where
the spirit was to appear. All wore large brown robes with green markings for
their individual emaion loyalties. Some began playing their panflutes, while
others rang small bells. A drum pounded slow and steady. Hoyoche walked
to the center and drew his knife on the young bomog. It keened weakly just
before Hoyoche gouged its throat, then squealed and bayed and gargled.
They of the circle raised their hands and chanted for Izilblisk the Cruel, with
Hoyoche holding up one of the small bannered trinkets, a cloth with feathers
and withered flower buds, over the dying bomog as it gushed blood onto the
grass. Hoyoche chanted, and they followed suit. Fal'iek understood none of
this, but when the climax was reached, he saw the faint glow, like a large
shadow, in the figure of a great owl with milky white eyes and symbols on
its feathered body. Izilblisk the Cruel regarded them silently, motionless, and
not as tangible as would be normal for a summoning. A third eye opened on
its forehead, more piercing still, before the faint emaion faded away.

Silence fell. Disappointed, the chamands began talking of changing the
setup to try something different, although Fal'iek found himself secretly
glad it had not worked. Calling any of the emaions was playing with fire,
and the Cruel wasn't even the worst of them. The summoners shook their
heads, conferring. *Say what you will about their ways, but they understand
community better than anyone else.*

Thoroah sighed. "There is no salvation for us now. There is no hope
for blind seers. The Tree of Doom drains us, and we must find our own
way, away."

---

72 *ibid, 3*

"How far have any of you gone from the village, testing the range?" Fal'iek asked.

Hoyoche examined the circle and answered, "All the way to Mantlgrym. We sent messengers there to discuss the problem. They experienced no change, so it appears to be done to us and not the location. The timing is most disturbing, since all but two of the known summoners were in the village for their river of stars festival."

"Who are the two? Can we contact them?"

"You're welcome to try if you can find them. One is the witch of the Kourii bogs—good luck with her—and the other wanders the mountains since we expelled him, probably half-mad if still alive."

"We don't have time for either anyway. How soon do you expect an attack?"

"There is always attack," Thoroah said. "Or there is never. May it be we are not the targets, but at least we know our own names. All except the traitors. We will fight."

Fal'iek stroked his chin. "And you've heard nothing in relation to a band of robbers dressed as carnival performers? Cantlgrym was attacked by a rebel group last night. That's where we just came from." He related everything he knew about the attack to them.

"Our scouts have heard nothing of this." They watched as the mess of the ritual was cleaned up. The bomog's body would not be used for food but burned.

"They did have a demon, apparently, although I've never heard of a demon doing anything like this or taking orders from humans. I suppose if the same group hit you, perhaps they just wanted to get your capabilities out of the way. Have you considered retreating to Voium? Or perhaps nearby if they don't let you in?"

"No." Thoroah turned to face Fal'iek, who wondered if he'd caused offence. "All here are trained warriors and hunters. We take care of ourselves. Others may yet need us if attacked from below."[73]

Past Thoroah, Fal'iek saw the dark, lithe form of Tek'ouk running through the village amidst some hurried summoners. Fal'iek called out to him. Tek'ouk turned and began toward them. Qosku said quietly, "This is more happenings. More of the bad."

---

73 *Likely refers to the Underworlds.*

"There's been sightings of a black fog at Voium," Tek'ouk said as he neared them. "They're preparing a team now to leave to catch it, and I've put us in. But we have to leave now."

Fal'iek nodded his agreement and, with a look at Thoroah, said, "Good. Let us grab our packs and some light food for the road."

After mounting with their packs ready, the three rode off with their mewil'ishyuuks and the four other riders of the coven, heading south.

CHAPTER EIGHTEEN

The Judgment Sword

Based on *Leyta's Journals*, cc bastica 48;
Annals of Syago, cc bastica 30; *Scars of the Martyrs*, cc bastica 938;

unknown day of Septimosk, 246

"What would you have me do then?" Leyta demanded. Arms folded, she looked at Syago expectantly.

"Anything!" Syago threw his hands up. "You could hurl food at them and I'd feel better than if we just sit and read their books and wait to be rescued."

"I'm sick of it too. So if you've a better idea that will actually work, I'd love to hear it." In the three days of their captivity, he'd supported her against the other agitators, and they'd even become friends, which was why she found his recent burst of impatience so frustrating.

He opened his mouth and stopped.

Before she could press him further, Mungo was in the doorway beside them. "Deir highnesses wan all of you upsdairs righd now."

They looked at each other, then followed him up, along with all the others.

Mungo led them out of the dungeons to the spacious great hall of the crumbling Castle of Covadongar. Daylight shone through windows and broken walls to reveal what they'd not seen before: Small vines covered everything, threatening to break the castle even more than it already had been.

Queen stood in the broken doorway that opened to the bridge. This skeleton of an old, great castle overrun by the wiles of the forest bore no major signs that a rebel group hid beneath, save for the armored giant standing as a lone sentry at the end of the bridge, still and silent as a statue, grand cleaver at the ready. The bridge stretched over the rocky moat from deep cliff to deep cliff. Leyta could see an abandoned chapel on the opposing cliff.[74]

---

74 See *La Epica Eluveitia de Sepultura*, 66

"Welcome, my lovely non-subjects," said Queen, the costumed focus of Leyta's real anger. A mock dainty voice hid the power she held. A scepter in her hand warned of it, though Leyta had seen her move fire without it and wondered at the change.

Queen continued. "You'll appreciate my lovely garden surrounding our tower and notice it's festering with these awful vines and flower corpses. But I only want red ones, so you must eliminate the white ones and domesticate the red ones so that they stay put around the outside. Even worse are the snails. Rid them from my sight."

The "garden," or, rather, the surrounding forest, now thronged with rose alerhas, both red and white, and snail monsters almost as big as she. Their greenish-yellow poison-coated bodies slid across the brush with a disturbing slowness toward the tower walls. Black bulbous eyes on the end of long stalks swiveled, and a round mouth sucked at the air. The rose alerhas ambled mindlessly toward the castle, some in the rocky ridge that surrounded them. The snails were drawn by the alerhas, which they ate, and both now threatened the castle's peace. Having gone unchecked, a large group had amassed to swarm the place.

As Mungo and Guilliom organized everyone into groups, Leyta was startled by Queen shoving something into her chest—the scepter. Leyta could hardly believe her fortune, being given exactly what she needed to break them free.

"You'll use this," said Queen sweetly. "And I'll be right behind you to help you use it correctly. Can't have you making a mistake and ruining my garden, of course, so I'll have my own fire ready." She moved to put Leyta between the infested woodland and Queen's scepter-less fire power, hands ready to burn her at a moment's disobedience. "You may begin."

Leyta gave her a hateful smile before turning. She examined the scepter, feeling the symbols with her fingers, accepting it as her foci. But how could she break them free? Syago led a nearby group of three armed with butcher knives to the snails crawling over the bridge. The rose monsters were the greater danger, but attacking with small weapons such as knives wasn't feasible. So they went for the snails, which retreated into their shells and foamed up in self-defense, gurgling and reaching out with a slimy, barbed mandible.

Leyta called out to Syago, "Don't you eat these things in Tolgrym?"

He snorted. "Don't you eat lifeless in Cantlgrym?"

She entered the Vision. The forest had a light mix of red and yellow, mostly from the plants and monsters of the woodland. But it was really more of a blank slate ready to receive her sentiments. She focused on the cliff, where several snails crawled toward the fallen alerhas, and pushed the anger she'd built up into the rocks, aiming for a group. Reds flared and rocks flew haphazardly, difficult to control but still effective in crushing the rose corpse and pummeling the spiral shells of the snails. Shells protected some as they hid and foamed, but several others were hit hard enough that their shells cracked in a sickening splatter that threw acidic guts around that seared the surrounding area and burned the rose vines.

Syago's group hammered at the shells while slipping in cuts at any green they could get at without touching the deadly foam. Tomas's group stabbed at them beneath the shells. Leyta noted that although she was able to pin or break the alerhas, her rocks weren't cracking most of the snail shells, and Queen still hovered behind her. She switched to fire. Starting the fire took a strong burst of red anger, then switching to brown hate for its superior sustaining power. Being in a bad mood helped her with this, but she wanted to stop or turn it back on Queen.

Syago poked a stick into flames and brought the fire to the other one. Leyta shouted to Syago, "You're welcome!"

"I know," he replied in playful ingratitude. She laughed and nearly lost control of the fire. She felt a wariness seep in; not using dyne in the days she'd been here had diminished her control.

Before long, all groups were stoking fires around their snails while also beating at them and burning down the white rose bodies. Syago's group was surprised by a sudden burst of speed from a larger snail as it lunged at two of them, dousing the fire, the acid eating through their boots and pants to their skin. Katti rushed to treat them, and Leyta then renewed the fires, stoking them big enough to contain the snails. They were tough and stubborn creatures, disgusting to the extreme. An image not helped by the proximity of Queen behind her, watching and waiting for Leyta to attempt a break.

Why is she having us do this? Leyta wondered. *To test our capabilities or our complicity?* She stopped searching for a way out.

They worked at the snails with gradual success, thinking it done, when a yellow and black slug, as big as Leyta, reached over from under the bridge and latched onto her dress. She couldn't pull away as it sucked at the fabric.

Keeping a level head, she used dyne to throw rocks at it from the cliff, but they bounced harmlessly off of its gelatinous body. As it drew her closer, she felt a slight panic seep in and called out for help. Milemeron pulled at her, and Tomas jumped in, beating at it with his rocks, even attacking its eye bulbs, until it finally released her in a faint squeal. It hissed at him before reaching with that sucker mouth, but he stepped back, allowing it to miss before laying into it again.

Then Leyta noticed the alerha of a malwolf lumber from the burning pile on the bridge toward him but before she could call out, the vacant head of white rose buds and twisting vines lurched forward and bit at Tomas's leg. He yelped and tried to wrench free, but it held on. Leyta set it on fire, hoping to the angels that the pollen hadn't gotten into his bloodstream, and burned off the attacker. He pulled his leg free. Fernandeon and Syago, the only two with knives, finished off the giant slug in an odious splay of acidic foam and guts bleeding out onto the bridge.

"Herbs for the cure, we need herbs!" Leyta shouted, wishing she knew the specific name of the herb needed. But Queen stood behind them, doing nothing about Tomas's predicament. They started carrying him into the castle, but he began trembling so much that they dropped him. Then the sneezing and coughing came, and then blood—it was too late. Leyta again shouted for help as the others gathered around Tomas. He could no longer cough, as though he were suffocating. His skin rippled, and small greens crawled out of his leg wounds, a white rose bud bulging until Syago ripped it out, and Tomas's bloody wound expanded.

Leyta raised her scepter once more, thinking she might try something with water, when Queen put a hand on the scepter.

"Child," she said kindly, "there's only one way to take care of these." Before any could stop her, she blasted Tomas with fire. Wordless, he fell down, all aflame. All quietly watched him burn, a mixture of sorrow and horror on everyone's faces. Syago choked on a scream, the others having to pull him away.

Before returning to the dungeon, a moment of truth flashed in Leyta's mind as she faced Queen, scepter in hand. Queen stood still, then held out her hand. After a moment's hesitation, Leyta placed the scepter there, and Queen immediately burned it, letting its ashes fall before turning to precede her downstairs.

Syago stood in the broken doorway of the tower, Knight watching from a parapet above as sunlight streamed through the forest and castle remnants. As far as he could tell, the rumor that Knight was a giant armored lifeless appeared true. Nobody had stopped Syago from coming above ground, he could run if he wished. The approaching dusk allowed him to see the smoldering corpses of those loathsome snails on the bridge and castle floor, in between old skeletons and piles of leaves. The snails were near useless too, barely edible and only after a cleaning process to eliminate the acid.[75] He kept thinking that his father, or even Fal'iek, wouldn't have let this happen. If Syago had Alexandre, then he too could've stopped it. Despair and his sorrow for Tomas weighed him down. Tomas, along with Matias, deserved better than their horrible deaths. Tomas's ashes had mixed in with the snails, rustling about in the wind through the ruins.

Perhaps even worse, after the task, he'd returned to their sleeping chamber to find his medicine jars gone. He'd searched everywhere, asked everyone, but most had no idea what he'd even been talking about. No note, no sign, no nothing. Just gone—and all his hopes with it. He wanted revenge on Jester and the others for what they'd cost him. If he was to lose Elisabet and his friends, then he at least demanded punishment.

As Queen had dictated, they could leave at will but obviously wouldn't survive the hell outside, unequipped as they were. Such had been the way: freedom to do anything within the limited options provided. Thornwood in darkemorg, a twisted woodland that promised only death, dared Syago out of the castle. But he would need a weapon to survive. Based on hunting experiences, he knew the forest fairly well. His home lay southeast several leagues, but even better, the grove of Alexandre lay directly south, probably only a league, if that. Syago's confident eagerness pushed him out, and fear called him back. But the fear was markedly less now than before—yet still reason reminded him that he wasn't equipped for this. But if Queen thought that would stop him, she was mistaken. He would run to Alexandre, take up the Judgment Sword, and rescue his friends.

---

75 Snail acid, which the Kimoc had made use of as a kind of weapon slicked on arrows or in gourds, and shells occasionally served purposes as well.

Another reason he didn't like waiting was that almost every night here he'd woken to see the agony, Knave, watching them from that one cell window. Other nights, he'd glimpsed it outside on a thornbranch, whining in pain from some unseen affliction, scratching and grimacing in a mixture of catlike yowls and girl-moans, unaware of its surroundings. In between dealing with Jester's "pranks" and Queen's "ethics lessons" and King's "battle training sessions" as they'd called them, they were left to read through a ruddy collection of political books. Syago grew impatient with searching for a way out.

But the tales he'd heard in his history lessons with Rociol back in Tolgrym of vanishing armies scared him. During the last war between the Kimoc and Asturions, it was said that both sides had sent out armies to challenge the other in battle. Neither army returned and no sure trace of them was ever found.[76] If that could happen, then how could he expect to be found in the tower? So Syago planned in solitude, growing impatient as the days passed.

It grew dark; the bodies would rise soon. He pulled up the old trap door and descended down the stairs to the dining hall for supper.

Walking into the room put Syago in even poorer spirits: taking food from the enemy, dining as if friends. The others sat about the table, talking, getting too comfortable for his taste.

He sat across from Leyta, the one aspect of this place that he'd begun to like. As plates of dead bugs were placed in between them, his eyes caught hers, and they both smiled, a faint laugh shared over unspoken jokes about the food. Eating meat after dark, during darkemorg, meant eating meat that moved. It was perfectly edible, if you could stomach the squirming. Even cutting it up to fine pieces couldn't prevent minute wriggling. King and Queen said this was necessary for their schedule and to toughen up the young ones. Jester merely seemed to enjoy the spectacle, which they suspected to be the real reason.

Next to the plate of struggling beetle corpses was a plate of large skinned rabbit, hard-cooked and nailed to the platter, and around it sat skinned and roasted rats that squirmed. A rat body bounced off the plate, rolling

---

76 Hunting and gathering expeditions vanished about once a year, but the Missing Battle of the Vanishing Armies is the largest on record.

toward Syago and Leyta. Seeing the skinned rabbit brought back memories of hunting the large beasts. The things were a terror to encounter. Syago had once seen a white rabbit rake a man's face off with its foot claw.

Syago pushed some nuts into the tortiya and ate a chunk of it, allowing the crunching sound to resonate loud enough for Leyta to hear before saying, "These bugs are actually really good if you mix them into the tortiya."

She eyed him. "You didn't."

"No, really, try it. You just have to bite fast before they claw your tongue out." He spoke with full mouth to give the appearance of the lie.

Her eyes narrowed.

"What do you think?," he asked. "Am I telling the truth this time? What's Leyta's verdict?"

She returned her attention to her plate while failing to hide a smile. "I don't believe you." But then she eyed him, grabbed a wriggling beetle, and ate it.

He chuckled, shaking his head, and brushed away a dead rat that pressed at his plate. She soon spit the beetle out into a cloth, laughing. He liked making her laugh; her face was beautiful with a smile or blush. Tricking and teasing her proved a blessed respite and enjoyable challenge in this hole they'd been trapped in.

She held up another wriggling beetle lifeless, stuck at the end of a fork, and smothered it in gravy—still it squirmed. Syago stuck a bug as well, then held his up to hers. They pressed their bugs together in a mock fight. Leyta's won, her larger beetle ripping off the legs of the other. Syago clapped his hand on the table in defeat, the sound drawing attention from the others. Remembering that they weren't alone, both looked down. But the other keepers reverted back to eating in self-pitying silence or playing games of their own.

"IT'S YOUR FODING FAULT HE'S FODING DEAD!" Robertobrus suddenly shouted, lunging at Queen with a fork while she remained in her seat, staring at him with that expressionless mask. Gabriol tried to hold Robertobrus back as Fernandeon joined him in attacking Queen.

Jester promptly rose from his seat, grabbed Fernandeon by the hair, and smashed his face into a plate of food. The boy's arms flailed as he grabbed at things to throw at Jester. Robertobrus pushed Gabriol away and stabbed at Queen three times before a bolas from Jester lashed around his body, tying his arms to his torso. Syago ran up to them, thinking to help. Queen rose with torn clothes but was otherwise unperturbed. Syago halted.

"Jester," said Queen sweetly. "Take Robertobrus to your playroom, won't you? He needs to learn how to share and play nice."

"Oh goodie, oh boy!" Jester clapped his hands, bouncing on his feet. "We'll have so much unfun together, I can hardly wait!" Mungo walked over to shove Robertobrus into the back hall, where Jester disappeared.

"I'm sorry," Robertobrus said, eyes desperate and pleading. "I won't do it again, I promise." His plea was ignored, and he was marched behind the curtain.

The incident ended any fun Leyta and Syago had been having, replacing it with dread for their friend. Syago finished his meal in silence, then left for bed without another look at Leyta or anyone else.[77]

That night, Robertobrus did not return. The prisoners held a small, private mass in their cell before tucking in, all of them worried. Syago slept fitfully, dreaming of failure. He awoke and reflexively looked to the window. But this time, instead of seeing the white agony watching from the window bars, he saw something dark move away from him. Syago sat up. The dark phantom from Mantlgrym watched him from a shadowy corner. He'd almost forgotten about it in the events since his medicine theft—but he could never forget those candle eyes, that penetrating gaze that held him in the dark. He felt a chill at the thought that it'd followed him here and watched him sleep. Ghost-quiet, it was darkness itself coming to greet him in the evil hour.

"Was it you who took my medicine jars?" Syago whispered, forgetting his fear in his anger. The eyes narrowed, menacing, then the form moved to the window and slipped outside, so swift and silent that Syago wondered if he'd seen it at all. But no, he'd seen it before, and the paralyzing gaze was real. *Is it a ghost?* He couldn't imagine what else this could be, save another minion of the Royal Chaos. It reminded him of an old folk rhyme that chilled as it ran through his head: "Dyne your emblems and pay your prayers for when day fades come the grimshades. To strangle parents as they sleep and steal children as they weep."

He gazed at the window and decided he'd had enough—it was time to act. He moved to the window. It was early morning, and some moonlight shone

---

77 *See Luskmord: Atrium Carcerio, 7*

through the clouds with sufficient visibility, though a light fog covered the snowy ground. Soon, dawn would swallow darkness. The pair of twinkling stars, those candle eyes, gazed at him from the forest's shadows on the other side of the rocky moat, the eyes of a hunter: intelligent, paralyzing.

"What are you?" Syago whispered, and the eyes disappeared. He slipped out the cracked doorway and into the empty hall, taking a patchwork blanket with him to tie around his neck as a cloak. He a lit a torch in the kitchen, where he also grabbed the best blade he could find, a rusting cleaver.

Perhaps it was the anger, perhaps it was the need or determination, or having greater experience, but he no longer knew fear of the outside as before. With cleaver and torch in hand, he broke into a run out of the broken castle late in the hour of creeping. The bodies, slow and clumsy, would actually be his cover, as he could outrun them long enough for the grove; it was the monsters he feared, but they hid from the lifeless during the Grave's Night. The cold, foggy air burned his lungs and clawed at his arms and legs, a thin layer of snow crunching beneath his boots. Knight did not follow; nothing jumped at him as he wove between bramble stalks. The only sound was the hooting of owls above. He began to wonder where all the lifeless were; Thornwood should be full of them, and yet he'd never seen it so quiet.

That silence set warning bells off in his mind, and he slowed to a halt. A quiet forest... his stomach twisted into a knot, and he considered turning back just as he noticed shadows following him. They stopped above him, so he ran again, faster. The shadows kept up. One even darted in front of him so quick he almost didn't see it, and the candle eyes met his for the briefest second. No, two pairs of them.

Then he noticed another shadow to his right: A pack of malwolves ran with him. All but one had fur, but whether black of hair or black of skin, malwolves were nearly invisible in the dark, rulers of the night. Each bigger and quicker than he, more fierce, and just as cunning. Their yellow eyes, all pupil, reflected his torchlight. Panic engulfed him. If the lifeless had been out as they ought to have been, the malwolves wouldn't be hunting. He wouldn't have tried this otherwise. He turned to run back, but one followed behind and he instead veered left. They then rapidly closed in on his left side.

Syago berated himself for his foolishness. They howled, a call to the moon during their hunt. Shaking like mad from fear, Syago backed against a thorntrunk. They would tear him apart and play with his limbs.

While swinging torch and cleaver to keep their snapping jaws at bay, he prepared to climb. But the trunk he leaned against moved. Then he realized it was the thick leg of a monster so big his torchlight showed only the bottom of its bushy body and gigantic claws. Moonlight hinted at a towering figure of some kind of bird, cracking branches high above with a beak that chirped. Just then, blue lightning shivered down its feathery body. A claw from the darkness crashed down on the malwolf that leaped at Syago, crushing it into the snow-laden ground with a loud crunch and splatter. More blue sparks crackled as the claw withdrew, and Syago soiled himself in the grip of panic.

Snapping out of his shock, Syago ran as two malwolves turned on this new, unknown terror. Two other malwolves pursued Syago, but the crashing of the branches followed them as the titanic monstrosity plowed through the forest, too big to be a natural resident of Thornwood. Malwolves barked and yelped. Looking back, Syago saw briefly in the illumination of blue shockwaves a thornbranch falling from a razor beak as it knocked away the malwolves, their hollow yellow eyes flickering. Well, if it accidentally helped him, he wouldn't complain, but it then charged him too, its beak nearly reaching him. He halted to wave his torch at its cold eyes. It hissed, and Syago forced himself forward on trembling legs, pressing the fire.

The monster reared, then let out a shrieking chirp, blotting out the malwolves' snarling. Syago ran around the nearest malwolf to put it between the monster and himself and set their attention on each other, a useful tactic in group tournaments. The malwolf snapped at his arm, but the maneuver worked, leaving it to fight the thunderbird creature with the rest of its pack. Syago saw his break and bolted away from the chaos.

As the din fell farther behind him, the forest ahead thinned into a small clearing, in the middle of which sat a small, brick-laid platform with overgrowth encroaching its borders. Atop the platform was a stone pedestal, a magnificent sword sheathed halfway into it, a two-handed claymore soulblade, angelic with a crossguard that slanted toward the blade and a pommel with a sun cross and etched fire.

Alexandre.

Syago sprinted toward it. The sounds of the fight faded as he entered the clearing, a small sanctuary of holy ground. He fell to his knees before his dream, his heart pounding.

It carried no scratches but felt ancient. It was a little small for a claymore, almost enough to be wielded in one hand, and he'd heard that its power adjusted the weight and balance to allow such an action. The pedestal bore the familiar inscription:

Here resteth Alasandair,[78]
May Justice and Trvth prevail and evil be vvanqvished
And the wicked bvrn at its touch
Thus is the will of the Judgment Sword

He always thought it strange that it specified only those without evil in their hearts, yet the priests taught that all have evil in their hearts. Then how could anyone touch it? Either way, the sword chose its champion. Another monstrous trumpet among the howls in the distance brought him out of his reverie. He stuck the cleaver and torch in the snowy dirt just off the platform and walked up, placing his hands on the sword hilt in anticipation.

With a deep breath, Syago pulled.

The sword didn't move.

Thinking the cold made it stick, he pulled and twisted even harder, and nothing happened. He tried thinking to the sword, hoping it would understand his thoughts and wake up. He finally said, "I am Syago, son of Odiru de Tolgrym. I have need of you."

As he put his hands on it again, Syago looked past the sword to see those living shadows with their candle eyes watching him from the dark, waiting, haunting.

"Who are you who haunts me?" he yelled. "What do you want from me?!"

The eyes stared, then vanished. The malwolf howls drew closer, and Syago refocused on the sword and thought of what might be the problem. Did this mean he wasn't worthy? Why wouldn't he be? Was it his mixed blood after all? He was old enough, as old as his father had been when he took it. It'd been several months since he'd tried last and almost a month since he left Tolgrym. And everyone spoke of how like his father he was. What noble virtues did he lack? He sincerely needed it for something the

78 Called Alexandre more recently. The entire inscription is translated from old Asturion.

sword would willingly fight for. This stung at him much more deeply than he cared to admit even to himself. It even appeared willing to let him die here in the outside. The torchlight simpered out.

He heard the malwolves approaching, their run slowing for more caution. He prayed: *I am mastozon, but I've completely forsaken any remnant of my savage, pagan heritage. I'm a true Deovan, and with good works and motives. Yet it refuses me still, the first mastozon in the family line and the first to be refused.* Frustration welled up in him. Syago grabbed Alexandre by the hilt again and pulled with everything he had and yelled, "Why won't you come to me? I am worthy of you and the cause is just. You are my heritage and my right, now serve me!"

This time, the grip shocked him, burning his hands. Syago fell back onto the hard, cold bricks. A single hot tear crept down his face, then more. Not for the malwolves or the cold piss on his pants, but for the dream that now refused him.

The malwolves strode into the clearing, three now and wounded; blood covered their black fur. The strange beast bleated far away, leaving him to his fate. They slowed at the sight of Alexandre, growling, but they didn't stop. A weapon sheathed meant nothing to them. Syago closed his eyes, bracing for the blow. But a deep pounding in the snow-covered gierra preceded the oncoming attack, and Syago heard a sickening crunch. He looked back to see Knight standing there above a malwolf cleaved in half, silent but expectant, his vacant corpse face dimly visible in the helmet under moonlight. Syago got to his feet, brushed himself off, and followed Knight back to the castle.

CHAPTER NINETEEN

CANDLE'S INFERNO

Based on *Leyta's Journals*, cc bastica 50;
The Nordvargor Testaments, cc bastica 732;

unknown day of Septimosk, 246

Leyta woke to Syago entering the cell at the morning's first glow. He looked cold and wore his blanket hanging from his neck, wet and torn; he must have tried to escape. His face was drawn and distant, though none else in the room noticed, too wrapped up in their own despair.

She threw her blanket over him. "Syago, what did you do?" she whispered. "Don't want to talk about it," he mumbled.

She shook her head and left to steal him an early bowl of warm soup from the kitchen. She hid her unease. *So even Syago is letting this place get to him.* She kept a strong front for the others, especially the younger ones, but she couldn't support them alone. If Syago was breaking, others would follow.

She hadn't told anyone except Katti of her plan to get them out. She didn't want to risk any of them acting on her plan before it was time. For now, she had to act as though she had planned nothing, and the continued absence of Robertobrus and the deaths of the others pressed on their minds.

She scolded Syago in her head but also felt some resentment toward him for doing more than she had to escape. Fortifying others was something she'd normally do, being the leader, so it bothered her to have it reversed.

Once in the kitchen, she scooped some porridge from the warming pot into a wooden bowl. Crestina ignored her, as usual. She returned to the quarters to find everyone gone except Syago, who sat against the wall staring at the window, his face an expression of utter despair.

She placed the bowl in his hands. A tear fell down his face.

She sat beside him. "Syago..."

"Please, just leave me alone." He wiped the tear and turned his face away.

"You need to talk about it, Syago. You can't bottle up your feelings. Especially when you're risking your life and ours."

He said nothing.

It was rare that she'd feel compassion for a man, but she needed his help, even if he'd brought this on himself. She was about to stand and leave when he said, "You ever have a-a dream thrown in your face?"

"A dream?"

He turned slightly so she could see his face, but he looked ahead. "As in, you had a certain image of yourself. You were important, some incredible destiny belonged to you, and you had an important task to accomplish. But then you realize you're not so great and you fail at the task. I was important. But now I'm nothing, and she's dead. They're all dead, all because I wasn't the hero I thought I was."

"Who's dead?"

"My cousin. I was bringing the cure to her, and now it's gone and I have no way to save her." He wiped his face again, then cleared his throat and stood. This was more than he'd ever divulged of himself, and she found that she wanted him to go on. She also felt a twinge of shame for judging him so quickly. He was deeper than she'd thought.

"I'm sorry you're going through this," she said, rising next to him. "Don't give up hope, though; she may need you yet. We need you."

He nodded, still not looking at her. "We should go break our fast before Jester decides to season my eggs with rat fingers again."

She stifled a laugh, unsure, but added, "Or my bread with squished worms."

"That actually wasn't so bad."

Then she did laugh.

After morning cleanup, Leyta entered the study room. It was small, with two bookshelves, a small table, and chairs, all of it old and weathered. At the farther bookshelf, she moved some books to reveal her project: A makeshift scepter she'd carved out of a broken chair leg. To make a dynal foci, she needed three things: some material, usually wood or bone, crafted into an elongated shape; the appropriate symbols etched on it; and another foci.[79]

---

[79] *Moonspell Hell Light de Lostregos gives a review of dyne, it's pagan history, and the political aspects of it. I agree with his conclusion that scepters require not specific symbols, only ones that are meaningful to the bearer.*

The last one would be the hardest to obtain, as she would have to either find or steal one. Archemy provided similar issues for the archemy keepers. Her plan involved the more likely option of stealing it from one of the royalty. They obviously had at least one. King and Queen used dyne without a visible foci, so she understood them to be hidden beneath their costumes. Of course, she likely couldn't just use the enemy foci once she had it—they would have ways to stop her—but she could use it to finish her own.

The scepter was almost ready. She'd participated in making one only once before, her staff now laying in Cantlgrym. A mistake could be disastrous, so Katti had been a tremendous help with her knowledge of symbology. But without another functioning foci to endow it with commanding power, their efforts served as nothing more than a work of craftsmanship. The same was true of the faith pendant Katti worked on.

She shuddered at what she would have to do when she finally had a working scepter. Memories of burning that man alive were never far from her mind, the sensation of sending hate out of her and into the fire as he screamed and squirmed churned within her. To take her mind off it, she taught the youngest, Kel'feq and Sabela, how to play ahedreth. A strategy game would do them good, and tutoring children would relieve her; young children always eased her heart. But they couldn't pay attention, eventually running off and leaving her with an odd riddle she found scrawled on the underside of the gameboard.[80]

> *Seven owls sit watch at night*
> *One owl marks the soul*
> *Two owls drain the fight*
> *Three owls bore the hole*
> *One owl is the light*
> *Of the hole*

Leyta didn't understand it, but it reminded her of the lockpick set she'd collected. At this time in the morning, she might have a better chance of getting into a locked door than at nighttime, when Knave stalked the halls, purring, giggling, and eating rats alive. In the middle of the day, the crewmen

80   See *Luskmord: Atriom Carcerio*, 13

walked around too much for her to be discreet. She hid the tools under her dress in a pocket she'd made, ignoring how dirty her dress was getting.

She went first to the decorated hallway. She hadn't bothered with the first set of locked doors because she felt sure those rooms held only storage. She hid in the curtain of the next door and began her work. Sounds of footsteps approached and she stopped, holding her breath. She saw their figures faintly through the curtains; the footsteps came from not one but several men carrying heavy boxes, and she recognized the forms of Arrochor and Mungo. The first few boxes were stacked like supplies, but the next few boxes were long, carried by two men on each end, like they were carrying a coffin.

A chill went through her.

Several of these passed by her toward the surface door. Then, the figure of Jester stepped in front of her, following the line of workers, and stopped. She saw the bell tails of the head turn toward her. He stared; her pulse quickened and skin prickled for what felt a long time, not daring to breathe, hoping he only saw the curtain. She fought to hold her breath until he turned and resumed walking with the workers down the hall. She waited a moment longer to let them leave before turning back to the lock.

To her surprise, the padlock clicked open with relative ease. Gently prying the lock off, she opened the door and slid inside, closing it behind her. Realizing her mistake of not bringing something for light, she debated leaving and grabbing a candle but feared the risk. She felt around, hoping to stumble on something she could use. She felt shelves and on the shelf something round... a skull. She pulled her hand off and it hit something metal: a candle plate. She grabbed it to hold it steady and felt around. Something brushed against her feet, and she fought the urge to climb onto the shelves. Maintaining control, she managed to light the candle using the archemical markings on the tray, thankful for just that much dyne and wishing she could do more. Wielding the flame as she needed wouldn't be possible from a candle without a foci.

The candle cast dim light on the dusty room, creating many shadows and the flight of gleaming vermin. The shelves held at least ten entire skeletons. *A collection, or storage to make something?* She saw also numerous blocks of wood, carving tools, and scrolls. She unfurled one to find sequential drawings of a human body, first of the skeleton, then with muscles, then with skin. At least the bones appeared clean and the stale musk of the room smelled better than rotting corpse pieces. The other parchments were blueprints of craftsmanship relating to furniture and toys, mostly dolls. The rest of the shelves had nothing resembling a dynal foci.

As she turned to leave, something caught her eye: A glint from the candle touched the visible tip of an old key in the corner of the doorway. Standing in any other place, she would have missed it. Covered in cobwebs, the key must've been dropped and left there ages ago. She picked the silver key up and tucked it away in case it proved useful then carefully exited the room, locking it behind her.

In the study room, Leyta found Katti examining the scepter. She looked up and smiled. "It looks incredible, Leyta. I think it's ready. It feels ready to me, like it really signifies something. And my pendant is almost done."

Leyta nodded, deep in thought. Katti asked, "What's wrong?"

"Nothing, I just... I found something," Leyta said and explained the room and the key. "It was really creepy. I've seen skeletons before, but not collected like that. What if they were old prisoners?"

Katti remained silent for a moment. "I think maybe Deova is trying to show us something. Either that we need to run or that we need to search more for a lock to fit the key."

"Perhaps," Leyta said. "We do need to search more. I've found one piece of the puzzle. And anything we can learn of our enemies will do us good for a fight if not an escape."

"Yes." Katti nodded. "We can beat Queen and show her we're the iron people. Our Lady of Salvation won't let us fail in this. Now what of that key? Can I see it?"

Leyta pulled it out of her pocket and handed it to her. "A key like this looks important. I tried it on a couple locks in this hallway, but it hasn't worked anywhere."

Katti examined it closely. "Well, it's definitely of royal make. I can't tell what clan, though. If we're in the forest, what barony would this have been?"

Leyta shook her head in uncertainty.

"Well, I say keep looking for its lock," Katti said. "You've done more than anyone else here toward getting us out of this mess." Her face fell a little then, reminiscing.

"Mariacarmina died full in the holy revelation," Leyta said. Katti nodded. "You saw what happened, with the light. She was clearly blessed by the Holy Spirit of Deova Bondua."

"The Lady bless her," Katti said.

Nevermore had seen many gangs and conflicts between peoples, but not since the Razhod had a foe so peculiar been brought to bear. If humans already endured the hate of the creator, adding to it by attacking each other made no sense. They wasted that energy on each other with oppression and conflict instead of nature, both in beast and lifeless curse, which deserved more of their fight. She was reminded of an old work: *I fear not the maligned theories and theologies of petty bishopesses. I do fear the diminishing will to fight and let our world dominate us, including our own human world.* Written by a young philosopher who later murdered his father and became the slain Dark Sage of the Inferno, Barthandeon.[81]

She didn't agree with the Dark Sage's politics, of course, but felt that he'd had many good insights about the problems of human society and the struggle against creation—a thing she could never point out to more dogmatic thinkers such as Katti. But they still had each other's support and a general gnostic faith in common.

Suddenly, Fernandeon and Gabriol walked in, arguing loudly. The younger Milemeron trailed behind them quietly.

"Leyta," Gabriol started, "he says you have a secret plan."

Fernandeon's eyebrows rose in an expectant glare at her, but he said nothing.

Voice sharp, Leyta said, "If I do, it ought to remain a secret."

"How can you let him in on it and not me?" Gabriol said in dismay. "I'm better to you than he is!"

Fernandeon laughed. Leyta wanted to hit both of them but instead said, "I'm not *letting* anyone in on anything until necessary. And I have to treat all of you equally."

Fernandeon, who had learned of it by eavesdropping on her and Katti, drew a sly smile. "What she means is your feelings won't get you any extra treatment. Not even of the most special kind."

She raised an arm to slap him. He flinched, and she stopped herself, lowering her hand. *Don't lose control, Leyta. A dynast who loses control loses everything.* Fernandeon, smug, made to leave, and Gabriol followed, glaring

---

81 *The Writings of Barthandeon,* which, fortunately, were not left with *The Philosophies of Night.* Those were burned shortly after his defeat on *The Nascendante* in the fear that any reader might follow in his path.

in betrayed anger. The boys passed Syago entering the room, eyeing the other pair, Milemeron lingered as well.

Turning to Katti and Leyta, Milemeron observed, "Sometimes I wonder if you two didn't become priestess and dynast because you couldn't get betrothed."

"Or you didn't want to..." Syago trailed off at the look of disdain from Leyta.

"I gave my heart to our Heavenly Mother," Katti began, "because Her Holiness fills me with the light and love I need. Don't assume that what I have is a last resort. We neither need nor want your pity."

Milemeron looked stunned. Syago blushed and muttered an apology and Milemeron echoed it.

"Anyway, we wanted to ask—" Syago was interrupted by a noise in the hallway—

... [82]

—tears poured down Leyta's face. Katti sat next to her, rubbing her back to offer comfort. On the other side sat Syago with an arm around her shoulders, his drawn face becoming hard.

Once she'd dried her tears, Syago helped her up then left. Katti and Leyta talked about it some more, then went to mentor the younger children on what they should've been studying back at Cantlgrym. The sweet innocence of children always alleviated her struggles and seeing them improve renewed her hope.

---

82 Nearly three whole pages are blotted out here. It appears they even did it twice and tried to scratch the words off the papyri in some areas. This time, a single word has been written at the top of the first page in the margin: **No**

CHAPTER TWENTY

NIGHT WITHIN NIGHT

Based on *Writings of Qosku*, cc bastica 50;
Annals of Syago, cc bastica 12; *Scars of the Martyrs*, cc bastica 950;
The Nordvargor Testaments, cc bastica 680;

23rd of Septimosk, 246

Qosku again rode with Fal'iek while Tek'ouk rode a separate mewil'ishy-uuks in the group headed for Voium where the reported black fog already came into view. The four mastozan chamands rode just behind them, letting the trackers lead. He didn't know them well at all, but he could tell of their prowess as warriors by the way they carried themselves. They rode through the outerwilds with caution but not hesitation. He'd also deduced that they were two pairs of sisters: Melonih to Melizah and Floar to Reyna. Qosku felt a tinge of jealousy toward them, all of them together and so well trained, at that. It didn't help that Qosku's would-be partners, Fal'iek and Tek'ouk, held little regard for his opinions or skills. Fal'iek had invited him but then overlooked him most of the trip, the same way most everyone did. Qosku tried not to let it bother him. A central principle of dyne was to not let others affect ones' state, that would give them power over him and weaken his own powers. But he was still human, and affect him it did.

They rode till the day drew late. The black cloud hovering over Voium grew bigger until it filled the sky over them in their approach of the city, blocking out any light of star and moon—a True Night. The wooden wall with stone towers already concealed much of the town, but the black fog poured over its thirty-foot height, obscuring what ought to be visible. He hoped the cloud led them to the Royal Chaos. Qosku had mainly been concerned for his friend Leyta and hoped to find the rest unharmed as well. In seeing the fog now, he felt a greater sense of immediate danger more unstoppable than the group that had so effortlessly knocked him away that night.

The group drew up to the large doors of Northgate and stopped. A wall sentry should have greeted them, but when no call came, they shared wary looks before dismounting.

Fal'iek and Tek'ouk wordlessly pulled vines out of their packs and pressed them against their foreheads, running their hands along them. Qosku watched as the vines slowly came to life. The hellhunters threw them up the wall, where the vines timidly slithered then wrapped around a hold, allowing the small hooks tied at the end to catch. Once they'd checked them for stability, Fal'iek motioned for Qosku to go ahead beside Tek'ouk. Qosku grabbed the vine and used dyne to speed himself up the wall. Powering his weary limbs with extra energy, he sped past Tek'ouk. Hoping he'd impressed them enough, he slowed down near the crenellated battlements at the top. Pulling himself over the top of the wall into a crouch, he regained his breath. Fal'iek reached the top not long after and shot him what looked like a disapproving glare in the darkness. The moment passed as they all pulled onto the ramparts and surveyed the area before them.

Black fog filled the town. Only a pace ahead on the walkway was visible, and nearby buildings couldn't be seen. Qosku sensed nothing in sentiments from the cloud, save for a stale, ashen scent. This chilled him, for at a minimum he should have been able to see or feel the sentiments. Instead, he felt only the ones flowing through his own body and those generated by his companions. A deafening silence filled the city.

Fal'iek walked the obscure path to a stairwell and descended quietly, with Qosku and the others following. The shadow cloud enveloped them as they entered; by the time they reached the floor, they couldn't see their hands in front of their faces. Such pure, impenetrable darkness unnerved Qosku, who'd worked the mines, and he thought on the rightness of calling it a True Night. He felt vulnerable as never before. The black fog filled them.

The group spread out, relying almost as much on their senses of touch and movement as on hearing. Qosku had done some training in darkness fighting and suspected the others had as well, though being blind would still be a severe disadvantage.

Qosku heard a faint whistle from Fal'iek, and they walked toward the empty town square. Fal'iek whispered, "I connected to the city rats. They fear the fog but also an unnatural presence here that they don't like."

Tek'ouk responded, "I felt the same."

"We're all still blinded to the spirits," Floar said.

Fal'iek said, "I'm going to call out and see if we can get the village's attention. If that doesn't work, we'll break into a home. This is too strange." He cupped his hands around his mouth. "HELLO!" he yelled. "I AM A KIMOC CAPTAIN AND HAVE COME TO HELP YOU. CAN SOMEONE PLEASE COME AND SPEAK WITH US?"

"We are here." A cold whisper behind Qosku—no, surrounding them. Qosku turned, his arms up in tight guard position.

"Who are you?" Fal'iek demanded.

"Old friendsss." The voice cut quiet and forced, like it barely had the lungs to make as much sound as it did. *"From your bleakessst nightmaresss."*

Qosku listened and felt. The voices moved, but he heard no footsteps. No rustling of cloaks or even breathing—and no sentiments. Qosku moved out of the circle as slowly and quietly as he could, hoping to get a position they wouldn't expect. He used no sentiments in his movements, lest they sensed it.

"What do you want?" Fal'iek asked. "What have you done?"

"We want you." This one sounded different, its voice a little harder, metallic even. *"Frienzzz leave or die."*

"Why?" Fal'iek said after a pause. "What does the Royal Chaos need me for?"

"Not Chaozzzz."

"Who then? Are you of the Razhod?"

"You killed our masterzzz. Will pay for it."

"Now," said another, and Qosku's heart pounded, body sweating and trembling for fear of any number of unseen enemies that seemed to be everywhere and nowhere at once.

"We ssseek remnantsss," lisped another. *"Give artifactsss."*

"No," Tek'ouk said. "You'll get nothing from us but retribution for any wrongs you've done. Return Bokhor its powers and leave this land—"

Something thumped to the ground, the thumping of a body to the ground. Qosku reached out instinctively, feeling something cold and slippery but dry.

It slid between his hands. Something wrapped around his legs and pulled them out from under him, then swung him against a wall. Stars burst in his head from the collision. Managing to slip his foot out before a second swing, Qosku rolled to a crouch. All was oppressive darkness.

"*No fight,*" said one like a firm hush. "*Killed summonerzzz. Continue more die.*"

"You bastards!" Reyna shouted. "You killed her!"

"*Give or die.*"

"You have our answer," Fal'iek growled. "We give you nothing."

Qosku heard movement and sprung at the nearest spot of someone struggling and gasping for breath. Warm blood gushed onto Qosku, and he clawed into something soft and cold but solid. He tried to wrap his arms around it in a tight hold, but it slipped out and grabbed his leg again. As Qosku grabbed at it, something smacked him hard in the face. He fell to the ground and twisted in a short spin to free his foot. However, this time, it was ready. It stopped his spin and threw him against a wall again. Qosku used some energy to shift momentum and spread it out. He collapsed to the floor.

Somebody screamed in pain. The mists moved, and some visibility returned. The thing wrapped around Qosku's neck in a choke hold. Qosku struggled against it and got slammed to the floor. Although, it didn't feel incredibly strong, the speed and durability of what felt like a tentacle held him prisoner. The sounds of struggle died down to silence. The pain in his head from hitting the ground swelled and lack of air made the fight even harder.

The mists lifted, revealing the town square. But a black fog gathered into a single spot, where moonlight revealed five tall, shadowy human figures, standing around the central statue. The shadowmen looked at Qosku with eyes like the midnight sky, stars within a void. *Deepwraiths?* he wondered. Their arms turned to wings as they leaped silently into the air and flew away.

The tentacle arm wrapped around his neck. "*Now sleep,*" it whispered in his ear, not long before he fell into unconsciousness.

He dreamed of his betrayal, before the sacrificial murder of his sister Chaska. He sat in his hut, a manacle tight around his neck, chained to other unfortunates. Rain pattered above. He wondered if any of the iron in the chain had been pulled out by him, if he'd inventoried it in the forge;

how much of his own captivity had he built? No doubt Chaska was also chained elsewhere, but both were soon to be released for labor.

An Asturion soldier brought him and the other boys he was chained to out into the rain. It soaked them fast. They were taken up the stairs, along the drainage chutes and reconstructed buildings, to the count's manor near the plaza and sat down inside facing a table. He sat next to old Machutec, who had been a Unakan priest, although one couldn't tell for the manacles and lack of his sacred vestments, just as the manor had once been a temple rimmed in gold. Now it bore the clumsy, inglorious, and dull style of the palemen—or palebottoms, as they were derided in secret.

A mastozon priest came in and sat down, a guard remaining at the door. He began speaking to them in passable Unakan, one priest for six students. Qosku'd gotten used to their sermons, usually from women, but this man was new. Qosku's mind began to wander into what Chaska might be forced into and how to reunite with her, when suddenly his attention snapped back to something the priest had just said.

"—you see, we must execute some for example. You are chains now because you cause too much problems and so you will stay in chain in different yaqta from you family and others execute. But occasion, we are exception. If you pledge faith and seek the insight from hanan pacha and are baptized, you are exception because you now Deovan."

That word, *Deovan*, the all-important justifier and his way out from a threat he'd not realized he'd been under. On the discovery of his and Chaska's deceit in the mine, they were told they'd just be separated for a time, but it now appeared they'd be permanently separated. Killed.

The priest rambled on, and Qosku interrupted him. "I want the revelation. How do I get it?"

It took a second for the words to translate in the priest's mind before he finally lit up. "Aha, praise Deova Bondua! But it is not... yet good. You need strong desire. You need sacred revelation in answer to strong prayer." As the man struggled finding his Unakan words, Qosku wondered if Deovan conversion might actually fix him into a full man, if this prayer really was magic like they claimed. Praying and offering to the other eternals hadn't done anything for him, but maybe this one would.

He stood up and shouted from his chest, "Save me Deova Bondua! Purge my evils I beg of thee." The priest beamed. Qosku breathed in and out, but he felt no different.

A soldier entered the room and motioned for them to come out, tugging on their chain. Walking through the rain again up to the main plaza, Qosku passed a home where a woman suddenly fell out of the hut. She stumbled, half naked, into the wet stony steps, and Qosku had to step over her weeping form. Though Unakan, he didn't know her. But he'd gotten to know her husband, Andrast de Barascon, who stepped out behind her. He was Qosku's favorite Asturion guard because he was the most lenient, either out of depression or laziness, or both. Though it appeared he now repudiated his woman.

High walls of tight stone bricks and large windows surrounded them in the central plaza, a mighty waka altar in the middle. They were led to the execution stand.

He'd seen the hangings and public racks to warn against rebellion and crime. He turned to Machutec beside him and asked, "Priest, if we're to be killed, is it possible to dedicate it to the Great Ones as a sacrifice? To turn our shameful extermination into a glorious ascension?"

The old Unakan grunted, almost a chuckle. "You've never seen a sacrifice, have you? Well, even I never got to see many. It involved a whole ritual that I can't duplicate here. If their priestesses would let me and I remembered it all, sure, but not likely no. There are rules to it all, and they are not in our favor."

Qosku looked ahead at the gathering of priestesses around the gallows. The count on the stand was also the executioner. He said in Asturion that their crimes warranted punishment and it was for the peoples' own good to root them out. But this was a mercy, a break in their days of hard labor. Not under whip at the mines but under law and custom of the palebottoms. And only one was brought up to the noose; the rest would be separated from their families and stay in chains, even during labor. He then went on to explain that he would eventually increase their pay, rejoin their families, and loose the chains for compliance to their contracts. They weren't slaves after all. *Nor will we all be summarily executed, just left with no option but to work ourselves to death*, Qosku thought. Everyone's forlorn expressions reminded him of a poem he'd been working on in his head.

The chain tugged at his neck, keeping him in line with the others until Andrast came along to swap out their chains. Qosku rubbed his chafed neck skin; the pain was minimal compared to what was to come. The mastozon priest was pleading with the count to let him go, being a potential convert. He tried not to get his hopes up until he saw Chaska among those getting released in a different line. Qosku's stomach lurched. He looked around, thinking that he could make a break for it, but she wouldn't be able to run or fight like he could. She was tough, but she hadn't been trained, and any of the dynasts present could blast them as they fled.

Instead, he broke the line, slowly and calmly so as not to raise alarm, and walked up to her. They embraced and he took her hand and led her up to Andrast, offering it to him. "You need a new wife, yes? Please, take my sister. She is young but a full woman and will be good to you."

Her eyes widened in horror at him, and he hastened to explain. "Please be good to him, it is better than death and torture. If you are very good, you can gain power and privilege." He spoke with his eyes as much as words, hoping both sides could agree to it well enough. For Qosku had already noted that the former spurned wife was not among the crowd to work in chains.

Andrast's passive expression turned annoyed, then amused. Chaska, eyes on the ground, didn't nod but didn't refuse either. The priest was yelling things at him. Andrast, nearly twice Chaska's height, gave a slight shrug and pulled her off to the side to sit her down. Qosku turned back to the line to be racked, but Andrast pulled him away and kicked him toward the hill. A hill that led to the road out of Izquchaka.

"Go," he said. "You'll be banned and exiled instead. Do not let us see you again."

Exile, the mode of execution cast as a mercy because it lent the obscure and fanciful hope of survival. Yet it was certain that none ever did survive being out alone. Another soldier approached to enforce his flight, so Qosku scrambled out, taking one last glance at Chaska, who was picked up and flung over Andrast's shoulder to be taken to his hut. He stopped again as her eyes met his. *Is that fear for herself or me? Hate and anger for me or for him? What have I done?*

Rain turned to pelting hail as his tears fell. He ran to the tambo, where he'd find and then lose her body, if it was her at all.

Qosku jolted awake on the streets of Voium to find himself leaning against an inn, early morning light shining through the empty streets. First, he noticed the stiffness of his body, bruised, and shook off the awfulness of that dream. Then he noticed the dead bodies lying in the street, blood pooling around them, and the horrible memory of what he'd just somehow lived through returned to him.

He pushed himself to his feet and stared at the bodies of Reyna, Melonih, Floar, and Melizah, twisted and broken. The two Roah'riik were gone. His stomach twisted, and he wondered at why he'd been left alive.

Qosku dragged himself down an alley and knocked on the first door he saw. No response came, so he broke open the door and went in.

He located a bedroom, finding two people dead in the bed. With the blankets ruffled and marks around their necks, he guessed a suffocation struggle took place, hitting both at the same time. The shadow creatures had done the same to him, but he'd survived. The vacant children's bed didn't offer any comfort, even at the lack of blood and children gone.[83] Qosku felt sick, remembering stories about the deepwraiths coming for bad children and strangling parents. A childhood folktale made real.[84]

---

83 About a quarter of the town's homes were hit in this manner. The rest were only made unconscious.

84 There appears to be parallel folktales revolving around these creatures, indicating a history of their practice in both communities. Little is traceable beyond the lore, however. Whatever connection they have, it is very old.

Syago walked down the plush, decorated hall of the upper floor toward the dining hall but stopped, turned around, and began walking back. He stopped, paused, turned again, and continued to the dining hall. It wasn't yet supper time. It was three days since his arrival and time for him to do something real. To save Elisabet, whatever the cost. *Whatever the cost? I've already stolen for her. What if the cost was to murder a defenseless person? What price will I have to pay for what might already be too late?*

The dining room was empty, the table already cleaned from dinner. Running water and dishes clacking could be heard from the kitchen. Syago approached the leaders' curtain. It was forbidden for him to pass, and while he wouldn't normally care about flaunting their rules, it was important that he get on their good side for this. So he shook the curtain and yelled until Jester's hooded mask poked through. What hid behind that facade?

Jester's bells jingled dully. "Yeeeessss?"

"I, uh, I need to speak with King." Syago backed away involuntarily. "If he's available. Or Queen."

Jester's head tilted. "Are you sure you didn't come to play with me?"

He stepped back, unsure when the clown joked or threatened. "Yes. I'm sure. I have a matter of great importance to discuss."

"You're sure you're sure?"

"Please."

He disappeared behind the curtain, head-tail bells jingling. Syago stepped back as King and Queen came in and sat at the head of the table. And, of course, Jester flopped down in the chair just behind Syago.

Trying to ignore the clown behind him, he turned to King, who'd usually been the most rational, if that could be said of him at all. "I know you have my jars."

"You do not!" objected King. Queen shook her head. Both looked slightly disheveled; their costumes were askew.

Syago resisted rolling his eyes and kept them locked on the garish, obscure masks, wishing he could see their eyes, see anything of their faces. "Why did you take them?"

"I didn't take any medicine."

"I didn't say it was medicine. But it was, so clearly you have it."

"Phooey!" said King, shaking gloved fists. "I liked the jars and wanted them for my dissection collection."

"Dear, I told you not to," said Queen. "You already have too many jars and no place to put them."

"I didn't take them." King motioned to Jester. "*He* took them so he could poison then cure the children for a prank-lesson."

"I don't care who or why," Syago said, firmly keeping his face pleasant and voice calm.

King folded his arms. "Good. Because you can't have them."

"We could make you part of the collection." Jester leaned forward, mask inches from Syago's face. "That way, you'd always be with the jars, be *in* them."

Queen nodded and King gestured toward Syago for his response to the offer.

Syago rapped his knuckles on the table to enunciate. "No. You promised us you'd not hurt us but would help us. I need that medicine."

"Oh, who needs medicine?" said Queen, waving a hand. "You probably stole it anyhow."

"My little cousin in Tolgrym needs it. Without it she and the other women will die."

"Phooey! Well, that's really selfish of her then."

Syago steeled himself, breathing deep to ventilate his rage. "How about *I* make *you* an offer. You can keep the jars if you take the medicine to her. Or let me go do it. It's not too far."

"No. We need you here and demand a greater price to be your errand runners." King's voice lowered. "Make us a real offer, boy."

Syago saw then that he was no longer dealing with the gruesomely childish and playful rebel leaders he'd gotten used to. These were those who had burned Tomas alive, took Robertobrus to the bad room, and killed Lügos and Henric before stranding them in the woods.

He leaned forward, throat dry. "What do you want? I'll do anything you want to save her."

"That's better." King raised a gloved hand to Syago's face, smoothing the side then cupping his chin. Syago's skin crawled under the touch. "Any good story has a hero being asked to sell his soul to a classical villain. We're your villains, aren't we? Give us your soul."

Deova help me! "All right. I pledge—"

"No, child," said Queen gently. "We want your soul, not lip service. Your allegiance for when things turn bad, for when Leyta fights us or the Kimoc find us. And should you turn on us, just remember, we'll know where your cousin lives, and Jester needs more playmates. That's our insurance on the bargain. We'll present you one of her belongings as proof the medicine was given. We'll treat you with greater liberty and mercy than the oppressive conqueror's system you've bought into. Now swear us fealty. We know you've done it many times to your lords in the church of make-believe. Do it here, now."

King motioned to the floor, and something in Syago sank, shriveled, and died: Dignity and pretense to being a good person, to his honor, his word, friendship to Leyta, and duty to Count Toriacus.

For Elisabet.

A moment passed of his inability to move, to complete it. Fighting the burning in his eyes, Syago dropped to his knees, bowed deep, then kissed the rings on King's proffered gloved hand, holy relics taken from Cantlgrym. *Deova forgive me!*

King took Syago's hands in his. Syago choked on his words before they came spilling out, damning him. "I-I, Syago de Tolgrym, son of Odiru, swear to you King, Ice King, that from this hour in the future I will be faithful to you with regard to your life, and the members of your body, in good faith and without deception. And neither this castle nor its territory will I seize from you, not I, nor any man or men, woman or women, acting by my advice or instigation. And I will help you to hold, have, and defend against all men and women who might wish to seize or deprive you of all these abovementioned things. And all that I have said will I hold and observe faithfully and without deception, by Deova and these holy relics."

He hated how easily the practiced oath rolled off of his tongue.

I'm sorry, Leyta.

King's voice dropped to a growl. "Your fealty is accepted, now rise."

CHAPTER TWENTY-ONE

In Shadows and Chains

Based on The Hunter's *Parchments*, cc bastica 220;
Scars of the Martyrs, cc bastica 960;
The Nordvargor Testaments, cc bastica 701;

unknown day of Septimosk, 246

Fal'iek woke to sharp pains in his feet. He saw only darkness but felt the cold stone floor beneath him and smelled the mustiness of a dungeon. His body, especially his back and ass, ached against wood column he'd been tied to and the hard floor. He tried to focus on what woke him, testing his wrist bonds and the strength in his legs. No, he wouldn't be walking anytime soon.

Still he struggled, and in his efforts, he noticed the star-twinkling midnight eyes of the shadowmen watching him from across the room. They winked out, then reappeared closer.

"Where are your treazurezzz?" The familiar cold, grating whisper startled him. *"Fall of masterz remainzzz hidden. Lozt relicz, lost piezez, lozt zecretz. Where?"*

He tried to place the location of the voice in the dark, but as before, it was everywhere and nowhere. Nor were there any other movements he could detect. Such powerlessness threatened to make him panic and weep, but he fought it down. "I told you." He coughed. "I don't have what you seek."

The twinkling eyes leveled in front of him, the only visible feature of his dank cell. *"You have knowledge. You know zecretz of your peoplez. Give me that."*

"I wouldn't tell you if I did know. And—" Needles of pain shot up and down his legs and arms of such intensity that he trembled and struggled against his ropes. The agony relented, and he slumped, breathing heavily.

The eyes stood over him, and another pair, looking down on him. He felt sick.

He said nothing, bracing himself. Air escaped his lungs as the black mist poured down his mouth. He closed it, but the fog only rerouted through his nose, burning and filling with a stale, ashen taste. He held his breath, but the fog made him cough, then gasp for air. His head throbbed and consciousness wavered. Then the mists withdrew, to his great relief.

"Now."

"Golk Darc'uk'milaq!" he spat.[85] The stinging and suffocating continued, but Fal'iek maintained his will. But eventually, mercifully, he lost consciousness. He dreamed of the Razhod, black eyes with red irises that glowed in the dark, of their blades and pet devils and lifeless that obeyed them. Of fighting their creatures amidst piles of mangled bodies and watching the Hellfaces tear people apart. Of running from the swinging scythe of old Devilface, Barthandeon himself, through empty corridors in some dungeon. Of seeing his friend suddenly turn on him in a violent rage, screaming fealty to the witchlords. So many failures. The torture resurrected too many of the memories he'd buried.

On occasion, he dreamed of Lil'iek and their children, at times happy to see them, and at times fearful for their well-being in his absence and severely sad that he'd never see them again. Tears fell. The nightmares were interrupted by torturing sessions or respites for food and bodily relief. These sessions continued for many days, possibly weeks. He failed to keep track in such opacity. They didn't even provide light for his disgusting meals. Memories of family and hope of survival kept him breathing. He had to endure. And the tortures brought more nightmares.[86]

He woke again. Too soon, he felt. His body dripped sweat from a nightmare where he fought against Barthandeon outside Voium. Now awake, he could see some light, faint and far away in the dungeon hall through the cell bars. Then the light moved, a small candle being carried. He heard no footsteps, which made him shiver. The candle entered his cell in the claws of one of his shadowy captors. It walked sleekly, holding the candle at a distance from its person, and wore a ragged cloak pulled tight over its slim, black body out of which peered gleaming eyes. In the other hand

---

85 See *Gybiaaw Blackbraid: Born in Winter*, 13

86 See *Luskmord: Atriom Carcerio*, 8

was a small cage of rats. It set both down and snuffed the candle, plunging him into darkness once more.

It whispered, *"Ready for truth?"*

He set his teeth, said nothing.

"Ratsss."

Fal'iek felt two rats land on his lap, a new method. They ran over him with small claws and grimy, wormy tails until they found open skin and began to tear at him, one on his foot and another at his abdomen. Starved, they hungered for his flesh. Unaccustomed to urban animals, he feared this more than the previous tortures. City rats weren't particularly large compared to rodents in the wild, but they could be quick and vicious and, in this particular case, desperate enough to eat him. Their greasy fur and tails titillated the skin around where they gnawed at him. It was slightly less painful than the needles but more repulsive. He reached out to their souls. He preferred using skulls, which were safer, providing a buffer between him and the creature's minds. He was experienced enough that he could connect directly with physical touch, bringing full exposure to the awful rabidness existing within. Their biting and clawing distracted his concentration, but he focused regardless.

"We wait." He felt another land on him, then a fourth. *"Another. and another. They come till you tell us."*

The added clawing snapped him out of it. Again, he tried to think of something to say, a lie or some truth that might relate to their search, but for the pain and exertion of calming the rats, he came up with nothing. He attempted a spiritual connection again. He perceived creatures in pain; miserable, afraid, and hungry. He showed them his common sentiment and intoned that salvation lay in gnawing through his bonds. Their savage hunger raked at his mind and their bloodthirst became his. It took some pressure and massive concentration to not get lost in that suffering and repugnance. Finally, one snuck away to work at the rope of his hands. Another migrated to the tie around his feet. Any relief he might've gained faded when two more dropped on him. Both went for his face and neck. He clamped his head down to protect his throat. A faint squeak as they sniffed, then clawed and bit at his cheek and lip.

He pushed them into fighting each other over a spot on his face while maintaining the other two cutting his bonds. The rest continued to scrabble about his clothes and bite at skin. Their dirty bodies rolled around his chest, frantically fighting for survival. Finally, one bit the other in the throat. It bled out on his chest, twitching feebly, while the other resumed its pursuit of his lower jaw.

With his mind full of rat, he could take it no longer and bit down on the creature. Its furry, grimy body struggled in his mouth as blood and guts burst out and little bones crunched. The rat in him exulted in it, craved it. He convulsed, his body aching to swallow, to eat them all, but his mind refused. Calling out for himself, for his sanity and humanity to come back, he spat it out. His stomach growled and chest heaved as he sputtered.

Then his torturer hissed. Two rats squealed as it pierced them with black claws, his ropes unfinished. Fal'iek forcefully pushed on all the rats to attack the shadowman. They obeyed readily and, with a great strain of his muscles, he burst the remains of his ropes. As he rose, he felt something grab him by the neck and slam him against the wall. Grabbing one of the rats, he wrung its neck and used the head as he would a skull, forcing any nearby rats to attack the shadowman. The shadowman hissed, and the hold loosened. Fal'iek saw through the minds of the rats their frantic attacks. He twisted out of the slippery tentacle's hold and ran out the cell gate. A sharp pain whipped across his back, and he stumbled.

"Die!"

He ducked, and air whooshed above his head as he dropped to his stomach. He rolled and kicked back, hitting something soft. It connected but felt like his hit simply slid off its willowy form. Another shadowman entered the cell. He reached out through the dead rat and called for more to come, then hit his head on a candle lantern. He quickly clicked the flint switch. Fire sputtered into life, illuminating his gloomy dungeon. Rats flowed in like a river in heed of his call, and now there were too many rats, starving and cruel. A moving floor, they crawled over him, covering him completely, and he moved away from the door. They turned on him till he was covered in the awful swarm. Staying his trembling hands and ignoring the slimy prickings of their assault, he knelt down and focused through the rat body in his hand, breathing deep to focus. He pushed his anger into them, to pit them against each other. Slowly, they turned on each other. He stood up, struggling to maintain control of the whole group, still covered in vermin, until they passed to fling themselves at the shadowmen, who darted about in avoidance. One shadowman leaped to the ceiling, while another came for him. He dashed through the sea of vermin to the door and exited.

He recognized his pack in the hall, piled with Tek'ouk's bag. He grabbed both and drew a knife. He turned for the shadowmen's expected attack but faced Tek'ouk instead, almost stabbing him as he rounded the corner. Tek'ouk halted, their eyes met, then they hurriedly took up their packs and ran the direction Tek'ouk had been heading.

"You've had your own fun, I see," Tek'ouk said as they ran. "You don't want to know what I had to do. I think I scared them off, though."

"They wanted the same things from you? Old relics from the days of their old master?" Turning down the left corridor, they came to a door that opened to a staircase to an upper room illuminated from daylight.

They looked back down the dungeon corridor to see two pairs of candle eyes watching them before winking out.[87]

"Tek, why aren't they pursuing?" Fal'iek asked quietly.

"I can't imagine, but I won't argue it either. Let's go."[88]

87 ibid, 9

88 No accounts say which city they'd been held in, but a Voium cellarway seems most likely.

CHAPTER TWENTY-TWO

RIOT ROT

Based on *Writings of Qosku*, cc bastica 56;
Scars of the Martyrs, cc bastica 1020;

7th of Octubre, 246

Angry people filled the streets of Mantlgrym, yelling and pounding on doors. Nearly too much commotion for Qosku, who could squeeze between people but got jostled and shoved about easily. The latest publications of rage prose had all the tenants and laborers, both mastozon and pale, united into a torrent that thrashed the main square. A widowed mother with children at home and who cleaned meat for the town pounded on the doors of the Court of Ashor, demanding the barons and the count show themselves. Another mother who worked all day as both a seamstress and midwife yelled at the doors of the chapel for her alms back. Numerous men in hide tunics raged about being made to leave on daily expeditions that the lords never accompanied.[89]

Various penal instruments stood erect with men and women tied to them. A wooden priory head-locked a man named Kask for shame-filled display; his head and hands protruded from the wood and iron binding and were splattered with rotted food. Others locked into similar devices shouted back in anger at the people, but he stared dispassionately. Qosku had talked to this Kask and liked him not at all, and yet despite his crudeness, Qosku felt the thief deserved none of the public torture. But at least he'd survived, while others were put on spiked chairs, coffins, or beams used to break the condemned.[90]

---

89 See also *The Schiltron of Magodeoz*, 88

90 See *Losnin Liberado Kani*, 26

Qosku didn't speak Asturion well, but their words in this fury were clear enough to him. He moved toward the main square, squeezing and sliding between people to where he knew his prey to be waiting. Thirteen days since the True Night of Voium and he hadn't been able to find Fal'iek or Tek'ouk, but he did find a lot of strange activity taking place in Mantlgrym. The horrid demon, Knave, appeared some nights, taking Qosku on a chase in vain and foiling all of his traps with animal and human carcasses, laughing at him. He hadn't intended to stay this long but had to know what the Royal Chaos was up to.

Tired of pushing through the crowds, he climbed a statue to view over their heads. He caught sight of Tek'ouk and Fal'iek running across the rooftops and felt a flood of relief that they weren't dead. Climbing down from a roof, they leaped onto the wall of the Ashor building and deftly slipped into one of the windows. None of the crowds gave any notice, so Qosku decided to follow.[91] By the time he'd ascended a building, jumped into a window, and sneaked downstairs, the mob's sounds had grown angrier. He exited the room and collided into a guard.

"Assassin!" the guard yelled.

"No, I no kill. I follow Fal'iek." Qosku ducked under the guard's spear and gauntleted hand, then darted past him as two more appeared. A sense of panic welled up in him; he could easily dispatch these men but didn't want to hurt them. They only served their families. He hesitated only a second and prepared to go the other direction when Fal'iek emerged between the two guards.

"Oh, I can vouch for this young man too," Fal'iek said as Tek'ouk appeared behind him. "That is, if you agree that I am here in the service of our alliance rather than subterfuge."

"Dreist, bring them all downstairs," said one, clearly the captain, judging by the marks on his shoulder plates. "See what 'ey think."

The men nodded, as did Fal'iek, at Qosku, who fell into step behind him. They entered the council chamber, a discordant room of numerous important people, all bigger and more stately than Qosku cared for. He could tell some were merchants, others military leaders, and all in finer clothing than those out in the mob. He found a new source of scorn for this society, the opulence of these in the face of the rest.

91 *indistinguishable scribbles*

"Warchief Fal'iek!" a bulky, surly gentleman bellowed and waddled over to them in a suit of fine wool. "My good man, come here. You must help us out of this."

"I'm not sure I can do much, Count Gallegom," Fal'iek replied. "However, if it's related to the Royal Chaos or black fog, I'm more than willing."

"Yes, well, you see, that group with their clown and their little pet, they've been spreading lies about us, sending out smear posts and fake letters about me and my barons, and now the town is in an uproar. We've got half our guards in here, the other half out there yelling at us."

"So I noticed," Fal'iek said, eyes hard. "Do you think it wise to have so few on the walls?"

"If those people outside want to hate our governance so much, they can experience life without us. See what happens when there's no wall coordination."

"But you risk losing more this way. If not from monsters then the Royal Chaos themselves could be coming in. Is Alfonsor still captain of the guard?"

"Yes, yes, he is. Listen, I know you don't agree and it's not your place to, in any case, but that gang is threatening everything! This rebellion they're trying to push is a threat to the foundation of our entire civilization. Normally, I wouldn't worry about some intrepid band, but somehow they've ignited this foolishness among the people. And look what they gave us a tenday past." Gallegom handed Fal'iek a worn parchment. Qosku peeked past his arm at its ugly scrawls.

> *Hi.*
> *I, Jester, message in behalf of the Royal Chaos:*
> *We're heer to end the rein of all powers and secrets*
> *And we know youve got more secrets than youve got powers*
> *I may be a clown, but yore the joak*
> *Your punchline is cumming*
> *Your slipknot is slipping*
> *The people are your krops*
> *You reave them like korn feelds*
> *With nine inch nails and chevels*
> *Disturbed at yor deftoned fails*
> *From your fancy spancy mansons*

A ministry that is old and korupt
Will end abrupt
Fiasco atmosfearo
Notorius public enemees
We profets of rage 4 see
That the bell tolls for thee
A rotting chrisis
A breaking of the benchmen
Gobsmacked and slayered
Now face the rath of Truth
Or start telling it
And abdicate your thrones
Or dye on them

Signed
Mourning Jester
Nether Knave
Thunder Knight
Fire Queen
Ice King
The Royal Chaos
Nas los nin dyabol[92]

Qosku noticed that Fal'iek resisted a smile in the corner of his mouth. *Is he trying not to laugh? Why is it funny?* Tek'ouk hid his face by looking away.

Qosku blurted, "Is any of it truth?"

Gallegom sputtered, "No, of course no—wait, who's this? Get him out of here!"

"He's with me," Fal'iek said. "And of no concern to you. But this letter resembles what happened at Cantlgrym."

Mercifully, the tall and thin Captain Alfonsor de Braga, wearing a gambeson, strode over and cut in. "We could use skilled eyes and hands such as yours in rooting out the enemy, which I believe is already inside the walls and on the attack. We're tied up in here at the moment, but otherwise there's no way out of this and it's their move."

Tek'ouk moved up beside Fal'iek, and Qosku caught the hard look

---

92 The scrawl here, on the preserved letter, is hard to distinguish. It might be another language, but one theory is that it's an odd and illegible attempt to say, "Not of/with the devil."

between them before Fal'iek said, "You realize how this will look, right? You'll be saved by two Kimoc warriors and that is how we must have it. We'll get better treaties honored for this."

Tek'ouk's eyes shifted to the captain; both Roah'riik gazes pierced. Demanding.

But the captain and count were unfazed. Warriors to warriors, they nodded and turned to a map spread out on a table. Qosku stood next to Tek'ouk, who'd hung back as an outsider with disdain that shone clearly to Qosku, if not everyone else.

Gallegom pointed at several marks checkering the city on the map. "We've sighted the group, or some of its members, around here," he said. "If they're not out yet, they will be soon. It is only difficult for us to leave the building with the crowds as such."

Fal'iek and Tek'ouk nodded thoughtfully. Qosku knew them to be experienced trackers, though that was in the wild; in a city, it would be different. On their way out, Tek'ouk muttered to Fal'iek something about how they always end up doing the dirty work for the palemen, and how they were siding with the wrong side, and Qosku gathered from his meager Kimoc that they debated which side, people or nobles, was best to aid in this.[93]

They decided on the troupe. The three left the way they'd come in, climbing from the window to the roof, then running along the roof to an adjacent one, when fire burst out to their left above the town square. The rioting hushed.

"Greetings everyone," came the loud, dynal-enhanced voice of Jester. "I'm pleased that we could meet here today. The time has come for a reckoning. Our priests, rulers, and aristocrats have much to account for, do they not?"

A murmur of agreement shivered throughout the crowd as the warriors searched for the speaker. Jester hopped up onto the top corner of a building and splayed out his arms, pointing at King and Queen at both ends. Jester continued in the ethereal tones of rage. "Today, I come not to mock or mourn, but to avenge."

Qosku and the two Roah'riik ran the rooftops toward the enemy. Qosku jumped to the outer side and continued running. Fal'iek and Tek'ouk soon joined him.

"As carefully detailed in the letters you've been reading," King began, "the charges brought against these messers are many and most disturbing. First, we must hear their defense. Defenders?"

---

93 See *Losnin Liberado Kani, 23* on the Saqra's Cult.

There were none, as the accused stayed behind their locked doors. Continued King, "Silence is the sign of guilt! Very well, then it is time for a verdict and I judge them guilty. What say you?"

Sparse cheers rose from the crowd, who now gave full but wary attention. A deep hum came from Jester, subtle and quiet at first, almost imperceptible, unless you knew to listen for it. Qosku had prepared some cloth stubs exactly for this to stuff in his ears and muffle the sound. Fal'iek saw him do it and followed suit. Qosku smiled inwardly that he did have tricks to teach the veteran.

The King's voice crescendoed. "They're supposed to be your principal defenders at the gates, yet the reality is you've defended them more! They make you go into the hell outside to hunt and gather, then they glut on it while parsing out sparings to you. They take indulgences and lock you down or hang you high for your own evils. They've kidnapped the children of Voium and come for you! These rotten imbeciles are dirty and rancid—can you smell it? We've smelt and refused them with raised fist. They have cheated, bribed, stolen, lied. This bad religion keeps us under their feet. This is hell."

Every word seemed to punch out as he spoke, and the Song of Fury enthralled them now, bringing out exuberant cheers to every syllable. Fal'iek led Tek'ouk and Qosku along the rooftops around their backsides to stay out of sight.

"We'll make this a day to remember and bless the fall of Northlane as it burns red.[94] These nobles lie in bed pretending we won't notice the affair, but we've peeked. They lord over us in their council hall, a coffin for misers. They preach at us from their stone chapel, a tomb of bigots." The crowd roared under the momentum of Jester's tune. King raised his arm to emphasize each line. "You have died for them. Worked for them. Fed them. Listened to them and obeyed every little law they throw at you. And what have they done for you? The nobility is useless in the best of times. Now they're as good as slavers, blasphemers, murderers! TYRANTS! NO MORE NOBILITY!"

The mob roared in unison.

---

94 Northlane was a street name where the nobility lived. Calling it Northlane indicates a deep understanding of the people's mindset.

"Burn the coffins!"

The mob roared.

"Topple the tombs!"

The mob roared.

"Kill the tyrants!"

The mob charged.

Like a dam breaking, building doors fell inwards as the people pushed in. Moments later, the mob dragged out quivering noblemen, merchants, and priestesses. One or two barons appeared, struggling in terror against their captors. One of the barons almost directly below them screamed, and Qosku thought of how he might pull the man out, but the circle tightened and several clubs swarmed in until all that could be seen were the bloody sticks swinging. At another spot, a priest's body was held aloft over the crowd, bloody, twisted, and unmistakably dead. Qosku saw Kask break out of his hold, but the mob paid him no attention, too frenzied to even bother with the instruments on their new prey. Above the din of it all lay Jester's angry hum. Qosku wondered at how the people failed to notice the manipulation they were under.

A sick mixture of joy and rage composed the cheers as Jester danced on the rooftop, singing. Qosku, fighting those invading sentiments with his own, arrived to it with Fal'iek and Tek'ouk beside him. Queen turned and a flame burst from her small white gloved hands toward them. Fal'iek dove to the side and almost slid off the roof, but he grabbed the ledge, hanging.

Before Queen could fire at him again, Qosku jumped at her with a swipe from his clawed gauntlet, using the rage fueled by Jester's song, while an arrow snapped in from Tek'ouk's bow. Queen whirled and the arrow sank into the thick bell of her dress. King shot darkfire at Qosku, who slipped, rolling once, then catching the edge of the roof. Tek'ouk now exchanged fire and arrow with Queen. Fal'iek shot at the dancing clown.

Shifting to hate, but more focused than the wildness in the song, Qosku ran up the shingled roof toward Queen. She deftly sidestepped with a twirl, and he reversed direction in a quick switch to rage to come at her, sliding under her fire with a ground kick to her legs, but she hopped back. Then darkfire was coming at him from behind. Arrows flew.

"Attack Jester!" Fal'iek shouted. "Stop the riot."

Qosku let himself roll down the roof, the only way out of the crossfire. Fal'iek continued his fight with King, arrows to fire blasts. Tek'ouk still fought with Queen, ducking and striking. Jester pranced atop a different building. Qosku made as if to charge King, briefly drawing his darkfire, but turned and, nearly slipping on the ice that now coated the roof, redirected to Jester's side.

Jester danced as if Qosku were not about to claw his arm off, but when Qosku did come in, the clown nimbly skipped to the side and kicked Qosku in the leg, toppling him. Jester continued the song, one that seemed to fill the whole city, and threw a dagger at Qosku. He barely snapped his arm up in time to deflect it, bursts of anger sentiments giving him speed, then he jumped for a spinning kick, putting that energy into it at the last moment, accelerating the kick in the air. Somehow, Jester ducked under it and was back on the top of the roof. He threw a bolas as Qosku slid his landing. Without time, Qosku then jumped up in a forward dive and caught it as it zipped under him. He landed on hands and knees, threw the bolas back, then sprang forward, up the roof like a mountain cat full of sentimental energy. Jester sidestepped again but missed his dagger thrust as Qosku dug his right claw in Jester's torso. Jester gave him a hard shove.

He bounced on the roofside once, failing to grab it, and slid off into the mob below. Their presence softened his landing. Fueled by Jester's song, they took ire with him, grabbing him. He tried to worm free, but there were too many, a swarm of hands grabbing, yelling, pulling, punching. A new panic gripped him, for they were everywhere, irrational in their anger and hate. They punched his stomach and slapped his face. At first, he resisted the urge to fight back in full; he didn't want to kill them, but the more he resisted, the more they continued, calling him digger, dirtskin, and savage. Old trauma returned, but he maintained focus.

They began pulling him closer to the center of the square, to the gallows. He struggled, but they only tightened their grip, twisting his arm to stop resistance. Hands everywhere, faces snarling. Trembling in panic, he reached within himself, swept aside the fear and focused on the anger, on the memories, pushing it into his limbs and twisting himself. As his limbs broke free, they came in again, grabbing, swarming. Weapons fell, blood everywhere. He tried ducking and slipping between their legs, but they blocked him. Arms on him, he began using his claws. Slashing, cutting, kicking them away. They grew feral, snarling, pressing in despite the pain. Blood sprayed. That wild look in their eyes frightened Qosku more than any monster he'd seen outside.

He felt drained of anger but called up the last of it to charge through, pushing them aside, heading for the alleyway. People grabbed and yelled, tried to hit him with broken bottles and clubs, sometimes succeeding—he wasn't sure. He felt many things in the mass of chaos but focused on powering toward his escape, hurting as many as was necessary.

The crowd thinned, as did their efforts to take him, and finally he cleared into an alley empty of people, gasping. *But what of the fight above?* He ran around the building, still limping slightly, in search of a way to climb up. Suddenly, there was a crash in the garbage pile further down, and Fal'iek crawled out.

With a frantic look at Qosku, he asked, "Where's Tek'ouk?"

"I no see him," Qosku said. Then sounds down the alley drew his attention; the mob saw them and shouted, pointing. With a look at each other, Qosku and Fal'iek ran the other way, the crowd charging after them. They wove in between alleys but soon moved to the streets, where more took up the charge. Qosku struggled to keep up on his wounded leg, but it wasn't long before Fal'iek brought them to the city wall.

They scaled the stairs and, with Fal'iek's vine, belayed down quick enough and with little danger due to the lack of guards. Once down, Fal'iek called for their mewil'ishyuuks using a piece of a skull, and Qosku asked, "What about Tek'uk?"

"Tek'ouk," Fal'iek corrected. "He took a wound and fell off the roof. If anyone's capable of getting out of there alive, it's him. But we have something more urgent..." He pointed at the sky. "We have more pressing matters."

Qosku saw Knave carrying something low and slow from the weight—Jester. Fal'iek took his bow from his shoulder and drew his last arrow while breaking into a run.

Qosku had an idea. "Wait, we follow. You track them."

Fal'iek slowed and regarded Qosku just as the mewil'ishyuuks sauntered up. He nodded, returned the arrow and bow to his shoulder, and they were off, keeping pace far behind. It was not long before they passed Westgate when it cracked open. To the immense surprise of the two warriors, people began pouring out. Qosku recognized Count Gallegom, Captain Alfonsor, and even Dreist the guard amongst the dignitaries and civilians—evidently having escaped the raging mob through a hidden back tunnel. Looking at them, Fal'iek slowed his pursuit briefly before running ahead. He released his last arrow at their fleeing quarry, falling short as it began to glide away.[95]

95 The controversy of the event and those following have led to questions and skepticism. Numerous other writers deemed reliable corroborate the accounts of these warriors. All written accounts around it are mostly coherent with each other, wayward orations notwithstanding.

CHAPTER TWENTY-THREE

REFUGE IN THE WILD

Based on *The Hunter's Parchments*, cc bastica 223;
Writings of Qosku, cc bastica 40;
Scars of the Martyrs, cc bastica 950;

7th of Octubre, 246

Fal'iek turned to the group of roughly sixty Mantlgrymians, and a deep horror set in. They'd escaped through Northlane's hidden understable entrance and were fleeing the city without the protection of a wagon or a sufficiently large garrison, putting themselves in mortal danger outside the walls.

He looked up at the fading demon and its cargo. *So that's the demon*, he thought. It looked like a pak'ak of Kimoc lore, but more animalian, and clearly headed for Thornwood. Motherwood.

Sounds of shouting snapped him back to the situation at hand. Women were screaming and crying about being outside the walls, and the men looked equally frightened. Those more in control worked to calm the rest, even though the gate had been pushed shut and locked by the rioters, dooming these people to exile in the wild. He cared more to go back for Tek'ouk than aid them but re-entering would be difficult and he trusted in Tek'ouk's own ability to hide or escape.

Violent cries could still be heard from the other side. The mob had turned on itself, a city insurgency and smaller counter-insurgency.[96] Chaos as King and Queen tried to regain control in Jester's absence.

Well, either way, it's of no concern to me anymore. And what do I owe to this group now stranded here? His current hunt outside Quoak had long outlasted

---

96 I doubt it happened so immediately.

its intended duration, and the Quoarn'riik would be furious, no less Lil'iek. But if they were to need help in the future, they had to give it now. He protected his people by protecting everyone. *If one of us isn't safe, none of us are.*

He turned to them. Outside, in the shadow of the wall, peasants and workers were yelling at the nobles and guard captain. Some priestesses and wealthier merchants stood aside, willing to let them take the heat for the current course of events and stay on the good side of the workers. But one worker, a large blacksmith, rounded on them too. "Wipe that smug smile off of your faces, this is your fault too. You worked deals with them at our expense. You cheated us just as much as them!"

"Yeah, and now we're in the outside!" said a smaller man, a cobbler if Fal'iek could place him. The shouts riled up the others, becoming an indiscernible din.

Fal'iek looked about uneasily. Nothing yet stalked them on the hilly plain.

A large woman stormed up to the count. "Is it true that you're behind the kidnappings?"

"Wha-no, of course not!" The count tore his gaze from the hills to meet her eyes, his hand already fingering the scepter in his hand.

"What are you even doing out here?" The blacksmith pointed his finger into Count Gallegom's chest, an act Fal'iek knew none of them would've dared do under normal circumstances. "Your fight is in there. The rest of the resistance, those who couldn't flee like us, are still in there fighting for YOU! You don't get to flee and hide!"

Fal'iek didn't like the direction this was going. "If I may—"

"You stay outta this, dirty birdhead," the blacksmith snarled as he turned to push away Fal'iek, but he was suddenly on the ground, with Qosku on top, twisting his arm. Although impressed by Qosku's drop, Fal'iek thought it wouldn't help matters. A woman muttered to others about the "two savages."

"I shouldn't have to remind you that you're all in serious, immediate danger," Fal'iek began loudly. "We don't need to help you. I'd prefer tracking the true enemy. But you have more to worry about than each other right now. Right now, you need each other. We need to get everyone to a walled city. It's still morning. If we start now, we can reach any of the three nearest cities by nightfall."

"Birdhead's right," said the cobbler, looking at the others. "If we don't start now, we'll not reach a city by dark."

A mumble of agreement swept the group. The slurs annoyed Fal'iek more than hurt; however, it did signal an attitude that would prove problematic if they needed to listen to him. He would have to tread lightly here. "Which town will take all of you in?" he asked.

"Voium would take us in," Gallegom said, puffing his cheeks in an odd attempt to look unshaken, already out of his element in every possible way.

Alfonsor and the merchants nodded their agreement.

"Not Voium," the cobbler said, shaking his head. "Not with what happened there. That place is cursed like Bokhor now. I's not for touching it. As well the road runs by that damned forest and is a longer walk, *and* I's thinking I not going with *them* either." He nodded at the count and his wealthy companions. "I say we go to Maolgon, I got family theres."

A carpenter added, "Voium's full of them arrogant scholars. Maolgon's more like us." Others nodded.

The blacksmith, who Qosku had let up at Fal'iek's silent gesture, said, "No, I think 'es right. Voium might take us longer and by Thornwood at that, but it's by far the safer bet. Maolgon 'as no room and they's not welcoming. They never liked us either."

"Yes." Gallegom cleared his throat. "In fact, I urge you to come with us to Voium, even Tolgrym is more welcoming and open than Maolgon despite my best efforts with Count Guilliomachen. Though they might open for us if I pay and pressure them in person, but only if my standing remains..."

"Your standing is worth mounds less than what it's been before," snapped an old spinstress and midwife.

"Whatever it be," Gallegom said, watching the skies, which had grown thicker with blackbirds by the minute, "it better be done now. Right then, those for Voium over here with us, and petty pickers for Maolgon over there."

The crowd divided up, with Qosku walking to the Maolgon side.

Fal'iek gaped at him in disbelief.

"They will need help," Qosku said. A truth, for though they had more men, and armed ones, they also had more women and children, also armed but far less so. "And they refugees like I was. I not let them die like my friends."

"Qosku, listen to me," Fal'iek said firmly as Gallegom led his group west and the Maolgon group departed for the north, "you can't save them. Even with you, it will not be enough. They will be denied at the wall and die to the wild outside."

"Then I attend them and carry their tale," Qosku said firmly. Alone on the plain of mounds, the pair stood, the wind blowing in rainclouds from the sea over Thornwood. "If I not save refugees, I no let them be forgotten. I am they and they are me."

Fal'iek felt as though he was seeing this boy for the first time. He was wise beyond his fourteen years, and braver than any man. "All right, then, I hope you survive to carry their tale. Go with the fury of the wild, my brother." They clasped hands and hugged briefly before joining their groups.

In the Voium group, anger had faded to fear—a death knell, for anger provided fuel to inner fire, one they would desperately need in the coming hours, as opposed to fear, which made people do terribly stupid things in moments of crisis.[97] The weight of the group pressed Fal'iek down as they hurried among the plain's rocky mounds.

And it was not long before the rain began. *Of course it would rain, why would the blessed wild make dying even remotely pleasant?* The rain fell light, then grew harder, turning their path to mud and puddles. He watched the people ahead: afraid but determined, willful, tough, and strong. Holding up the rear, he found himself evaluating and estimating them through heaven's tears, as the Asturions said. He still hated them, but they were stout, as all of Nevermore had to be. Even the wealthier group defied Kimoc views that placed the Asturions as soft in their comforts. Of course, Gallegom, the most unfit of the group, had been trained in his youth. He was a dynast but one largely out of practice. Merchants traveled all the time and so were competent enough in their own right. The youngest child was six, with a knife and small shield; the women were similarly armed. Of himself, he was prepared with human bones as a shield against the bodies and skulls of vermin and carrion feeders, but nothing that wouldn't keep a herd of daemog or pack of malwolves from tearing through them like leaves in the wind. At least darkemorg meant fewer creatures.

In times such as these, he wished there were eternals or creator spirits for him to petition for aid, and to blame. *But no, we are our own mistakes, our own responsibility.* He was encouraged by how they went from fighting at the wall to supporting each other on this dangerous path.

Fal'iek should've seen it coming but for the thick rain, being in the rear,

---

97 *See Luskmord: Atriom Carcerio, 10*

and the thing hiding by Thornwood: A blackwood willow tree of furacán size, the biggest he'd ever seen, charged them with alarming speed.

The towering monstrosity lashed at them with long, leafy tendrils hanging from the ends of knotted branches. With a gurgling shriek, it attacked, whipping and grabbing hungrily at the screaming, fleeing crowd through the rain and mud. Tentacle-branches snatched people off of the ground as they dispersed in panic and either stuffed them into its roots or sucked them somewhere into the branches while its roots crawled it along the ground.

Arrows would be useless against its bark, so Fal'iek drew both knives and ran at it. He maneuvered around the lashing tendrils. The tree hissed and caught him in three leafy tentacles, too quick and strong for him to avoid. It whipped him up to the branches with another, the blacksmith.

Nearly panicking, Fal'iek cut through the tendril that held his leg and fell to the base of a branch, managing to hold on with his knives to a mossy malwolf skeleton. At least three maws cracked open between branch arms, but he was more surprised to see their resemblance to human mouths: lipped and flattoothed. *Why do they get stranger as they grow bigger?*

The blacksmith was pulled in by several tendrils, yelling as he struggled to fight back, but it was a fight cut short as a set of jaws caught him. He screamed as the blood splattered onto Fal'iek and continued to do so until his body was munched into the hole; the screams died on his gaping face. Folding in on himself, the spine snapped with a crack. Before Fal'iek could stop himself, he vomited all over the knobby branches in front of him. The mouths gurgled in delight as tendrils pulled the body out and threw it away, seeds latched onto the blacksmith's back—the mouths on top weren't for feeding but seeding.

Fal'iek considered throwing something into the maws to wound it, anything to keep it off the fleeing people, but he struggled to keep hold and not fall to the same fate. The branch he clung to heaved and moved, trying to shake him. One thought remained clear in his head: *Defend your species against the rest.*

Holding on for his life, he threw one knife into the nearest hole, aiming for the softer tongue deeper down. The blade of bone stuck, and he lost his grip in the effort, but the creature's gargling turned to a whimper of pain. Fal'iek fell as it flailed, landing hard on a large, gnarled root but softening his fall with a roll. A tentacle from beneath caught his arm and began dragging him under. He cut at it with his remaining knife but had to shift focus to avoid being crushed by the larger leg-roots. They beat and clawed at the ground around him as he rolled and tucked, then he was under the tree at the edge of its feeding center with another who'd been pulled in. Instead of a maw, a web of thin roots came down on them in the suffocating orifice. Wiry brown stems needled at him, searching for the sustenance of his body. The other man screamed and fought back in a frenzy.

Fal'iek began cutting a way out. The tree hissed angrily, and the roots wrapped him up, binding him, while he slashed desperately. In feeble light, he saw the other man get drained of fluids and flesh by the roots that laced him, his body withering into a husk. As the feeder-roots pricked and pried into Fal'iek, the veteran Roah'riik panicked and started cutting at the roots that bit into his skin. The tree shrieked and roots invaded Fal'iek's flesh as his arm weakened. Blood drained and nausea came; he was losing strength.

He made a final effort to connect to the tree's frenzied mind and prompt it to remove its wounded roots. As his first time bonding to a furacán he was immediately hit by a wall of screams in its twisted mind, stealing his breath. Swimming in its pain-filled shrieks and wails he gritted his teeth, trembling, and forced the prompting through. Though clinging to sanity and self he soon found himself babbling nonsense. Finally, the roots gave in and released him, spraying tree-blood and saliva all over. He deftly rolled out of the mouth, getting pummeled by the lip and surrounding leg-roots.

He stumbled away, delirious from blood loss, and pulled out the feeder-roots that'd taken hold of his body and been cut loose, growling in pain. Rain cleaned off the blood but not the sticky saliva, and he now fought to keep up with the half of the group who'd survived and were now fleeing. Behind, the tree released a gargling howl.

Once the tree was out of sight, they slowed, several people even stopped, sobbing and saying they couldn't go on. Fal'iek and others prodded them forward, encouraging them to fortify and strong forth, for this was not only about them but also those who depended on them. The road above all is no place to weaken.

The rains abated, finally, and the day waned, as did everyone's energy. But they were a tough people, such that even when night descended and Voium was in view, but still too far to make before the lifeless came, they did not lose heart.

As they neared Voium, come the bodies did, slow and thin at first, but building as the large group drew attention. The armed men on the outside cut down those that approached, only as necessary. Paces away from the wall, bodies of beast and man thronged the group, though thinner than what Fal'iek had expected, to his relief. Banging on the gate at the late hour, unannounced, the people waited breathlessly for entry, almost without hope. A wounded Gallegom pled their case through Eastgate as Fal'iek and the other warriors defended their outer edge.

Eventually, the count prevailed, and Fal'iek closed ranks as the group retreated into the cracked gate, where exhaustion and gratitude hit him with sudden ferocity.

Qosku followed the group of city workers and soldiers through the rain and mud. He remained no more than an observer, a silent guardian to them. He took interest in the children, having been one himself in his time as a refugee. The parents wouldn't let him near them, though, clinging protectively to them, looking around constantly in fear of attacks. Any sliver of resentment he'd held toward them vanished. Running between two women, he briefly imagined himself one of them. But the ache was too much, so he focused on being present, and male. The lack of attacks surprised him until the rains abated. Then the birds came.

It started with smaller quervosk blackbirds, then larger gurows joined in. They dived and pelted the people, pecking and clawing at them viciously. Qosku did what he could, but the birds had an aerial advantage. And so the air around their heads filled with black and bloody feathers, beaks, and claws. The assault flurried until the group crouched down and slashed upward, together driving the blackbirds away.

Finally, they exited the Mounds of Fury and emerged onto the Catalor Plains, where Maolgon sat distantly in view. A few leagues of grassy terrain separated them from safety. They ran, reaching Southgate just as the evil hour neared. Some grew wary of a growing dust cloud on the horizon and prayed, signing the sun cross over their faces and chests. Qosku prayed to his ancestors and the eternals, wishing he had the mountain leaves with him for the complete ritual.

The wall guards watched them, stone-faced; they did not open the door. The peasants insisted on speaking to Count Guilliomachen, but the guards said nothing. Finally, a baron and a bishopess appeared and heard out the arguments. Qosku understood little of what was going on, but felt cold and anxious—he knew they weren't going to be let in.

As the dust cloud grew, mixed with daemog smoke from the herd now faintly visible, the people began shouting. The cobbler pointed at the approaching herd. "If you don't let us in, we'll die. You're killing us."

"I'm sorry," said the baron from the wall, "but, family or not, we can't risk letting in rebels from Mantlgrym. And we've no room either."[98]

"But we're not with that gang!" called the cobbler. "The clown tried to have us killed. It's because of them that we're even here instead of our own homes."

"This is insane!" an older woman shouted. "You would let us die because you're afraid and inconvenienced!"

"It's a risk we can't afford," shouted the baron. "I have to put my people first. You really should've thought this through beforehand. Or maybe you, in traditional Mantlgrym fashion, thought we owed you everything and *must* let you in." The bishopess nodded alongside him.

Qosku looked around at the group. He hadn't thought of them being Chaos spies or rebels. They didn't look it to him, but he supposed that wouldn't be an easy thing to spot. Yet surely they'd let in the children. Growing impatient with a debate that seemed more and more petty in view of the immediate danger that approached, he cupped his hands to his mouth and yelled, "THEN SEND AID TO FIGHT OFF THE DAEMOG HERD!"

"We shall help you from up here," the baron tried to return a more positive and encouraging tone, but people shouted back in protest. "For we'll not risk our men for another count's people, no less one who shies on our trade and hunting agreements. You should've known we at Maolgon fortify strong against immigrant robbers and cheats. And we've no tolerance for violent rebellions. We owe you some sympathy but no aid, aid we give only as a kindness."

His last words were barely heard over the deafening thunder of hooves and furious bull snorts. Wreathed in smoke, dust, and ember, the herd halted

---

98 *ibid,* 13

several feet away, glaring with hollow eyes. The herd circled the terrified humans, bleating in a hellish haze. Qosku joined the front line of armed men. Mothers shouted up to the guards, pleading for the children's entrance as the daemogs finally charged. Their pleas were ignored as the guards released a volley of arrows and dynal attacks at the herd. But a herd of daemog in full charge heeds no attack nor front line of protruding weapons. Their tough hides, skulls, and horns plowed in, and the screams began, mixing with the callous baying and bellowing of the vengeful beasts.

Qosku crouched and, despite his uppercuts to the beasts' softer under areas, was soon kicked and tossed by horn.

Hollow eyes glared and fire snorted out of the daemogs' nostrils in a frenzy of savage bucking and kicking. Qosku had barely risen from his fall when he was tossed again, this time into the wall. All was chaos. He could fight many foes at once, but here he was powerless in the frenzy. He tried to strike out again, but his clawed gauntlet only grazed the monster before he was knocked back. All around him, the daemog herd pressed without any tangible resistance, pushing and trampling the people against the wall and burning all as they went. Blood, smoke, mud, and bodies flew, and fires burned. Next to Qosku, a man was smashed into the wall and gored as the bull's horns ravaged him. Qosku reflexively ducked under an airborne burning child. A woman got caught between two bulls and was smashed between them. He tried to launch off the wall at them but the storm of haze and death was impossible to aim at.

For what felt like endless hours, Qosku watched then attacked forward only to be shoved back in a daze as the herd massacred the group of refugees. Attacks hit the daemogs from above, but they were so vastly insufficient, even hitting some of the people by accident, it added to Qosku's feeling of dissonance, a complete lack of coherent sense in the world.

As the massacre subsided, Qosku slid from his position leaning against the wall to sitting among the bodies. Devilborn shapes moved through the smoke and dust, further trampling the destroyed bodies. He considered hiding under a corpse but felt too weak and in shock as he'd never been before. In the fading torrent, a daemog approached him, its vacant eyes no less than a hand within his. It stamped a corpse and snorted embers, violence never diminishing. Qosku didn't even wince, exhausted and resigned and numb. The dull eyes looked at him, and Qosku got a sense of meeting the monster, the outerwild. He wondered why it hated him so much. But those soulless eyes made him feel that the animosity was imagined. *It doesn't hate; it's vicious by instinct and appearance, but inside indifferent.*

He was sure it would finish him too but instead it snorted smoke in disinterest and disappeared into the burning field. The daemog herd left the gate untouched. As the herd stormed off into a red sunset, Qosku found himself on his knees, the only one still alive. Weeping and aware that within an hour the bodies around him would begin to rise, he still could not bring himself to leave. He didn't feel as though he could ever rise again.

CHAPTER TWENTY-FOUR

A Face Full of Masks

Based on *Leyta's Journals* cc bastica 60;
The Hunter's Parchments cc bastica 228;

17th of Octubre, 246

Leyta flipped the key through her fingers absentmindedly. It hadn't worked on anything, and she now kept it more as a memento than for any practical reason. She'd broken into a few other doors like the first—they were mostly basic supplies and strange objects she didn't understand. Not even a weapons room. She deduced that the dynal-related possessions had been entrusted to more secure locations. It didn't help that this was an old castle with everything changed to accommodate hiding underground. She was beginning to wonder at the unexplored areas of that small cavern under the dungeon and the curtained-off area behind the dining room.[99]

Both she and Syago had made several unsuccessful attempts at counter-pranking the Royal Chaos. He'd unsuccessfully rigged their chairs for collapse, and she'd spoiled the food, and they acted as though they hadn't noticed. Of course, the masked leaders didn't appear to truly eat anything in the feast-tea parties. Befriending the crew and thugs hadn't accomplished anything either. Aside from that, Syago had dropped all mention of escape or overthrow and even urged her to just wait. She supposed his near-death failure had really changed him.

Her commanding rod, however, was mostly completed. She'd added eye marks on the bottom, representing wisdom and knowledge. The final step would be endowing it with one of the Chaos's foci. She felt certain

---

99 *See also Reptilium Nimrød, 76*

229

that they had one beneath their costumes, or how else could they use the powers that they did?

She heard a dull bell toll thrice: suppertime. She stuffed the rod under her dress and entered the hall to walk with the others—and perhaps overthrow some royal pretenders.

In the dining hall, she took her usual seat near the head of the table, between Gabriol and Syago, who stared despondently at the head of the table, where empty seats sat. Leyta frowned; none of them had come in the past four days. *Where are they? Why aren't they here?*

Suddenly, Jester walked in. A few days past, Syago had seen him enter the tower with a shredded tunic, but now Jester wore a new one. They guessed it to be from a malwolf or white rabbit from outside, lamenting there was no further damage done to the damn clown.

"Jester," Leyta said, clearing her throat to get his attention. "Where is Robertobrus? What did you do to him?"

The room stared at him as he stood silently. He threw his arms out wide and said, "How about a joke? Why did the boy drop his candied fruit?" No one answered, so Jester shouted gleefully, "He was mauled by a mabin'guarik!"

As always, silence met his anti-joke, and he bowed before taking a seat. Then Chester and Mungo placed trays of food before them, and after poking and smelling it for safety, she and the others began to eat. Though often barely tolerable, the food given to them at these meals were a lot better than the evening meal—the most repulsive.

Leyta decided to start putting things in motion, saying, "You want to know a good joke?"

"Is it you?" replied Jester, vacant mask not really looking at her, but still seeming to.

"No, it's this place. Why don't we have some fun to cheer ourselves up more? I propose a—" She stood and picked up her plate in one hand. "Food war!"

She threw the plate at Jester's face, mostly hitting the target. She put one hand on Syago's shoulder, giving him a stern look, and threw some of his food into his astonished face. She then walked along the table, throwing food randomly at others. Syago picked up the clue and joined in, throwing food at her and the other kids. Leyta got to Jester, who'd tossed the plate over his shoulder and risen to his feet. Leyta threw another at him while pulling the scepter out from her dress but keeping it wrapped in cloth to hide her intent—to touch it to Jester's commanding tool, probably located inside his tunic. She neared and thrust her scepter forward, but something rammed into her and held down her arms.

"Stop," said Syago into her ear. "Not now, they'll kill us."

She looked into his eyes, a mix of fury and betrayal filling her. "What are you doing?! They'll kill me for this." The half-hearted food war stopped as everyone stared at them.

"No, you have to offer yourself to them. Trust—" He cut off as several plates clattered to the floor behind them. Knave walked onto the table, prowling toward them with its girl's face menacing and gleeful. Its tail lashed from side to side, claws shoving things out of the way.

Syago released her. The others backed up to the wall. Jester stood watching, dark mask all a quiet mess of food. Knave sat back on its haunches in front of Leyta and leaned in close to her. Hot breath covered her face; its long, rough tongue slid across her cheek.

"You were warned," the agony's soft girl voice whispered. "Any betrayal, and we give you to Jester. No restraints on the clown. A pity I don't get you. Maybe when he's done."

"Oh yes, oh yay!" Jester clapped. "We're going to find so many new ways to cry, I can't wait."

A shiver ran through her as Jester turned his mask to her, but she forced herself to stand tall.

"You can't hurt her yet," Syago protested. "Make her the same deal you did me."

Deal? Leyta glared at him, raging inside. *I trusted him!*

Jester wagged his finger. "We promised not to hurt your cousin or your friends in exchange for you controlling the Leyta. You did, but only after her failed attempt. Perhaps I'll have to relocate your cousin for a playdate after all."

She understood then; he'd been all for her trying something like this until days ago. They were holding everyone hostage against everyone else. But the fool still should've told her.

Mungo and Chester grabbed her and stood her up as Knave began licking a claw. Jester watched her blankly. She spat at him, and Syago protested behind her, trying to push forward, but was blocked by Arrochor and Guilliom. His frightened, apologetic face met hers as she was pried away.

"Come with me," said Jester. He yanked her rod away and walked to the forbidden door. Suddenly, he turned to the rest. "You may continue the food war." They didn't, and he said in a low voice, "I *said* continue."

Fernandeon picked up some food to throw but stopped when he saw that still nobody else did. Jester left the room, and the brutes pulled Leyta roughly through the curtained doorway at the back whence the leaders always entered, one she'd never been allowed to enter before.

They pushed her into a chair and tied her down. She didn't fight it; what could she do? Where could she go? The bulky men then left, walking past the lanky Bard of Sorrows. That mask watched her, hollow. Then he walked up and slapped her hard across the face, turning her head and sending spears of pain through her left cheek. A moment's pause, then he did it again with the other hand on the other cheek. Then again, and again, until she lost count and almost lost consciousness.

Eventually, he stopped, leaving her head swimming, swelling, and stinging. But she wouldn't cry; she fought the sobs and kept straight, dignified in her victimization. Hate burned in her, a fire that would consume unless vented.

She opened her eyes. He was nowhere to be seen. Sounds of shuffling from behind told her he wasn't gone—he was preparing, preparing for something worse than the beating.

"Pretty little twit." Jester's voice seemed to echo about the entire small chamber. Then she felt his gloved hands on her neck, sliding gently up and down around her shoulders, head, and then down toward her left breast... but he halted short and withdrew. The horrible breathing, deep and heavy, continued however. "Obstinate, gullible, delicate, pretty."

He came into view, a wooden box in hand. "Let's play." He turned the box upside down, and onto her lap fell five large black, yellow, and purple spiders. She bit her lip, refusing to scream as they scurried over her dress, arms, and hair with prickly legs. Each finding a spot, a niche to sit in and hide. One came to rest on her forehead, with hairy legs reaching over eyes and nose. Loathing and repulsion ate at her.

Breathing heavily and beginning to sweat, she tried to calm herself. As the spiders scurried, settled, scurried more, Jester held up a knife, dragged it lightly across her aching face, and sliced the bonds around her hands and feet as the spiders moved. She knew the game: Remain still or get bitten.

"You like my friends? Because they like you; in fact, they're looking for nesting spots to plant egg sacks beneath your skin. How about a joke for educational perspective?"

"I don't want any of your stupid jokes," she growled through clenched teeth.

"What's worse than a dead baby?" He paused. "Ten dead friends in the next room!" He laughed his sorrowful sob.

"What's worse than a poisonous spider bite? ... A thousand spider bites!" And he dumped another box. This time a dark-green mass of smaller spiders fell on her and spread, covering her in their itchy awfulness. Prickling on her skin beneath her clothes, no personal space remained safe from their searches. Tears fell unbidden down her face. Some of the larger spiders pounced on the smaller ones, eating them off of her skin, but they eventually stilled.

Jester moved around her, sobbing again. "I do love playtime."

He hummed, and the spiders moved all over her, even crawling over the tears on her cheeks.

Shutting her eyes tight, she couldn't help herself. "WHY?!"

"Finally, the right question." He hummed, and the spiders stopped. She forced her eyes open; the spiders had moved from her vision. Then, Jester's arms reached up and pulled the hooded mask off his head. She stifled a scream.

His hairless head had no face. Mottled skin covered where there should've been eyes. In place of a protruding nose was two holes that flared in fury. A lipless mouth revealed yellow teeth. The skin had a purple hue. No eyes—he was blind. The mouth spoke. "On *The Nascendante,* I worked as a young crewboy. I aspired to rise above my meager station as full bard and court jester. I loved story and song, and making others laugh through tricks. Especially little children, just as your clowns do today.

"Then, in a great feud between the crimson coven and the royalists—your parents, in particular—the ship was destroyed, along with my future. That explosion burned my face off. I wouldn't call it luck that enabled my survival, because living was hell. I spent my younger years living off of the pitying, wasteful, and careless of Nevermore. A vagabond of the streets akin to rats. Ridiculed or ignored, harassed and beaten, I survived. Nobody would take me in, nobody aided me. Not Cantlgrym, not the city leaders, not the priests, not the Kimoc, nobody except to throw me scraps to be rid of the sight of me."

"The play," she whispered through gritted teeth upon realization. "The play was about you."

He resumed without acknowledgment. "All the children mocked me, calling me Uglyface and Noface, until the adults picked it up too. I was imprisoned at age thirteen—thirteen! Although unsuitable for any kind of habitation, at least there I didn't have to beg and steal for food, and when they didn't feed me, I caught rats. After, it was that stupid asylum for the insane, where people are sent to die out of sight or labor as a slave, hardly better than prison. All our workers here have similar stories. Many mastozons have similar stories, the freed slaves have even worse. Nobility living well on the backs of their conquered. Your society is a failure, girl. What you defend is evil. Your motive is ignorance, your weapon is a feckless piece of wood—" He held up her scepter and threw it into a nearby burning fireplace. She twitched in reaction to save it but the spiders shifted like an extra layer of crawling skin—they were still on her.

"Hint: Your plan wouldn't have worked anyway. A terrible joke with a boring punchline. If you weren't so dependent on your societal structure, the best joke around, you would succeed more often and actually make something worthwhile. You haven't learned the art of trading lives, of sacrifice and necessary murder. I didn't learn anything either from these teachers, these manipulators. But what I couldn't teach myself, I learned from the darkness. The Royal Chaos cared for me where none others did. In the East, I found power. *I* did the work. *I* rescued these people. The Chaos society deserves the rule, and I would see your world burn before I let it go without."

"After all that you've done," she forced the words out, "you deserve it, in retrospect."

He drew a mortifying smile, then pulled the mask on, resuming his playful tone. "You asked after Robertobrus. Well, here he is."

He held out his hand to indicate the far side of the room where Robertobrus stood, facing the corner. Jester hummed and Robertobrus turned. Leyta's eyes widened, and again she held back a scream. Robertobrus was dead, his body pale except for dried blood and emptied eye sockets. Jester adjusted the humming to move him toward them. The body moved slowly, stiff, to stand in front of her. "Now kiss your lost love," Jester whispered in his humming.

The lifeless leaned down to where a spider sat on Leyta's face, bringing the foul smell of rot to her nose. With a jolt in the tune, the lifeless bit at it. Hairy arms clawed at her face as the spider struggled. Dead jaws squeezed the arachnid, and its innards oozed out, squirting yellow and green onto her face before being pulled away by the lifeless. Robertobrus's body stood munching on it until the pieces dropped from the mouth and the rest dribbled down the chin.

"Now that you've gotten comfortable," said Jester, "I think I'll leave you two to it." He then left her prisoner to the spiders with Robertobrus's corpse standing mutely in front of her.

Seeing his body wasn't so much of a surprise—she'd already suspected he was dead—but she hated that it was being used in this way. Her eyes fixed on the fire, where the scepter was ashes now. Spiders hated fire. But could she make it there? She needed to. She would not die as Jester's toy. She would fight.

Commanding herself to fortify, she stood—slowly, deliberately—and breathed deep. Spider legs moved, but only slightly. She inched toward the fire, moving around the motionless body and its gaping face holes. She increased speed subtly as she gained confidence, then paused as they shifted, one coming onto her face. Her breathing shuddered. Once near the fire, the spiders fled down to the floor, running away. She let her hair fall in front of the fire, touching it to the stone floor so the spiders hiding there could escape. Once she felt sufficiently certain they'd all fled, she stood straight again but couldn't shake that sensation from her mind that some still hid beneath. Still, she breathed deeply.

Straightening herself, fingering the key with a quick look around the room brought her attention to an old, large halberd hanging on the wall and beneath it a trap door bound by an old lock. Her heart skipped a beat, hardly believing it could be possible. She knelt and pulled out the key from her underpocket.

It fit perfectly, but the lock, stiff with age, wouldn't turn. She wrestled with it to no avail. Casting about for another solution, she saw the old halberd and brought it back. She chopped at the trap door, pausing only to make sure Robertobrus wasn't going to attack her, then resumed hacking until the opening revealed a small wooden ladder descending into the dark. And into the dark she went.

Crouched in a branch of the northern corner of Thornwood, Fal'iek concentrated on his bond with the gurow until it flew. Midday provided good lighting, and the rain gave extra cover. It'd been a frustrating past few days: Tek'ouk was still missing, King and Queen now controlled Mantlgrym, and Qosku had shown up at Voium alone and badly injured. They'd had to wait for his recovery before moving on to Quoak and out in search of the Chaos hideout in the region of Thornwood he'd seen Knave fly. They'd eventually located them in the broken castle of Covadongar, right under their noses.[100]

His group of sixteen Roah'riik edged in toward the ruined castle, moving through the forest, their home. Its broken towers and crumbling walls revealed only Knight standing guard on the gatehouse buttress over the bridge. Short of scaling the deep rocky moat, the bridge was the only viable entrance. So Knight was their target.

They moved into position.

Leyta emerged from the trap door with the only thing she needed: an intact scepter, taken from among other ancient treasures. Old and dirty, it proved its sufficiency when she flared the fireplace, infusing it with her rage. With a torch in one hand and scepter in the other, she entered the hall and came face-to-face with a servant, his mouth open in surprise. She incinerated whatever he'd been carrying with her wrath. Ashes fell through his fingers, and she glared a warning, then turned and entered the dining hall. No Jester, but the kids sat eating, so she burned the table.

"My friends, it is time we fight," she said. Syago looked at the burning table and snapped his head up suddenly. He rammed his elbow into Guilliom, then slammed a chair against him, breaking it and knocking him out. Some others broke chairs and still others grabbed their forks. They were going to find Jester and punish him.

Leyta burned the tapestries, then returned to the chamber from whence she'd come. She burned the wooden doors further down the hall and re-entered the

---

100 See Gybiaaw Blackbraid: I Don't Conform, 15

one from before, burning it too. As she lit it all up, Jester seemed to magically appear in the middle of the blaze. He snapped two daggers at her, sending them flying through the air. One pricked her in the gut while the other thunked into her scepter. Clutching her wound, she pulled the dagger out of the scepter, hoping the latter was still intact. But Jester lobbed an archemical flask at her, and she threw herself backwards, avoiding it as the small thing exploded. Darkfire swelled, and she moved fire at Jester, putting all her fury into it, letting her hate for him destroy. In the Vision, the room hated both him and her, swirling around in a blaze. She directed these sentiments at him.

Jester walked through fire and smoke toward her. Ignoring her fear, she waved her scepter to move the fire at him. The inferno raged with the dark hate she pushed into it. She jumped as a hand clamped on her shoulder, striking at it before realizing it wasn't Jester but Syago. He yelled for her to calm down as she sent another blast toward Jester, neither able nor wanting to stop the hate running through her. The fires in the small room swelled, and she realized her mistake, sweating from the heat and choking on the smoke. With a flash of fear, she realized she couldn't stop the hate from leaving her. Everywhere she looked, she made the flames blaze, catching Robertobrus's body and the rest of the furniture. She singed Syago, who yelled at her, jumping away. Where flames had surrounded the clown, black smoke now obscured him.

She tried to shift her flow to weaken the fires, but the only thing left was fear and that spread it more. Then suddenly Jester grabbed her, shaking her violently. He dropped her and nimbly jumped back as Syago picked up the halberd and charged him. Without slowing, Syago thrashed it back and forth, forcing Jester into a swift retreat. They vanished into black smoke, which again blinded her sight of the room. Still, her hate flowed out beyond her control.

Then Gabriol was beside her, trying to help her up. "No!" she shouted, but too late. She ignited his clothes and he screamed, trying to brush them out, but they spread more quickly, powered by her mix wrath and fear. She kicked him to the floor, yelling for him to roll. She looked around for something to smother the fire with, but all was burning. Gabriol stopped moving.

She turned and saw Syago on his hands and knees, coughing. He doubled over on his side. Fearing she might burn him too, she ran but tripped on a rug aflame. It nearly burned her, but she rolled away, snuffing out her own dress.

She lay, smoke and heat all around, suffocating. She had to focus—panicking would only further this leak of sentiments. The bodies of Robertobrus and Gabriol lay motionless and burning beside her. She calmed herself, using the sorrow she felt for them, and rose to her feet. She ran to Syago and helped him up. Arms around each other, they headed toward the door.

He choked out, "Think I got 'em."

She didn't respond. There was no sign of the clown, and smoke and fire were everywhere. Robertobrus and Gabriol were gone—she'd lost control and all was burning. Syago coughed out an apology for the betrayal, and she told him to focus on breathing.

They stumbled through the hallway to the dining hall. The rest of the children cowered against the wall and under table. Knave flew about the room, hitting, screeching, and whipping its hooked tail around. It had created a panic, and even with a coordinated effort, it was unlikely that they could take the demon without a special hellweapon.

Fal'iek stared grimly at the towering figure of Knight, who gave no notice of their hidden presence. Qosku waited below to enter the castle at first opportunity. At Fal'iek's waist hung the hellknife, made of bone and leather. It was one of the few things able to permanently slay fiends like the demon that stayed with the enemy.

The scouts signaled to him. He motioned for the three-point start. Three counts for him, two for the positions on the side, and one for the position opposite the tower. The timing worked: Acid-tipped arrows from all sides shot at Knight, ropes hooking around the ridged armor. The vine ropes tightened, and the giant straightened and began to struggle. The pull held, but his men began to lose their position to Knight's strength. Even the points that anchored against brambletrunks began to sway.

"Second wave!" Fal'iek shouted through the rain.

Before they could continue, a supernatural shrieking sound tore through the sky, bringing their hands to their ears and knees to the ground, incapacitating them. Fal'iek cracked open his eyes and saw Jester standing atop the broken tower, unmoving. The voice weakened and cut off as Knight, having torn free of the hooklines, dropped from the gatehouse buttress with a tremorous thud and charged across the bridge to where Fal'iek hid with his bow. Qosku slipped across the bridge to enter the castle.

"Second phase!" Fal'iek yelled, scaling up to a higher branch, narrowly avoiding the cleaver's shearing of the thornbranches as Knight cut through.

Fast and strong, Knight swung again and again with that massive blade, chopping thick branches. Fal'iek darted quickly along the thorny boughs. He threw hand-axes and knives down at the eye slits, but they availed nothing against that vacant skull. *What could possibly stop this thing?* Jester's evident ability to incapacitate them shook his confidence in having an advantage with the terrain.

Smoke billowing out of the tower made him redouble his efforts. Time was running out. He had to prevent Jester from unleashing another sonic wave and rescue the captives before the fire killed them. A near cleaving brought him back to focus.

He led Knight away from the tower but saw him turn to the other men instead of continuing the chase—he'd caught on to the ploy. Fal'iek rushed back, leaped directly onto Knight's armored back, and began sliding knives through crevices in Knight's armor, trying to cut those dead tendons. Knight shook his body, and Fal'iek leaped off to another branch, bone armor shielding him from thorns. He saw his men struggling to get into the tower as smoke poured from it.

Then a mabin'guarik appeared, beating its chest and chasing two Roah'riik through the brambles with a companion behind. *Of course,* Fal'iek thought, *why plan or try to control anything in Thornwood?* Suddenly, an explosion rocked the tower, and he saw several brutes emerging with large sacks over their shoulders and weapons in hand. Knight charged ahead, cleaving a path for them, and the white demon flew out of the tower, carrying Jester, who dropped a flask that exploded in purple smoke, effectively obscuring their flight. Jester's voice boomed through the forest. "Go ahead and keep the tower and your cooked friends, I now have a whole city to entertain. Not a bad trade, actually. Woohoo!" They flew north to rejoin King and Queen in the new Chaos stronghold: Mantlgrym.

He almost called for one group to pursue them, but they were occupied with two mabin'guarik that had suddenly attacked. Instead, they split into managing the struggle above ground and going below.

Leyta tried to pick herself up after the destruction that she'd caused. Her ears rung and head hurt, but she'd lived, slumping against a wall with Syago. Qosku had appeared, seemingly out of nowhere, and was now trying to revive them as Katti prayed. In a great miracle, the flames vanished instantaneously.[101]

Leyta rose on shaky limbs, using the wall as a support. "Is anyone else hurt?" she said, her voice laden with sorrow.

"Is anyone injured?" Syago asked louder.

Groans came as the only response. Leyta waved away Qosku's concern, and he went to others. *Where did he come from? Maybe he was a recent capture.* Realizing she was clutching something tightly—the scepter—she breathed in relief: It looked intact. She coughed and waved it to clear the room of the black smoke, keeping it circling to create a constant airflow that pulled the smoke out of the room.

"That was insane. I can't believe we're alive," Syago said, then stopped when he saw her expression.

"Most of us, anyway," she replied quietly and again had to sit as the weight of the senseless deaths she had wrought rolled over her.

"It wasn't your fault, Leyta," Syago said, his gaze soft but direct.

She didn't know what she was supposed to feel. She wanted him to hold her, and she wanted to be left to cry alone.

"I..."

"You lost control. Jester attacked you, everything was chaos. Anyone could lose control in that. Even if you made a mistake, it wasn't intentional, and you're not beyond redemption. You hear me?"

She nodded numbly, feeling grateful for the words she needed to hear, though it did little for her pain. Her mind turned to another anxiety: If the masters at Cantlgrym learned of this, she could lose her dynasty, maybe even all of her elementist rights. But if Syago didn't say anything, then she might be able to continue and... what? Go mad with power again? It wasn't very honest in either case. She looked at the scepter, wondering if she'd just lost her dream. Perhaps she should destroy it for the safety of others.

---

101 *Miracles through the conduit of the priesthood seem common to Katti but this was most experienced priestesses. Her nomination for sainthood didn't win on that alone.*

Just then, Fal'iek ran in and her confusion mounted. But as he gave orders and began checking with the youths till he saw Syago, whom he quickly
embraced. Then newer appearances fell into place: A rescue team.

As more Roah'riik filtered in, Fal'iek said to the children, "We're taking
you to Quoak for the night."

CHAPTER TWENTY-FIVE

The People of the Sky

The Hunter's Parchments, cc bastica 216; *Annals of Syago*, cc bastica 80; *Leyta's Journals*, cc bastica 77; *The Nordvargor Testaments*, cc bastica 870; *Scars of the Martyrs*, cc bastica 976;

18-19th of Octubre, 246[102]
17-18th of Octubre, 246

Thick fog hid their path, and growing darkness obscured the village of Quoak above. They had only seconds before the lifeless in surrounding areas would rise and encroach. They hadn't time to reach Tolgrym before dark, a fact that scared the mostly unarmed Asturions more than taking refuge in Quoak. Fal'iek secretly felt pleased that they could bridge over that fear and meet his people, assuming they'd be well received.

Climbing ladders unfurled as soon as Fal'iek blew his daemog horn.[103] Qosku stood beside him, looking up nervously as Leyta and Syago went up. Inidividually, none were a problem to anyone, yet the associated groups could make it a problem if they weren't careful. The Unaka were old Kimoc rivals but got the worst of the Asturions. They'd been a major contribution in the war against the Razhod and supplied most of the minerals of the region. The lad annoyed Fal'iek and sometimes made foolish choices, but he'd been a competent companion every step of the way, almost like a younger Amaruc in the way Syago was a younger Odiru. Of the four companions-Fal'iek, Odiru, Matias, and Amaruc-the latter had been the firmest and most valiant, up until his brutal murder. If Amaruc of old was Qosku's potential now, Fal'iek realized he ought to put more effort into

---

102 Fal'iek's date disagrees with the others' and so is probably incorrect.

103 See Gybiaaw Blackbraid: *I Don't Conform*, 16

bolstering him instead of merely using him. He motioned for the lad to wait and ascend last with him.

Fal'iek looked up high at his home, the hanging city, and fingered his feq'uok. In his brief return before the castle raid, he'd greeted Lil'iek and would now have to confront her and the Quoarn'riik on his extended stay outside working in Asturion lands. At least he'd get to see the children.

"You have nothing to fear, Qosku," he said. "You'll stay with my family, we'll keep you well." Qosku didn't look very reassured. "And I need to thank you for your help in finding them—the captives, I mean. You did well."

"Thank you," Qosku said.

Once he reached the bottom plank and several Kimoc hands pulled him up, Fal'iek was reminded of the impressive network of wooden planks, ropes, and canvases that made up his people's Quoak. A manmade web in this younger, greener area of the barbed woodland where dead leaves rustled through their homes. Feeling that wind, he regretted leaving so often. All was wooden platforms hanging by ropes and vines, with some bones in place of wood or as decoration, all of it hooked to thornbranches. Anchoring platforms and bridges onto each other and numerous branches meant that swaying of one or another would have a minimal effect on the rest. All around hung streamers that whistled and pointed in the direction the wind blew.

Qosku clutched the side of the platform.

Fal'iek laughed. "Would you like to climb onto my back?"

Qosku refused the offer and walked to the rope bridge, hiding the trembling in his limbs, and forced himself across while holding on to the nearby thornbranch the bridge was tied to. Fal'iek slipped past him and stopped at the end of the bridge. He called out and pointed to a small canvas hut, painted figures of beasts and warriors covering the fabric. "That is my clan's woshik—come and be at home with us."

He turned to see Lil'iek coming toward him across a plank bridge. They embraced wordlessly, though he sensed a looser hug, even more than the night when he'd come for reinforcements.

"It was urgent. I'm sorry," he said, preempting a rebuke he felt coming. Before he could say more, his three children shouted for him from above. He smiled and caught them as they jumped from the post, one by one, in a great hug.

He knelt on the narrow platform, the three kal'muq around him. The youngest, Mosh'iek, clung to him. "Look at you, my little monster! Bigger and stronger than ever. And it's only been a month," Fal'iek teased.

"Papik, where were you? We missed you," Mour'iek, the eldest, murmured. "Mamik cried, but I didn't."

"We thought the grim'iik took you away," Shoq'iek, his second, said.

"Or a shadowman," Mour'iek said.

A chill shot through Fal'iek. *So they've been here too.* He ran his hands over the sides of their faces, feeling their softness, straightening the vest of one. They also ran their hands over his bone ornaments and battlescars, their touch so tender, so deeply missed. "They had me, and I broke free. They can't keep me yet, not while you're here waiting for me."

"Nothing could ever keep you, right, Papik?" Shoq'iek asked.

"Not quite, only most things."

"What could keep you, Papik?" Shoq'iek asked.

"Not his wife, apparently," Lil'iek said, standing behind them, arms folded. "Now go see friend Syago so Mamik can speak with Papik."

They squealed and ran off down the plank, both holding hands of the youngest. He stood regarding his wildflower. Standing in the shade, her dark eyes and lips, thick and luscious, were inscrutable now.

"You just promised no more long wanderings for at least a month. Why do I get the feeling that these guests will change that?"

"We're not safe here either, Lil," he said quietly. "The ones that tortured me were focused on us, these... shadowmen creatures. And they're threatening to come here, maybe Jester too. But I do plan to stay and defend this time."

Her face softened; it was beautiful, with sky-blue lines painted across cheeks and forehead, black lines tattooed on her chin, and beads and feathers in her dark hair. There was an eternal intensity in her brown eyes. She hugged him, and they touched minds. Hers was calm but gloomy, yet allowing him to do it was a good sign. Of course, it let her feel him too; the vulnerability always went both ways. He sensed she was holding back sobs. The hug loosened.

"I'm sorry you had to go through that again," she said. "You know I am, but it also hurts us. Having you return doesn't make it any easier when I know it's not the last time."

"I am sorry too that you go through this. I'll stay longer this time," he said, looking into those fierce dark seas. He kissed her gently, though she hardly responded, always hard to win over. He released the hug, but they stayed close.

Putting his hand on her shoulder, he cracked a mischievous smile. "Do you remember the first poem? The one I wrote before you liked me?"

She leaned into him gently and whispered, "Vaguely."

He began to recite what he'd written over ten years before, just after they'd met:

Do you know that your waves
Come at me and will not stop?
Do you know that when your waves hit me
I drown trying to drink every drop?
Do you know that your waves
Are pulling me in?
No escape and no excuse
Hard to refuse
Can't you see
Your waves wash over me?
I want to fly through your ocean doors
And burrow through your ocean floors
Do you know I tried to swallow your sea?
I want you to swim through my skies
I wish I could fly into that starry night
Inside your eyes
Let your midnight find me something new
In you
Do you know that when your waves crash upon my shores,
I drown as I pull them into my pores?
Have you any idea what your waves do to me?
I seek nothing more than to bathe in you
Your smiles love like waves
One way emission flows
That run up all of my caves
Slowly hypnotic
Your aura
Softly despotic

Did you know that your waves,
Left me stranded at sea?
As long as it's your ocean,
Your waves can take me away
Let all your tides come
Till I am left numb
In your sea
My plea[104]

He let the last word hang in the air for a moment.

She looked off to the side, then met his eyes. "You can sleep in my hammock tonight," she said as she walked into the woshik.

He sighed. An improvement, he supposed. But he dreaded his next challenge: going to the Shouk family to explain Tek'ouk's absence.

So he was surprised to find Tek'ouk already inside the woshik, sitting with his two children on a fur mat. "Hello, my friend!" Tek'ouk greeted Fal'iek's stunned face.

"Tek? Well, of course you'd be here!" Fal'iek laughed. "Why wouldn't you be? How did you escape?" Fal'iek stopped on realizing Tek'ouk wasn't rising to greet him. Tek'ouk's right leg was severed just below the knee.

Fal'iek knelt by him as the children were ushered out by their grandmother. "Tek, I'm so sorry."

"It's healing well. No infections, they say." He sat up, grimacing.

Fal'iek wanted to help or ask about it but wasn't sure how.

"It wasn't even that clown group," Tek'ouk continued. "They knocked me off the roof and I caught a window seal, breaking my fall. But the mob grabbed me. Those golking palemen beat me till the other group, the resistance to the rebellion, pulled me free. But the broken leg was already infected and we severed it once I got up here." He gripped the wooden braces with one arm and a crutch in the other, stiffly rising on his remaining foot.

"I wanted to go back for you, but—"

Tek'ouk grunted, moving around toward the door. "Save it. I don't blame you. You did what you had to, but I do blame them, who we were only

---

104 It's unknown if Fal'iek wrote many poems or just this one. Either way, it has many characteristics of traditional Kimoc poetry and song.

trying to help. So you can keep your usual excuses for them. I'm not help-ing them anymore. Couldn't even if I wanted to."

Fal'iek didn't say anything.

Tek'ouk turned at the door. "You remember when the shadowmen tor-tured us, they asked us about the Razhod relics?"

"Yes, and we didn't know."

"I asked when I returned yesterday with Mour'ikik. He'd gone to Mantlgrym and the group that saved me got me out with him. Anyway, when I got back, I remembered the ancestor relics by the center. I think that's them."

"Let's go see them, then," Fal'iek said without thinking and rose to fol-low, but Tek'ouk's slow pace made him wait. A well of pity and sadness filled him to see his once-nimble friend struggle across the plankwalks of Quoak, nearly falling off several times and refusing help. The experienced warrior could no longer serve as Roah'riik and had other difficult choices ahead of him.

They arrived at the shuq'uok poles in the center of Quoak. Each wooden pole was ornately decorated with feathers and beaded necklaces that also carried teeth and clips of hair. Some had pieces sealed inside a wooden or leather case. Each was sacred but looked eerie in the setting night.

Everyone had clan monuments for their families, but both went to the shuq'uok post for Clan Unknown. *It has to be this one*, Fal'iek realized. It held unplaced pieces and mystery objects. There'd been speculation that some of these were pieces of Barthandeon or that they were cursed by evil spirits. One of the fangs was long for a regular human, but too short for any beast.

Tek'ouk's face scrunched up in puzzlement. "But how did they know about this? And why do they want it?"

"But they didn't know it was here, or they wouldn't have asked us. Think of it, these pieces have hung here, all but forgotten. If we were barely aware of these, then how could they be?" Fal'iek fingered them, examining each piece. "They only knew of them, if these are even it."

"But why? What use have these to them?"

Fal'iek shook his head. "The only thing I can think of is that these crea-tures miss their old master. Or have come to worship him. But that was so long ago and these shadowmen weren't even there. I can't—"

Movement caught their attention. From the darkness above, an arm blacker than the abyss stretched forward, then withdrew from the shuq'uok, the trinkets in its claws. They shouted and both threw knives, which vanished into the night. The ember eyes were unfazed.

Another dark arm knocked out Tek'ouk's crutch from under him; he dropped and caught himself on a vinerope. The shadow rose up over him, gleaming eyes glaring, and Fal'iek couldn't move. Beads of sweat formed on his body; he feared losing Tek'ouk, at being powerless once again before these things. All hope was gone, and they would drink his soul-

Tek'ouk's remaining leg kicked Fal'iek's leg, jolting him awake to his shouting. The shadows slipped away, Fal'iek unable to keep up.

Tek'ouk said from behind, "At least now we know why they let us go."

"True," Fal'iek sighed. "But the next question is: Are we done with them?"

The following morning, Syago gathered his things in preparation for the migration. Unlike Asturion towns, which were stationary and sent expeditions to hunt or gather food, Kimoc villages migrated to farm new locations.

Because of the undertaking, slightly more difficult for Quoak since it hung from branches, the rescued visitors would have to follow along and even help if they could, then leave the following morning with armed escorts for Cantlgrym and Tolgrym, respectively.[105]

Syago feared what he'd find on his return. Will Jester have already taken Elisabet by then? Even if they hadn't gotten to her yet, they would soon, and he might not be able to do anything. And what of Eliana? If they had control of Mantlgrym as Fal'iek had told him, what had become of her? Even if they didn't know of her relation to him, she was caught in the middle of that rebellion.

Elisabet and Eliana were lost to him.

Lügos, Henric, Matias, Gabriol, and Tomas were dead.

Alexandre didn't want him.

Syago had never felt such despair.[106] He broke his fast with Qosku on the

---

105 *Typically preceded by planting seeds below and on the branches that would grow to fullness by the time the village rotated back to the area.*

106 *See Thy Light, Therion!, 63*

floor of Fal'iek's woshik to Lil'iek's excellent cooking, although they themselves were still fasting as part of the traditional move. Fal'iek took pride in telling Syago of the giant muru'unkuy he'd killed. Hunting remained their principal commonality, though Fal'iek always had the better stories and made Syago wish he enjoyed it more. Lil'iek occupied the children, cajoling corn and beans into Mosh'iek's mouth and reciting a song with them. Syago helped clean up so Fal'iek could play with them.

After, they prepared for the move. All woshiks were collapsed into a sizable bundle that hung from several vineropes. The main village structure of planks would be left in place, and everything else would be moved along the constructed path to the next site, whose planks were already laid down. A day of this would get them over a league; several days could move the village ten leagues if no complications ensued.

Elisabet and Eliana were lost to him.

His friends were dead.

Alexandre didn't want him.

A light breeze blew leaves through the folding village, and an unusually clear blue sky was visible through the brambles. Syago helped Lil'iek wrap up their canvases, using them as bags to carry belongings while Fal'iek, as Roah'riik chief, went ahead with scouts to ensure that no blackbirds or mabin'guarik would be in the way. Syago sensed displeasure in Lil'iek over this and began to suspect marital troubles. He wanted to support them but didn't know what to do about it other than make conversation.

"What does your family farm?" Syago asked her as they unhooked the ropes of another large tent bundle.

"We harvest nuts and fruits during darkelan, corn and shrooms during darkemorg," she replied absentmindedly, her focus on packing and carrying everything in balance. "We only harvest, as any herding or hunting requires a husband, and mine's always patrolling. Put that line there and then move that one there." She indicated the spots while moving others herself.

The kids waited nearby on a side plank with sacks slung over their shoulders. The flock would be moved by Lil'iek's adjoining sister, Qio'iek, and Leyta, who, he noted with curiosity, eventually asked to switch from a more distant group to this one with him. Qosku took her place and worked farther down with the caged birds, alongside Milemeron. Everyone was tied to the part they moved, and each part was always connected at least halfway to the branches. In this way, no accident would result in the fall and death of any participant. On seeing that the process of migration actually worked, it was easier for an outsider like Syago to imagine how life in the forest sky village succeeded.

Elisabet and Eliana were lost to him.

His friends were dead.

Alexandre didn't want him.

"How do you farm like this?" Leyta asked, tying off her end of the tent bundle and lifting it with Syago to carry. Her bushy hair looked beautiful in the wind, even with leaves getting caught in it. "I'm still trying to grasp the logistics of this... impossible way of living."

"What way of living isn't difficult?" Lil'iek replied, looping a rope around a branch, hooking and tying it in one quick motion. "You mostly need to know how to innovate. That's the key to survival in a harsh reality—adaptability. We harvest everything by hand, hanging and jumping from each branch. But we do use the ground a lot as well."

Syago saw below, on the forest floor, several people moving with the mewil'ishyuuks herd. One had his scythe out, and he cut and bundled up the grainy grass as he went. The blade swung in hypnotic circles, slicing perfectly through windy bush and grains in between brambletrunks, watching for threats all the while.[107]

Lil'iek continued, "It is peculiar, really. It seems like there should be an easier way, or at least that it could be different, in another world, maybe. Yet, I can't imagine a world without friction, decay, and strife. Any world that has gravity will drag you down, require you to resist in order to stand up and move. Existence can only be painful, I think."

"Yes," Syago mumbled as he fastened a hook. His thoughts kept returning to Alexandre, one thing that could be different in a better world. The legendary sword and family relic that he wanted desperately, but it didn't want him back. And because it had rejected him, because he'd been found unworthy, he'd failed to keep Elisabet from the walking grave. He began shielding himself from the sun, standing in shade, hoping that doing this would lighten his brown skin and he'd be more worthy, or at least look better.

---

107 Farming only works for the Kimoc because they migrate, rotating land use, and keep warriors close. Asturions can't farm because the need for walls restricts land availability.

"How often does someone fall?" Leyta asked, balancing awkwardly as the plank wavered back and forth from the move. She leaned to avoid a thick, thorny branch. "Tell me you still worry about it sometimes."

"I've lost one child that way, actually," Lil'iek said indifferently as Leyta gasped an apology. "Dropped him by accident while doing this. Three months old. We've moved on, mostly. You never forget something like that, but you have to live with it, like it or not."

"I suppose," Leyta said, her eyes staring into the distance. Looking back in time at the losses she'd caused, Syago supposed. He crouched under a branch as they swung the bundle underneath it, always keeping an eye out for predators and considering what he'd do in each situation. Using his knife wouldn't be as impressive as Alexandre.

"What's on your mind, Syago? You're too quiet," Leyta said.

"Nothing, just... things," he said. After a pointed look from Leyta, he continued. "Just I miss my cousin and wish I could've been there when she'd passed is all."

"She could still be there," Lil'iek said. "You never know—Motherwood has mysterious ways of granting."

He shrugged. "I don't see how. Even if she did get the medicine in time, Jester promised to take her if I betrayed them. Maybe it wouldn't be so bad if it hadn't been my fault. I ran from the castle one morning, I went to Alexandre's grove, to draw and wield it. I told myself that drawing Alexandre wasn't just about me—it was for Elisabet too. And everyone else. But I realize now that I was wrong. It was always about me, and I was the wrong person at the time."

Elisabet and Eliana were lost to him.

His friends were dead.

Alexandre didn't want him.

They said nothing but watched him intently. He shrugged. "I don't know. If it didn't elect me, then maybe it won't ever. It's been a dream of mine. I grew up hearing stories of my father wielding it. By my age, he was already a prominent knight in the war against the Razhod. It's not exactly a family heirloom, we don't own it, but it may as well be since it's been wielded in my ancestry for generations. I just assumed it would come to me like it did for them." He stopped and sighed. "I've done everything I can to be what it's looking for, thought I deserved it, that it was my due, but maybe not."

"I'm sorry," Leyta said. "Dreams are hard to give up and even harder to achieve. But you did really great in the tower. I can even forgive you for your treachery," she looked at him slyly, and he laughed. "Truly, though, you were better than I could've hoped. I was terrified for my life, if that's any consolation."

"It's not." He shrugged again. "Maybe that's all a dream is, imaginary. A good idea that would've been nice and fun."

"Only the unrealistic ones," she said. "If within reason, it's something to aspire to, to be motivated by. My dream of being a powerful dynast fell in the castle when I lost control. But my expectations were more realistic. Instead, I fear I'm more in danger of losing what I've already won."

Elisabet and Eliana were lost to him.

His friends were dead.

Alexandre didn't want him.

He grunted with a nod and resumed his work. She said nothing else on the subject and the conversations sporadically meandered through various subjects as they worked. Near the end, he felt the sun on his face, looked at his skin and sighed, disappointed. As if it could've lightened in so short a time, he'd need to cover up more, do more than just stay in the shade.

Trying to shake thoughts of Alexandre, Syago noticed Kel'feq, the young Kimoc girl who'd been captured with them, nearby with another family. She looked much more in her element now. Being of Shouek, she'd found her cousins here and was due to meet her parents soon. At least things had panned out for her. The closest family he had was in Tolgrym, but he was glad for someone more vulnerable to be blessed. He could take joy in helping to achieve that.

Having arrived at the new site, they secured all ropes and planks as night took over. Leyta enjoyed the long work; it helped her work through her storm of emotions. She'd murdered Gabriol. Her charges, Navidsom and Robertobrus, died or were lost under her watch. Thus did her thoughts and feelings roil within her. Her dynast training helped immensely with this. So much of it included ways to avoid and push back against insanity, depression, bitterness, and any other possible trauma that the study and practice of dyne might incur. She felt she was handling it well, yet she'd thought that and failed. So she worried. Syago was right—killing Gabriol was a mistake, an understandable one, given the circumstances, but the consequences haunted her all the same.

Immediately following the final move, everyone broke the long fast and prepared for the settlement ritual Quo'mook. Earlier, the Kimoc priests smoked chuosh, from which they claimed a heightened awareness and even visions in preparation for the ceremony. This in the village center, where the entire community could look on from platforms and walkways. Leyta and the guests stood farther back. An altar plate in the center would hold their offering in thanks for the tolerance and support of the Mamak Yoaom and request for safety in the new location.[108]

Leyta stood next to Syago, and on the other side stood the Sequo'iek clan. Small torch lamps hung about the village, burning on smokeless fuel and enclosed by a small cage of rat ribs and bird legs to prevent the flames from escaping. The lights provided a warm but haunting glow to the hanging Kimoc civilization. They began with a dance: Two men and two women, decorated in feathers, furs, and bones, painted and beaded. The colorful figures moved to the steady rhythm of drum and chanting around the altar. As they moved, they used feathered fans to blow smoke about the area, sanctifying it from evil, Fal'iek said. Leyta leaned over to him. "What are they offering?"

His eyes shifted to her briefly, then back to the altar as he held his youngest in his arms. "A child."

"A child?" she asked. "As in..."

"We take of the forest to eat," Fal'iek said in a low voice as Leyta put a hand to her open mouth. "And in appreciation, we must give back. The beasts give to us their children, and we give back. In the wild, everything is give and take, or you rob it and incur its wrath and that of its spirits. The Great Ones require blood to sustain the world."

Leyta's face twisted in horror. She'd always heard the rumors, but this couldn't be true. "But you don't believe this, do you? You don't believe in those traditions."

The cold stoicism in his eyes and voice unnerved her. "I believe they serve a purpose. They provide meaning and a safe structure to the world for people who need it. Help them ingest difficult choices."

---

108 Motherwood, usually called Mamak Yoaom, was one of the Kimoc eternals. Part of the Kimoc beliefs held that nature spirits walked the world, keeping it growing and dying.

They placed an infant on the altar. Despite the dancing and music, the child did not cry; it'd been given calming herbs. Seers chanted and waved fern branches and bone scepters, decorated with feathers. Women hummed. The father, a Quoarn'riik, began the dedication.

"How can you justify this?" Leyta tried to keep the disbelief out of her voice. It wouldn't do to offend the entire village, but she felt appalled. Fal'iek's dispassionate expression told her he'd already confronted this himself. "How can you let your own people do this?"

"What would you have me do to stop it, Leyta? I can stop it no more than you can stop the rebellion in Mantlgrym. I'm not particularly pleased by it, but the alternative is also frightening. What's being sacrificed tonight is Wilq'olq's deformed infant. Kel'olq offers him in place of a healthy boy. In that way, it is both generous and pragmatic."

"Pragmatic?" she asked, incredulous. "Some struggles are worth the cost!"

"I agree. But don't think that killing the baby is not also a struggle. It's sacrifice in more than one way, for we hate doing it and a part of ourselves goes with it. I don't like it but I'm glad that we rarely do this and that when we do, it's of the ones that would burden us and have a hard life."

All hushed as Quoarn'riik Wiq'olk held aloft the ceremonial knife. He shouted, "Shamak'qul, diek'faim'olq!" and plunged the blade into the chest, jerking it about to open up the body to the wild for Mama Yoaom. Leyta thought briefly of trying to save it but knew it was folly. She forced herself to watch and was surprised by a sudden gust of wind that filled the area when the deed was completed.

Fal'iek was the only one unfazed by the sudden wind. Noticing her looking at him, he resumed his thought. "Consider what life would be like here in Quoak for the baby lacking four useful limbs. You have all of your limbs and yet can barely navigate this place. Then imagine that on a larger scale, a hanging village full of wounded or malformed people for us to take care of. Even fully grown, they're rarely useful to the community here; they can't guard or hunt, and need assistance moving. Some of the ones better off can craft, but we've no shortage of that. We could not survive the way we do otherwise. We wouldn't be able to farm, hunt, or move as needed. Even healthy children tax us but still take care of themselves as they grow. There are stories of Kimoc societies that tried it another way, and all failed in it.[109] Your church calls this world our hell, our punishment for the evils of a previous life where we must work out our redemption. But this to me is the definition of hell, when you only have bad options to choose from, however much I prefer the other way. Maybe someday we'll be able to give them a chance at life, but not yet."

They'd finished a final farewell to the child and began lowering the mutilated body on the plate to the forest floor below. Music and dancing began again, melancholic. Leyta looked at Syago next to her, leaning on the rope in front. His face told her that he'd known of this, maybe had even seen it before. She understood the crossroads of consequences Fal'iek laid out for her, but it still repulsed. "I don't know how you can do this. There has to be another way, maybe give the child to Mantlgrym..."

"You think they would take them?" Lil'iek asked suddenly. She'd been watching Leyta while holding her two children's hands, amused. "Your cities don't even take care of their own deformed. Wasn't that part of King's point?"

"But we don't *kill* them," Leyta said.

"Don't you?" Lil'iek pressed. "Not feeding them, keeping them chained... even the better-off ones are imprisoned by their rich parents or made into mummer fools to entertain. They die, and when they don't, they hardly live."

"Look at it this way, Leyta," Fal'iek said, eyes still on the silent procession in the beginnings of a mantra and slow dance. "You said you could never do this, but you have, have you not? To become a dynast, didn't you execute a man in front of a mob? Sure, it was a criminal and not a baby. But not all criminals are truly guilty of the crime they're convicted of. You accept the deaths of those innocents as a necessary sacrifice in pursuit of justice, and every society finds ways to eliminate its burdens, its undesirables, so it falls apart. You know that your system kills innocents as well as guilty, but you consider it more worth it to continue, and so you do by sacrificing those innocents to stave off the rest."

He had a point. Davagis had even used similar reasoning in preparing her for the trial. But there had to be another way.

Fal'iek continued, "The result of ours is that we don't starve, we don't lose the children in more tragic ways, and the rest of the children can thrive. No society desires to do this, so it creates elaborate rituals, be they

109 He must be referring to folk legends, but I find no record of this.

religious ceremonies or legal courts, to sanitize it against their consciences. At least in both our cases, we've picked the ones that either deserve to die or deserve a better life than what they would've had alive. Even he," he nodded at Syago, who kept his attention forward, "had to put down his hunting companion, his morwolf, when it took a bad wound. He couldn't save it nor afford the burden of taking it back to Tolgrym.

"It's not always justifiable, if at all, but at least it's preferable to Maolgon denying entry to the refugees, effectively sacrificing them for security, or the Amoyara ridding themselves of infant girls out of preference for boys, or the Unaka offering virgin women to feed their eternals."[110]

"But now you're judging by the same," Lil'iek pointed out.

He nodded and shrugged. "Everything can be a metaphor for something else when the path and consequences are similar enough. Or why else do we tell stories? Our tales convey these same messages even when we don't intend them to."

Leyta felt a pang for Qosku, who stood silently with them. She'd condemned both Kimoc and Unakan the way Fal'iek said. All Asturions did, and though she didn't share everyone's urgency to convert them, she now thought setting up missions in both a viable option. But she also thought on that day she'd killed a man she'd never met. Trusting that he was indeed guilty and deserving of death, she used her hate to burn him alive. The sight and sound of it still haunted her, though now it was overshadowed by the burning of Gabriol. Was war really that different from execution? And was the execution really any different than ritual sacrifice? One repulsed her more, but she knew that gut feelings were not a viable ethical standard.

She glanced over at Lil'iek. She wanted to ask but knew she shouldn't. Instead, Lil'iek smiled and answered for her. "I have done it. Offered our first, the child that fell survived for the small drop but with permanent injuries, and it was the hardest thing I've ever done. But I take relief in that the memory spirit resides with us, in the embrace of Mother Yaom, while the body rests in the World Below, and the child spirit walks with the other children of the tribe in the World Above. A better life than she would've had with us."

"Do you at least try to change it? Perhaps we can negotiate something."

---

110 In fact, the Unaka do this the least and the Amoyara the most, unless you count the Asturions who could be the top if you include all their executions and wars. But these are all vague estimates.

Both Fal'iek's and Lil'iek's eyes flashed like a whip. "Why would you assume that we don't? Are we too savage or pagan?" Fal'iek asked coolly. "Perhaps you'd like to come in and solve the rest of the problems of a people you've just met. No doubt you've been taught such arrangements have worked great in the past."

Such biting sarcasm surprised her and stung. She was only trying to help and didn't feel this response was deserved. Only the glare from Lil'iek and a warning in Syago's eyes stopped her from an equally sharp retort. She held her peace. *Help me, Heavenly Mother. Humanity is violence.*

Fal'iek had grown accustomed to the ceremonies, but still irked by the superstitions. So it surprised him that Leyta's arrogant questions bothered him more, and Syago's cowardly, neutral silence second, pushing him into defending something he wasn't proud of.

After the ceremony, Syago, Leyta, and Qosku ate dinner with his family, in quiet tension, when Reed'luk rushed into their tent. "Chief, they're missing!"

Fal'iek stood quickly. "Who's missing?"

"The lifeless," he said. "The floor is clear. We didn't notice it the night before because of the fog. But we can see now, they're gone. Nothing moves below."

Fal'iek left the room, and Leyta moved to follow him. He turned and held up a hand. "I'm afraid you have to stay here. Village rules. Because of limited space, only the man of the family goes and then reports back to the home." *Well our women can go, and sometimes do.*

"Can women go in your place? Could Lil'iek?" she said before he could turn away, her eyes narrowing. "I would hate to have everything important filtered to me through someone else, least of all for it to always only be a man."

He stared at her in disbelief. "I'm not arguing this with you. I must hurry."

"But I'm from Cantlgrym and their leader," she said. "We deserve a presence, a representative."

He put a hand to his chin, considering. "All right. Syago, come along."

"WHAT?!" she shouted as he turned away. The surprise on Syago's face told Fal'iek he didn't like being pulled into this.

Syago shrugged at Leyta as he left. "I didn't make the rules," he said.

"No, you just support them by following them!" she called after him, her voice fading. "You can start..."

As Fal'iek made his way toward the Quoarn'riik woshik, he thought about what Leyta had said. She was really starting to irk him; using his wife was going too far. Kimoc women chose the Quoarn'riik. Wasn't that enough? He admired her fire and actually sympathized with what she said, but it had never bothered Lil'iek. Or had it? He'd never asked; maybe he should have.

The emergency session convened just as Fal'iek arrived. He chanced a glance down to the forest floor. The dim torchlight showed haunting emptiness. He pushed through the gathering crowd and entered the Quoarn'riik ring. The woshik was stretched over a broad platform that folded as a spiral. The ten Quoarn'riik sat in a half circle around a small burning brazier. Each Quoarn'riik was dressed in the usual furs and leather with an ornate headband of feathers and beads. Paint lined their serious faces.

He looked behind and saw the usual cluster of village men gathering. Syago's head appeared in the back, and he noted a serious and downcast expression. Was he bothered by Fal'iek pitting him against Leyta? No, he'd been uncharacteristically withdrawn the entire time in Quoak; perhaps he should ask about it later. *He's been through a rough few months but still needs to fortify if he's serious about being a Knight of Nevermore and wielding Alexandre. It's not as though mine have been any easier.*

"Warchief Fal'iek," Quoarn'riik Link'ouk called, and the din of conversation hushed. "We expect an impending attack."

"What?" Fal'iek asked. "But they're gone. What's attacking?"

"The Royal Chaos," Quoarn'riik Link'ouk continued. "We received threatening messages from them many days past. Because of their charades, it wasn't serious to us. They tried to turn the people against us, but the people are strong and undeceived. Now their promise of the lifeless rising, I fear, is true."

"You received threats and didn't tell me?" He made no effort to hide the anger in his voice.

"This came many days ago." The Quoarn'riik waved his hand. "While you were gone. When you returned, we had other things to do and it didn't seem important anymore. Now, we've seen the bodies disappear. It might only be a low point in the season, but the wind has stilled, speaking danger, so we'd best be careful."

"This is impossible," Quoarn'riik Wiq'olk said. "Only the Razhod have ever driven that many bodies. And we can't be reached up here, anyway."

"No, I've seen it happening," Fal'iek said almost too quietly, remembering now, then speaking louder for all to hear. "On the forest floor, I saw them moving in a single direction, though I didn't understand it. It has to be the Royal Chaos; they have a lot of strange abilities. They're powerful, much more than they look. They've been collecting the bodies into a group somewhere in the forest to mount a concerted attack, using them as an army because they lack a real one. This also indicates that it was they who desecrated our graves."

"But they can't hurt us," Quoarn'riik Wiq'olk said. "We're too high up."

"Normally, yes," Fal'iek said. "But they or something did draw them, and if it can do that on such a scale and with such stealth, then it might be able to bring them to bear against us. I think it most likely that they'll use other means, hit us with fire and darkfire, cut our ropes and topple us onto the lifeless. We must prepare now... and our homes here won't stand well, so we must plead Tolgrym for refuge."

"We can't go to the castlemen!" Quoarn'riik Link'ouk almost shouted it. "They have never been fair, never kept a promise to us. We let them into our lands on the mounds, and now it is their lands, stripped, with us hiding in the woods. Remember the lore? How they had us fight each other and used us in their own wars? How they took our children after massacring the parents? Better to fight on the forest floor than trust them or put ourselves below them, admitting weakness and need."

Quoarn'riik Yano'creeh added, "They'd not like us bringing this problem to them. They'll leave us to die or kill us themselves before helping. We're better off not asking."

Syago nudged Fal'iek, "Are they talking about Tolgrym?" And Fal'iek recalled Syago didn't speak enough Quoak to understand, so he explained.

Syago then called out, "They'll accept you with me." Fal'iek cringed as his friend stepped forward, breaking the woshik rules, but he translated for those not understanding his Asturion. "You rescued us and took us in. If you deliver us safely and offer to protect Tolgrym from a malevolent force, they'll accept all of us."

Fal'iek could tell that none of the Quoarn'riik liked his breach but considered his words. Quoarn'riik Wiq'olk mentioned using the alliance as an opportunity to mend trade relations between the two and guarantee cooperative security of the region. Unspoken was the additional thought that the Asturions of Tolgrym likely would be attacked next, if they were not already under threat. Its main strategic importance was as a wood resource and a link to the sea, but the port was little used now. Fal'iek saw the potential alliance as another opportunity to bridge the two peoples. It was a far cry better than the useless rituals and prayers they would otherwise do. *Nobody saves us but us.*

To their arguing about the strength of the Kimoc, treachery of the Asturions, and doubt about the danger, he said, "If you truly value your children, the time has come for us to show the true strength and courage necessary to do what no other people has. We must bend our pride enough to ask for help, and we must be empathetic enough to help them in return, or we lose all."

"It's too risky," Yano'creeh continued. "We're safer here, alone and hidden."

"That's the love of weakness that we can't afford," Fal'iek paused, looking them all over, seeing for the first time what this sacred circle had become. "Is this what we've come to? Passive and soft? Aggressive only when it comes to betraying our allies? What happened to the tribe known as the greatest warriors in the land? We hunt the wild, ride it as an extension of ourselves, and you would have us cowering in our homes while lesser armies sow their sweat and blood in our defense. What of Kimoc pride and ferocity? I don't want to hide from the palemen, I want to command their respect with my truth and superior capacity. We carry the legacies of our ancestors as warriors. Hunters. Roah'riik! Does the wolf cease the hunt because plants might infect it? Does the serpent shy from the prey that fights back? You masters of the wild, I ask what happened to your fangs? When did you lose your thick hides? This is not of us, not fitting of Quoak. Where's your claws?"

The circle was silent for a time. Quoarn'riik Wiq'olk asked, "You're sure of this? The winds haven't warned us..."

"I'm not sure of anything," Fal'iek said. "None of us are. And that is why we prepare for everything—we prepare for the worst."

"And if-when they betray us?" Fer'iik asked. Syago stood beside Fal'iek, unaware of what was being said.

"We prepare and turn it back on them."

The Quoarn'riik gave a unanimous vote, and the meeting broke into even greater activity than the heat of the move.

CHAPTER TWENTY-SIX

THE BATTLE OF TOLGRYM

Based on *Annals of Syago*, cc bastica 12; *Writings of Qosku*, cc bastica 70; *Leyta's Journals*, cc bastica 89; *The Hunter's Parchments*, cc bastica 207; *Scars of the Martyrs*, cc bastica 999;

19th–20th of Octubre, 246

They spent the rest of the night preparing departure and left at dawn, taking little to none of their belongings and moving fast through their home woodland. It wasn't far to Tolgrym from the new location, a few hours of hurried march, but they were burdened with children in Thornwood where any number of surprises could lurk beneath woodland tranquility. They paused briefly in rest by the Grove of Alexandre. Syago stared at the grove, a patch of sunlight in a dark forest. He walked into the grove, slow at first, with others following to look at the legendary, sacred relic. *Do I dare try again? Is it worth repeating the disappointment?*

The sword gleamed beautifully in the sunlight. He grasped the handle and, as thrice before, it didn't budge from its pedestal. He sighed and turned away. But behind him Milemeron walked up to it, grabbed it, and pulled it out. Everyone gasped in surprise, including Syago. But while the others looked on in respectful awe, his was of stupefaction, then horrified pain as they gathered in, cheering. Milemeron, a boy with three years less than Syago and mild battle prowess, had been chosen by the Holy Judgment Sword. Was it the noble birth or white skin or something else? Answers eluded Syago, and evidently Milemeron too as bewilderment contorted his face. The brilliant, shining blade lit up the grove like a great halo, before dimming slightly. Eyes shifted to Syago, the denied one, and he could take it no longer. Walking out of the grove, he could not stop the tears from flowing. Death would've met a sweet welcome from him that hour.

They arrived at Northgate, where Fal'iek and Syago made the plea to Count Toriacus. Though they were both shocked and delighted to see the safe return of so many of their young—and with Alexandre, no less—the ever-cautious count conferred with Bishopess Myrian and Baron Roberochester and asked a number of other questions, but the acceptance was evident. The Kimoc people were admitted on the provision that they keep to the designated areas and follow the lead of the town leaders.

More cheering around the legendary sword began, new songs for their new champion. Of course, Syago was pleased to return to Tolgrym, but it felt mixed with bitterness and sorrow. Anger at Alexandre and sadness for Elisabet. So surprised was he then when she ran up to him through the crowds and leaped into his arms. He twirled, swinging her around as tears streamed down his face once more, glad for something to feel good about.

"How?" he croaked as he let her down. "I thought I'd lost you."

"The medicine," she said excitedly, jumping.

"What medicine?" he asked, pretending to not know.

She pulled on his hand to lead him out of the crowd to their home. "Come on, I'll show you!"

It melted his heart to see the normally quiet, even timid girl so animated. He thought he should speak with the count soon but couldn't say no to her pulling him away.

After stopping to greet other villagers along the way, they found their way to the cottage by the graveyard. She pointed at their window, where two empty jars sat. "We found these jars with the medicine here one morning. We used the medicine on everyone who was sick, and Grandpa said I was almost gone but they saved me and everyone else."

He pulled a jar off the windowsill. "But how did they get here?" What he really wondered was why the Royal Chaos hadn't come for Elisabet yet. It'd been days since he'd crossed them.

Elisabet shrugged at his question.

He looked at her, not smiling anymore. "Elisabet, have you seen any strange monsters watching you at night?"

"Hmm, no. Bishopess Myrian said this was divine providence. She said it was a gift from the angels of Deova. She heard our prayers and saw your valor!" she announced.

Syago couldn't help but smile at seeing her out of her shell, although he remained disturbed.

"Syago, my boy." Goidiberic walked up behind them. "The others were just telling me what you came from, and what a tale! All the grander with you getting out of Mantlgrym when you did."

"Fal'iek told me of the rebellion there. Have we word of Eliana?"

Goia sighed. "I'm afraid not. She may still be there or she may have escaped, though it's unlikely. I'm not sure which is worse though, that she be on their side or against it. I suppose it depends on Theordoric."

A new sorrow hit Syago then, dampening the joy he'd felt at seeing Elisabet. He'd hoped that the blessing of Elisabet's well-being had held true for her sister. "She helped me, Grandpa. She gave me this medicine. Somehow it got here from my dungeon cell, but I wouldn't have had it if not for her. Her husband, though, he was crueler than before. And with that rebellion, he's wealthy, so... well, I imagine she'd support him, and I think he was against it."

Goia looked at the jars strangely. Then he grunted and said, "I hope she's well. We can only pray to the Deova Bondua for her protection."

"What happened with the investigation here?" Syago urged. "Did they figure out who poisoned the water?"

"No. It might even have been an accident, though few think so."

"How can they not have any leads? Have they considered the Royal Chaos? Or..." He was going to say "phantom shadow people that look like grimshades" but caught himself.

"It's a good question, but I should think that a group as unique as that would leave even more clues, not less. We've no evidence. Fact, you best not mention it—it's become a sore spot among the villagers." His frown switched to a smile. "Come and eat something first, before the count needs you again."

They talked of the time between their parting. Goidiberic appeared impressed at how well Syago had done, saying he was the real hero and deserver of the sword, though Syago couldn't help but think this flattery paled in comparison to that of previous heroes. It wasn't long after the pleasantries were over that he set to help preparing the town with Fal'iek.

After the chaotic bickering and corruption he'd seen in Mantlgrym, Syago felt a measure of pride that the whole town had banded together, and with the Kimoc, to fight against this unholy threat. Even Donmal had sobered up to help defend. Out here, they took care of each other.

Syago told Count Toriacus of his oath to King. The earl, barons, and archbishopess all agreed that it had been done under duress and therefore counted for naught, but they still allowed him to renew his oaths, kissing the count's and barons' rings. He also told them all he could about the rebellion that the Royal Chaos was trying to foment.[111]

After finishing a meeting with the nobility, Fal'iek permitted Syago to join their perimeter survey. The end of their perimeter run brought them to the crags overlooking the sea, some fifty paces from Tolgrym's southern wall. The river Masasoik that ran through Tolgrym emptied in a rocky waterfall near the stone watchtower on which Syago stood. A light fog blanketed the water, creeping onto land. All rivers perished into the rocky, dark-green ocean that licked the jagged shore. Overhead, where the distant gulls shrieked, extended a dull sky of evil green haze instead of gray. Everything about the ocean was wrong, Syago reflected. It spanned forever, went unspeakably deep, and held more mysteries than the mountains or forests of Nevermore. It was thought that the monsters of the sea were somehow even bigger and stranger than those of land, though he felt it hard to imagine.

Only bad things came from the sea, fomorion barbarians and the Old Plague had, and anything that ventured out was cursed. It was the Criod's barrier to them, one of many cruelties of creation levied against them without explanation, without reason. Only occasional trade ships to and from Cantabryn took port below, a reminder of when his parents escaped in secret on their ship.[112] That was another thing that was wrong about this wretched expanse of water. It had swallowed *The Nascendante.* As a boy, he remembered seeing the masthead and back end of the ship protruding out of the water not far offshore. Then one day, when he came to the tower to see it, the ship was just gone. The sea even regurgitated bodies as lifeless during darkemorg. Water, like land, served as a grave that completely immobilized lifeless unless they washed ashore unburied, as happened with his father's corpse.

<hr>

111 *See Luskmord: Atriom Carcerio,* 14

112 *ibid,* 16

An evil wind blew at him from the sea, and he spat at it before turning back to find Fal'iek also watching the quiet expanse. Unforgiving for him too, another of the few that had survived. "That day, your parents only cared about a world where you didn't have to fight the Razhod. It wasn't about them anymore, only your future. That's what they both said before we got on the ship. It was like they knew, somehow."

"Well, at least someone got what they wanted." He meant it as a joke, but it didn't come out that way. He regretted wasting so much time and energy on that fool's dream and pushed it away, turning back to the horizon. He thought it odd that Fal'iek would say something like that, the kind of thing a Deovan might say instead of an unbeliever. "I've never asked you before," Syago began. "Why do you think the bodies rise and attack?"

"I don't know," he said. "I don't think anyone does, despite claims to the contrary."

The waves lapped the ground below, increasing with the tide, a haunting sound that softly disturbed the silence around them. "Then you don't think their souls are trapped in the bodies?" Syago asked.

"I really hope not, and at least the chamands don't think so. We live on a sea of ignorance; I'm only concerned with surviving it without becoming a monster."

"Doesn't it bother you though? Having all these mysteries and no answers?" Syago pressed.

He shrugged. "Life is full of unanswered questions. I think our fables and folklore do us a disservice by tying everything up in a nice bow at the end."

"But if certainty could be had? And hope to come with it..."

Fal'iek's eyes flickered from the sea to Syago and back to the sea. "There's more benefit in low expectations than a false hope. In the end, all we really have is our actions and the moment we're in." He turned to see Mour'ikik, Reed'luk, and Yarok emerge from the trap door leading down, ready to leave. They too looked out on the sea warily before nodding to Fal'iek, who muttered, "Let's go."

Syago wanted to continue the conversation. *But what if the knowledge is the key to surviving?* It was such with his faith that spiritual knowledge is a path to salvation, but it wasn't the time for another debate. At least for himself, he found insight and hope far more inspiring than Fal'iek's depressing skepticism.

Mour'ikik reported that the scouts to Quoak found nothing changed other than some birds picking through the place. They returned to Tolgrym and waited for nightfall. No attack came that second night, so they used the extra time to plan and prepare.

Syago, avoiding the city's talk of how wonderful it was to have Alexandre back, put himself on wall duty. He caught himself nodding off and stood up to stretch when he noticed the white figure of Knave in the branches over and above. He almost called an alarm, but it made no move to attack, only watched him with that abominable child's head, the way it did in the dungeons at Covadongar. It smiled—one for the nightmares. Such a wretched creature.

"I renounced you," Syago yelled, his voice disturbing the stillness of midnight. It licked its paw. "Tell them my oath was invalid and I renounce it, you hear? All of you stay away from her, YOU HEAR ME?!"

Other guards ran down the wall toward him, looking into the woods. It flew away.

On the third night, it came.

Qosku initially felt relieved. The experience of leaving Quoak for Tolgrym had terrified him in its resemblance to fleeing Mantlgrym for Maolgon, a travesty he still nightmared on. Thankfully, Tolgrym had admitted them, and they would all stand together. Yet this only made the slaughter outside Maolgon more tragic. This kind of acceptance could happen and work well, but it hadn't then; it was too late to go back and change it. He wished those barons and priestesses had been here to see this harmony. In fact, he'd felt welcome. The way everyone had taken him in and trusted him as their ally meant far more to him than they'd realized. These were people who cared for each other, people he could protect. He could even possibly escape his guilt over Chaska here, among the other secrets and buried demons from which he fled. He'd barely thought about being a girl at all, though that had more to do with the unending race against death he'd been on since the carnival.

He crouched between Fernandeon and Syago with other soldiers along the parapet, including the one with the glowing sword. The families huddled securely in the middle of the town and along the walls, where they planned to help with supplies and care for the wounded. Behind the lines of soldiers stood archers, ready with fire arrows, and elementists. Leyta watched with them farther down the wall by the gate. Tek'ouk was also among their small number of nine, in spite of his earlier protests.[113]

Qosku's relief quickly turned into anxiety at the absolute silence of the forest and the thick evening fog that blanketed them. The soldiers waited quietly, certain this would be the night, for no other reason could explain the stillness in the surrounding woodland. He wasn't sure how the struggle would go; he'd never been in a siege before and wasn't trained in wall tactics.

Even Qosku, who didn't know the forest as Syago or the Roah'riik, felt it coming, an approaching tremble of the outerwild. Sounds of movement broke the silence—sticks breaking, stones clacking—and eventually the quiet mass of animated bodies appeared, a faint malefic wail driving them. They came from the southwest, by the coast. Fog concealed the silhouettes until lantern light revealed desiccated monsters picking into a clumsy run, many tripping in their attempted haste. The awful smell reached them next, this time strong from the volume of its source.

A mabin'guarik lifeless, ragged, gigantic, and pockmarked with holes, crashed into the wall, its arms easily reaching over the ramparts until being hacked off. Over the spike-riddled moat and against the brick-laid barrier, they fell. They didn't get far, falling, then trying again in wet silence. Other, less complete bodies merely thumped into the trench to be stepped on. They were bodies of men in the remains of rusting armor or shredded clothes. They were beasts strange and lethal in life, horrid in after-death. Wolf, bird, mewil'ishyuuks, rat, rabbit, and mabin'guarik, mangled and rotted, caked in moss and mud; their skeletons retained varying degrees of flesh to propel them and repulse those fighting. All with eyeholes and mouths that gaped in eerie silence.

The swarm gathered, and Qosku felt numb at how many there were. He couldn't see the forest floor, only a moving mass of rot as they completely surrounded the west wall and moved toward the other walls. For the moment, it looked as though the moat and wall defense would be sufficient. Then they felt the song—a haunting melody that grew stronger but still distant and swaying, cajoling.

113 See Luskmord: Atriom Carcerio, 18

"Stuff your ears!" Toriacus shouted. Qosku and all along the ramparts they shoved wads of wet cloth in their ears to little effect. It clawed at the inside of his mind. Qosku even found himself moving with it again; he stopped and saw that the bodies were piling up along the base of the wall, creating a mound for the rest to climb up. Soldiers shouted war cries and slung stones wrapped in alcohol-soaked cloths to carry flame while elementists threw fire at the piles with their foci. But the fires didn't catch; most were smothered in the churning mass of rotted flesh.

Qosku put his sling to expert use with the rocks he'd collected, yet even the best shots only slowed the bodies instead of stopping them. Jester's song grew in strength, becoming more guttural and throat-shed. It drew nearer from an unseen location as the bodies ascended over each other. Bodies of mabin'guarik led, followed by freshly dead birds and rats, all with hook claws. Qosku wondered in awe and horror, *What manner of bard is this that can sing to the lifeless and they heed him?*

He assisted the soldiers with a cauldron to drop boiling pitch, letting it eat at limbs and sticking the bodies to each other, but it was still too little—many stumbled, only to become the step to another unharmed. The corpses of the forest charged on, weaker but resolute in their mindlessness.

"Prevent them piling up!" Milgalic shouted.

The longspears prodded and kept them at bay. Qosku jabbed with his, roughly succeeding at preventing a fresh malwolf lifeless from gaining a higher handhold. Then he heard the rustling in the branches, not far off, as something broke through. The Roah'riik called warnings that weren't heard over the din of the bodies. Trees emerged from the foliage, dead and rotting, but still moving. Though they were less mobile, their height was an obvious threat. Six tree lifeless approached the wall, pressed on the piles of bodies, then fell against it. Fire flew, but bodies were already clambering up them, either snuffing the fire out or catching it and becoming a burning siege weapon.

A large rabbit lifeless got over and embraced Qosku in a hideous hug, trying to bite him with a toothless mouth. One of the barons knocked it loose, then tossed it off the wall with stones thrown by dyne. The baron nodded at him, the outsider defending his town, and Qosku felt a brief sense of belonging and acceptance he'd been yearning for. But as he rammed his spear into the lifeless of a girl, and it clawed at him, he had another moment of clarity. Chaska was his responsibility, dead or not. And he'd have to face the consequences of his actions, give account before the eternals, and also face his own hidden female self, the shadow of his twin. He kicked the girl lifeless off.

All the soldiers were now switching to swords, axes, and hammers for the closer combat. Alexandre flared bright in Milemeron's hands, and the dynal blasts from the count and barons tore through dead flesh below. Qosku punched and clawed with his gauntlets but found this offered too little reach against the clawing, burning arms. Eventually, he was shoved back behind the line so that those with shield and sword could work the wall more effectively.

Dismayed, Qosku could only watch the horrific scene unfold before him. The flaming bodies were bashed away by shields, but this only scattered their burning parts, which fell along the walkway. Qosku and the soldiers scrambled to put them out while maintaining the line, but the swarm continued. A wall of putrid smoke and fire grew as the flames finally took hold, making it difficult to hold the line and anticipate what came. Bodies fell over the ramparts.

A flaming arm grabbed at Qosku's leg as a malwolf head snapped at his other. He kicked them away, smashing them against the wall and stamping out the fires, but there were so many, he was hard-pressed to keep pace behind the line of shields. A flaming mabin'guarik lifeless pinned him to the ground, embers searing his skin, but he punched it away until he was free. He panted heavily in a brief break.

The song moaned from above, moving through them. Qosku felt it stronger, the driving force. Then Qosku saw the Bard of Sorrows, in the dark of the forest, singing and dancing a song of necro-mastery.

"Anytime, rulers!" King's voice echoed over them as they fought the tide. "Give up your authority, make us your protectors, and the bodies will retreat forever. Never again to pervade your lives."

"The ruin this brings isn't worth it." Queen's voice now surrounded them. "I do so love your little homes. What a shame to trample them so, all to make a point."

Qosku noticed an ash-covered Syago standing next to him, panting. The two stepped forward to stanch the tide of bodies flowing over the brim of the wall. But the tree branches suddenly grabbed them, hoisting them into the air. The tree toppled backwards, and they fell directly onto the mound of writhing decay. Qosku sprung free and pulled Syago out, though another soldier was caught by the arms of the lifeless. Claws and teeth tore at the spaces between the man's armor, and he shouted and hacked wildly with his mace as Syago and Qosku tried to pull at his legs, but the soldier disappeared in the mass of death. A tall human skeleton, with just enough flesh to give the bones mobility, stumbled toward Qosku, and he broke its legs and arms, but rat and bird bodies were assaulting his legs with rotting fang and claw. He smashed them away, backing up as more left the swarm at the wall to pursue him. He crouched and swept his leg around to clear the space around him. When he turned around, what he saw frightened him.

Syago stood beside two deepwraiths, all three unmoving as he gazed into their midnight eyes, held by their unwavering stares. They wrapped him up in long shadow arms and moved into the dark of the forest. Qosku ran after them. "Syago wake up!" Syago snapped to attention but couldn't break the hold. One of the deepwraiths turned to slash at Qosku, who ducked and sprang up. It nimbly dodged his aerial kick and moved again, this time bringing an arm up to wrap around Qosku's neck. The deepwraiths deftly drew them into the thornbranches as Qosku lost consciousness.

Syago made a hard spin, peeling himself out of the grimshade's grip while pulling on Qosku as he fell. He held Qosku tight and fell past the other surprised grimshade as his leg snapped into its head. On landing with a roll in the grass, a quick assessment told him he had no broken bones, Qosku was unconscious, and there were nearby lifeless coming at them. He picked up Qosku and ran from some desiccated malwolves that charged them.

Just then, a massive corpse with fleshy chunks covering its skeleton appeared, tusks jutting from an elongated head. Carrion bugs crawled through holes where eyes should've been. Syago recognized it as the large muru'unkuy Fal'iek had described killing—the old shortspear remained stuck in the gaping mouth. It charged, smashing through one of the mal-wolf bodies but then slammed into a thorntrunk. Too big and clumsy to navigate the forest well, it rebounded from the trunk and careered toward

Syago, who thought, *Why hadn't Fal'iek completely dismembered the corpse after killing it, as is mandated of all?*

Flashes of light caught Syago's eye, and he realized that Milemeron was coming to their aid with the shining blade of Alexandre. Syago had to avoid the ambling bodies who crashed, reoriented, and charged again. Milemeron attempted to cut them down while Syago searched for any weapon. In slightly oversized armor and the two-handed sword, the lad still looked too young. His attacks on the lifeless were clumsy, and he somehow kept missing. Syago shouted for the lifeless and moved away, distracting them. But as they left Milemeron for him, the grimshades approached the boy. He waved Alexandre at the creatures threateningly, charging one only to have it easily dart over and around him.

The remaining malwolf caught up to Syago on the right, snapping mindlessly at his arm. He moved to the left and got knocked forward by the brunt of the muru'unkuy tusk. Luckily, his armor protected him against the tusk and bite.

The grimshades had Milemeron flanked, and they were playing with him. Syago tried moving closer, but as the boy circled around trying to guard his back and front, one clawed him across the skin exposed between helmet and neckguard. He screamed and stumbled, flailing his blade and clutching his bleeding face, which was already being healed by the sword's power. He fought on until the other grimshade turned its arm into a long blade and stabbed him in the leg. Syago shouted and ran around the muru'unkuy toward him. The boy fell, dropping Alexandre, and the grimshades moved in, stabbing and stabbing and stabbing until long after the boy died. Then their candling heads of darkness turned to Syago, and he halted. The muru'unkuy charged again, and this time it knocked him over into thick grass. He rolled, feeling something sharp jab him in the leg. The muru'unkuy body charged past him and crashed into a thorntrunk.

Lying in the grass, he scrambled for a fallen axe or at least a loose rock when he saw Alexandre on the ground. He rolled over and grabbed it; instead of getting burnt by the handle, he was able to lift it from the ground.

The lifeless barreled toward him. Syago stood up, the sacred blade amazingly in his hands. No time to relish in the dream achieved, or mourn the boy, he swung the glowing blade at the large, stumbling lifeless. He missed; the blade slid through the air faster than his arm had moved it.

The overreaching lunge put him closer to the charge, and it brushed him, knocking him backward. It felt as though the sword was trying to leap out of his hands, cut before he intended. He eyed the blade, took aim, and swung at the back legs. Missing again, he stumbled because of the eagerness of the blade, realizing he could sense that mentally. Something inside it had a motive and its own strategy... *But what strategy?* He tried to press at the forefront of his own mind the urgency of the task and that it needed to trust him, follow his lead. Otherwise, this would kill him.

He gripped the sword tight and swallowed. The muru'unkuy body smashed into a thorntrunk behind him, so he turned to the malwolf. He swung slower, more measured, and Alexandre still swung faster than he was prepared for, the divine blade slicing through a foreleg. The lifeless hobbled toward him. Frustrated, he swung repeatedly in a frenzy until the skull fell off and the front legs were gone. The remaining pieces struggled to get him but were too useless to threaten. *Now I know why Milemeron couldn't strike them.*

The muru'unkuy skeleton charged, and Syago came in with a hard swing that shot down too fast, so he turned it into a thrust. Thrusting into the ribs didn't cause any harm, but waving the blade back into the legs did. It slowed, and he sliced off its back leg with a side cut, but the momentum took the blade into a large stone, where it sliced in then got stuck as soon as the momentum faded. The muru'unkuy stumbled from losing the leg and turned to drag itself into him. Syago tried to pull the blade out but the cut wedged it tight. As the muru'unkuy neared, he sawed it through to cut its way out, then yanked it and nearly fell to the ground as it broke free. He stood and stepped back, away from the sliding muru'unkuy. Moving slow, he cut the left tusks and severed the front left leg, then the neck. It collapsed, right legs struggling uselessly.

Anxiety for defending Elisabet, for Tolgrym, banished the thought. He had to hurry but for the moment, Qosku needed him. He ran to where he remembered being knocked down. The light of the moon and Alexandre's blade showed him his path. Finally, he saw gleaming metal to his right—Qosku, just as more lifeless approached through the fog. Sword in one hand, he picked up Qosku on his shoulder, feeling a wound in his side as he straightened. He put his hand to it and saw the blood in an opening of his armor, yet the sword wasn't healing him as it had Milemeron. Grunting, he made toward Tolgrym, broken lifeless shuffling after him.

A mix of emotions roiled him now. Relief that he'd gotten Qosku back. Elation that he now had Alexandre. But both tempered by a deep frustration with the sword—he could barely wield it. It would suffice against large, lumbering targets, but against smaller or more agile creatures, or in a duel, he was doomed. He would have to retrain with it before he could be considered nigh enough competent with it. But for now, his mind could only worry about Elisabet and the others, under heavy assault. He took heart in the thought that if he took up the fight on this end, someone else protected her better in there. The battle was a cumulative community effort.

Movement above drew his attention. He saw the grimshades shift in the branches, watching. He raised Alexandre and, in a voice more confident than he actually felt, said, "I'm ready when you are." Qosku stirred, then twisted out of Syago's arms to his feet, armored fists ready.

The two grimshades circled, assessing them, then fled swiftly and silently into the night.

From her spot on the ramparts, Leyta pointed her scepter and pushed a stream of fire down at the seething mounds of bodies thronging the wall, all the rage she felt about the abuses she witnessed as a child going into it. She was careful to avoid the soldiers and Roah'riik that had gone down to dismember the trees, but it seemed futile. Her fire was only making it worse, reigniting her fear of losing control of it. Fal'iek and others in the brambles had turned their attention to Knave, who flew at them from the shadows in hit-and-run attacks, terrifying the soldiers. Following the count's cue from further down the wall, she ignited a darkflame in her water flask and began freezing the smaller bodies in place. She hoped at least that King and Queen would not be entering the assault; she knew little of their powers but whatever they be she couldn't compete with them in this frenzy. The swarm encroached all below, mindless and foul.

"This cannot continue, sweeties," chided Queen's voice as lifeless now crawled along the ramparts. "All you need to do is chain your leaders up and let us in. At least think of the children."

If King and Queen are here, why aren't they attacking?

"We can't win this way," she yelled to the soldiers along the walkway. Fal'iek, barking orders to those around him on the branches to deal with Knave, couldn't hear her. She turned to see Jester now standing at the northgate. Further north in the woods, she saw malwolf eyes shimmering in the nighttime fog. Not corpses, but live ones waiting for the lifeless to finish their damage. People below maintained braces on the gate and put out fires from Jester's flasks, but no soldiers on the wall had gone after him.

So she ran toward him, shooting darkfire at him from her flask while looking for cover. She still feared losing control on the soldier and Kimoc running ahead. Jester raised a pouch to throw at them, and she raised her scepter to stop him, blast him away. But she hesitated, fearing herself, then as the pouch was launched she thought she saw the soldier shove the Kimoc from behind. The man stumbled into the pouch, catching its flames in full, then tumbled limply off the wall as the soldier advanced on Jester. She was too shocked to scream for the dying man but quickly focused on aiding the soldier in his pursuit of the clown.

Jester hopped across the gateway and threw a pouch at him; she snapped back to put wrath in the air to compress it, then blew the rest of the fire away from the soldier. But out of the corner of her eye, she saw the soldier lurch forward. Knave had caught the soldier with its tailclaw through his armor and ribs, pulling him down the walkway, screaming. She threw a spread of darkfire at both Knave and Jester, but a pump of its wings pushed back the darkflames. It perched on a wall crenelation, the tail stabbing the man again and again as she tried air, then finally a spark of lightning that got it to hop off and vanish below, the soldier already dead. She stopped another pouch and blew its purple smoke back with a hate-filled gust. Jester cackled some anti-joke she couldn't hear, her head still tumbling with the deaths she'd just witnessed. She turned the mix of anger, fear, and sorrow into power and threw darkfire at Jester, catching and freezing him around the legs.

Before she could press the advantage, Knave returned to the battlements behind her with a small captive in its clawed arms: Elisabet, Syago's cousin. Leyta raised a hand to stop the soldiers who'd finally come to help her. Licking Elisabet's terrified face, it watched Leyta with that odious child mouth. *"Where you going, Miss Pretty?"*

It then dropped off the other side of the battlement, leaving the screaming child down below, outside the wall. Her first inclination was to make a quick attack. Stopping Jester would end the fight and so justify the sacrifice. But what if she failed to stop him? And she could never do that to Syago, or the girl.

She quickly descended the nearby stairs as Knave picked Jester up to fly him away. They were vulnerable, a perfect target for wind or fire, but they moved out of reach and she had to hurry into the gatehouse to slip out. The women and children barricading the portcullis door, which groaned and cracked under Jester's exploding flasks, now watched her in alarm. No time to explain, she rolled the crank to raise the portcullis a crack, then slipped out and grabbed Elisabet. The portcullis clanged shut behind her, sealing them outside. She pounded on it, screaming. Bodies approached from along the wall, and malfwolf eyes leered through the dark, closing in.

Leyta felt paralyzed; she had dyne but she couldn't stop all of them. The malwolves were too big and fast, and the bodies too many. The black beasts darted in growling, plowing into the bodies, tearing and tossing them about. Then a Kimoc woman was in front of her, axing down the limbs of the encroaching lifeless.

"Come on!" It was Lil'iek, holding a giant malwolf skull to her head with her other hand. "I can't hold them much longer."

Lil'iek had raised the gate, and a woman of Tolgrym held it until they'd slipped back under. The woman eyed Lil'iek suspiciously then apologized to Leyta and ran back to the barricade.

"Are you hurt?" Lil'iek asked, rising to her feet, knees trembling. Leyta shook her head more in disbelief than in answer, eyes falling on the burnt body next to them. Lil'iek looked at it. "He was Kanche'maq, and I'm sure he died bravely, one with the wild. But you shouldn't go after Jester alone like that—"

Leyta followed her eyes to see Fal'iek pursue Knave and Jester up to the brambletops. Leaving the malwolf skull on the ground, Lil'iek quickly ascended the stairs, handaxes drawn, before disappearing over the top. Leyta looked at the Kimoc corpse with remorse. *She doesn't know. But what if I didn't see him shoved? With the Asturion dead and me as sole witness, it could stay that way. The truth a small sacrifice for peace between us. Ah, but now I'm sacrificing. I wouldn't offer the girl, but I will the dead Kimoc I've never met.*

I suppose they were right, and I'm collecting too many dark secrets.

The lifeless now pressed the portcullis. Women and warchildren gathered to renew the braces. She called for them to move so she could move stone and dirt to pile up a better defense. But in the din, they couldn't hear. The iron gate bent, and the people screamed as the door cracked and caved inward under the weight of the clawing bodies.

They ran, pushing and shoving, knocking down Elisabet. Leyta ran as someone stepped on Elisabet's arm and another on her back, pushing the young girl into the dirt. Picking her up, Leyta braced against the last of the fleeing people as lifeless poured in. Once they were past, Leyta turned and raised her scepter in a fury and threw up dirt and rock at them, blocking the gate momentarily. She ran with Elisabet to the nearest house and banged on the door, screaming to be let in. The door cracked, and they slipped inside.

The small cottage was nearly full of people huddled together among chairs and tables, knives at the ready. A fire in the fireplace burned low. Leyta looked out the window and saw bodies roaming about. Not far off, a malwolf howled into the night and some in the room cried out.

"Let me in, let me in!" A woman's voice called with pounding on the door. Almost everyone protested but none stopped Leyta from letting the woman in, one offered her a shawl. The woman's safety relieved some of Leyta's guilt for not being out, supporting the fight. But what could she do as one dynast against so many? What if she burned the village down? Gabriol's face floated in her mind, shocked, burning.

Leyta peeked through the wooden window shutter: Dim glows of fire shone along the wall but little else, and she began thinking of how to help. Then violent scratching at the door rattled it, and everyone gave a start. The unmistakable snarling of a malwolf followed the clawing. Though they barely knew each other, Elisabet clung to Leyta.

"Snuff the fire!" hissed a woman. "Put it out!"

"No, don't," Leyta said, but they didn't heed her. She could protect them but not without light. "Leave the fire!"

They put it out, and the room went dark. A couple more scratches sounded in the darkened room. Then it fell still, a silence that lasted until the beast's head burst in through the window, throwing wood and pottery everywhere. Its large head, hairless and black, save a tuft of fur on top, hid well in the dark room as it wriggled its bulk to get in. Several women ran to attack it. It snarled as Leyta quickly threw darkfire in its face, but it snapped at the chairs and knives the women brought to bear with jagged fangs, then slipped in the rest of the way with a crash, all but vanishing in the small, dark cottage.

Leyta huddled with Elisabet against a post, hearts pounding. The massive black beast savaged through the darkness, snapping and snarling through the screams and crashing of furniture. Dying gurgles followed as objects flew everywhere, and the hunter darted from victim to victim. Blood sprayed Leyta's face. She pushed away her fears and set the chair by the broken window on fire. Now there was more light—and a weapon. She brought rage to bear, using it to throw fire at the monster moving through the shadows. Its jaws clamped onto a boy and whipped him back and forth like a ragdoll. Leyta ducked under the flinging blood and pushed fire at the beast. Under the flare, the malwolf tossed the boy, and came for her with a deep snarl.

She shoved Elisabet down and away while diving to the other side and, with all that she had, pushed the fire at it. It crashed into the far wall. Smoke filled the air. The beast whined then growled, a deep rumble stopped by a cough from the smoke. She made the fire pop, having power remaining for little else now. Singed all over its furless skin, it fled out the door that someone had opened to escape. She hoped that many had, or her failure would be great. Over the carnage and wreckage of the room, she checked on Elisabet, who threw herself into her chest, weeping, and Leyta heaved a sigh of relief. They went to another locked home, and Leyta left her there to help clear the village.

Lil'iek pursued Fal'iek, who pursued Jester to the top of the brambles. She saw Fal'iek get caught by the clown's bolas, then jump to a nearby branch. Jester met him there. She drew an arrow for a surprise shot but couldn't get a clear aim with the branches between them. She ascended, still watching.

Fal'iek cut in half the rope but a kick that clipped his head had him hanging from the branch. Finally near the top, Lil'iek shot her arrow, which Jester narrowly dodged. She noted a wound on Fal'iek's side in a gap in his hide and bone armor that prevented him from swinging up. She jumped to his thornbranch and pulled him over.

The joy on his face at seeing her quickly vanished. "Why aren't you in the town? Who's with the children?"

"Someone we trust," she replied, notching an arrow. "Though if we lose, it won't matter."

She released it, replaced it, and did it again. The singing had grown to a rougher, throat-shredding howl. She glanced at Fal'iek's side. "How bad are you hurt?"

"Just the surface. But don't worry about me till he's dead."

"I scared him away."

"No, he's got more tricks up his sleeve. Lil, you don't know him like I do. Go back—"

A cloud of smoke burst at their side. A dagger flew out of it; she deflected it with her bow, but a second came right behind. Fal'iek threw his arm up and caught it but received a small cut.

"Stop that," she snapped. "I have this."

"No," he growled as he rose from his crouch to stand beside her. "*We* have this. Circle the gurow?"

She nodded, then they split. She started her undulating warcry and darted over the brambletops while Fal'iek mirrored her direction over the uneven, thorny stalks. He drew his bow and arrow and began shooting with her. One of her arrows stuck Jester, then another poof of smoke hid his escape. The song continued.

Knave shot out of the dark below and dropped Jester, with dagger in each hand, by Lil'iek, then dove at Fal'iek. The Roah'riik swung under the branch, emerging on the other side behind Knave. He jumped, baring his knives and grabbing Knave's tail above the claw. He yanked and slammed the creature against the branch, though its wings beat and slowed the hit. It snapped the tail free, nearly cutting him but for his foot, stomping the agony down. Lil'iek feinted flight from Jester; she shrieked as she reversed direction, driving her shoulder into his gut and handaxe to his arm, disarming one dagger while using her shield to stave off the other. Jester hopped away, and she pursued, attacking with her small handaxe and round shield against his single dagger. Behind, she watched Fal'iek lose hold on Knave while preparing his hellblade to finish the demon. He ducked as Knave flew past him and grabbed Jester's hand, lifting him in a steady glide away from them while the clown wept loudly, no longer singing. Lil'iek's thrown handaxe missed him, but two arrows still protruded from his costume, marking him as severely—if not fatally—wounded.

They flew away underneath the clouded moon, escaping while the concentrated rush faded down below. Cheers could be heard below as the tide of battle turned—the song was over.

Lil'iek turned to her husband, and they embraced at their shared victory. Over Fal'iek's shoulder, shadows shifted in the thornbranches, and Lil'iek stepped away, trying to understand what she saw. The shadow lurched for her, and she ducked under its attack.

But the shadow hadn't been aiming for her at all. Her heart stopped at the sight of the black, spear-like arm protruding from Fal'iek's chest. The surprise on his face would stay in her mind forever.

The shadowy being withdrew its bloody spear and turned to a winged form in flight. But Lil'iek had no thought of pursuit; she caught her husband, her love, as he fell and pulled him onto the branch. Blood came up from his throat.

"My torturers," he whispered. "They caused the blinding and—"

"Shh, don't worry about that now. Just be here with me." She touched into his mind, feeling him weaken.

Each word a belabored breath. "I guess I go to wander as a lifeless now instead of the river of stars?"

She opened her mouth, but no words came.

His voice grew more feeble. "I'm just glad you're safe. Don't worry about me. I'll..." He dropped his hands from her face, but the other hand clutched his feq'uok.

She had hers too but kept stroking his face, touching his mind. "You will be fine, whatever happens to you. I just... I'm losing you now after so much time, but so much more that... and the children..."

"Please don't grieve long. At least we had-had the moments that we did. Treasure them and—and move on."

His body emptied, limp in her arms.

She nodded through tears, pressed his head tight to her chest, and hummed a prayer to the Great Ones for him.

CHAPTER TWENTY-SEVEN

BEHIND OLD SHADOWS

Based on *Annals of Syago*, cc bastica 90; *Scars of the Martyrs*, cc bastica 1023; *The Nordvargor Testaments*, cc bastica 880; *The Dark Fortress of Mephorash*, cc bastica x;

20th–31st of Octubre, 246

As the lifeless lost focus in the absence of Jester's song, the allies dispatched the rest with fire. There was some elation at the prospect of a darkemorg mostly void of lifeless, but that only meant an extended darkelan. Syago aided in the burning, putting out fires that reached beyond the wall of ash and smoke. Alexandre eventually conceded to heal his wounds and stayed with him instead of returning to its pedestal, as it was known to do when its wielder died. It had chosen him after all.

Milemeron's death led to a difficult, even awkward, oath-swearing to the count. Although Toriacus had already accepted his oath earlier, somehow Syago succeeding his dead son to the legendary relic threw that into question. The sword belonged to the boy's father, the count, according to the count, yet it'd refused him. And his other son, Andras, wasn't present to try it himself. The barons helped smooth it over and Syago had no qualms about bowing the knee, again, to his lord. However, it hadn't done anything to ease his own confused pains and left him feeling still a lowly tenant of Tolgrym and the count's squire who must go on hunts and prepare food for his lord. Not the hero knight he was supposed to become. The Kimoc also appeared to have a falling out with Tolgrym nobility, accusing each other of betrayals and selective fighting during the battle. Syago wasn't clear on the specifics and guessed that both sides only had suspicions and no proof. Even this he only heard as third-hand whispers after a meeting between leaders when the Kimoc abruptly called the rest of their tribe to cease aiding in the cleanup and prepare to leave, not staying for the vigil planned that night. They had lost surprisingly few in the end, considering the wall breach. And among the townspeople, there was a solemn unspoken harmony in their mourning and rebuilding together.

That night, the hollow held a mourning vigil. The village square filled with people standing together in black, holding candles. After a prayer from Bishopess Myrian, the women began their song, a wail for lost sisters, mothers, and daughters. Goidiberic stood with Syago and Elisabet, who wasn't singing. Goia pressed her to join them. She did so quietly, looking at Leyta, who sung hers nearby.

Syago would never forget the sacrifices of those who fought beside him. Same for those of Cantlgrym who were slain, or of the Kimoc who fell defending theirs.[114] Syago grieved for Fal'iek above all. He would miss Fal'iek's clever jibes and advice; the warrior wouldn't be there to train him on Alexandre as he'd promised. Deovan theology held that Fal'iek, unenlightened and uncleansed, had gone to one of the lower hells. Syago prayed to Heavenly Mother that she would at least make an exception for him. He also prayed for Fal'iek's family.

"It's time you go," Goia said. Syago looked at him, but his grandfather's eyes remained fixed on the priestesses and the small choir that led the wail. "To Cantlgrym, I mean. With the enemies out there and you having Alexandre, you need to train and serve. There will be war, Syago. They won't let the rebels keep Mantlgrym, and that troupe won't be content with only Mantlgrym."

He gazed out onto the sea of candles. This was a dream fulfilled, Alexandre and Cantlgrym, but now he hated it. He had changed.

He looked at his family. "I don't want to go anymore."

"The sword did choose you, Iago. It chose you instead of returning to its post, thanks be to Deova and Her angels. So it doesn't matter what you want—it's providence and duty."

"I can't leave you and Elisabet now. Not with them out there and the town weak."

---

114 Because of the number of deaths among the allies and some uncertainty about who died where, when, and how, the author didn't include all of their names in this dramatic narrative, as it's not the focus of this work. They're better honored in the accompanying *We Paid It All*, compiled by Bartolome de Sart. Rebellion deaths are also chronicled there.

"The town will rebuild soon enough," Goia said, clamping a hand on Syago's shoulder. The men began their moaning hum for the lost brothers, fathers, and sons. "We'll be fine. You'll offer us more safety out there, trained and fighting, than you will sitting here. Go, but come back."

They joined in the low-toned wail until it ended. Silence fell as the candles were stifled and they dispersed to sleep in their shared houses and tents. Syago and the rescued of Covandongar left for Cantlgrym some few days following the Battle of Tolgrym. After circumnavigating Mantlgrym, now under King's control, they arrived, exhausted, to a small but ecstatic welcome among those remaining at Cantlgrym. They feasted and danced and mourned some more.

Many days later, Syago sat at supper between Andras and young Lügos, with several others of Tolgrym. He felt more attached to them now, being gone from home for so long.

Down at the masters' table sat Alkant, whom he'd heard much about but had never met.[115] Roza and Anaruth were arguing amiably with Davagis and Bishopess Gladys Yanet. Balgor and Virgow focused on their food. They'd all won his respect in the few days he'd been there.

Still troubled by his experience with Alexandre, Syago didn't speak much. After so many rejections by the Judgment Sword, and then being passed over for someone else, it'd finally accepted him, but proved extremely difficult to wield. Syago carried Alexandre everywhere mostly to continue familiarizing himself with the entity within, to connect with its presence—a difficult experience, especially when sparring. Its mind was strange, uncommunicative, and holy. He'd gotten several questions about Alexandre—and even more curious stares—things he'd dreamed of, but now he felt awkward and unsure.

Qosku sat alone. Pity welled in Syago, but then left when he saw Leyta sit by the lone friend. He marveled at how good she was with minding other people's struggles and supporting them, wishing he was better at it. As those around him burst into laughter at a joke he'd missed, he got up to join Leyta and Qosku.

When he sat, Qosku turned to him. "Leyta said you were promised to her as a child. So now that you save each other from Royal Chaos, you can marry!"

<hr>

115 *Moonspell Hell Light de Lostregos*

Syago sputtered in his cup.

Leyta laughed but didn't completely hide the flush in her cheeks. "I didn't say it like that!"

"If you say so," Syago said, drinking from his cup to hide a grin and any flush in his own face.

She eyed him from her cup. "As if I'd keep the promise anyways, dead or alive."

But before Syago could say anything else, the great hall's doors burst open, clanging loudly. Everyone in the hall froze as a wild-eyed man ran in, shouting, "We're under attack! It's the demons—the demons have come!"

Mayhem broke out as everyone jumped up. Alexandre in hand, Syago ran with the masses to the courtyard, wishing he had his armor on.

The crowds slowed at the door, staring at something he couldn't yet see. Pushing his way through, he finally made it outside, his heart stopping at the sight.

A thick black cloud encompassed the entire castle grounds, stretching from the wall to the sky and encasing the whole clearing in a darkness held back only by torches.

The guards had descended from the walls in fear of the fog that thickened and swirled, hiding expressions of awe and fear as they took up defensive positions around the edges of the courtyard. The gentle clanking of metal, the patter of footsteps, and crackling torches brought the only sounds. A stale, ashen smell touched Syago's nostrils. Alexandre hummed with unease in his hand, glowing bright.

The wind blew, and a massive dark form swooped down from the eddying clouds to perch on the wall. Arrows and crossbow bolts flew into the winged form of the grimshade. It shuddered, then stretched open its large mouth and regurgitated the projectiles.

A line of soldiers approached, shields up, as the dynasts began an assault of lightning, but the creature retreated back into the clouds. The soldiers halted, uncertain. The clouds swirled again and moved forward. Shouts rose, and the soldiers retreated.

Syago pushed farther to stand at the front with the guards. The dark clouds shifted violently inward and retreated to just behind the wall—far enough to reveal eight figures standing atop the wall where the winged grimshade had been.

All eight dressed in varying combinations of armor and black leather and had a large weapon strapped to their bodies. Four were Asturion and four were Unakan. Three released the slain bodies of wall soldiers lost in the black fog. The bodies thumped to the ground.

Scars and calm hatred covered their white and brown faces. They stood with calm confidence. Some were bald; others had short hair, while two had long dark hair. All looked as if they'd waged many a long, hard battle.

One spoke. "You and your predecessors slew our masters whom you named the Razhod, the witchlords, and the Hellfaces. We, their faithful disciples, now come to reclaim our stolen heritage and, in time, to exact atonement for the crime."

Syago squinted at the leader, thinking he looked familiar but couldn't remember from where. The realization of what was happening set in, regardless. He recognized their dress from stories of the Razhod, but they lacked the eyes. Once a disciple took the Crimson Covenant, it changed his eyes to black with red irises, or so he'd heard. These then were cultist disciples, followers who lacked the power to call on emaion spirits or their hellish soulweapons, and not yet full Razhod.

"Religious fanatics that can't let go," Alkant said loudly, stepping forward from the crowd. "That's what you are, and it will gain you nothing from us. I've faced down your so-called masters, now long dead. We can take care of you if need be. We stopped them, and we can stop you. You may leave now or die at our hands."

"Alkant," the leader, Syago supposed, began. "You deserve the first penalty, above all, as you were a lead opposer to the Great Lord of the Deep. Splaying your blood may yet please him such that he will return and grant us our glory due. Perhaps the master of masters would return and make us Razhod."

"And how do you plan to exact this revenge?" Alkant strode closer to the wall. Davagis and Anaruth trailed behind, each with scepter or staff at hand. "What army have you that could possibly match us? You are not even full, true Razhod. You haven't the Crimson Covenant. This is a fool's—"

Without warning, Davagis rammed a long knife into Alkant's back.

Everyone gasped.

"They don't answer to you, pitiful gowk," Davagis said. "And for the first time in too long, neither do I."

"Dav... why?" Alkant pleaded as he dropped to his knees.

"I tire of pretending for you," Davagis said. "And your philosophy of liberty a lost cause. I'll see to it that all you've accomplished has been unraveled."

He yanked the blade out as Anaruth snapped out of her shock and turned on him in a fury, scepter raised. Darkfire burst at him from her water flask, but a pillar of dirt rose up in front of the traitor, blocking her shot. Davagis moved another formation to skewer Anaruth's belly. She fell dead.

Bolts and all manner of fire and lightning flew at Davagis, but he'd already fled to the wall, where a grimshade lifted him up and away from the assault. He joined the others at the top, out of range, making them nine. In a fury, many continued to break ranks and charge forward.

With a booming roar, Balgor led the way, throwing explosive flasks, followed by Roza and Constantin, and Syago and Qosku charging behind.

Two grimshades flew in front, absorbing much of the offense, while Davagis and another waved their scepters. Lightning crackled around the assailing group, bringing Balgor and the soldiers to their knees. Syago and Qosku assisted Balgor to his feet and retreated with the others, watching for what came next.

"I know them," Qosku said quietly, beside him. "Zupayk's Cult. They no have mask and yellow robe like when I see them in the mountains, but the symbols. They are Zupayk's Cult. I think they make me kill my sister." Syago looked from him to them but said nothing. "I think they have her body."

It began to hail. Hard, cold ice tore through the black fog.

The cool gaze of the lead cultist fell on Syago, hail melting on his hair and shoulders. Syago recognized him. "Kask?!"

Kask smiled. He replied in a voice that was no longer raspy, but clear and strong. "Yes, I've been one for nearly as long as I've been a vagrant. Seeing the underbelly of the city showed me the truth. You may join us followers if you'd like. We accept those with potential, after some trials and special rites. You'd have to surrender that holy sword, though. We don't get along."

"I'll kill you for this," Syago yelled, but Kask ignored him.

"Now," Davagis shouted, "we have a demand that you bring out the Relics of Aram Ghaal, the Maps of Lustmord de Gallowbraid, the Diabulus in Morda' Stigmata, and the writings of Barthandeon. Bring that and we will leave. I know you have them. Do it now, or the executions continue... starting with the youngest." His eyes seemed to glint at making them do for him what he could've done himself.

"Traitors, heretics!" Leyta shouted, pointing at them with her staff. "The old war is over and we haven't changed. We'll not bow to you."

Bishopess Yanet's voice boomed over the field. "The Holy One will not tolerate your blasphemy. She will cause you to be smote down as before, as always!" Katti and others crossed themselves, nodding and whispering, "Amen."

The fog on the right swirled as a grimshade stepped out. Humanoid, it towered over them some twenty feet. Its head of candle eyes gazed down at them. It reached a long thin arm and grabbed Mariaciela before anyone could stop it. Leyta and others raised their staves to hit it with lightning, but the timid sparks affected nothing. Mariaciela's screaming followed her into the fog of the other side before stopping abruptly.

The cultists kept silent. Syago saw Leyta, Balgor, and the other masters look at each other before Leyta led several people into the castle to retrieve their demands. The fanaticists stood patiently on the wall, like sentinels sent from the underworlds.

Leyta returned with some small books in her arms, leaving them on the grass near the base of the wall. She then stood beside Qosku, glaring at Davagis.

Davagis smiled at her, a grotesque sight on the man who had never smiled while pretending to virtue and loyalty.

Some large scrolls, the maps, were brought next and also laid on the grass, as well as a small, dark wooden chest.

Davagis said, "If this is not all there is—and I will know—we will return on less pleasant terms." He nodded as the black mists from behind enveloped them again. Everyone backed away as the clouds reached down and took the items before retreating, swirling, and fading away into gray skies.

Wet, cold, and defeated, everyone went inside. Alkant's and Anaruth's bodies were carried in, and Syago helped take in the slain soldiers as the hail thickened around them.

The sorrow in the castle didn't last long, but soon caught afire with rage. Syago had endured and overcome a great many things in the past few months and building a closer bond with the Holy Judgment Sword could only augment that. Leyta led the hall in a toast to the fallen and to honoring them with the fight they'd learned. They were not done, they would have justice for the treachery dealt them.

First comes faceless One
Unbidden, unknown, uncaring
Then forms Two against you
Undeniable, unkind, untame
Till Three will burden thee
Unrelenting, unsafe, unholy
And then follows the rest
Unwise, unfortunate, unclean

DEFINING OUR TERMS

ANDREW WROTE THIS PART

Angels: Beings of the overworld Kingdom in Heaven, Halls of Celos, embodied in various forms. They come from the classes of Seven Virtues: Chastity, Temperance, Charity, Diligence (Devotion), Patience, Kindness, Humility. These parallel similar classes of Seven Blessings by the lesser known Celestians, neither which are as safe and innocent as they sound.

Alerhas: Plants with pollen that infects lifeforms' wounds to germinate, then grow roots in the body, usually killing it. The alerha then drives the body to infect more and spread its pollen.

Apus: A type of eternal or "god" for the Unaka, based on specific mountains in the Apugakas, their name for the Barbathors.

Archemist: Using dyne and alchemy to manipulate the elements, the needed symbol is etched into an appropriate object which then activates when touched. The person touching use their sentiments to power it.

Archdynast: A dynast at the top of the dynal hierarchy, including elementists who are not dynasts such as archemists. Like all dynasts, they require a foci, usually a scepter or staff, that lets them aim and direct their sentiments into the elements. *See Dyne*

Asturions: Called the palemen by the Kimoc for their whiter skin, came from overseas several hundred years ago. They brought castles, swords, and more monsters according to the Kimoc. According to the Asturions they brought peace and prosperity.

Bards: Minstrels, musicians, poets, story perfomers, dancers, jesters, fools, and the like. They specialized in using music and/or art to convey sentiments into people and animals. Dyne puts the sentiments into the art that then seeps into human bodies through perception.

Barons: Minor lords within towns or cities, generally under a count with the absence of kings. They're responsible to fund expeditions and defend the domains.

Baw'kook: Fomorion in Asturion, these half-human half-animal were giants and usually only seen raiding. Included the ukuku, ohancanu, wookalar, goatmen, wolfmen, and so forth.

Bolas: Stones on the end of a cord that when thrown wrap around the target, binding them.

Bomogs: Bomok in Kimoc. Burly bulls with thick fur and curling horns used for meat, wool, fertilizer in the outside, and pulling warwagons.

Chamands: Summoners and necromancers accepted of the covens in Bokhor, they summon spirits with a bell but can also be warriors. Shunned summoners were witches, or witchlords in the case of the Razhod.

Claymore: A type of two-handed sword.

Counts: The lord of a town or city by male birthright. Wife would be countess until husband dies. They're usually over barons, like lower level lords. The count typically must be an archdynast to lead the defense of his domain and fund the expeditions.

Crenellations: The blocky, peggy lining that runs along the ramparts/ battlements of a city or castle wally wall.

Culicida: Legendary carnivorous fungi that exhales poison gas.

Daemogs: Thinner bulls that run in bigger herds and snort fire. Their farts also are flammable.

Deepwraiths: Grimshades or shadowmen in other languages. An odd shapeshifting shadowy creature of stealth and death.

Demons: Otherworlder monsters like devils but from The Vast Abyss, an arctic oceanic underworld. They're classified by the Seven Afflictions: Agony, Terror, Despair, Violation, Sorrow, Bondage (Slavery), Destitution (Starvation), and Insanity.

Deova Bondua: The Sanator, The Holy One, Our Blessed Lady in Heaven, Sofia the Savior, The One True Path, and the Eternal of the Palemen (Kimoc wording).

Devils: Underworld monsters like demons but from The Infernal Hellpits, apparently a mostly subterranean otherworld. Classified by the Seven Deadly Temptations: Greed, Gluttony, Lust, Wrath, Pride (Arrogance), Envy, Sloth, and Hate and Apathy.

Duende: Urisg brownies or the Kourii are other names for them, not to be confused with the Xanas. This tiny people are said to be dangerous and live in the marshes.

Dyne: Originally the power to move the elements, like a ruler over them as dynast or but also through archemist and bards. The real power is through sentiments identified in the Vision: Red is anger, hate is brown, fear bright green, anxiety less bright green, sorrow is blue, joy is yellow, pride is orange. But note that only some are used while others have less useful effects or are just not as explosive, common, or sustainable.

Dynfist Monk/Friar: Like a dynast or bard, they use dyne to shoot their sentiments into something. In this case the careful practice of putting it through their own body for greater bursts of speed and strength. Deleterious health effects may follow. It's more distinctly religious, called Takanaku among the Unaka.

Elementist: Anyone that can use dyne.

Emaions: Greater spirits with specific but broad powers, such as a Belfegor the Behemoth or Nimrød the Reptilium, that can be summoned. Spirits of fire, lightning, shadow.

Eternals: The Great Ones "gods" of the Kimoc, Unaka, and Amoyara pagans. But each group views theirs differently. Often associated with natural features.

Feldinal: Furacán in Kimoc, Amoyaran, and Unakan. They're oversized animals often with strange humanoid mutations, similar to demons and devils but less lethal.

Flambard: Two-handed sword with a wavy blade, like flames.

Foci: Usually a scepter or staff serving as the tool of a dynast to guide their sentiments in the practice called dyne. For archemists the foci would be the object they write on, for bards and dynfists it's their bodies.

Fomorions: Baw'kook in Asturion, these barbarian giants were half-human half-animal and usually only seen raiding by humans. Tribal collective that included the ukuku, ohancanu, wookalar, goatmen, wolfmen, and so forth.

Gierra: What the Asturions call their earth.

Grievore the Violator: A flambard soulweapon greatsword, maybe just short of a greatsword. But two-handed life-draining soulweapon wielded by the Razhod.

Grim'iik: Gigantic blackbird that stalks Thornwood and mountain valleys and is worshiped as an eternal.

Grimshades: Deepwraith or shadowmen in other languages. An odd shape-shifting shadowy creature of stealth and death.

Gurows: Large, vicious crow-like animals.

Hellfaces: Tauntname for the Razhod who'd had black eyes with red irises that glowed in the dark, these helleyes along with scars earned them it. Barthandeon, their leader, had one more unique: Old Devilface.

Hellweapons: Handcrafted by shamanic, necromancer figures specifically to slay otherworlders. Different materials grant narrow but spectacular abilities, usually at a dark tradeoff. Not to be confused with Soulweapons.

Kimoc: The tribal peoples of the land of Nevermore. Even though the desert canyon peoples and the forest peoples are quite different, the Asturions call them all Kimoc to simplify things.

Lifeless: Undead, animated by forces of one religious narrative or another. Or by forbidden magics. Oft called zombi by the Bokhor summoners.

Mabin'guarik: Fearsome forest beast with a vertical maw on its chest, bulky clawed arms, and a cycloptic eye on its head.

Machicolations: The extensions of the wall battlments that enable soldiers to shoot down through a small hole at siege assaults or battering rams while staying covered. If in a shooting mood.

Malwolves: Large wolves with tusk-like teeth, yellow eyes, and either thick black fur or no fur at all but hairless black skin. There's probably some reason for this.

Mastozon: Mastozan for women specifically, who'd be second class of an already second-class word meaning mixed blood/skin. Of both Asturion and Unakan/Kimoc ancestry.

Mewil'ishyuuks: Basically a huge sacred deer with wicked antlers. For some reason they let the Roah'riik ride them and worship them.

Mordios The Reaver: A soulweapon warscythe used by the Razhod. Said to kill instantly on touching blood. Had been a favorite weapon of Barthandeon.

Morion Helmet: Openfaced helm made to go with armor that has a collar. Morions have a rim around the edge and a small crest or fin along the top.

Morwolf Hounds: Smaller wolves that somehow cooperate as pets and hunting companions.

Mother/Mamak Yoaom: The motherwood, or eternal "goddess" of the forest, but like she is the forest.

Muru'unkuy: Massive boar-like animal with tusks and extra bad smells.

Nevermore: The Kingdom Republic of Nevermore is the undisputed(?) name for the largely unmapped realm herein which we find ourselves.

Ohancanu: Barbarian giants who are the most human of the Fomorion/ Baw'kook collective, would be human except for their size and cycloptic eye. Balgor is sole proof they can be intelligent and peaceful, not that you've given them a chance.

Osmos: A mystic cosmic gate that connects gierra to the otherworlds (overworlds and underworlds), for a price. The osmosis of the cosmos. Do NOT summon unless prepared to pay a toll.

Otherworlder: Any being from the otherworlds, typically broken down to overworlds and underworlds, though gierra is sort of considered an underworld as well by the Church. Either way, better just not summon Osmos at all.

Ozor: Even if you think you can pay, or have nothing to lose, don't summon Osmos. Oh and ozors are just extra large angry bears.

Pauldron: Basic medieval terminology you really could've looked up on your internets. But guess I shouldn't complain you're here instead. Pauldrons are shoulder plates of armor.

Penaga the Slaver: Penaga the Punishment, as well. A barbed warwhip soulweapon wielded by the Razhod.

Pillory: Same, but medieval arm and neck brace to punish criminals, expose them for public mockery.

Piory/Abbey/Monastery/Convent: Sorry I'm not doing four of these, even if there are minute differences between them. They had monks, friars, abbots/abbesses, and sometimes priests and bishops. Religious communities wouldn't be so isolated in Nevermore anyways, but cloistered in some corner of a town or maybe on a mountaintop fortress.

Quelk: Like an elk, but with a q and more sinister.

Quervosks: Like big ravens with extra temper and razor beaks.

Quoarn'riik: Like a chieftain among the Kimoc, but also shamanic and usually elected by the women. This varied by people and tribe.

Razhod: Witchlords, the Crimson Coven who held the Crimson Covenant. When alive, they were called Hellfaces as well due to their hellish eyes. Not to be confused with their followers in the cult.

Roah'riik: Hellhunters and helltamers among the Kimoc, more so the forest tribes, who use bones as a telepathic medium.

Saqra: An eternal of the Unaka, but one that can be summoned and so also emaion or greater spirit. Known for dark tricks, he also had a mysterious cult.

Soulweapons: Weapons with greater spirit emaions in them. The powers of the spirit are then embedded into the weapon pending good relations between wielder and weapon spirit. Not to be confused with hellweapons, these are sentient, durable, and select who can wield them. They also have extra sharp blades, control over weight and balance, and can fly. The Razhod destroyed all but Alexandre who in turn destroyed them.

Tamboc: Unakan fortresses usually on the tops of mountains.

Takanaku: The practice of dynfist as found among the Unaka.

Ukuku: Ozormen Fomorion/Baw'kook, so ozors are like large bears and these are even bigger and more half-human bearmen. Said to be the most peaceful giants.

Unaka: Mountain dwelling peoples that worshiped the sun, moon, and mountains as eternals and supplied the entire realm of Nevermore with metals while barely getting credit for it.

Warscythe: Since scythes were used to shear harvests during a gathering expedition, these are only different in that the blade was retrofitted to point more up. Not a common weapon.

Witches: Outcast summoners and necromancers, different from witchlord Razhod who were a class of their own.

Wookalars: Boarmen of the Fomorion/Baw'kook barbarian giants. Large hairy walking swine with tusks.

Woshik: Various home arrangements of skin canvas, often with furs or art on it.

Xarampions: Lizard-like creatures with frills and long hook claws. Also smell terrible.

Yactas: Unakan town or village, usually mountaintop or plateau.

Zupayk: Another Unakan eternal that can but should not be summoned. See Emaion greater spirit.

Zurrogiath the Desolator: A great-axe soulweapon light for its size. It rapid rusts and rots anything it touches. Wielded by the Razhod.

www.ingramcontent.com/pod-product-compliance
Lightning Source LLC
Chambersburg PA
CBHW031143160726
47991CB00004B/1548